To Rule as in Days of Olde

Denae Dassow ↢ ⊙ ↣ Book 1

Dale Denton

The characters and events portrayed in this book are fictitious. Any similarity to real persons, living or dead, is coincidental and not intended by the author.

ISBN: 9798872380740
Cover by Dale Denton

For Bryce

Acknowledgments

This couldn't have become a reality without the help of several people. Thanks goes to The Carrollton League of Writers, Worthy Lafollette, and Alijah Ballard, who all offered advice on portions of the book during the editing and rewriting process. Thanks also goes to The Trinity Presbyterian Men's Book Club, who put up with reading a later draft and provided ideas for me to follow up with.

Special thanks to Christy Williams acted as my alpha and beta reader on this book, catching all of those things, obvious and not so much, that passed my viewing, and also for reading the following two books of this series, helping me maintain continuity from book to book. Special thanks also goes to Carol Johnson, who critiqued my first draft, furnishing me with many suggestions that improved the early form of the story.

And thanks to my son Bryce, who suffered through multiple oral readings of the story, and provided his own suggestions and insight that helped Denae become the character she is today.

Chapter 1

The Bear

"Mom, I got some rabbits." Denae loped into the kitchen barefoot and plopped four furry carcasses onto the counter. "Can I have one of the skins? The biggest one?"

Mom glanced at the floor as she set a potato back in the sink with the others, and Denae smiled. It'd been years since she'd forgotten to wave her feet clean, but Mom always checked. She watched as Mom examined the rabbits. "This should work for supper with the older boys gone. I think your Aunt Tilda wanted as many pelts as she could get…not sure what she's making, but it sounds like a full coat or something."

"Oh…in that case…."

"I'll ask her, but don't get your hopes up." Mom looked up from the rabbits. "All of these are headshots. You've gotten nicely accurate with that stone-shot spell. Why do you want the skin?"

"A purse, or pouch, really…hang it off my belt. I'm getting better at sneaking up on them, too, so that helps."

"Your new snakeskin belt?" Mom smiled indulgently.

"My massasauga belt, Mom." Denae had just finished making the belt and today was her wearing it into the forest. She twirled slowly, hoping the scales would shine to full effect in the light of the kitchen lightstones.

"My old belt pouch…." She tugged on the large worn suede pouch on her belt, "it doesn't look good with this belt. The rabbit skin's the right size and would look so much better. I'll use a piece of cowhide on the back to stiffen it."

Mom laughed. "I'll ask."

"Mom, didn't Aunt Tilda say something about wanting a fox for something? I petrified one while I was out."

"No, she got what she needed a few days ago, so go back and un-stone that poor creature. You enjoy doing that a bit too much."

"Yes, Mom. And it's fun, especially with little brothers."

"You didn't?" Mom turned, smile fading, facing her fully.

"Not recently," Denae replied, grinning, "but I've got to practice."

"You know that spell well enough already." Mom gestured at the rabbits. "You're not getting the rabbits from near the house, are you?"

"No, Mom," Denae sighed audibly. "Other side of the lake. They breed much faster there than I can hunt them down."

"Are you going to the movie with the boys? I think they're heading into town in about fifteen minutes."

Denae shook her head with a grimace. "Lucas said they're going to see The Omen. Really? They may want to see it, but I'll stick with Island at the Top of the World or Doc Savage. Besides, it's rated R, so I can't go anyway…not for almost another year."

"That's why we picked it." Lucas swaggered into the room, followed by her brother Jude and cousin Bradley, who gave her a smug smile. "We didn't want you or Bin tagging along. It should be a good comedy since I'm sure they won't get any of the magic right."

Denae groaned. Lucas might be her most annoying brother, but Bradley was her most aggravating cousin, and the feeling was mutual.

"Don't worry about me tagging along to that Carrie movie either," Denae snapped back. "You fooled me once with horror. Never again."

"Don't worry, Sis. Carrie's rated R too, and you'll still be sixteen in November. Besides, you haven't bothered getting a driver's license. Even if you were seventeen, we'd never be able to pass you off as being over twelve when they card you." They laughed, then Lucas turned his attention to their mom. "We'll just grab supper in town."

Mom nodded. "You'll miss out on roast rabbits, but that's fine. Is Anton going with you?"

"Nah. He's getting spritzed up for a date. Been home for summer break a week, and he's already got him a new girl." Lucas nudged Bradley and winked as they turned to leave. "Maybe he can give me some pointers when we room together at Madison this fall. I'll be a sophomore, so no dormitory ever again."

"Hey," Binesi said from the living room before joining them in the kitchen, his blond hair contrasting with Lucas, Jude, and Bradley's dark. "What's in these movies that makes it so I can't see them?"

"Oh, you know," Lucas said with a smirk. "Bad words, blood, gore, maybe a decapitation. Things a fourteen-year-old just can't handle. Maybe even some sex or real breasts." He smirked at Denae when he said that.

"Lucas," Mom said.

"We gotta go. You two have fun staying here," he said before disappearing with Jude and Bradley through the doorway.

Mom shook her head and bent down to prepare the rabbits.

"I've got a fox to un-stone," Denae said, turning toward the backdoor. "Bin, you want to come?"

"Sure."

"Dad wants you to help him in the workshop," Mom said. "Remember."

"Right," Bin said. "Sorry."

He looked back into the living room, hand moving slightly, and sneezes echoed back. He stepped away from the doorway, a grin on his face. "Gotta practice," he said in a low voice.

Mom chuckled. "I need both of you to work at the warehouse in the morning. Don't forget that."

"I won't," Denae grumbled. That would be a trip to town. She'd rather stay out here in the forest.

"Denae, you can go to town, you know. It's not like you're seven anymore. You know how to behave yourself."

Like when she was seven and sent that town boy floating into a snowbank. She thought he'd like it, but it caused her to be banned from town for a year, and she still wasn't that interested in spending time there.

"I know, Mom. I like the forests better. Less noise and clutter."

Mom smiled. "Go take care of the fox. Love you."

Denae dashed out to the patio, Binesi following her. She was irritated at Lucas but happy to have another reason to be back on the other side of the lake. Lucas might be right about her looking like a twelve-year-old, but he didn't have to point it out, especially her barely-there breasts. She'd get him for that, saying it in front of Bradley…sometime when Mom wasn't around.

"Lucas is an asshole," Bin said, and she nodded.

"Thanks. What're you doing with Dad?"

"Maybe lathing wand blanks or working on the tractor. He didn't say, so I really don't know." He waved as he headed for the workshop.

She jogged back down the hill, her broad earthy yellow braids brushing her collarbones until she pushed them back. Great-Aunt Namid had plaited them Ojibwe-style after their shared heritage when they were over at Papa's and Granmama's last weekend. Still, even with her tan and high cheekbones, nobody would think of her as any sort of Indian with her hair or her equally dark yellow irises. Binesi said they were the color of yellow citrine gems, but she was sure he was trying to be nice.

Of course, her German and Swedish heritage wouldn't be in the running either. People didn't know what to make of her with her weird hair and eyes, so she tried to keep them hidden when she had to go into town. The rest of her family might have streaks of color in their hair, but their eyes were all naturally colored, even if a few had more brightly-hued eyes than most people.

Denae stopped, remembering Bin's *gotta practice*. So did she.

She pictured the beach by the small lake a few hundred yards away. She'd try it without words, using only gestures. A slight risk, but she was close enough, so it should be minimal. Besides, that's how you learned. The beach in her head, she curled a couple of fingers slightly, twisted her hand, and shifted.

Cold water splashed past her knees, and she caught herself from falling, levitating above the small lake. The bottom of her sundress was soaked, but that wouldn't be a problem for long.

Denae looked back at the beach. Missed her mark by thirty feet. The words would've gotten her closer, but no big deal. She'd eventually hit it even without a gesture.

She smiled, knowing she could squeeze in another swim after the fox was unstoned—no need to get back until suppertime, which was a few hours away.

Northern Wisconsin didn't have many months of swimming, so she wanted to get in as much as possible while it was warm enough. One day, she'd go to the Florida Keys or some other tropical place where she could swim year-round in warm water, but for now, she'd take what she could get.

She floated in the air, moving slowly across the lake, just a few inches above the rippling surface. The wet hem of her sundress left a small wake behind her as it dragged through the water. She'd hang the dress up to dry once she got to the other side.

She liked spotting the fish swimming along, and she'd skim above the surface following their movements. Her cousin Justin saw her doing that and now sometimes called her *weird one*, but he smiled when he said it and didn't say it when others were around, so she didn't mind. He was Lucas's age but her friend, sometimes protector of her or sometimes those she was upset with, and he could talk to her when everything seemed to be going wrong.

She followed some fish for a while but got to the opposite side and started down the trail. Once she got a little away from the lake, she stripped off the wet dress and hung it in the stone kiosk she'd built a little off the path.

Denae stretched, feeling the cool breeze on her body. Total freedom again.

After putting her belt back on, she stepped back for a moment to admire the simplicity of her kiosk design. Two vertical stone slabs at right angles to one another, with a third slab laid horizontally on top of them. And, of course, a thick stone foundation that stepped up from the forest floor.

Getting everything positioned and flattened to the proper thickness took a few tries, especially that horizontal one. It was tiring to hold the earth properly before turning it into stone. Granite worked well for the final product but was more challenging than limestone. She'd melded the three slabs together to make a single piece of stone, then molded stone hooks to hang her clothes and stuff and made sure there were plenty of overhangs to stand under if it did rain.

She'd built it during the spring once the snow melted, and it'd been quite handy ever since. Hardly anyone came down this trail in the summertime. They had to cross the lake or take a long way around. By that point, there were better trails to take. Few of her extended family levitated or flew, so hardly anyone even knew the kiosk existed. She'd build a few more around the family lands in out-of-the-way places, mainly for her benefit.

A branch scratched her side while Denae jogged down the trail. She'd done the same thing this morning…she should know the branch was there by now. A little dab of healing salve would fix that and any others she might get, and she'd trim it on the way back. Her freedom now was worth much more than any scratches she might get.

She surveyed the trail…the fox was over a half-mile farther down, past the cutoff to Oma's. It had taken almost an hour to lure it close enough to stone, but it was okay that Aunt Tilda didn't need him. While the pelt would be nice, she didn't need it, and hanging his tail off the back of her belt would only get her laughed at. He'd be happy to be back hunting, if maybe stiff for a few minutes. Then she could get back to the lake for a swim.

A deep pulsing growl brought Denae to an abrupt halt. She'd come around a slight bend, about halfway there, and that big male black bear was down the trail at the blueberry bushes. He'd either heard or smelled her. She hadn't been paying much attention to what slight breeze there was in these woods but thought she'd been relatively quiet.

Denae had seen the bear plenty of times, but he had never growled at her before.

She stopped.

He stood on his hind legs and pulsed out another growl.

She backed away, raising her arms to make herself look taller. This was silly. Still girl-child small compared to him.

His front paws slap the trail. She gasped at how fast he charged toward her.

Stoning spell, like the fox.

Casting. Was there enough time?

Hot breath. Spell done.

Pain. Falling.

Blackness.

↢ ↢ ⊙ ↣ ↣

Denae awoke to semi-darkness, looking up through tree branches.

Everything hurt—felt ripped from the inside out.

I guess I'm not going swimming, came floating through her brain, and she laugh-grunted against the pain. Oh, that hurt. Her vision dimmed to pinpoints for a moment before slowly returning.

She wiggled her toes and fingers while she lay there. It hurt to move anything…they ached even without moving them but worked. She lifted a hand up. The fingers were there, but bloody… dried blood covered the hand and down her arm. So heavy. She dropped it with a grunt, head swimming.

She closed her eyes…tried to focus on what hurt.

Everywhere.

Her breath was heavy…wet…her guts hurt. Her head pounded—it all throbbed. At the same time, everything seemed intact…whole.

What happened to the bear? The spell worked, didn't it?

She lifted her head slightly, gasped, and dropped it. She tried to scream, but only a faint gurgle came out. He was on top of her, jaws open above her belly, paw by her hip, but all marble.

She pushed, kicking against the ground, trying to slide out. Her knee banged something hard as her insides wrenched. She twisted, spewing out the contents of her stomach. Blood. A part of her mind registered what had happened while she spewed out more.

The spell had worked. She gagged on more. It hurt more than she thought it would, but then he was big…so much bigger than anything she'd ever tried to stone before. She'd hurt herself slightly in the past, but nothing like this. She fumbled with her pouch, wanting her jar of healing salve, but gasped again and fell onto her back, blackness overwhelming her.

↢↢⊙↣↣

Liquid flowed down her throat as she opened her eyes again.

Ah…it was already doing its magic…healing draught from somewhere. She could feel herself getting better, her insides knitting up. She swallowed the final bit and started pushing herself to sit. Bin's face came into view as her vision cleared.

"Slow down, Denae." He pushed her back down gently.

"Let me up!" Her voice was stronger now. Could she even speak before? She couldn't remember. "I can sit up now."

"Okay, okay." He released her shoulder and held his hands up. "Okay."

Denae pushed herself up, sitting. Her head spun a little before settling down.

"We need to get you to Oma's so she can get you healed."

Denae nodded slightly, putting her head into a spin again. The bear was marble in front of her but not over her. Had she kicked her way out, or had Bin done that? She began to shake, looking at the bear, his mouth open, fangs bared. He'd fallen over, on top of her in mid-swing to rake her with those immense claws.

"You stoned the bear?"

"Yeah. He charged me. I don't know why." She slipped back toward the ground, Binesi easing her down. "Everything hurts." Not the same way as before. She felt more mended, but the pain was sharper now.

"Your eyes look better."

"As in how?" She blinked reflexively.

"They're not blood red now. More like bloodshot from a weekend bender."

"That's a relief." She wasn't sure her sarcasm had gotten through.

"Yeah, it is. Your irises are your normal shade of yellow now."

She snorted at that. Too bad the blood couldn't dye them something else.

"Your skin's crusted with blood. It's like it came through your pores, and it's been leaking out elsewhere, aside from where you puked. Not sure what your insides are like, but your pulse and breathing are better. I only grabbed one draught, so don't think you're anywhere close to fine."

"I have a salve."

"Let's hold off on that for now. I don't see anything specific to put it on. Let me get you to Oma's."

He scooped her up, grunting slightly as he stood, then started down the trail.

She tried to focus, at least on the trail to Oma and getting better. She could maybe teleport there. It'd be faster, but no. She had no energy, so she'd just hurt herself more, would miss the mark, and needed Bin to carry her inside anyway.

"What happened with the bear? He's never bothered any of us before."

Denae shook her head, trying not to wince with every step. She shouldn't shake her head either. Now she was dizzy…nauseous. Things might be better, but he was right...they were nowhere near good.

"When he saw me, he growled and charged. I wasn't even close to him. I backed away. I'd never heard a growl like that."

Has anyone found Denae yet? Mom was sending out a blanket telepathic call, her thoughts anything but calm.

Denae was still trying to put words together when Binesi answered. Her brain seemed so slow.

I have her…taking her to Oma's.

What's wrong?

Long story, Mom, Denae added, brain finally kicking in. *Tell you later. I'll be okay.*

Bin? What happened to her?

That bear in the woods here tried to attack her. She hurt herself petrifying it.

Mom, I'll be okay.

Denae could feel the sigh come through.

Dad will meet you there. I'll be there in a few minutes. Love you.

Love you, too.

"Mom's finally learned when not to press you for details," Bin said with a chuckle.

"It's made life easier, but I'm sure questions will come once I feel better."

Talking made her tired, so she closed her eyes for what seemed to be only a couple of minutes when Dad met up with them on the trail. He obviously hadn't bothered with his Suburban and simply teleported there. She maybe could've left the bear behind, but probably not. No telling where she would've gone with a panic teleport, assuming she even went anywhere. She most likely would've just tired herself out going nowhere.

She closed her eyes again and reopened them, now feeling the cool hardness of Oma's examination table. Her grandmother's concerned face looked down on her as fingertips touched her sternum and navel. Healing warmth began flowing into her.

"I think I'll keep her overnight, Jerok."

"That sounds good, Mom. Riann will be here in a few minutes to help out since Ebby's dealing with a colicky baby." Denae glanced over, following her dad's voice, and smiled at his worry-etched face as he stood close, hands in his pockets. She felt a warm wetness on her foot and raised her head to see Oma-ma bathing it. Her great-grandmother ran the wet cloth along her ankle before wringing it out. It felt good, though the wrung water was dark red.

"But of course." There was humor mingled with concern in Oma-ma's dry, breathy voice while the healing warmth kept flowing from Oma. "Riann will have to see her only daughter, make sure she's okay, and of course, find out the how's and why's of what Denae did to herself this time."

"She didn't have a choice about petrifying the bear," Binesi responded. "When he finally came to a stop, he was on top of her. If he'd fallen differently, he would have crushed Denae. Another second, and she wouldn't have gotten the spell off anyway. He would definitely have mauled her badly, and there isn't that much of her to maul."

"I can hear you, you know." She moved her head more easily to find him, his shirt and shorts filthy with her blood from carrying her here.

"You disagree?" Binesi flashed her a smile.

"If I can get one more growth spurt, I'll get to five-foot."

"Hope springs eternal," Dad said, and she saw a smile form on his face, which probably meant that she was looking better enough that he was out of crisis mode. "And, of course, you were running the trails in the buff again?"

"Of course. It's not like a sundress would've protected me from the bear or what actually happened."

Oma-ma's hand stopped bathing her leg. "Jerok. You know you're never going to stop her." For reasons Denae didn't understand, her great-grandmother always seemed to take her side on this argument.

Dad gave them a wry smile. "I know. I think even Riann's given up on trying to turn Denae into a proper lady."

"That would be for the best." The warmth of Oma-ma's cleaning began again, moving up to her knee as the sound of tires crunching on gravel caused them all to look out the window.

Oma smiled at Denae. "Do you want to talk to your mom now or in the morning?"

Denae shook her head slightly, not feeling the spinning now. Everything was feeling better, but not that good yet. Bin could tell Mom most of the story.

"Morning."

Her grandmother ran a finger down from her forehead to the tip of her nose, and Denae felt her muscles relax and sleep flow into her.

Chapter 2

The Tipi

"That wasn't nice," Denae said, glaring at her little brother while she tread water. Her mind had been on last night's nightmare about the bear that attacked her last summer, and he'd slipped one of his body control spells in on her.

"You just told me I need to practice more, so I did," Binesi responded, annoyance sounding in his voice. "We're in the lake and away from the rest of them." He glanced over at their other relatives swimming a little away from them. "So what if I made your bladder let loose? I didn't think cramping a muscle was a good idea at the moment. You usually block me anyway, so I'm having to come up with sneakier ways to do my body control spells, and this actually worked."

He gave her a big grin, so she hit him with a reverse levitation, dunking him. She considered holding him under for a while, but he had successfully snuck one in on her. However annoying it might be, it was what he was supposed to do, though the bladder releases were a bit juvenile. She released him after a couple of seconds, and his head broke water, arms flailing.

"You need to work on your resisting, little one."

He snorted as he shook water from his blond hair, the silver streak in it sparkling in the sun. At fifteen, he might be two years younger, but he'd broken the five-foot mark by well over a half-foot while she was still a half-inch shy. "I can't block you on that…never could."

"That's why you need to try," and she dunked him again, re-releasing him almost immediately.

After he came up, she said, "You are getting better with your control on those spells. I didn't even feel that one until it was too late."

"You weren't even supposed to know I did that." He laughed. "You should've heard the cussing when I hit Lucas with that when he was in the shower. He didn't even know I did it until I told him later. He didn't seem to be sure whether to punch me or praise me but finally said it was nicely done and hasn't done any payback yet."

"Oh, it'll be coming, and I want to be around to see it when it does." She hesitated, then continued." You want to see what I've been working on out in the woods?"

"More kiosks?" She'd put up a few more stone kiosks around the forest over the last year and shown those to him.

"No, something bigger."

"What?"

"Come see." She grinned at him more broadly than she really felt but was far enough along on it that she didn't think he would laugh.

"Where?"

"Where I was attacked by the bear last summer." Her stomach did sink in voicing that memory. That attack was the cause of her recurring nightmares and the reason she was building in the forest.

"Sure. Let's see whatever you're doing there."

Denae glanced to where their clothes and towels lay on the bank, thinking she should put a kiosk there, too. Later. Reaching out a thought, she lifted her belt with its knife and rabbit-skin pouch from the top of the pile and floated it above the small lake toward the trail they'd take as they began swimming in that direction.

↢↢⊙↣↣

"Seriously? A stone tipi?" Binesi shook his head and took a step back as he surveyed the large four-foot-tall circular slanted stone wall from several yards away, a sour look on his face. Denae stood next to him and wondered why he seemed disturbed by this. She knew it was a little weird, but this wasn't like him.

"It will be when I'm finished," Denae declared. "It's twenty feet in diameter and will be about that high when I get to the smoke hole. The stone walls are two feet thick, and since it's a cone, it's self-supporting."

"But why?" He fidgeted, each tiny step backing him up slightly.

Denae took a deep breath. "A few months ago, I woke up lying here…right here where I'm standing. Lying in crunchy, dirty snow."

"How?"

She nodded. "I apparently teleported myself here in my sleep to get away from my bear nightmare."

Binesi whistled as he took another step back. "I didn't know that was possible."

"Neither did I. I've done this five times now, and I hit my mark exactly each time. I can hit my mark better in my sleep than I can when I'm awake. I'm surprised I was never sleep-flying or levitating to get away before. I wasn't, was I?"

He shook his head, his brow furrowing. "Have you told Dad?

"No, and don't you tell him either yet."

"So, you're building this because you teleport here in your sleep? This still isn't making much sense." He took another step back down the trail.

"I'll have a safe place here when I sleep-teleport. Away from the bear."

"If you say so, but Dad, Anton, and a couple of the uncles hauled the bear off to the other side of Minnesota before Uncle Leonard turned it back to flesh. It's hundreds of miles west of us. You're safe, even without the protection wards you've put on it."

"Protection?"

He looked back at the tipi, though this seemed to take him some effort. "Oh yeah. I have to force myself to even look at the tipi, but it's hard, and I really don't want to. I guess this is good training of some sort, but if you hadn't told me where it was, I would never have even looked that way. I would've kept going down the trail."

"I don't know how to do those," Denae said quietly and saw him shrug in response.

She knew that people could sometimes do more than they thought they did with something, and she really wanted this to be safe for her, especially in the middle of the winter. It already felt inviting at only a fifth of its total height. She'd tried other designs, but they didn't seem stable enough. However, this concentric ring design was working quite nicely.

If she could get a set of faucets so she'd have hot and cold running water, she'd be happy to live here. But those magical faucets were so expensive that she'd have to carry water and melt snow for years. She supposed she could get a wand to create the water for her, but she'd have to get someone to recharge it for her on occasion, and that someone wouldn't be Lucas. Until she figured out something, there would be no bubble-baths for her out here. She stepped forward and floated herself over the sloped wall. "So, can you hop over and come in?"

He took a hesitant step forward. "I don't think so. It's more intense now. I have a great desire to go back to the lake. I'm very sure I left something I need there…or at Oma's."

"That's not good. While this is my place, and I don't want at least some of the family here, I want you to come in. I really do."

Binesi staggered forward slightly. "Well…that made a difference." He inhaled a slow, deep breath, seemed to relax, then took the few steps effortlessly and hopped over the sloped wall. "That dropped the wards, at least for me. You should get Jude out here. He can tell you what you did with this."

"I'll do it…after I'm finished." Jude would be okay, and he could keep a secret, unlike her other two older brothers.

"So…show me what you're doing."

Denae smiled, hoping he'd ask. He was getting adept at controlling body and mind but did nothing with the elements, not that she did anything with them except for earth. She leapt over the back wall, sliding down the slope, and walked about a hundred feet down a path before stopping at another small clearing. Coaxing a length of earth to slide off the side of a wide trench as Binesi got there, she sent the line of dirt creeping back down the path. Water had seeped into the bottom of the trough, leaving behind a muddy pit. The earthy fragrance of freshly turned soil and the way it flowed over her feet made her smile.

Binesi stepped out of its way, then followed her back up and over the tipi wall. At the same time, Denae lined the earth several inches thick on top of the tipi wall, following the arc several feet.

Denae handed Binesi a long wooden triangle with a bubble level attached to one end. "Run that slowly along the outside while I straighten the dirt, then again on the inside. That way, I'll keep the angle right all the way up."

Binesi nodded and did as she asked. Once she was happy with how it looked, she made a gesture, and it all turned to stone as more energy left her.

Binesi grinned at her. "That last took it out of you. You're all sweaty."

Denae nodded and sat down on the ground. "Give me a few minutes to catch my breath, but that's how it's done. Turning it to stone is harder than simply moving the dirt."

"Do you use your amulet for this?"

Denae looked at the beetle-shaped amulet that hung on her chest, its wings iridescent in the sunlight. Papa had made that for her after her attack by the bear so she'd have more available energy if she needed it. It was similar to Mom's, though not as strong. She shook her head.

"I tried, but it takes too much time for it to charge back up to make it very worthwhile for a big task like this. I'm saving it for when I need a lot at once, like Papa said."

Bin looked a little sour. She knew he'd like one, but only Anton had one as a present from Papa and Granmama for graduating college. The rest would have to wait, and while Granmama always acted like Denae never measured up, Papa made up for it by doting on her. This amulet was an excellent example of that. Of course, since she wasn't going to college anyway, maybe this was just an early equivalent gift.

As Binesi ran his fingers over the rock, she continued. "I'll meld that new bit to the existing rock later, once I have the entire ring done. The good part is that each ring going up will take less time, though I'll have to levitate while I'm doing most of the rest."

"Of course you will," he agreed with a laugh. "Why bother with building scaffolds or anything like that. You'll have this done by the end of summer?"

"Unless Mom and Dad send me back over to Papa and Granmama's for training, though I'm getting good enough with the teleport that I could still come here and work on it. I come out before daybreak and get a layer or two done, then again at lunch, maybe breaks if I have the time, and then again if I can get away in the evening. If I could sneak away more, I'd have it done in less than a month. I don't want to wake up out here in a snowstorm because I teleported in my sleep unless I have someplace to go quickly."

Binesi sobered with that. "That nightmare is nasty. I wish I heard you more often so I could come help."

"I'm glad you can do it now. That first time you tried…."

He shuddered. "Yeah, I got trapped in the dream with you until you woke up. Sometimes I still feel the claws slashing into my back."

Denae got up. "Let's start walking back. I need to try practicing that entombment spell on something small. A squirrel or rabbit or something."

"And when you get good enough, I'm your guinea pig on that one, too?"

"Of course, just like I'm yours. I am getting tired of you trying to release my bladder, though, so try other things."

"When you don't successfully fight me off on that, or any of the things I try. You're harder to get through than any of the bubs, and they're all older. At least I haven't tried releasing your bowels."

Denae glared at him, then softened it some. "I'd say not to try it, but I'm so stressed about teleporting in my sleep that there are times that if you could send it through the bathroom door, I wouldn't fight it at all."

"I'm trying to get Aunt Issa to teach me something that will give a more peaceful sleep, but she keeps saying 'not yet.' She thinks I need to work on other mind spells before I progress to that, but maybe I can convince her to let me start that sometime soon. That's one I'd like to practice on you."

"I'd really like that. See if you can get her to teach it to you so that you have it down well enough before the first snowfall."

She was about to head back down the trail to their small lake when she had a sudden idea. From the glint in Bin's eye, she was pretty sure of the source of this inspiration, but it would be more fun to go back to the trough and wallow in the mud than fight his spell. She was sure that was a part of his whole suggestion, but she could dunk him so that he was as dripping in mud as she was going to be, and she could be washed off at the lake long before he could walk back. At the lake, it didn't matter if she missed her mark by a few feet.

Chapter 3

History

"You're doing quite well with your history abilities, Denae," Aunt Gaia said. She was only nine years older than Denae, and brilliant, if a bit absent-minded. Kids called almost all of their extended family's adults aunts or uncles. However, Gaia was one of her biological aunts…her dad's youngest sister. Gaia's streak was spread throughout instead of the simple streak in her hair like her dad and brothers, giving it a two-tone mix of red and copper. Much more lovely than her own earthy yellow hair that was nothing but streak.

Aunt Gaia smiled at her. She was in her usual gauzy gown, the oranges and reds matching her hair, and Denae smiled back. She liked having these one-on-one classes with Gaia despite the tangents her aunt tended to wander off on while teaching. Sometimes they were trips to la-la-land, but at other times, they were more interesting than what Gaia was supposed to be teaching her.

Denae found that history could be fascinating, though she had to be careful with it, especially on people. You could easily find out things you really didn't want to know. Plus, it was just plain rude. Objects were safer…usually…from that aspect, at least if you stayed away from weapons. Aunt Gaia used a beautifully made antique knife as an *object* lesson for that.

She'd warned Denae that it had a bloody past before letting Denae history it. What she didn't say was that this bloody past included human sacrifice. After they'd cleaned up Denae's puke from where they were sitting, Gaia had explained that this could be a problem even with objects…you never really knew their past until it was too late.

She at least didn't recognize either the wielder or the victim, and neither seemed to be family. And it'd happened a decade before she was born. The problem was, she knew it happened a little before midnight on April 6th, 1950, under the darkness of a new moon. That date was now stuck in her head forever.

Aunt Gaia was reticent about who the wielder was, though her eyes went steely when she said he would never need the knife again. She kept the knife stored here in the library strictly for this lesson on history.

"My question today is this. How far can you go back with your history?"

Denae blinked, bringing herself back to the present as her aunt set a black alder box on the table that seemed heavy for its size and was well over a foot square.

"Let's try this item and tell me what you can see." Aunt Gaia undid the latch, opened the lid, and took out a square of black velvet, the edges hemmed in gold. She spread the cloth on the table. Next, she pulled out an ornate gold circular stand that she set on the black velvet cloth. It had a look of age about it. After that, she lifted a heavy, clear orb which she unwrapped from another gilt-edged black cloth and set it gently on the stand. "This has been a family heirloom for a long time. Relax your mind and tell me about it as you delve back."

Denae looked at the crystal ball a moment as her aunt slid it closer on the black velvet cloth it sat on. She saw nothing but the distorted clearness of the crystal sphere, which she supposed was as it should be. The stand, however, intrigued her, with the woodland scenes around the part of the base that she could see. There were rabbits, deer, birds, and a dryad or nymph or something like that at the trunk of a fully leafed tree. She looked away briefly, aware that she was supposed to be discovering the history of the ball, not admiring the superb craftsmanship of the stand.

She held her hand over the orb, quietly speaking the words she needed to focus the spell, then took a breath and relaxed as the vision began to coalesce in her head. She hadn't gotten good enough yet to be able to do the spell silently without the words, but she was getting close. She wondered how old this really was. The initial feelings she felt stirring were of something ancient. Things started to clear as she saw her aunt in her vision.

"I see you using this. You seem concerned about whatever you saw, but that was only last March. You've used it several times, learned on it a decade ago, nineteen-sixty-seven, with Oma-ma when you were almost my age."

"Is that Dad…much younger…twenty-five years ago or so, again with Oma-ma. He seems frustrated…there's another man. Opa, maybe? He looks family. Dark hair and golden streak right of center…seems to know what he's doing, and this is like forty-five years ago." Denae continued on like this, never seeing what they might be seeing in the crystal ball but describing the people as she went. Their styles of dress changed as she went back a century, then two, three, four. Except for teaching, it seemed like the people were always alone while scrying with the crystal orb. It seemed like almost all the people involved had some sort of streak in their hair. Were they all in the Dassow line?

"This one's different." Denae didn't spare a glance at her aunt that might break the connection, which was becoming tenuous. "This man has a heavy apron on. He's actually shaping the orb. It's hot. Now…heat…fire. Fourteen-sixty…I think the year is somewhere around there. I'm not getting anything more exact, but that's when the crystal ball was made. The man looked to be Dassow based on his spread streak, similar to yours, though blond, and he's balding." She broke the spell with a look now, seeing her aunt beaming at her.

"Most excellent, Denae. You're the first to be able to take it all the way back in a long time…since me, in fact. According to family records, it was made in October of fourteen-fifty-nine, so you were very close for that gross distance in time. The man was your many, many times great grandfather Gotfrid Dassow. And yes, that was Jerok trying rather unsuccessfully to learn how to divine using this crystal ball. Your dad didn't have the patience for it. I'm hoping you will."

"You mean?" Was this her next training with Gaia?

"Yes, I do. Take this home with you."

"Won't I be studying it here?"

Gaia smiled. "I have another here that we can work with. Take this one to your room and work with it there. Divination is a personal study. I can give you some direction, but most of it is simply you clearing your mind, looking into it, and working to see something. I can only get you so far. Jerok never saw anything, but Anton did."

"I didn't see Anton in this."

"He has a different one. I trained him when he was home for the summer between college semesters. We weren't going to send anything as precious as this into a mundane college environment, so he has a much more modern orb of crystal that works just about as well. Besides, he wouldn't have had the appreciation for this one that I know you will."

"And you trust me with this?" Denae stared from Gaia's smiling face to the ancient family relic. She wondered if the forest-scene base was the same age or different, but she could find that out later.

"Your dad said that if you could history it all the way back, then you'd understand its value and treat it with care. Your outdoor wanderings are curtailed some with the snow on the ground and early darkness, so your personal studies at home with this should carry you through Yuletide. It is not easy, and it is not quick, but you can scry interesting happenings and futures if you keep at it."

"Futures, as in the plural?"

"Indeed. Maybe I should say possible futures, probable futures, but nothing is carved in stone. The past may be fixed, but the future is quite pliable, and visions from a crystal such as this can help make it even more malleable." Gaia gave a mysterious smile, then asked, "What's this I hear about you having a tipi out in the forest?"

Denae jumped slightly. Did everyone know already?

Gaia laughed. "Jude let that slip a while back when we were going over the protections on the library, but asked me not to tell anyone else. So tell me about it."

"Twenty feet tall, all of stone, except the door flap, and that's deerskin. White on the outside, and I've painted the inside."

"And these protections you've done on it?"

"I don't know," Denae said, shaking her head. "Jude says they're nothing he's familiar with. He thinks my anxieties from the bear and some of my cousins have become manifest. I was building it for my protection. I know I poured my heart and soul into it."

"Not literally, I'm sure," Gaia said with a laugh.

Denae shook her head. "I'm safe there. I sleep better there than anywhere else, and Bin says there's a comforting quiet there. Only he and Jude are currently allowed inside, and Bin's the only one not off at college."

"You have so much talent about you that you haven't even explored, and at the same time, you can't even get a match to light without a mundane striker. So intriguing. You'll have to show me this tipi sometime. Oh, and with those invitations you did for Bin and Jude…can you turn them back off?"

"I don't know," Denae responded, her brow furrowed. "I haven't tried."

Chapter 4

Town

Why had she bothered with this stupid divination? Aunt Gaia was sure she had the gift, but Denae doubted it. She'd been trying for weeks. Most of the time, it was nothing or misty fog. If she was lucky, the mists swirled. On those rare occasions when there might be something, it was snowier than it had been outside last night, just vague shadows. She simply didn't know what she was seeing or if it was really anything at all.

Gaia insisted it took practice…lots and lots of it, apparently. Dad never said she was wasting her time, but he'd never seen anything in it. Still, Anton had, so she should be able to do better than him like she'd done with history. She would've asked him for some hints, but he'd gone over to Uncle Mawk's after breakfast to help with some maintenance on the house there. If nothing happened soon, she'd grab him this evening.

It had to be tonight. Anton was heading north tomorrow after lunch back to where he worked now. She suspected that a girl was the real reason he was leaving earlier than he needed to. Mom didn't scry in any manner, nor did any of the other bubs, so they'd be no help.

Denae settled back to the orb that seemed to be laughing at her attempts and took a deep breath. She was supposed to not focus on anything. Clear her mind and allow it to wander.

Well, the wandering was easy. She was getting expert at that. Keeping it off her dreams about the bear and getting this idiotic ball to give her anything coherent was something else entirely. From what Aunt Gaia said , she'd probably have no clue what it meant even if she got a vision. She said that it took a while to gain discernment in the perceiving, assuming you even got them. She'd rather be down in the parlor practicing eight-ball on the pool table than staring at this oversized cue ball.

Bin wasn't helping, playing Casey Kasem's *American Top 40* on his boombox. Casey was doing a New Year's Eve rundown of the top hits of 1977 since this was the last day of the year. It wasn't that she didn't like the music echoing down from Bin's room. She probably would've been listening to it herself, but she needed quiet to help her with her practice. How he could study with the racket was beyond her, and the start of that thumping beat of *We Will Rock You* definitely wasn't helping. She hoped his batteries would run out soon. She'd taken the last D-cells yesterday for her own boombox.

She'd been sitting in her room staring at this antique crystal sphere for hours…enough time that even her stomach was distracting her with thoughts about lunch. She needed something more concrete than this insane divination.

Earth was solid to her…mud, dirt, or stone. Auras weren't supposed to be concrete, but they were to her. Like levitation, but then she'd done both of those since before she could remember.

And why was it so incredible to her that they could listen to songs from Hollywood out here in the forests of Northern Wisconsin? If she'd ever seen Hollywood, she could teleport there, so sending music should be relatively simple, shouldn't it, but that was a totally different sort of magic…one she didn't understand, like sending voices or electrical power over copper wires.

Even so, that was solid compared to the divination. She reminded herself that it had taken years to master teleport, after stone-shot, flying, and many other spells before even starting to learn that one. Plus, she'd ended up in some unknown places before she'd figured it all out completely. At least she'd found her way home and hadn't ended up in an ocean like her dad did when he was learning it.

It was the base of the crystal ball that intrigued her more than this divination. She did history on the base and found that it was made at the same time by another ancient relative, and Aunt Gaia told her it was her many-times great aunt Elspeth. She looked young, not as old as Gaia, with gold and blond hair intermixed like her older brother Gotfried. Elspeth came through more clearly than most anyone else. Probably, most of the time, the people were either pulling it out to put the orb on it or putting it away. They weren't spending time doing anything with the base. Elspeth, on the other hand had actually created it and spent a lot of time crafting the intricate details of the woodland scenes.

Large animals carved so life-like in the gold… a stag, a wolf, and the standing bear that gave her shivers when she first saw it. There were birds and smaller animals throughout, with a couple of men and a child scattered about. There was the dryad or nymph and other alfar or fey or whatever they were. A couple of the smaller ones had wings and were flying, and the larger ones seemed earthbound. Denae studied the child for a while, but dressed as it was with the clothing of the time, she couldn't tell if it was a boy or a girl.

Denae found a fascination with Elspeth, in part due to the likenesses between them. They were both small and slight of build with long fingers and strangely colored eyes, though Elspeth at least had jade green eyes that were more pleasing than Denae's, just like the blond and gold hair. Denae wondered if the family had any other antiques that Elspeth had made. She'd like to find out more about her if she could.

She was straying…her mind wandering, not focusing, but that was what she was supposed to do, right? There must be something here besides the fog and fuzziness.

Open your mind…yeah, right. She tried yet again, looking at the orb instead of the stand.

Then something, for just a second, then back to fuzziness. Someone. She looked familiar. It came again. Leah? walking? Snow? Where? Fuzz again.

Leah was a town girl…a mundane…who treated Denae okay. She was about her age, though Denae was pretty sure that Leah thought Denae was much younger. Blonde and on the plump side, Leah was a senior in high school and waitressed some evenings and weekends at Fred's.

Leah seemed friendly, talking with her on occasions when Denae's family ate at Fred's, not that Denae had much in common with her or anyone else in town.

Leah chatted when she didn't need to as a part of her waitressing. She even gabbed when Denae was by herself. Leah would talk to the girl with the weird hair and eyes like she was ordinary, though Denae always wore her tinted glasses when she was in town to hide the yellow of her irises. People didn't like looking at her eyes, not even her cousins. Spooky, they said. Eerie…worse than the polluted Lake Erie, they'd tease.

Denae focused again on her crystal ball, letting her mind sweep, trying to ignore the lyrics of disgrace and being put back into their place. She could concentrate on Leah…work on what she actually saw. Leah was momentarily solid, but why?

Suddenly the crystal ball was clear, the vision of Leah wavering only slightly. It was in town—she recognized it. Leah by the snow-covered park—then outside The Evergreen Café—a truck sliding on ice, careening out of control—blood—body under tire—death—darkness. It would happen soon…very soon.

She had to stop Leah…save her…now.

Denae stood and shifted to the middle of that park. That's where Leah would be and where she was, fifty feet away at the corner, waiting for the light to change so she could cross the road to that next block, the one where the café was.

"Leah!"

Leah jerked, turning on the icy sidewalk. She lost her step slightly but caught herself again.

"Stay there," Denae yelled. "Don't move."

Leah just stared at her, mouth agape for a moment.

Good…stay surprised. Don't move.

"What are you doing there," Leah yelled back a moment later. "You're…you're—"

"Just stay there," Denae continued, waving one hand wildly, her other skimming the chest-deep snow she'd landed in. "Just wait a minute."

She was sure it was less than a minute away.

The light turned green, but Leah had already started to push through the snow toward Denae. All for the better.

Then came the crash Denae knew must happen. Metal against brick. Glass shattering. People yelling…screaming. Leah turned, staring back where all the noise came from.

People were probably hurt, maybe killed, but Leah was okay. That she didn't mess up. Leah wasn't dead.

"You're fine…you're safe now," Denae said to herself, then turned her back to everything, her bare feet suddenly aching. Her cold, wet nightgown clung to her, twisting as she turned in the chest-high snow, more light snow coming down into her hair and face.

She had to leave, but she couldn't do it here where the town people would see. They may have already seen too much. Leah definitely did. Maybe the wreckage would distract the others. Most of the people had turned that way when it happened.

She pushed forward, fighting her way through the snow away from Leah to the next street. She punched at the snowplow's head-high dirty drift, hurting her hand, then clambered over the icy snow, her long nightgown snagging on the ice chunks. This would've been easier naked, she thought.

She heard her name called…Leah's voice, she was sure, as she slipped over the top and fell onto the street. A scrape on her cheek burned and another on her hip, but it didn't matter. She had to leave.

Denae pushed herself up and shuffled, her gown wrapped around her legs. She heard more distant yelling and screaming…some obviously in pain. She had to get home—get behind the next building, out of sight, and shift there.

She shouldn't have come to town, but Leah would've died. She barely even knew her, but she liked her. That made it okay, didn't it? She wasn't sure her family would see it that way, but they'd have to accept it once they heard. It was done. She was scared that word would somehow get back to them that the weird cousin with the strange ochre yellow hair and eyes was in town half-dressed and screaming. She didn't see any of them, so maybe she got lucky, but that kind of luck rarely came her way.

Her feet felt frozen as she slipped and slid her way around the building, then into a plowed alleyway. She thought she heard footsteps and looked both ways to make sure she was alone. She couldn't jump inside the house, or any building, without possibly breaking something, or maybe herself, but the front of the house would be close enough. The front was closer to the stairway so she could get back up to her room unseen.

She shifted and suddenly was even colder and couldn't see anything but white. She inhaled snow as she gasped—thrashed around, coughing, snow everywhere. She kept punching, making an opening around her. She couldn't move her legs. They were stuck somehow. She knew she was twenty feet from the porch. She was also trapped, as frozen as her feet.

Then her mind clicked…stupid, stupid, stupid. She'd panicked. She went here like it was summer. She should've remembered that the snow drifted here after every heavy snowstorm like last night when the wind was out of the northwest.

Stupid.

She put a hand over her mouth, took in a cold gulp of air, and rose into the air. The snow pulled on her gown, her legs. It tried to hold her back, but she powered up above the snowbank. She floated herself onto the porch, feeling a deep shiver start.

Her hand shook as she grabbed the doorknob and let herself in, closing it quietly behind her. She felt somewhat drained by the two jumps but exhilarated by what she'd done.

She almost got to the stairway when Mom looked out the kitchen door, saw her and the wet footprints she'd left from the front door.

Crap.

Denae could see the wheels whirling quickly in her mom's head while she tried, futilely, she knew, to round the corner and go up the stairs.

"Stop. Now. Wait. There," Mom said, spitting the words out as she processed the scene.

"Mom, can't I just go up and get dry," Denae asked, though it came out as more of a chattering whine.

"No," came the reply. "Get that thing off. By the fire. Now."

Great, Denae thought as her teeth began to chatter. At least she'd thaw out quicker in front of the living room fireplace. She could step inside that fireplace without even having to bend over, something even Binesi couldn't say now. Little brother was too tall.

She slogged off the wet nightgown, gave it over to her mom's outstretched hand, then trudged over to stand in front of the fireplace, her body shaking in earnest now. Her feet ached from the cold now as she made the walk, her teeth chattering harder. The heat felt good, like life itself at the moment, even if she looked more like a half-frozen twelve-year-old than only a week away from turning eighteen.

Mom threw an afghan over her shoulders, then disappeared back into the kitchen.

Denae dimly heard a slight clatter as she absorbed the warmth of the fire, and then her mom was back, handing her a hot mug of coffee, suitably sweet and creamy. Denae sniffed the wonderful scent, warming her hands and trying not to spill any of it with her shivering.

Mom pushed a chair close to the fire for Denae, then slid the ottoman up for herself. "Sit," she said. "Where did you go?"

Denae winced. "To town."

"In your nightgown…no shoes. Not even your belt?" Denae rarely left her bedroom without her snakeskin belt with its pouch and knife.

"No time," Denae replied. "Not even for that." She let out a sigh. "At least I was wearing my nightgown."

At her mom's upturned eyebrow, she explained what she had seen while scrying the crystal ball, why she'd had to go right then, what she did, and how she got back. She managed to bite her tongue and left out the part where she landed in the snowdrift.

"This was all because you saw it in that crystal ball?"

Denae nodded.

"You jumped into town because you saw something for the first time in that orb?"

Denae continued nodding vigorously, trying to get it through to Mom that she'd done the right thing…that she hadn't messed up. "It was a true vision. Leah was right where I saw her, about to cross the street. I stopped her, but we both heard the crash less than a minute later. Everyone on the street heard that crash. The truck hit the building. Leah would've been in front of the truck if I hadn't stopped her."

Mom stared into the fire for what seemed like minutes, her expression unreadable. She was going to ban her from town again. Finally, Mom's shoulders drooped slightly, and her gaze softened.

"So, you saved this Leah," Mom said. "I guess I should be glad you were at least wearing something." The upstairs area was where they didn't have to wear clothes, and really, the only reason Denae was wearing her gown this morning was that it was chilly in her room. If she'd only wrapped a blanket around her, she would've dropped that before she teleported.

Denae nodded in return, not meeting Mom's eyes, and sipped the hot coffee. Her feet ached and throbbed worse than ever.

"Let's see your feet." Her mom examined the toes, declared no frostbite, and then dabbed salve on her cheek, hip, and knuckles. "You said that no family saw you? Hopefully that's the case, but if someone did, I'll try to head them off. You may have to answer questions if word does get around about this."

Denae understood. With as large of an extended family as they had, it wasn't that unlikely that someone was close enough around to have seen and recognized her. It wasn't like her hair color and braids were hard to spot at a distance.

Denae glanced at the fire. "I'm going to lie down on the hearth and warm up here for a while first."

Her mom smiled and nodded. Denae took another sip of coffee and set the mug down, the afghan falling to the floor. She stretched as she stepped close to the fire, feeling the heat begin to permeate her body before curling up on the warm stone hearth.

Questions may come, she thought as her front warmed quickly, but she couldn't be in too much trouble if they did, could she? She'd saved someone from dying. Gaia said that the future was malleable with this scrying, and since Leah would've died without her seeing and acting, that was right. But this was scary. She'd played God in a way, and what about the others. She thought about the screams of pain. Despite the warmth, she shivered as a chill flowed down her back. She was sure there were others that she hadn't saved.

Chapter 5

At The Arcade

"It looks like you got away with it." Binesi gave Denae a grin. "Blipping into town in your nightgown and back." Looking at the packing slip for this order, he slipped a jar of Aunt Berti's Bath Salts into the box, wedging it securely between the packing worms. Denae thrust her hand into the worms to make space and slid a pump bottle of Issa's Body Lotion in next to it, then laid the slip on top.

"Yeah. Nobody saw me. Mom hasn't heard anything." She folded the box shut, and Binesi grabbed the tape gun. "Nobody important anyway."

It'd been two weeks, and at this point it'd become apparent that she had gotten away with it, aside from a talking-to from Dad. Even that had been more of a conversation about being careful and watching her priorities, but that saving a life was a high priority.

"Leah's important," Binesi said. "She's alive, I mean. You said she wouldn't have been otherwise."

"Yeah. That's what saved me. Mom and Dad understood that I'd saved her life. Some of the rest of the family wouldn't have cared."

"Still, this is the first time Mom's asked you back down to work in the warehouse in two weeks." He glanced at the empty clipboard on the table. "Is this the last order?"

"It is." Denae looked around. They'd caught up on boxing up the mail orders and already had the new products stocked. They didn't have a storefront or even a sign out front, but they had a good-sized load for the postal truck every day.

"You want to go to the new arcade?" He grinned across the table at her.

"You think Mom will let me?" She wasn't sure she would be allowed free run of the town yet.

"One way to find out. I'll go ask if she has anything else for us to do or if we can go."

He ran off to the vault area while Denae levitated the last stack of mostly mundane packages over to the loading dock. He was more likely to get a yes answer from Mom if he asked anyway.

Various family members of her rather extended family made magical, alchemical, and mundane items and products. The mundane products often had tiny amounts of one or both of the others to make them even better, so they all called those mostly mundane. She'd been helping out fairly regularly for years when she wasn't doing her studies.

Binesi had been talking about this game arcade enough that even she was interested in seeing it. If nothing else, she could play pool while he played the other stuff. He was much more interested in what went on around town than she was. Give her the outdoors, hiking or skiing the forests, books to read, and a warm fire, and she was happy. The town was more of an annoyance, the warehouse a necessary pain for her so they could make the money needed to live as they wished. Despite Binesi's complaints about moving into the twentieth century and getting electricity wired to the house so they could have television and not go through boxes of batteries for their boomboxes, they seemed to do better than most people in town. That is, if she judged the size of their home against most of the houses in town. Magic seemed to suffice for most of their needs if you didn't include radio and television.

Binesi returned from the vault where the valuable magical and alchemical items were stored, a broad grin on his face.

"We're golden. Mom was deep in conversation with Aunt Issa, and I think only half-listened to what I said. Let's get out of here before she thinks of something else."

Denae smiled and grabbed her parka as they made it out the door and through the wooden fence of the front entrance.

They walked the few blocks through the snowy downtown. A shiver rolled down Denae's back when they got to the boarded-up front of the café where the truck crashed through. The stores on either side looked undamaged but had been long vacant. Dad said that a lot of the downtown had moved out to the edge of town along the highway.

Binesi stopped and looked.

"This is it?"

Denae nodded, feeling a tightness in her chest.

"Paper said the truck plowed through the window…driver was drunk and going too fast. Lost control."

Denae nodded again. She'd read that, too, and that the café had their usual lunch crowd then. People had died and others injured, though she had saved Leah.

They walked on to the next intersection, and she saw the park.

"You were really out there in the middle of the park up to your butt in the snow?"

She nodded…swallowed. "Deeper, really."

He scanned around as he nodded. "Yeah, they'd have to be fairly close to see you, with those shops across the street. You wouldn't have had more than head and shoulders above the top of the snow. Still, you got lucky. Family could've banned you from town for a year or more."

"Wouldn't be the first time," Denae muttered, remembering that had happened about a decade ago. It'd been more of a problem for Mom back then. If she wasn't doing schooling with family, Mom had to get some cousin or aunt to watch her while she handled the warehouse.

"The new snowfalls have completely covered up your indiscretion," Binesi said with a laugh, and Denae gave a weak smile in return. She still expected some aunt or uncle to jump out and ask what she thought she was doing in town.

Past there was Fred's Diner, and Denae breathed a sigh of relief when she didn't see Leah waiting any tables. She had no clue what to say if she did see her.

The new arcade was in the next block, taking the place of an auto parts store and a run-down washateria. All the clear glass had been blacked over, with lots of fluorescent paints advertising the games.

Loud noises assailed her when Binesi opened the door. There were lots of machines, high-pitched beeps and blips, flashing lights, and a couple of pool tables toward the back that seemed a little smaller than their table back home. She almost turned and went back out. It was all so loud.

Still, she followed her brother inside, hoping she might get used to it all. She reached up and made sure her tinted 'town' glasses were in place. No sense freaking out people with her eyes.

There was music. Some group was singing about some dancing queen who was seventeen. She liked that song and started moving to the beat of the music. She could get into the mood to dance with this, so focused on it to try to block out the noises of the games.

She followed Binesi around for a few minutes until he settled on a pinball machine. He'd just dropped a quarter in when she heard someone behind her. "We need to talk."

Denae winced as she recognized the voice. She turned and nodded.

Binesi glanced over, also hearing the voice over the noises of the games, or at least feeling the other's presence.

"We're going over there," Denae said to Binesi, pointing the direction with a nod of her head. She pulled a couple more dollars out of her coat pocket and laid it on the glass top of the game.

Binesi eyes widened as he saw Leah, and Denae saw that Leah had caught that.

They walked to a small table near the pool tables where the noise level was lower. "Boyfriend?"

"Brother," Denae responded. "Little brother, though not so little anymore," referring to the fact that he was closing in on the six-foot mark while it looked like she would never reach five feet. They sat down on the stools.

Leah leaned forward on her elbows. "Where do you live?"

"About fifteen minutes north of town." Denae thought this was a strange question, considering that everything Leah knew about her was from eating at Fred's.

"I thought so," Leah mused, then leaned into Denae's face and spat out, "So why were you in the middle of town in your nightgown yelling at me to stop and going all Carrie on me?"

Denae flinched back, wiping spittle off her face. She could feel tears coming to her eyes, but fought them back. Leah glowered at her, not moving, eyes boring in.

"I had to…had to save your life," she finally said, the last in a rush.

Leah leaned back suddenly, confusion on her face. "Save my life?"

Denae took a deep breath, thinking, here goes everything. "If I hadn't yelled at you…gotten you to stop, you would've been…been…in front of that truck…that truck…when it crashed." The last words just spilled out of her mouth, and she covered her face in her hands and sobbed.

Denae didn't know why she was crying now… the vision had replayed in her head over and over. She'd been woken up by it instead of the bear for several nights but never cried. Why now?

Why wasn't Leah saying anything? Denae looked up through her bleary eyes, and Leah wasn't at the table. She glanced around, panic starting, then saw her at a tall machine that read PEPSI in blue block letters. Denae had seen the pops at the grocery store, but Mom didn't want that sort of trash drink at home. Water, milk, tea, or more recently coffee were what all she had at home, with maybe chocolate or strawberry Nesquick, and sometimes lemons for lemonade in the summer.

Denae took advantage of the time to take off her town glasses and wipe the blue-tinted lenses hiding her dark earthy yellow irises, then wipe her eyes. Her hair color matched her eyes, but Leah had seen that plenty of times at Fred's. She shrugged her coat off and hung it on the back of her stool, then slipped her glasses back on when she saw Leah walking back with a couple of cans that looked to have a similar design to the machine.

"Here." Leah thrust one of the cans in front of her, then pulled off a little handle on her own and took a drink, setting the opener thing on the table. Denae copied her, fumbling at it before hearing the pop as it opened and peeled the thing off. She drank down a bit of the fizzy liquid, coughed a bit, then took another sip, then looked at the can while the tingling in her mouth competed with the noise and lights of the arcade.

"You've never had a Pepsi?" Incredulity was playing with amusement on Leah's face for a moment, then going serious as Denae shook her head. "You're not in one of those religious cults or something like that?"

Denae shook her head again, thinking that Leah really had no clue as to both how close and how far away that guess was.

"So, you saved my life," Leah stated. "How did you know?"

"I just did," Denae said, knowing how weak that sounded.

"How?"

"Vision," Denae said. No sense bringing in the crystal ball. "I had a vision of that happening." She felt her shoulders sag as she said it. She needed to stop herself, but she wasn't sure how…how to keep this snowball from causing a complete avalanche.

"Vision?" Leah looked at her. "You had a vision of me dying, so you popped into town, yelled at me to stop and held me there until the truck crashed, then broke through a snowdrift, ran down an alley and popped back home?"

"I just got there before you so I could stop you."

"In your nightgown?"

Denae nodded, feeling things crashing around her. That was weak. She never could lie.

"You have these visions often?"

Denae shook her head. "My first one."

"This was your first vision?"

Denae sat still…squeezed her eyes shut. She wanted to leave, just pop back home right now, but that'd just confirm everything.

"I talked with Daniel."

"Who's Daniel?" Denae didn't know that name.

"He claims that when he was seven, you made him fly," Leah said. "He said he was chasing you, you fell down and pointed at him, and he flew over your head and landed in a snowbank about thirty feet away. You were four or five, he said."

"I was seven, and it was barely fifteen feet," Denae said before she could stop herself. She put her head in her hands as she saw Leah draw up.

"I went looking for you when you ran off into that alley," Leah continued. "I was only about 10 seconds behind you, but you weren't there." She paused. "There weren't any doors close enough for you to go through, and you couldn't run very fast with that wet nightgown around your legs, and you were barefoot. Your butt was showing through, by the way."

Denae didn't care…she was waiting for that moment when Leah would start shrieking or screaming or something. Barry Manilow's *Copacabana* played over the noises. She liked him, wanted to lose herself in that music, but Leah hadn't stopped talking. At least she hadn't started screaming.

"I went back to where I first saw you," Leah continued, her voice quieter in the recounting. "I saw you climb through the snow going away. There was no other trail in. Nothing. Then I heard the sirens." Her voice trailed away. "I didn't know until later that it had hit the café."

"Three people died," came her whisper. "Four others were hurt, a couple of them bad." Another pause. "Jessica was screaming…the truck had pinned her leg down." Pause. "It's badly broken, but they think she'll walk again. So's the other one, but not as bad." Pause. "Broken ribs, pelvis, perforated lung, but she's doing better." Pause. "I was going to meet her for lunch."

Leah was silent for so long that Denae opened her eyes and looked up.

"Why did you stop me…save me? Why not Jessica or one of the others?" Leah's eyes were brimming with tears. "Why not them?"

"I saw you…everyone else was blurred." She took a sip of her Pepsi. Her mouth had gone dry. "I could save you, but not them…there was no time."

Leah stared at her. "Not even for you to get dressed?"

"No. Not even that," Denae replied, shaking her head. "I guess it was good I was wearing something. Sometimes I'm not wearing anything when I'm in my bedroom," she finished, her voice trailing off.

"You were in your bedroom somewhere...," Leah waved her hand for emphasis. "Somewhere north of town and literally just jumped...teleported like Star Trek or something. You left your bedroom and stood in the middle of the park, then went down that alley like...I don't know what, and went home?"

Denae didn't even breathe. She couldn't say no, and shouldn't say yes, but Leah seemed to read the answer.

"I've been freaking out these last two weeks. What happened couldn't happen, shouldn't happen, but it did." Her voice broke as she wiped her eyes. "I didn't die, and I think I should have...would've been walking in the door...."

Denae nodded. "That's exactly where you would've been."

"Why me...why did you even see me?" Worry was etched on Leah's face. "Why?"

Denae shrugged and slowly shook her head. "I don't know. I don't know the people in town, but I know you, know your name, and you've been nice to me." She shook her head. "I don't know if that made any difference at all, but if I didn't know you, I don't think I would've seen you or the vision."

"You saved me because I was nice to you?" Leah laughed a choked bark kind of laugh. "That's all it took?" She took a long swig of her drink.

"I don't know," Denae repeated. "I don't know how all this works yet, but yes, it might've helped, probably was the reason." She shook her head. "Not many people are all that nice. I'm the weird kid with strange hair and eyes. I don't really know how to act around normal people."

"Everyone's weird," Leah said. "Just in different ways."

"Not like me," Denae countered.

"Touché," Leah agreed. "Hey, look over there. Your brother works fast."

Denae swiveled around to look at Binesi while Leah took another drink from her can. He was chatting with a couple of girls his age, one dark-haired and petite though still a little taller than her. The other was only a few inches shorter than Binesi, shapely with light brown hair. The music had changed, something about losing a shaker of salt. The different lights in here made Binesi's silver streak stand out more in his blond hair. Why couldn't she have hair like that?

"He's discovered girls, and now he thinks he's a man," Denae declared, and Leah sprayed Pepsi out of her mouth, coughing and gagging.

Denae swiveled back to see Leah grabbing for paper napkins. Pepsi had been sprayed all over the table.

Denae pulled a handful of napkins out of the holder and gave them to Leah, then grabbed a few more and started wiping the table. Leah continued coughing while she wiped.

After another minute, Leah said, "That hurt...Pepsi went out my nose." She coughed a few more times, then blew her nose. "Sorry."

"Don't worry about it," Denae replied. She swiveled back to look at Binesi. "He's quite the talker, you know...the opposite of me."

"You speak well," Leah said. "Except for that comment, that is." She chuckled. "Caught me at the worst possible time, too."

"Yeah, that's me," Denae said. "Say things, do things at the worst possible time."

"Not always," Leah countered softly.

"Give him another year or so, and he'll talk those girls right out of their pants." Denae shook her head. "They won't know what hit them." She turned back to Leah.

Leah was holding her can of Pepsi, halfway to her mouth, looking at Denae. "You know, I don't think I'm going to drink anything else while we're talking," and set the can back on the table. "So, can he do the things you do?"

"No," she said, thinking that he did other things, including mental things, which was why the girls wouldn't have a chance if he wished it that way. She was pleased that she didn't actually say that out loud.

"So, you're special?" The tone was curious, not spiteful. "And you use your powers for good?"

Denae relaxed and laughed at that. "Mostly, unless my brothers annoy me."

"How many brothers do you have?" She had a different sort of interest on her face.

"Four, counting him," Denae gesturing at Binesi with a jerk of her head. "The others are older."

"And do they—"

"Let's not go there," Denae said, cutting her off. "Jude is a Sophomore at U of W Milwaukee, Lucas is a Junior at U of W Madison, and Anton's off working near Summit Lake, doing whatever."

"I've never seen you at school," Leah said.

"Homeschooled," Denae replied. "All of us." She spread her hands expansively. That was the official answer if anyone asked.

"And what's his name?" Leah nodded at Binesi.

"Binesi, but we call him Bin," Denae said. At her puzzled look, Denae continued, "It's Ojibwe for Thunderbird."

"He has Ojibwe blood with that blond hair…and is that a streak of silver there?"

"We all do, but the Viking won out over the rest," Denae said. "My older brothers all have dark hair," continued Denae, except for the silver or gold streaks in their hair, she thought, but managed not to say it out loud. Lucas kept his gold cut down to the skin and his hair long to hide it.

"And you?" Leah reached over and fingered one of her braids. "Where does your hair come from?"

"No," Denae said flatly, bringing her hand flat on the table for emphasis.

Leah drew her hand back. "Sorry, but you're interesting, and I'm nosy." She looked up, then at her watch, and said, "I've got to get over to Fred's for work." She looked Denae in the eye. "Come over and eat. It'll be free…forever. You saved my life."

"No," Denae said. "I'll come and eat, but I'll pay, and I'll tip. You owe me nothing." At Leah's crestfallen look, Denae shook her head. "Okay, you can buy me dessert sometime."

Leah's smile returned. "I'll do that." With that, she hopped off the stool, threw her coat and scarf on and waved a goodbye as she headed out the door. Denae grabbed her drink and walked back to where Binesi had found another game to play with the dark-haired town girl while women sang about a barracuda. She wasn't sure what the lyrics meant, though she knew they weren't singing about the fish. She smiled both at the song and at her talk with Leah. That went a lot better than expected. She at least didn't seem to have given anything away that Leah hadn't already figured out on her own.

↢↢⊙↣↣

Denae watched Binesi punch a few songs into the table-side jukebox radio thing for music until they got their food at Fred's. It was almost two weeks since she'd talked with Leah. She was relieved to see that she wasn't waitressing, then sighed when she looked over where the bells over the door were chiming and saw Leah come in.

Leah sat down next to Denae, pulling off her coat. "You got anything planned for Friday evening?"

Denae shrugged. "No. Why?"

Leah gave a slightly strange smile. "My parents are going to be gone for the weekend, and I don't have any hours here Friday or Saturday. You like to come over? We can have a girls' night."

"Uh," Denae said, picking at a chipped spot in the table's Formica top. "Um, I don't know." She looked from Leah to Binesi, who grinned at her discomfort.

"You really should, Denae," he said.

"See, even Bin says so," Leah said, gesturing grandly at Denae's little brother. He at least had the decency to go a little pink at the sudden attention of this older girl.

Denae sighed heavily at Binesi but was inwardly excited. She'd never spent any time alone with anyone not family, however distant. "Okay, I'll do it," more to herself than anyone else. She looked up at Leah, a smile forming on her face. "So what, where, and when?"

"Meet me here tomorrow at six, and we'll walk to my house," Leah said. "It's only a few blocks away."

"Okay," Denae agreed. "I'll be here."

"Great!" Leah beamed down on them. "I've got to get my apron on and get to work, but I'll see you then." She turned and walked briskly toward the back of the diner.

"Wow. She invited you over for a girls' night." He looked at her. "What does that mean?"

"No idea," Denae said. "I guess I'll find out."

Chapter 6

Girls Night In

When Denae stepped inside Fred's, she saw Leah standing just inside the entrance holding a large white paper bag. Leah smiled. "Got supper here, so let's go."

Denae turned and followed her back out. "What's in the bag?"

"Spaghetti, meatballs, salad, and garlic bread. Let's get home before it gets cold." They walked as briskly in the dark as the icy spots of cleared sidewalks would allow.

After Leah had dished out the food and poured some wine, they ate, and Leah told her about the different things that happened to her over the last couple of weeks.

"With Jessica at home for however long it takes her to get better enough to be able to go back to school, I'm the only girl in the chess club. I liked having her there for support since some of the guys are chauvinist dweebs, making up excuses when I mop them up on the chessboard, and that's most of the time. There's only a couple of the guys who give me a good challenge, and they're the cooler nerds that don't get upset when I do win."

"Doesn't that make you a nerd, too?" Denae was relaxing a bit, maybe because of the wine.

Leah grinned. "It does, as though my being good in math and science wasn't enough, and then I'm a science fiction, fantasy, and horror geek as well. Unfortunately, that narrows the field of guys quite a bit, and most of them aren't that interesting to me. I guess it's good in a way because while I haven't had many second dates, it does weed out those who are only interested in my boobs when I start talking."

"And the difference between nerd and geek?"

Leah laughed and set her garlic bread down. "Nerd is what you're good at, and geek is what you're interested in. So what's your nerd and geek areas?"

Denae chewed on her food longer than she needed to before answering. Binesi told her to stick to neutral areas and delay if she could. She wasn't used to talking to a mundane about more than simple things at one of the stores, and Leah already knew more than most mundanes did. "Can we wait on that? What are you doing after high school?"

"U of W Madison. I just got accepted there. I'm going to try pre-med, but I'm not sure if I want to be a doctor or a nurse, and I could be a nurse a lot quicker."

"I like that…either one should work. What do you need to learn for nursing?"

While she could get work with an associate's degree, Leah said she wanted at least a bachelor's and then started in detail about the classes.

Denae let all of that sweep over her as she sat eating. There was the strangeness of the house, much smaller than where she lived, but it had electric lights and the magic of television. It currently showed something black and white where some strange tall, round knobby metal thing rolled around chasing people saying, "Exterminate."

She wondered about the things that Leah took for granted and the differences. Denae's house had many of the same things, though they worked magically. The faucets were enchanted to provide hot and cold water, stones that continually put out light—that she effectively turned off by closing shutters or a lid or covering with a cloth. Other things, too. She came back from her reverie to hear Leah say, "And what have you been up to?"

Caught off guard, she said, "I was up at Uncle Alford's most of last week and the first part of this week. He was teaching me more about the spirit world…as abstract and esoteric as he makes it sound, I'll probably never use it."

"But you could like summon or control these spirits…if you wanted to?" Leah seemed excited.

Denae balked a bit. She needed something blander to bore her with so that she'd start talking about herself again. Oh well…she'd cover this, then switch. "Not really recommended," she said. "Most who try to do that end up in a bad way. It's supposed to be rather addictive, which is part of what brings them to a bad end."

"Then why do they do that?"

"Why do people smoke?" Denae countered.

"They like what it does to them?" Leah asked hesitantly.

"Yeah," Denae replied. "It makes them feel real good for the moment, but then they need it again…and again, more and more. It's not sustainable."

"Wow," Leah said, laughing. "Sustainable isn't a term I'd put together with magic or powers. Still, it sounds almost like heroin, or something like that."

Denae nodded, unsure what heroin was but relatively sure it was the right thing to do. She had read that it was something very addictive.

"That sounds like a movie I saw on tv a few weeks ago," Leah said. "The bad guy vampire was summoning up some infernal forces or spirits or something, and the good guys threw holy water at him that missed. It put out one of the candles and broke the drawn pentacle. The vampire got sucked up into that spirit world where he'd be tormented forever."

Denae looked up thoughtfully. "I guess he could do something like that, but I don't know why he'd bother, even if he had the powers to do that."

Denae felt a sudden silence, Leah's eyes wide as Denae looked back at her. "Did you just say that vampires were real?"

Damn. Leah saw it on her face. "They are, aren't they?"

Denae nodded. "There aren't many, and none around here." Leah relaxed a bit.

"Do you want me to talk about something else?"

Denae nodded again.

"Sorry. So, tell me about your brothers."

"Anton is my oldest brother," She started. This was somewhat safer ground, anyway. "Last year, he graduated from Madison and works a couple of hours northeast of here doing…something. I'm not real sure what. I haven't been out there yet. Lucas is a junior there, and Jude is a sophomore at U of W Milwaukee. I've been to the schools with them, but I don't really like the big cities. And you know Binesi."

"Thunderbird. I can believe that. Where are you going to college?"

"I'm not," Denae said, some disappointment sounding in her voice.

"Why not?"

"Learning more magic stuff. I'm way ahead of where any of the bubs are, so I'm learning the more esoteric things about magic. Also, they didn't say it, but they probably don't think I'd do well in crowded classes or even in a city, and they're probably right. I'm happiest outside in the forest.

"I thought you said your brothers, or at least Binesi, didn't have powers."

Denae shook her head and sighed. She'd let that slip out. "They don't do what I do."

"So, what do they do?"

Denae picked up her glass and sipped more wine. She hadn't intended to go quite this far. "Anton is heavy in the knowing. He knows what time it is, what direction is north, and can easily pick out magical things from the mundane. He sees auras and histories and does the divinations that I'm just starting, plus he's good at finding people or things." Maybe better than me on that, she thought, but managed not to say it out loud.

"He joined a Search and Rescue group where he lives now to help them out. We learned some of the same things. He can light a fire with a word…I still can't wrap my mind around even the simplest fire spell, so I carry a Bic with me when I'm out in the woods. Anton can do things with light, too. I see well enough in the dark that I never bothered with that."

"Lucas does a lot with earth and water and has dabbled a little in other areas. I started earth after him and quickly got better, which pissed him off. I didn't want to deal with him in the water spell classes, so I never bothered with those. I should give those a try sometime but haven't had the time."

"Jude's more into protection and such, though he picked up a little of a lot of different areas, probably the most in the empathy and feeling area."

"Knowing, light, earth, protection, feeling? This is your magic? I thought it was like sympathy, contagion, and that sort of thing." Denae looked at her, and she reddened. "I read fantasy novels, and a couple of them talk about magic that way. Others talk about ley lines and things like that."

Denae nodded. "I understand there is that sort of sympathy and contagion methodology out there, but it's not how we do it." She paused a moment. "For the most part, I guess, though there really is a bit of that, now that I think about it. There's something to ley lines, but I don't know what. That's totally foreign. From what I've learned, there are innumerable ways of doing this, some that work totally counter to others, some that shouldn't work but do. I understand ours, but not the others…not really."

"What is yours?"

"We learn by large groupings of related spells. Elemental magic would be one, though we break it farther down into its four quarters. Earth, air, water, and fire. Weather kinda falls into that as well. There are others for knowledge or knowing things, animals, plants, people, and magic itself. Some areas like weather straddle more than one of these." Denae shrugged. "That's it."

"Your teleport?"

"Moving. From picking up objects and moving them to levitating people to flying to that." Denae gave a hoarse laugh. "Moving objects and levitating living beings like people are supposed to be separate, but from age three, I'd do either as one and at the same time. This means I broke our system about the time I was potty-trained. Some of the family still resent that little thing," she finished, grimacing.

"I should probably quit asking questions, shouldn't I?" Leah looked apologetic. "I told you I'm nosy."

"Not a problem," Denae said, shrugging with a glance at the television furniture.

"Oh, that's Dr. Who on the public station," she said. "It's appropriately silly science fiction for a couple of weird girls like us." Then she smiled. "But first, let me get something from outside."

Leah brought in a snow-covered bottle. She wiped the snow off onto the carpet as she came back in, then grabbed a couple of small glasses and motioned Denae to follow her into the living room where the tv was playing.

"You know what this is?"

Denae shook her head, trying to read the label as Leah waved it slowly in front of her, but it didn't seem to be in English.

"Water of life," she said. "Aquavit, from Sweden, like our Viking ancestors," and she set the bottle and glasses down. Denae saw that one of the words spelled out something approximate to what Leah had said.

"You've had this before." She seemed to note Denae's stare.

"Um…no," Denae said. "We sometimes have wine with supper like tonight. I've tried beer but don't really like it."

"This is how it works. I fill these shot glasses with the cold life water, we toast each other *skoal*, and drink it all down. Then I refill, and we can sip and watch the Doctor."

Denae nodded in agreement as she thought of some of her family members doing that from time to time, though she didn't think it was with Aquavit. Uncle Aldo seemed to like initiating those sorts of toasts, but he enjoyed anything that involved alcohol.

She watched as Leah twisted the bottle open and poured the glasses, handing one to Denae and picking up the other. Lifting the shot glass to eye level, Leah said, "*Skoal!*"

Denae repeated the toast, watched as Leah tipped hers all the way and did the same, feeling an immense coldness go down inside her, then suddenly heating up.

Leah coughed slightly, then turned big eyes to Denae.

Denae coughed several times before everything started settling down some.

"Wow," Leah said after a moment.

"Yeah," Denae said with a slight wheeze. "You've never had this before?"

"No, but I'd heard about it and thought we should try it." She took Denae's glass back and refilled it. "We can sip now." And they did. It was smaller bits of cold going to warm, which was better.

Later, Denae poured the last of the bottle into Leah's shot glass, and Leah said, "Last drop here," and tilted her head back, tongue out. With the room spinning some, Leah's mouth swaying back and forth, Denae had problems holding her arm steady, the drops rolling down Leah's cheek instead.

Denae put the bottle back on the table rather heavily, making Leah jump. Denae had decided to go ahead and tell her about the bear when her stomach started rumbling. A burning hit the back of her throat. She lurched upright and belched out, "lavatory."

She hit her shoulder on the door jamb on her way out of the living room, then caught herself and used it to swing into the hallway. She'd have a bruise in the morning, something dully told her, but spotted the lighted opening she knew was the lavatory.

She slid along the wall toward the light, banged into the door jamb, turning. The contents of her stomach came up as the toilet came into focus. She tried to seal her lips for at least a moment, stumbled, falling to her knees, head going toward the water as it spewed from her mouth, again and again.

Once it stopped, she looked up. An ashen-faced Leah weaved in the doorway, looking back at her. Denae felt puke running down her chin as Leah lurched forward, tripping over Denae's ankles. She fell partway into the tub, retching.

Denae reached over to try to pat her back, felt another wave coming, turned back to the toilet. Her hand patted something as she swung back around…probably Leah's butt, a small voice in her head told her. Great, was her final coherent thought as the next wave hit.

A little later, she was still retching some, but nothing was coming out. She slid to the floor, the cool tile pleasant on her face, Leah still retching.

↢ ↢ ⊙ ↣ ↣

Denae woke, something jostling her. She could feel coolness on her.

She opened her eyes. Leah was in an oversized t-shirt, tugging on Denae's arm. They were still in the pukey bathroom, her nose told her.

"Whatcha doin'?"

Leah looked at her, pinked a little. "You have puke on your sweater. Any on your pants?"

"Nope," Denae said after looking them over for several seconds, then eyed Leah. "You changed."

"Puked on everything. Tossed it all in tub and rinsed them off. I'll deal with them in the morning. Your sweater only got a little. Put it up on sink."

Denae glanced up, her head swimming from the movement, to see the top of the vanity, then pulled her arms slowly out of her sweater. Leah grabbed the shoulders as Denae pushed it up over her head, then Leah placed it over the vanity.

"You're not wearing a bra."

Denae shrugged, then gestured at her tiny excuses for breasts. "No need with these little things. Don't sag, don't do nothing."

"I can get you something."

"Nah, this is fine."

Denae felt a pressure in her head and put her hand up to keep Leah from saying anything.

Denae?

Hi, Mom.

Were you coming home tonight? You never said anything one way or another.

Wasn't sure, but I'm staying the night.

Oh...okay. Is everything alright?

Yeah. Drank a little much, but we're fine.

Drank too much?

A little. We're fine.

Denae could feel the sigh come through.

Should Dad come to get you?

No. We're about to go to bed.

When are you coming home?

Hold on.

Denae opened her eyes and looked up at Leah's concerned face.

"When are your parents coming back?"

"About three on Sunday afternoon. Why?"

Denae shook her head slightly, making her head spin, and closed her eyes.

I'll be home by three on Sunday.

Is Leah okay with that?

Yeah, if she can put up with me that long.

If not, Denae thought to herself, I'll come home sooner. Despite how she felt right now, this was a new experience. She wanted to do it to the fullest.

Okay then…well…sleep well. Love you.

Love you.

The pressure was gone. Denae opened her eyes to find Leah squatting next to her.

"What was that?"

"Mom checking in on me."

"And…." Denae saw a couple of emotions pass through Leah's face as she absorbed that.

"I'm good until your parents get back."

"She doesn't know we drank ourselves pukey?"

"I told her we'd drunk a bit too much, but no details."

"She's not coming to get you?"

Denae resisted shaking her head, instead saying, "She offered to send Dad, but I told her we were going to bed. We are, aren't we?"

She could hear the slight pleading in her voice. She really hoped there was nothing else for tonight.

"Yes. So your mom can read your mind?"

"No," Denae replied. "That's…not something she can do." Denae was happy she managed not to say that was what Binesi could do, to a certain extent. "Besides, if anyone tried to do that, I'm pretty good at fighting it off." Though probably not now. Drinking messed with resisting things.

Leah nodded, quiet, so Denae grabbed the vanity counter and pulled herself up, feeling Leah lift her by her other elbow until she was swaying but upright.

Leah studied her jeans. "Those do look clean. You weren't as messy as me. Let's get to my bedroom."

Denae went to the side of the bed Leah pointed to and slid out of her jeans. She sat on the bed to pull them off the rest of the way and felt Leah's eyes on her.

"You're not wearing anything. I can get you something."

"I've still got my socks on," Denae said, then tugged them off. "This is how I sleep."

"Your mom lets you…."

"We all sleep in the buff. Healthier that way."

"Oh. You were wearing a nightgown…."

"That was lunchtime and my room was chilly, and sometimes I'm just wearing a blanket, so be glad you didn't see me like this in the park that day." Denae stood and gave her a half-smile. "I can go home."

"No. It's okay. I just wasn't expecting…let's go to bed."

Denae lifted the quilt and flannel sheet and slid into bed while Leah ran a brush through her hair. One advantage to my braids, Denae thought, though she could also see that it wasn't as okay as Leah made it out to be. Her aura showed that edge of fear again that had subsided early in the evening. Like Denae was somehow dangerous naked. But Leah said stay, so it couldn't be too bad.

Her eyes had almost closed when the lights went off, and Leah slid in.

"Everything okay?" Leah flashed her a tentative smile with the question. The room was lit only with a nightlight, so Denae assumed Leah didn't expect her to even see the smile.

"I'm good," Denae replied, giving Leah a smile she hoped was broad enough to see in the dark. That wasn't completely true since her stomach hurt and her mouth was rather yucky, but compared to a while back…no vomiting or dry heaving now, so she was good enough. Leah wasn't good yet, but her aura was better than even a couple of minutes ago, so she'd resolved something. "Let's get some sleep."

Denae turned her back to Leah and closed her eyes. She felt a light pat on her shoulder and a quiet "good night" before Leah moved in the bed, apparently turning the other way. Maybe she should've put something on, but she wasn't sure she could sleep like that, all bound up in clothing.

Chapter 7

The Morning After

Denae woke with light streaming in. She was on her back, her mouth so dry. She looked around Leah's bedroom while trying to work saliva back into her mouth so it didn't taste so awful.

Large posters covered the walls, clashing with the pink gingham curtains the light shone through. Something called Young Frankenstein, with a man yelling on one side and someone big and gray with a top hat on the other. Another with some sort of metal clockwork cowboy called Westworld. Another one was a drawing of a blue person with fins for ears holding a little person that looked human called Fantastic Planet…definitely weird. These were movie posters, but not any movies she'd ever seen.

There were others, but she had to pee and brush her teeth. Leah was sleeping on her belly, face toward Denae, her arm lying across Denae, hand by her hip. Denae lifted Leah's arm gently and slid out. She padded out to the lavatory, the throbbing in her head kept beat with her steps.

The stench in there took her breath away. Oh yeah…lots of vomiting went on here. She could feel her bile rising.

Her sweater lay draped across the sink, bits of dried puke visible. Further in, it looked like Leah had simply thrown all her clothes into the tub. There was puke both in and outside of the tub.

When she finished peeing, she grabbed her sweater and carried it out to the kitchen, laying it out on the counter.

She grabbed some kitchen towels and cleaner, then went back and rinsed out Leah's clothes and the tub, getting a shower in the process. When she finished cleaning the rest of the lavatory, she brushed her teeth. She'd eyed the single toothbrush in the stand, knowing it was Leah's, but found another one in the cabinet. It took twice before her mouth felt semi-normal again.

Leah had turned in her sleep, mainly lying on her back now. She wasn't sure how to wake her, or even if she should.

She shook Leah's shoulder. Leah moved slightly, then stopped, seeming to settle back, so she shook her gently again. Leah gasped and opened her eyes.

"Oh," she said, seeing Denae sitting on the edge of the bed. "You're still here," and she smiled, then looked her over. "Aren't you cold?"

Denae nodded. "You have something I can slip into now? It's a little chilly."

"There's another sleep shirt hanging behind the door."

Denae got it, Leah watching her as she pulled the oversized t-shirt on. It hung off one shoulder.

"You said everyone sleeps nude in your family?"

Denae nodded.

"So, you've seen Bin naked?"

"Not since yesterday morning."

"What do you mean?"

"He was brushing his teeth when I finished my shower, so I left the water running, and he handed me a towel as I stepped out." At Leah's look, she continued, "I assume this doesn't happen in your family."

Leah burst out a laugh. "It's been years since I've even seen my mom undressed. I'm not allowed out of my room unless I'm dressed. No pajamas at breakfast since I was about seven. Bra on since I was twelve. At least when they're not here, I can walk around the house like I am."

"You could walk around nude if you wanted."

"Unlike out in the country where you live, I'm in town, and not all the curtains are closed. However, I've been known to go from here to the bathroom without bothering with clothes when they're not here." She suddenly had a look of horror on her face. "Oh my god, the bathroom."

"Relax," Denae said. "I cleaned it. I was thinking about fixing breakfast for you, but I'm not sure I can work your kitchen."

↢↢⊙↣↣

Later, Denae went into the living room and sat down on the couch while Leah went to the lavatory and showered. Leah's sleep t-shirt was definitely oversized on her. She could keep it from sliding off one shoulder or the other, and it went down past her knees. Still, she supposed this was like at home, where you wore something when you went downstairs. She was hoping for a bit more freedom with no parents around, but as Leah said, they were in town, and the curtains weren't drawn.

The sounds of water stopped, and Leah came in, tying her bathrobe. "It was bad, wasn't it?"

"It was," Denae agreed, "but it's better now."

"I appreciate it. I probably would've puked again trying to clean."

"I wish I had breasts," Denae said, watching her.

"Oh, you have them," Leah countered. "Small, but they look nice."

"Barely even there breastlets that disappear totally when I stretch. Not like yours."

"You don't want these," Leah said, touching them lightly. "They're too big. They hurt my back sometimes, and I always have to wear a bra, and when I'm old, they'll hang down to my knees."

"Not that far." Denae thought of Oma-Ma, and how her breasts did sag to her waist.

"And the guys are always looking at me," she said, pouting. "It gets really annoying when you can't walk down the street without them staring and maybe someone whistling at you."

"People in town look at me, too," Denae said. "They wonder about my hair color and why I wear tinted glasses. The braids are all that keep them from thinking I'm a boy."

"I know," Leah said softly. "I've heard them. Your eyes are a strange color, but I like them."

Leah hesitated a moment. "Go sit in that kitchen chair. Let me grab a couple of things, and I'll take those braids out and see what you look like with your hair down. I think you'll look nicer and more feminine than those thick plaits."

Denae sat and let Leah work on her hair, feeling it hang loose for the first time in months…years really, for any appreciable time, as Leah brushed and combed it. It felt weird, having it all over, but if Leah liked it that way, she was willing to try it.

"Your hair is so straight. Not a curl or wave. I can't even see anything from it being braided."

"Don't even bother talking about dyeing or bleaching," Denae added. "It won't take either. Believe me, I've tried. Braids seem to be a good way to hide it under a jacket."

"Straight is good…feels nice," Leah said, and Denae could feel her running her fingers through it, down to the middle of her back. "It seems strong for such a fine texture. I didn't comb out nearly as many loose hairs as I thought I would."

"So, does it stay or go back in braids?"

"Oh, it stays." Leah took a few steps back and smiled. "It ages you by at least a couple of years, too."

"So I look fourteen instead of twelve now," Denae said reflexively, though inside, the thought of looking even a couple of years older thrilled her.

"At least," Leah replied with a laugh. "Tell you what. Let me check the newspaper to see when the early showing of *Close Encounters of the Third Kind* is at the theater. We can go watch that if you want."

"Um…sure."

"You have no clue what that is, do you?"

"I have seen a few movies," Denae protested, "but no, not that one."

"Let's go watch it, then. Please. My mom doesn't like me watching or reading speculative fiction and kept figuring out whenever I'd planned on seeing it during Christmas break. Then she'd plan some other crap so I couldn't go. It was all bullshit, then Jessica and the truck. We were going to watch it after having lunch." Leah shivered. "It's about to leave the theater."

"Let's do it."

↢ ↢ ⊙ ↣ ↣

"So…how did you learn to do that teleport thing?" They'd stopped by the grocery store, and Denae made up some sausage and cabbage for them. Leah got a bottle of German Liebfraumilch wine, and now they were having both, and Leah started with the questions again.

"That took a while," Denae said. "It's only been in the last few months that I've been comfortable with it."

"Comfortable?"

"You have to be able to envision where you want to go quite well. The spell is a quick one, though very tricky, but putting the vision well into your head is the biggest thing. Usually, you only miss by a few feet if the vision in your head isn't that good. I can do it quickly now…just think and go. However, I learned the whole vision thing the hard way more than once."

"How's that?"

"They say you can go somewhere using only a picture. Yeah…right," Denae sneered.

Leah quietly looked for her to continue.

"I wanted to go to Florida and even had one of those Key West picture postcards from one of my cousins. I'd studied it for days, making sure I had the beach there in my mind. I went to a bunch of sand, that's for sure, but there wasn't any water, and I was totally exhausted."

"Where did you go?"

"I wish I knew. There was a large flat place that was probably a dry salt-lake of some sort, but otherwise, no clue. I guess the sand color was about right, though. It was July, and it was scorching there. I was sweating tons by the time I'd recovered, so stupidly, I tried again. Got water with the sand that time, but still not where I was trying to go. Again no clue, but it was also hot, the water wasn't the right color, and there were all sorts of biting flies that just ate me up."

"Wherever it was, it wasn't nearly so far, so I wasn't as tired, so I just focused on home and went there."

"It gave my dad a good laugh when I showed back up, blood running from dozens of bites. I was wearing a crop-top and cutoffs. Lots of places for them to bite before I could get away. That's when I found out he'd ended up somewhere in the Atlantic Ocean when he was learning. He had to tread water while he got everything together to come home. There were other misses like that, but nothing so far away. On purpose, I haven't traveled farther than Madison or Milwaukee."

"Visiting your brothers?"

Leah poured more wine into each of their glasses.

"Anton mainly at Madison. Lucas got annoyed whenever I showed up, so I stopped once Anton graduated. I tried to be nice, but he hadn't forgiven me for turning him into a statue when he was getting ready to go on a date last summer."

"What?"

"We were fighting over who was going to take a shower first. He hosed me down with a jet of water and knocked me into the toilet, so I turned him to stone, brushed my teeth and took my shower before turning him back. He was running late, and an after-effect of that was that he was stiff in all the areas, except where he wanted to be." Denae chuckled at her joke, "or so I overheard later."

Leah goggled at her. "You turned him to stone, but you could turn him back, so not like Medusa?"

"Yeah," Denae said. "Assuming Medusa was real…probably a live woman practitioner rather than that snake-headed thing from mythology. Remember that she was supposed to be one of the Gorgon sisters, except that she wasn't immortal while the others were. She either didn't know how to change them back or didn't want to and was probably the only one around who knew anything about it. When Perseus killed her, nobody could bring them back."

"You learn a lot about mythology with this magic?"

"Some, but there's also the fact that…."

Denae paused, took a deep breath, and sighed.

"Perseus is the one who killed Medusa, and his dad is Zeus." She eyed Leah steadily. "The thing is, his mom was named Denae."

She stood up, threw her hands out, and took a half-bow. "Ta-da. For some reason, I'm named after her." She sat down with a thump.

"I missed something there."

"Denae was locked up by her father. That typical prophecy thing about her son killing her father. Zeus found her anyway, misted on her, and got her pregnant. You wouldn't believe all the ways my dear cousins have used that over the years to tease me."

"Ugh. I don't think I want to. So, you can turn people to stone and back again."

"That, or I can bury them fifty feet underground."

"Fifty feet? For how long?"

"Indefinitely."

"So they die?"

"No. They're held in a stasis of some kind, so they don't need to eat or breathe, and no time passes."

"Fifty feet down."

"That's what they told me. I never measured it."

"So, they could stay there for a thousand years before someone brought them back up."

"It's happened."

"I really don't know what to believe here. Turned to stone or buried."

"Well," Denae said with a grin. "It goes something like this," and made a gesture.

↢ ↢ ⊙ ↣ ↣

"Goes like what?"

Denae smiled as she heard the question. She stood behind Leah now and tapped her on the shoulder.

Leah turned around, eyes widening. "What's—"

"Look around," Denae said. "I've put up the leftovers and done the dishes. No time passed for you."

"You just buried me?" Denae heard the quiver in her voice.

"Entombed is the proper term, so you were entombed for about half an hour."

"So…this is real."

Denae smiled again. Leah lifted slightly off her chair, then floated her to an empty spot a few inches above the kitchen floor.

"Denae, you're freaking me out."

"Then put your legs down and stand up."

Leah did this shakily, her body quaking as she stood there.

"You've been so curious…I think you said nosy, and since you really wanted to know, I showed you."

"You did make Daniel fly back when he was little."

Denae nodded. "Got in big trouble for that, too. I'm not supposed to do magic in town, especially on the mundanes."

Leah was still shaking slightly but had a curious look on her face. "Mundanes meaning people like me?"

"Exactly. Those who aren't practitioners."

"Of magic."

Denae shrugged. "That's as good as whatever you might call it. Aunt Gaia likes to call it practical quantum mechanics."

"Whoa," Leah said. "You understand quantum mechanics?"

"No, though she has taught me some about Schrodinger and Heisenberg. She says that whatever we're doing has to be affecting things on the quantum level. She says we can't know exactly because the observer messes with the observation, except that we somehow influence things through our being, will, and training. It's the only way it makes sense, not that she's given me any proof, of course."

"Okay," Leah said, slowly retaking her seat. "Now my head hurts two different ways. Where did that floaty levitation thing go?"

"Once I was sure you weren't going to fall, I dropped it. All of this takes energy to do…well, not much with the levitate—I've been doing that since I was three, and it's easy. I can float myself around all day without getting tired. You're heavier and not me, so it takes energy for me to do you."

"So…this entombment thing you can do on anyone?"

"If I put it on another practitioner and he realized it, he might be able to fight it off."

"But if he was attacking you and didn't, then he's your prisoner."

"Definitely."

"This happens how often?"

Denae shrugged. "I haven't heard of anyone doing it in battle in my lifetime, though I've used it on my brothers some when they irritate me, and Bin's been my main practice partner for this and a lot of my spells. I just recently learned it. It's very complicated and definitely one of the hardest ones I learned…teleport being the other. Turning flesh to stone is almost as hard, and I almost killed myself using it on a big bear."

"A bear?"

"Yeah," Denae picked up her glass of wine. "Let's go sit in the living room or something."

Leah nodded, grabbed her glass, and led Denae to the couch.

Once they sat down and settled, Denae continued. "The bear tried to attack me."

"Where did you meet this bear?"

"Not far from home. He lived in our forest but never bothered us…until I was sixteen, anyway. He charged me, and I stoned him, barely. I didn't even have a second to spare. I also didn't have near enough energy, so I had to pull the extra energy from my body. That tore me up. Bin told me that I was bleeding from everywhere, leaking it out of my skin and orifices. Bin found me, got me to Oma, who healed me up, and Papa…that's my mom's dad…made this beetle amulet for me so I'd have more energy available." She smiled. "That's about it. Dad and some of the others hauled the bear off to western Minnesota and set it free."

She pushed the head, and the wings opened, showing off an opalescent gem.

"It's like my mom's, but hers stores more energy. This almost doubled mine back then, though my power's grown some in the last year and a half. I used it a little to help me build my big stone tipi there to remember the bear by."

Leah was reaching for the amulet but drew up.

"Stone tipi?"

"Twenty feet in diameter and slightly taller. You need to come out some weekend. I haven't managed to get running water out there yet, or I'd live there. I never learned water spells, and the faucets are expensive. Snow melted in a bucket suffices in the winter, though."

"A stone tipi…." Leah just stared at Denae.

"I've been meaning to build a wigwam farther north but haven't gotten around to it yet. It took me a while to get the tipi built correctly…it fell down a few times before I figured things out…I haven't had as much interest in doing the wigwam, even if it's more appropriate for here."

"Twenty-foot diameter…."

"Yeah. When I can't sleep, I go out there for the night. I sleep better there. Jude says I inadvertently put some pretty good protections on it when I built it."

"You have a three-hundred square foot tipi cabin of your own in the forest that you built out of stone that you could go live in. How many of your family live out in that forest?"

"I don't know…sixty people or so. Maybe more."

"Whoa. That many Dassows?"

"Or related. We have another smaller group that lives north of Manitowoc. My mom's family lives an hour or so east of here. There are other families around we've married into, plus a few mundanes married in, and a few have gone off to live elsewhere, some in the mundane world completely."

Leah nodded. "Another world all around me, and I had no clue."

"I guess that's true. I'd never really thought about it that much, except to try to avoid the mundane world."

"Why?"

"They don't like me. My hair is strange, and they really don't like my eyes, so I wear my glasses when I come into town so they can't see them. Even most of my cousins don't like them and can't look me in the eyes when I try to talk to them. I gave up on most of them, not that they were trying to talk to me anyway. I scare them."

"I can see why you'd scare someone like me, but them?"

"I didn't mean to scare you."

"It's okay. My heart's getting down back to normal."

"No, it isn't, but it's at least getting better."

"Now what?" Leah gave a resigned sigh.

"I'm just watching your aura."

"Of course you are," Leah said, suddenly sitting very still, "and what are you seeing."

"The expected. Fear, but that's subsiding some, until just now. Curiosity. That's been high all weekend and seems to be overriding the fear again. I'm glad about that. I do things sometimes without thinking, like entombing you. I was afraid you'd scream or tell me to leave or something when I brought you back. I'm glad you didn't."

"This is kind of like a dream, except I don't have the powers."

"No, you don't."

"You can see that, too?"

"Practitioners have what we call a spark. It's a faint small flame-like red-yellow-orange glow that comes from around here." Denae tapped Leah's solar plexus. "You don't have it. At the same time, don't have sex for a couple of days. You're fertile right now."

Leah jerked straight, a bit of wine spilling over her hand, then she sucked the wine from her hand as she stared at Denae.

Denae laughed. "What? You're fine with me telling you about the spark but shocked to find out you're in your fertile period?"

"I," Leah started. "I just don't…how did you learn all of these different things?"

"I'm precocious," Denae sneered.

"Meaning what?" Leah held her hand up. "Let me put my glass down first before you make me spill my wine again."

Denae shook her head. "Probably not as earth-shattering as knowing that you're fertile, but here goes. Most kids don't get their abilities until they're around nine or ten."

"I still haven't gotten mine."

Denae ignored her. "I got mine at age three. I may have been seeing auras earlier than that, but I was levitating things at age three. I broke Lucas's arm the first time when I was three because he was grabbing the toys I had floating and wouldn't give them back. I lifted him up and dropped him."

"The first time?"

"That's what they tell me. I don't remember it, but Oma's patched him up a lot from me doing things like that to him. The other brothers, not so much, but like I said yesterday, he and I just don't get along that well."

"Ow."

"Yeah, I was a real terror when I was little. I'm probably lucky I didn't kill anyone. When I was twelve, Bradley…he's a cousin who's Lucas's age. Anyway, he tried to drag me by my braids, so I bounced him and broke his collarbone. Oma fixed him. The next day he and three other teen cousins jumped me. One fire-hosed me like I told you Lucas did to me, and another caused my stomach muscles to spasm. There were a couple of other spells, but I fought those off. Then they grabbed my arms and legs and said they were going to pull me apart." Denae spread her arms and legs out, mimicking her words. "They had some enhancing spells on them, so they might've been able to do it.

"I freaked. Next thing, we were all in the air. I don't remember doing it, but we were. A couple of the boys let go right away, and I had them spinning. Bradley fought it longer, but I finally got him spinning so he'd let go, too. I lifted them higher and kept them spinning while lowering myself down. Some of the girls were watching and they screamed for me to stop, but I didn't, even when one of the guys started puking. I don't think I was actually going to drop them, but I definitely wanted to scare them. My cousin Justin ran in and talked me into setting them down, so I did, but they were sure I would've killed them otherwise. Simon had pissed himself, and since he was turning, he soaked his shirt as well as his pants." Denae gave Leah a satisfied smile. "They left me alone after that. Almost everyone left me alone after that." Denae slumped slightly, then took a sip of her wine.

"Who's Justin?"

"My best friend. He's a cousin, though he seems more like a brother. He's about the only one who didn't leave me alone, and he's also the same age as Lucas. In fact, they're rooming together in Madison this year. He's the one I miss. We've hung out together since I can remember. He can use my tipi without permission. Bin can too, but he doesn't know it, so he asks," Denae finished with a smile.

"Oh. Justin does sound nicer than your other cousins."

"He is. He's like six-foot-four and really broad in the shoulders…bigger than any of my brothers, but gentle. He's double-majoring in wildlife management and botany.

It goes with his focus on plants and animals growing up. He's the only one who'd stand up for me, and he was always big for his age, so he could get them to leave me alone. I was tiny, so he'd put me on his shoulders sometimes while we walked so I could see better."

"Sounds like you're sweet on him," Leah said.

Denae shook her head. "That'd be weird...not that I've had a chance at any other guys."

"You don't meet people in town, and you scared off your cousins," Leah said with a laugh. "I can see where you had a problem."

"What about you," Denae countered. "With your body, they should be all over you."

"I told you. I'm too weird and geeky. Did I say nerdy? To the guys, I'm boring, and I'm not interested in getting groped. I've got some guy friends…chess club and such…Jessica and I were the only girls in that, remember? I think there are a couple of them who'd like to ask me out, but they're too scared or shy. I'm not going to go out with them if they're too afraid to ask me out. There were more, but I trounced them too many times in chess and bruised their fragile egos."

"Whoa," Denae said. "Maybe it's just as well that I don't know hardly anyone in town. I don't know if I'm any good at chess. The only ones I've played recently are Dad and Bin. Anton taught me how to play but always played easy."

"Let's play. There's supposed to be a tournament in Eau Claire in a few weeks if my dad and I can convince my mom that I can go. She considers it or anything weird or cerebral as unladylike, so we'll see. Maybe this marriage retreat weekend will hold long enough for her to agree, and I can get it paid for. I think my dad's going to divorce her after my graduation. He's changed from the retreats, but she goes back to her old ways after about a week. It's been a nightmare but let me go get the board and pieces."

↢ ↢ ⊙ ↣ ↣

She ran. The trail curved ahead, the bear behind, chasing her. Hot breath on her neck, claws swishing, slashing so close, she could feel the wind. If she could get to the tipi beyond the curve, she'd be—

Her name was called, coming from the woods to her left. She stumbled, but the bear was farther away…gone. She opened her eyes.

Where was she…what was on her belly, moving around.

"Denae," came a soft voice from next to her. Leah. She was with Leah. It was that dream.

"You okay?"

Leah's hand was rubbing her belly…small slow circles.

"Yeah," she managed to say. Her voice sounded choked. She shouldn't go to the tipi. Not if she was with Leah.

"That was some nightmare."

"Yeah," she said again, her voice sounding more normal.

"What was it?"

Denae paused a moment. The circles on her belly continued, felt nice…calming. No tipi. This would work. "The bear. It's always the bear."

"You were running in bed, flailing your arms. You kicked all your covers off."

She could feel the coolness of the air but was warm…sweaty from the dream, still breathing hard. "It was chasing me…it's always chasing me. I wake up before it gets me, but it's getting closer."

"I guess that's good, anyway, that you wake up."

Denae nodded. "I'm glad you woke me up rubbing my belly like that. It was a better wake-up than most of the time with that nightmare."

Leah gave her a smile. "Do you have more than one of those a night?"

Denae shook her head. "It's too bad I had one tonight. You ready to go back to sleep?"

"I think so," Leah replied and rolled on her side with her back to Denae. "Goodnight."

Denae pulled her pillow over, slid against Leah and kissed her on her neck. "Goodnight."

↢ ↢ ⊙ ↣ ↣

Leah opened her eyes to light in her room. Not full daylight, so it was still somewhat early. She wasn't going to bother with Sunday school or church since nobody was forcing her. And somewhere in the night, she'd turned over, so she was facing Denae.

Well, kind of. Denae's forehead was on her collarbone, and she could feel the slow breathing through her t-shirt. She mainly saw that head of earthy yellow hair, and that was her true color…eyebrows and lashes, underarms, everywhere. She'd never used a razor…wasn't sure why she would. Mom would call her a hippy-child. In some ways, she was, Leah supposed.

The weekend had worked out how she wanted, though she hadn't expected her to stay Saturday night as well. She'd gotten a lot of information. Get a drink in Denae, and she'd tell you almost anything. She wasn't going to do anything with the information but wanted to know what was real. Now she knew that she didn't know much about the world.

She'd kinda liked Denae from before, but she did like her now. She was weirdness personified, but in some way, Denae was her kind of weird. Even lying here like this seemed okay, even though it shouldn't. You weren't supposed to be in bed with a naked girl…woman, really, though Denae was right that she looked like she was maybe thirteen at most, and that was all she was going to get.

Leah had more at eleven, but would be happy to trade half of what she had…she had more than she wanted. Jessica had it right…a C-cup was much better. Of course, she was back at the hospital after yet another operation to put Humpty Dumpty together again. That's what they joked about when she visited her, and Jessica wasn't too dopey with pain meds.

Leah started rubbing Denae's shoulder down to her shoulder blade…her scapula. She wanted to be a nurse…or doctor, so she needed to know the right body parts.

Her hand rubbed down against Denae's ribs. Petite didn't cover it. Denae was skinny…she could feel each rib. So unlike herself. She carried a layer of fat over her ribs…everywhere, it seemed. She felt Denae shift and stopped rubbing.

Denae looked up at her and smiled. "Hi."

"Hi," she responded automatically. "Did you sleep well?"

"After the nightmare, I did. Don't stop …that feels good."

Leah started rubbing lightly again, from her floating ribs up to her scapula and back. Denae smiled up at her like a little girl.

After a moment, Denae bowed her head and kissed Leah's collarbone...clavicle, then looked up with a smile.

"I'm glad you woke me up from that nightmare. If you hadn't, I think I would've woken up lying in the snow outside the tipi."

"You would have teleported in your sleep?"

"I've done it before. For a second, it feels like the bear got me. It's a shock to wake up half-buried in snow."

"Naked."

Denae nodded. "Usually, I wake up first, then teleport and sleep the rest of the night there, then come back in the morning. Unless I get lucky and Bin hears me having the nightmare. Then he comes in and calms it away."

"He can do that?"

"He has to enter the dream, so it's not great for him either. The first couple of times, he couldn't do it and was lying by my bed crying and shaking worse than me when I woke up, but he kept up until he could do it…save me from my dream. It worked, but so did you when you rubbed my belly, and that was nicer."

Leah got another of Denae's little girl smiles, and Denae kissed her clavicle again. Strange but pleasant to be kissed like that.

Leah kissed Denae's forehead when it came into view and pushed her down into the bed. "I'm going to fix some breakfast. Get some clothes on and come help me."

Chapter 8

Big Sister

"Denae, are we done for the day?"

Denae came out of her reverie, looking up from the book she'd supposedly been studying for the last several minutes. She set her translation wand down next to the sixteenth-century tome of Slovincian gothic script that described some of the daily life around Lake Lebsko and the Baltic Sea. Drawings of various interiors and exteriors of wattle and daub construction with magical reinforcements and waterproofings were not holding her interest. Neither was the mix of magical and mundane within their daily activities. Thoughts of Leah and showing her the tipi kept creeping in.

"Yes, Aunt Audrea," she said. "I think we are."

"Uncle Gunnar said you were having problems focusing yesterday, too." Her pointed face gave a small smile under the tangle of bronze-streaked dark brown hair. "Is everything okay?"

"It's fine," Denae replied, smiling at her. "I'm good." A little too good, she thought, since my mind is with Leah and not where it should be.

"I want to make sure everything's okay with the associated archeology and anthropology lessons we've been going over. They're only tertiarily involved with magic, but you said you were interested. And of course, this tome is rather dry in translation."

"I am. I'm just a bit distracted by other things. I'll do better on Thursday."

Aunt Audrea nodded and slid the large book away from Denae, hefting it up to put it back into the bookcase.

"Oh, and how was that girls' night you had with your new friend last weekend?"

Denae jerked up. Had Mom said something?

Aunt Audrea had her back turned, putting the old tome they'd been going over back in the bookcase, so she hadn't seen her reaction. Then Denae remembered that she'd been in the shop when Denae had told her mom where she was going. She was glad most of her training was one-on-one these days. She didn't need to be teased about having a friend in town.

She took a calming breath as Aunt Audrea turned around, then said, "I had a great time…we saw the movie *Close Encounters of the Third Kind*, ate spaghetti, watched tv, and…well…hung out." Aunt Audrea gave her a quizzical look.

"I'm glad you found a friend in town," she said. "She must be nice." The tone was friendly, but Denae wondered if Aunt Audrea had verbally omitted the word *finally* before *found.* There'd been the slightest hesitation there.

"She is," Denae agreed. "And we had a lot of fun together."

"I'm glad." She gestured Denae to get up, then hugged her, whispering in her ear, "It's good to have friends," then let go. "You want me to drive you home, or do you want to ski?"

"I'm going to ski," Denae said, and take the long way through the forest, she thought to herself.

"I thought you might," Aunt Audrea said. "You have that look about you."

Aunt Audrea was good with auras, thought Denae. I wonder if mine has changed since last week. Dad could see auras if he tried, one of the few knowing spells he'd bothered with, but Mom and Binesi hadn't learned. That would be a good extra for Bin. It would work well with his mind spells, but she was sure he'd at least thought of it. He was focused on other areas right now.

"I'll phone and let them know," she said.

"Tell them I'm going through the forest," Denae added. "It'll be dark before I get home."

"Will do."

Moments later, Denae pulled on her skis and started home. Yesterday afternoon, she'd cut her studies with Uncle Gunnar short because of her distractions and worked at the warehouse. She and Mom ate supper at Fred's. She knew Mom wanted to see Leah, probably chit-chat since Leah was now her friend.

Leah smiled nervously when she saw Denae and Mom but relaxed more as they conversed while she served them.

Denae wanted to ask Leah about coming out to the tipi but wasn't sure how Mom would take it. She had asked before she left on Sunday, but Leah had been non-committal then. The tipi was her alone place, but it'd be nice to have Leah there with her. When Leah came back to ask about dessert, she plunged forward.

"Leah, you want to come out to the tipi this weekend?"

She saw her mom stiffen slightly when she asked, but Leah seemed to miss it.

"Not this one, but maybe I can convince Mom to let me come next weekend." Leah looked over at Denae's mom. "If that's okay with you."

Maybe she hadn't missed it.

"That would be nice." Mom gave Leah a smile that seemed genuine. Was it really okay? She was sure she'd find out once they headed home.

Leah turned her attention back to Denae. "Oh, and I don't have anything going on Wednesday after school if you want to meet over at the arcade."

Denae glanced at her mom, who nodded, and she grinned. "Sounds great!"

↢↢⊙↣↣

"So, how much does she know?"

Mom had just put the pickup into gear. Her voice was light, but Denae recognized the undertone.

"More than she should, including that you do telepathy."

"I'd figured that out. I'd hoped to catch you alone, but that didn't work. Bin already told me that she'd pretty well figured out on her own that your trip into town wasn't normal in any way, and you confirmed it. Anything else?"

"We talked. She was curious, and I'm no good at lying."

"So that means?"

"She knows more about the family as a whole. I've also asked her not to tell anyone, which she already understood. She didn't want to be another Daniel."

Her mom turned a corner to the main road north before speaking.

"Daniel's the boy you levitated into the snowbank when you were seven."

"Yeah. You know his name?"

"He'd blabbed about you to too many of his friends by the time we found him, but Issa was able to suggest to his parents and a couple of his friends that he'd imagined it. She said his mom needed some reinforcement, but that quelled all of that."

"And made him a laughingstock at school, according to Leah."

"Actions have consequences, which also included you not being allowed to be left alone in town for several years."

"And me not wanting to be alone in town even after that."

"That, too, until a few weeks ago."

"I had to do that. I couldn't not go and stop Leah."

"I know."

"Is Aunt Issa going to visit Leah now?"

"Your dad and I discussed that over the weekend, and the answer is no. Not so long as Leah can keep the secret. You say she understands that. We hope that will be enough."

"And she's allowed to come to the tipi?"

"Yes, and the house."

"The house? I thought that was totally—"

"We talked about one of two things. Either Issa visits Leah, and you never see her again, or…because of what Leah knows and has surmised…Bin says she's pretty quick on the uptake…she gets more access to us and the house. The way you talked about the weekend when you came home, we were pretty sure the tipi wasn't far behind, so it's a risk, but a manageable one, and she seems to be a friend you need."

Denae nodded. The subtext she knew was that she couldn't screw this up to the point Aunt Issa needed to alter Leah's memories. There were enough memories now, with powerful ones from the days of the wreck and the arcade. That could mess up other associated memories as well…not a good thing with school and her other activities.

They'd turned west along the north edge of the town, mainly farmland to the south and the forests that marked the southern border of the family lands to the north. She sat quietly, watching the snow-covered fields go by for a few moments before speaking.

"I'm glad you like Leah."

"You're not a little girl anymore."

Denae let that sweep over her as her mom turned onto the road that went into their holdings. Trust and responsibility. That's what Mom meant.

"I also like that she got you to wear your hair down," Mom continued. "She's right… it does make you look older."

"I'm still getting used to it, but yeah, if she likes it this way, I'll keep wearing it down or in a ponytail."

↢↢⊙↣↣

Denae had barely gotten into her robe and settled in at her desk when Binesi came in.

"Mom said you two ate at Fred's, and Leah was there. I still haven't heard how your weekend went."

"What about you? You ended up staying the night at Oma's."

"Flynn was practicing his flying in the barn at his house, hit a beam or something, lost his concentration and fell, breaking a lot of bones and such. He'd been lying there for a while before Ebby found him."

"How bad?" At ten, Flynn was her favorite younger cousin, probably in part because he acted before he thought, the same as her. His mom was a decent healer, so it must've been bad if she took Flynn to Oma.

"Pretty bad. Ebby got the internal bleeding stopped before she moved him. He actually levitated himself to the car despite being hurt …he was rather proud of that."

Denae grinned in spite of herself. "He would be."

"Ebby could've fixed him up completely at home by herself, but she was sure she'd screwed something up and was a total basket-case by the time she got to Oma's. Sasha was screaming—"

"Two-year-olds are like that," Denae said, and Binesi nodded.

"She was upset because big brother Flynn was broke, and Mommy was upset. I eventually got Sasha to sleep, him semi-sedated, and Ebby calmed enough that she could continue healing him at Oma's."

"Impressive," Denae said honestly. Doing all of those at the same time called for some serious concentration. Little brother was getting good.

"Yeah…I was so wrung out by the end that I could barely stand. Sasha didn't want to sleep, Ebby didn't want to be calm, and Flynn was overly interested in everything happening to him. If I tried to put him under too much, he'd throw it off. It was easier simply to have him generally relaxed but conscious and move numbness to wherever they were working. He can fight the mind control stuff almost as well as you can."

"I've had a lot of practice," Denae said with a grin, "and pain can help with that."

"Yeah, well, I'm siccing him on you so you can hear all the gory details. That's payback for letting him see Sasha being born."

Denae winced. She'd been there to assist Oma with the birth…one of those things Oma thought she needed to experience, and she'd asked Ebby if Flynn could come and watch. She ran off at the nod to get Flynn, not realizing that the nod was the start of the next contraction and not a yes. Flynn got to see his sister being born, and Oma even let him cut the umbilical cord. He'd regale anyone who'd listen with the story, and Ebby still hadn't forgiven her for bringing him in.

"What about your weekend with Leah?"

"It was good. I really enjoyed it, and now I want to go to Wyoming."

"Wyoming?"

"We saw *Close Encounters of the Third Kind,* and this Devil's Tower Mountain was in it a lot. I want to go see it."

"That's the space alien movie. So, you're going to blip over and see it?"

"After the Key West fiasco, I'm not going to try to go anywhere via a picture again. Not even moving ones, though it seems like that would be easier since I see more."

"I understand they sometimes film the closeups that would give you better detail in totally different places than the wide shots. You might end up in a totally different part of the world if you went with the wrong one of those."

"Oh…yeah…thanks for the warning."

"So, what's Leah like?"

"Nice. She reads and watches a lot of fantasy and science-fiction stories, so I guess that's why she's pretty accepting of what we do. I had my bear nightmare, and she woke me up by rubbing my belly. That was really a nice way to come out of that."

"I bet so. How badly did you bruise her?"

"What?"

"I learned the hard way to stay away from you when you're being chased by the bear." He pointed to his cheek, ribs, and hip. "I had big bruises before I could get away."

"She didn't say anything."

"But she was right there, next to you. You should've seen the bruises by morning."

Denae shook her head. "She wears a big t-shirt when she sleeps."

"Oh." There was disappointment in his voice.

"You were expecting a report on her breasts from me?" Denae glared and stood up from her desk.

"They do look nice under her clothes," he protested.

"You can look other places," she countered.

"I look at the whole body," he said, sitting down on her bed and grinning up at her.

"I doubt that," Denae said sarcastically. "What color are her eyes?"

Binesi stuttered, the smug look wiped off his face, and Denae continued, "I'll believe you've looked at a woman properly when you know more about her face than her tits and butt."

"Right," Binesi drawled out. "That is good advice, but back to Leah."

"She may come out and spend the weekend at the tipi with me in a couple of weeks."

"Seriously? I'm surprised they haven't sicced Aunt Issa on her, but they're letting her come out here instead."

"Aunt Issa was discussed last weekend, but Mom said that it was decided to leave things alone so long as I didn't screw things up. I may need help." She sat on her bed next to him.

"I can do that. Oh, and I have something I want to show you, but don't tell Mom or Dad."

He fished a strip of photos out of his sweatshirt and handed them to her. The pictures were of him and the petite dark-haired girl from the arcade, both smiling at the camera in the first one, her closer in the second. In the third, she's kissing his cheek, and they're kissing each other in the last one.

He had a big grin on his face. "Her name's Olivia. That's from last weekend."

Denae looked again at the last two pictures. It seemed like there was something she was missing with those.

"I walked her home. There are some trees across the road from her house. We went back there and kissed some more before I took her to her front door."

Denae nodded, then the thought came to her…what she was missing.

"Wait a minute…hold on." She pushed him onto his back and pinned him, staring intently into his eyes.

Binesi's grin disappeared, his eyes growing wide at her gaze.

"What?"

"If you wanted to, you could magic Olivia out of her pants and make her think it was all her idea." She rapped him lightly on his forehead with a knuckle. "You could, couldn't you?"

"I didn't do any magic on her. The photos and the kiss were all her idea. The other kisses were…mutual. I didn't do anything like that. It was—"

"But you could."

He nodded with a gulp.

"And you've thought about it," she continued.

"I wouldn't do anything like—"

Denae thumped his nose with her fingertips. "Did you know there's a spell called partial petrification?"

He shook his head.

"I learned it about a year ago," she said. "Not sure how useful it will be, but understand this, Binesi." She grabbed his hair and pulled his head up until he winced. "If you do that to one of those girls…or anything they don't want to do, I will use that spell on your balls, break them off and throw them in the lake. Oma can probably grow them back, but I understand that it takes months, and there will be a lot of questions. I bet you'll be in more trouble than I will once those questions get answered. What do you think?"

She released his hair, and his head bounced onto the bed, the silver streak shining in the light as his blond hair spread over the quilt.

"Understand?"

He nodded, wide-eyed.

She rolled off him. He got up and almost fled out of her room. A smile spread over her face as she watched him go. Despite him being bigger, she was still the big sister and not to be messed with. She'd never really practiced with that spell, but it was the threat that mattered. With that, she grabbed her book and went to the bathroom to take a long, hot bubble bath.

Chapter 9

Meeting the Parents

Denae stood at the edge of an empty wooded lot about a block from the high school, waiting to spot Leah when school let out. She'd gotten to town early and didn't want to hang around the almost empty arcade. She knew she was being too eager, but she'd shift back to the fenced area by the warehouse entrance, get Bin, and walk to the arcade. She'd still beat Leah by at least five minutes.

The bell rang, and people started pouring out. Some went for cars, and others for the yellow buses, but many were walking. Leah said she walked, and after a few minutes, Denae spotted her. She resisted stepping out…Binesi said it would be weird when she told him of her plan, so she shifted inside the warehouse fence and went to get Binesi.

Binesi dropped a couple of quarters in his favorite pinball machine while they waited once they got to the arcade. Olivia was also coming there for a little while before her dance class started since it was only a couple of blocks away.

Denae watched as he took his turn with the silver ball, fewer dings, beeps, and other noises than there would be later, and no song going either from the jukebox. "You going to watch Olivia at her dance class?"

"No," he said, shaking his head. "She doesn't want the distraction, though they have a recital in May, and she does want me to come to that."

"Sounds like she plans to keep you around for a while."

He had the decency to pink slightly as he smiled. "That she does. Don't act so anxious when Leah gets here. You don't want to scare her off."

"What do you mean? With all she's found out, she doesn't scare easily."

"I don't mean that. Remember when Jude was dating that girl, and she dumped him. Anton told him it was because he was acting too needy. You're acting a bit like Jude today. You're not dating Leah, just being a friend."

"Like I know how to do that," Denae snapped.

"My point exactly. Relax a bit and remember that she wanted to see you."

"Where are you getting all of this?"

"Two places. First, psychology is a part of mental control, just like anatomy is needed for body control. Second, you've been agitated enough that you didn't notice me slip in a mental tracker on you earlier. I knew when the school bell rang and when you spotted Leah. I was glad you showed up back at the warehouse instead of running out to Leah like a little lost puppy dog."

"And you all cool and collected."

"Yeah. Until Olivia walks through the door. Then I can barely remember my own name."

Denae laughed. "Good. It's not just me."

"So get some pops for everyone and bring two of them to me. That will look like you're thoughtful toward Leah, another of your not-so-strong points."

"And you'll look thoughtful, too."

"I thought of it." He nodded at the pile of quarters on the pinball machine.

Denae sighed. And she wouldn't have at all. Not even after she'd gotten up and bought herself one. She wouldn't have thought about asking if anyone else wanted one. Maybe after, when it was too late. She scooped up some quarters and headed back to the machine. Leah liked Pepsi.

↢ ↢ ⊙ ↣ ↣

"You're an awful driver. This game has steering wheels and everything." Leah had just lapped her on the crude racetrack on the tv screen. She was having problems just keeping it on the track.

"I've never driven a car." She'd gotten it pointed right on the short straight part, and she was getting a little better on the curves.

"You don't have your license?"

Denae shook her head, focusing on the next two corners. "Never saw the need. I can go where I need to much faster."

"Like Devil's Tower or Key West. How are you going to get to those places?"

"I'll figure out a way." She hit a wall with her blocky video car and needed to maneuver out. She didn't want Leah to pass her again.

Leah laughed as her car zoomed even farther around the track. "It gives you a different sort of freedom than your way of travel. You can go see places you've never been to before."

"Eventually, I suppose I'll have to."

"You don't sound enthusiastic."

"It's scary. I'm afraid I'll hit something—someone, especially after what I saw in the crystal ball. Or that they'll hit me."

"Crystal ball?"

"The vision. I was trying to learn how to use it when I saw you and the wreck."

Leah was quiet for a moment. "Last lap for me. You're keeping it between the walls better. At least cross the line before me even if you have another lap to go."

Denae managed to do that, the screen flashing Game Over as Leah crossed seconds later along with the bad electronic music. She knew she could practice and get better at the game if she wanted.

Leah looked at her watch as they turned. "I'm going over to Jessica's in an hour. I'm taking care of her tonight."

"Taking care of her?"

"Yeah. Someone gave her parents a gift certificate to a restaurant and a motel stay in Wassau. They're heading off for a night away, and I'm playing nurse to Jessica."

"There's a problem with that?"

Leah shook her head. "It's just a little scary, being alone with her all night. Nothing's going to happen, but what if it does? What if she falls or something?"

"You'll handle it. You're going to be a doctor."

"Or nurse, so yeah, this is exactly the sort of thing I'd be doing. And she wants me to give her a sponge bath. I've never done that."

Denae shrugged. "Why not her mom for that?"

"She thinks I'll be nicer…gentler. Her mom's so frazzled by all of this. They're in a lot of debt from the hospital and surgeries, and Jessica's got at least two more surgeries. Her brother probably won't be able to do his senior year of college because there's no money for it now. Jessica's gone into her shell and fights with her mom all the time. It seems like I'm the only one who can talk with her, and that's when she's not too dopey from the pain meds. Otherwise, she's asleep or close to it. She loves dancing, and she'll probably never walk again without a limp, so she'll never dance."

Denae wanted to say something about magical healing and the salves and draughts that could help but knew that was a step too far. She wasn't even sure they would help with the injuries a month old now. Plus, doctors were involved, and apparent miracles didn't mix well from what she understood.

"I can help keep her from falling."

"Your levitate?"

Denae nodded.

"You'd have to be there. She doesn't want to see anyone new right now, and if the levitate was needed, I'm not sure how we'd explain it. I think it has to be up to me, but I have your number if I do need you."

Denae nodded vigorously.

Leah smiled, then looked around. "What next?"

"Billiards."

"Pool? You know how to play that?"

"We have a table at home, but these are smaller."

"I'm going to get my butt handed to me, aren't I?"

"I'll be nice."

↢ ↢ ⊙ ↣ ↣

"So, do you like Olivia or not?" Denae walked with Leah through downtown toward where Jessica lived. They'd talked with Binesi and Olivia before he walked her to dance class. Leah seemed a little annoyed with Olivia from the start.

"Olivia's okay, I guess. Her sister Cheryl and I used to be friends until she got into cheerleading. Now I'm not good enough for her, and she lets me know that regularly, so I don't know what Olivia will tell her and how she'll twist it next time I see her at school. Other than being a bit giggly, Olivia is fine and really likes Bin."

"It's mutual."

"Ah…puppy love. Something else I missed out on."

"Yeah…me, too."

"Oh, and that's Jessica's house, over across the street in the next block."

Denae looked at the small frame house with a nod, then realized she was at the wooden fence outside the warehouse's main entrance.

"Wait. Let's go in here a minute."

"Is this your family's business?"

"Yeah. I want to grab something for you."

"Uh…okay?" Leah eyed the eight-foot wooden fence warily.

Denae swung the gate open and ushered Leah in, then did the same with the front door. They stepped in, and Denae smiled as Leah gaped. There was an office to the right, but everything else in sight was rows of shelves with different bottles and boxes and packaging.

"Wait here," Denae said and dashed off out of sight behind one of the rows of shelving, reemerging a minute later, arms full of bottles, setting them on a small table.

"I've got you some of our Aunt Bertie's products for Jessica. I like the way the lavender and rosemary go together in our liquid body soap. This meadowsweet and spearmint shampoo is wonderful if you need to wash her hair, too. Also, some bath salts for her mom that will help calm her down when she needs it."

"And the other?" Leah was looking at the other bottles.

"The same things for you. There are very minor amounts of magic in all of these that make them work even better. Let me grab a couple of bags," and Denae stepped into the office.

She looked up from the note she'd written to see Leah looking at her. "Just letting Mom know what I took so the inventory stays correct. Here are the bags."

"You don't have to—"

"She'll just take it out of my pay, so it's no problem." Denae beamed at Leah.

Leah slumped. "I need to ask you a favor."

"Okay," Denae responded, still smiling but wondering what was up.

"I talked to my parents about going out to your place next weekend. They want to meet you. Come Friday night for supper. The thing is, Mom is going to recognize you just because of your hair color, so please keep your hair down. She doesn't like different things. Your glasses are a bit weird, but you should probably keep those on, too. Less weird than your eyes, and I really hate that I just said that."

Leah reached up to either side of Denae's face. "Maybe do a Marcia Brady deal with your hair and bring these side pieces to the back and clip them."

She pulled parts of Denae's hair to the back while Denae tried to understand all of this.

"Why?"

"To look more feminine. I know it's not you, but Mom's seen you with your Indian braids and doesn't like them, so if you can like wear a dress or skirt or something, and something nicer than your hiking boots, I might be able to come for the weekend."

"Okay," Denae said. "You want me to get girly to meet your parents."

"This sounds awful, but yes, and don't say anything about a tipi. I told them it was a rustic cabin near your parents' house. I should've just said I was staying at your house. Mom's worried about it just being the two of us."

"Seriously? We're both eighteen. I've spent lots of nights out there by myself."

"Mom's a city person. Even this town's a little too rustic for her, though she says she's adapted."

Denae looked at Leah. That wasn't the reason. She was lousy at reading people without looking at their auras, but it was apparent something else was going on. She didn't like to read people's auras in town. So many times it was like they were wearing masks or costumes. Their auras looked so different than what they let show. She wasn't going to do this with Leah, either. Maybe at times, but not now.

"There's more than that, isn't there?"

Leah stared at her a moment, then her face crumbled. "My mom's a first-class controlling bitch. She's not going to like you, but if you look nice enough, then I might be able to come over anyway. She doesn't like me spending as much time at Jessica's as I do, and I'm sure it's because Jessica is broken. She might see you as an unbroken friend to replace Jessica. That's terrible, but it's probably true, and you're not replacing Jessica."

Leah shook her head. "She doesn't even like me working at Fred's…I'm better than a mere waitress, but I took the job in part to get away from her. It's her idea for me to be a doctor instead of a nurse. I want this weekend away with you so much."

Denae watched as Leah started sobbing, not sure what to do. Bin had said something about being a friend to have a friend, but what did that mean now?

She took a step and put her arms around Leah's waist, then stood on her tiptoes and kissed Leah's wet cheek, the salty taste coming through a second later. She shifted, kissing her other cheek.

Leah stopped sobbing and looked at Denae, brow furrowed.

"What's that for?"

"Mom used to dry my tears like that when I was little. I think it worked." She kissed Leah's cheek again.

"And that?" Leah looked a little…Denae shifted aura sight on. More concerned than scared, she saw. Curious. Always curious with Leah.

"For you being you. Nursing Jessica tonight. For rubbing my belly the other night." Denae shifted again to the other cheek. "I probably would have disappeared from your bed and woken up in the snow next to the tipi if you hadn't done that." She gave Leah a final squeeze and dropped back down to her heels.

"What magic did you just do?" Leah's curiosity had overridden everything else.

"Nothing. Why?"

"I suddenly feel much better. You had to have done something."

"Nothing. Honest. I'd tell you if I did. I don't do that sort of magic. I'm better at hurting people with my magic than helping them."

"Uh-huh. Well…whatever happened, I'm blaming you." Leah kissed Denae on the forehead, and Denae felt a warmth radiate down her body that made her smile.

"I have a brown corduroy jumper dress and a white turtleneck. Will that work?"

Leah's aura lit up along with her smile. "That will do nicely. Modest and conservative. Let's get these bagged up. I really do need to get over to Jessica's so her parents can leave."

Denae felt a letdown knowing Leah was leaving. "Um…who's Marcia Brady?"

"Brady Bunch." Leah laughed at her confusion. "Never mind."

↢ ↢ ⊙ ↣ ↣

"Your family has a lot of property northwest of town, don't you?" Supper had gone well, and Denae was sitting in the living room with Leah's dad while Leah and her mom cleaned up after supper.

"We do, but I have a rather extended family that lives out there. Still, it's not like town. We're spread out a lot more."

"That sounds nice. I see deer many times when I drive the road south of your properties. Do you hunt your lands?"

"Sometimes, though we don't use guns. We treat the land as something of a nature preserve but try to keep the populations in check. Do you hunt?"

"Not in years." He gave what seemed like an unconscious glance toward the kitchen. "Bow and arrow?"

Denae nodded. Many of her cousins did hunt that way.

"Do you hunt?"

Denae swallowed. "A little. I got a deer once. It walked almost in front of me, but I still think mine was a lucky shot, and my cousin Justin showed me how to field-dress it." She was ad-libbing though not far from the truth. She'd broken its neck with a large rock instead of an arrow. "Mostly, I snare rabbits, skin and tan the hides and make pouches out of them. We sell things like that along with the bath and beauty products like what Leah brought home. Some of the family raise rabbits, so we have a steady supply of skins, but I like the taste of the wild rabbits better, so I hunt them."

Leah's dad smiled. He was chubby with thinning hair and easy to talk to…no real probing questions aside from the property so far. He was obviously proud of his daughter and had similar interests, from what she could tell.

Binesi and Mom had coached her for tonight at the kitchen table. Dad had stood farther away, leaning on the kitchen counter with an amused look on his face. No talk of magic or of saving Leah. It was easy not to say anything to Leah's parents about that since they were so obviously mundane.

Since Leah had never told them anything of that day except that she was running a couple of minutes late, there was no talk about the wreck. Denae didn't have to feign ignorance of it, and Jessica wasn't even mentioned at supper or afterward.

She had to pretend she'd never been in the house and asked where the lavatory was. Leah took her to see her bedroom before supper, so that was covered early. She'd complimented Leah's mom on the curtains in the living room and on supper and dessert and offered to help with the dishes, though Leah shooed her out to talk with her dad instead.

She wasn't sure about what Leah's mom thought of her. She smiled a lot, but the smile never went up to her eyes. It was easy not to try to look at her aura…Based on what Leah said the other night, Denae really didn't want to know any more about her than she had to. She was like some of those other town people with their faces hiding who they really were. Leah told her Thursday evening that her mom had borrowed the shampoo and liked it, so Denae brought a catalog with her. That did seem to help matters from the start. Aside from a few quick questions, her mom hardly talked to her at all.

"I've met a few of your family at a Chamber of Commerce meeting a while back. Jerok and Leonard, is it?"

"That's my dad and uncle," Denae said, excitement growing in her.

"It's an interesting process they described about their family business. It almost sounds like one of those hippy communes where everything belongs to everyone, and everyone contributes, except that yours seems to work."

"We get paid for our work," Denae said. "I've read about some of those communes, and that seems to be the difference. They assume everyone will contribute equally, but we get paid for what we do, and then expenses for housing and such get taken out. I get paid for every rabbit skin pouch I make. I get paid when I work at the warehouse. My aunts and uncles get paid when they teach the kids or make products to sell or for the food or animals they grow for the family. It is communal, but you have to help. Unless you're little or old. Uncle Mawk doesn't get around very well, so doesn't do much, but lives pretty well in his house, and we help out there as much as he'll allow."

"Like this cabin you're staying in?"

"His is much nicer. The cabin's a single room with a wood stove for heat and cooking. We'll melt snow for water."

"Outhouse?"

"Actually kinda inside…tucked into a back corner, but a pit toilet." It was really a slit trench, and there are no corners in a tipi.

"Leah know about all this?"

"She does."

"Know about what?" Leah padded into the room.

"Just how rustic this cabin is," her dad said.

"Denae's told me, and yeah, the bathroom facilities leave something to be desired, but I'm not seven years old now, so I'll cope." She flashed her dad a smile before looking at Denae. "You want to go over to the arcade?"

Leah's dad gave them a shooing motion and they went to put on their boots.

As soon as they were off the porch, Denae asked, "How was Jessica?"

One of those thoughtfulness things that Binesi coached her to ask. She'd almost forgotten. She didn't want to bring up Jessica first since Leah said her mom thought she was spending too much time there. She really just wanted to ask how the evening went with her mom, but Bin told her this was more important.

"It went well," Leah responded, a smile suddenly on her face. "We did some things her mom wouldn't have allowed."

"Like what?"

"Sounds silly, but I took Jessica out on the porch until she got good and cold. She said that she wanted to feel something real besides her pain with all the drugs, so we did that. Then I gave her the sponge bath sitting on a chair in the bathroom…not on the hospital bed like her mom wanted. Lastly, I shaved her legs…kind of. With the scars being so fresh, I couldn't do a lot with her right leg, but shaved most of her left. That we did on her bed instead of the hospital bed in her brother's bedroom, and she fell asleep before I finished. I didn't even get a nightgown on her, so she slept with a damp towel around her. She was happier than I'd seen her in a while come morning, just for those little rebellions."

"Why'd she want her legs shaved. That just seems weird, especially in her condition."

"Just because you're a little hippy child who's never used a razor doesn't mean the rest of the world is that way," Leah said with a laugh. "She wanted to somehow feel at least a little normal. Most women shave their legs and under their arms."

"I know, but I don't see the purpose. It seems like a waste of time."

"Maybe if you get a boyfriend, you'll change your mind."

"If having body hair will run him off, maybe I don't want him."

Leah chuckled at that. "You do have a point about the shallowness of some guys, and you pulled off that Marcia Brady look just fine. You have a clue about that yet?"

"Yeah," Denae replied with a pout. "I asked Bin, and he asked Olivia, and she fixed my hair in the arcade lavatory while telling me about the television show before I came over. It actually feels better than I thought it would, with the little clips on the sides. So what did your mom think?"

"Mom didn't dislike you horribly, so that's a plus. Dad enjoyed talking to you, so he'll probably go to bat for me for the weekend if only to see if I can survive without modern plumbing."

Denae laughed. "It's really just a slit trench. You have to squat."

"That still sounds better than risking splinters sitting on a cold wooden board with a hole in it and who-knows-what on the bottom side. Is there any privacy?"

"I have a sheet hung up, so it blocks sight, but not sound. It also blocks the heat a bit, so that's the chilly part of the tipi. You may not want to linger."

"It's going to be an adventure."

Denae smiled. "Yes, I guess it is."

Chapter 10

At the House

Denae stood on the front porch when Leah pulled up in her dad's '72 Olds Cutlass. Her mom drove the newer Buick.

"Wow, this place is huge." Leah surveyed the length of the covered porch, a grin on her face.

Denae smiled.

Finally, Leah was here. Her mom had been changing her mind about twice a day, though Denae only had to hear about it every few days.

Denae led Leah into the warmth of her own home, the first town person to enter in years. Her brothers kept their liaisons in town or out in the forest unless they dated a distant cousin. Mom and Dad didn't want the townspeople at the house, but Leah already knew enough that it really didn't matter much.

Leah oohed and aahed over the massive log frame house and large stone fireplace in the living room. Mom greeted her with a hug, taking her coat from her.

"Don't take that too far," Denae said. "We'll be heading out shortly."

"It's right here," Mom replied, "by her bag."

Denae's dad stepped out of his office and gave her a slight smile before turning his gaze to Leah.

"This is my dad, Jerok."

"So, you're Leah," he said, not giving Leah time to speak. "I do remember you from Fred's."

Leah seemed to freeze at his steady gaze.

"You're going out to your tipi?" he asked, not taking his eyes off of Leah.

Leah half-nodded while Denae said, "Yes, Dad."

"You're getting there how?"

"Snowmobile," she continued.

"You're staying warm how?" Jerok's eyes stayed on Leah.

"I already have a fire going, plus there's about a half-cord of wood between inside and out." She could see Leah fidget out of the corner of her eye, but she wasn't going to say anything to her.

"Food?" His eyes never wavered.

"I have some packed, plus several days there, and I can hop back and get more if I need to." His eyes did jerk over to hers for a second before settling back on Leah.

"Drink?"

"I have the makings for coffee, tea, and hot cocoa," she listed these off on her fingers. "We'll melt snow for the water."

"Booze?" Leah's legs seemed to wobble.

"Ah…," Denae started. "Two bottles of red wine, only to be drunk when we're settled in for the nights." She grinned. "No Aquavit for us. That turned out nasty." She glanced at Leah. "I told him about us redecorating your bathroom."

Her dad grimaced, and Leah gave a weak smile as he broke his stare at her, turning his eyes on Denae. "And the storm?"

"Unless it lasts over a week, we can ride it out fine," she said, returning his gaze. "For that matter, as Bin would say, I can blip back here for more of whatever we might need."

Leah spoke finally. "If the storm's that bad, they'll cancel school anyway, so there's not much sense in coming in." She looked over at her suitcase. "I have a transistor radio with extra batteries, so we'll know what's going on, and books and playing cards…and extra warm clothes."

He gazed at her for another moment, nodded, and gestured toward the door. "It's good to finally meet you properly, Leah. Go forth into the wilderness. Be careful, have fun, and stay warm. And Leah, leave your car keys. I'll put your car in the workshop before the storm gets here." With that, he turned and walked back into his office.

Leah looked wide-eyed at Denae. "I wasn't sure what to think with the way he stared at me," she squeaked.

Denae laughed. "I wasn't sure what he was doing either, but I think you passed the test." She was pretty sure he was watching Leah's aura but wasn't going to say that.

"You two need to get going," Denae's mom said, smiling. "It's already getting dark, and the temps are supposed to drop a good bit with that clear sky. I heard on the radio that the storm's going to roll in around midnight, so fasten the flap tight." Leah looked questioningly at that last bit.

"We'll be fine, Mom. Snug as a bug in a rug," repeating what her mom had said sometimes when she was little.

"Get off then, and whatever your father said." She pushed the back door open once Leah had put her coat on. "And Leah, keep Denae safe out there." Leah opened her mouth a moment, then nodded as she went out.

"Goodnight," Leah said as the door closed behind her. Denae felt her move close. "We're really doing this. It's scary, going out into the forest like this alone, but it'll be fun."

Denae simply looked back and smiled as they got to the snowmobile.

↢ ↢ ⊙ ↣ ↣

Shortly, they were cruising down a trail on the snow, Denae chatting about different things as they passed. She pointed out things Leah couldn't really see because of the dark, her voice coming through the speakers in Leah's helmet. They crossed the lake, frozen solid many inches thick, and went back uphill slightly as they went back into a trail. Denae had said she could see well in the dark, and this must be true because Leah wouldn't have been going faster than a walk despite the light from the moon.

This was definitely going to be rustic, then she saw what had to be the tipi, white and glowing in the moonlight against the darkness of the sky and trees. It was at least twenty feet tall and that wide at the base. Denae went past, made a wide circle cutting around some trees off the trail, and stopped in front of it.

After throwing a cover over the snowmobile, Denae hurried Leah inside the tipi and secured the flap against the cold. There was a fire going in the center of the…Leah supposed it was a room. It was almost down to coals, and the warmth on her face felt good as she pulled off the helmet.

Denae was soon out of the snowsuit as well, peeling off layers, so Leah followed suit. Leah saw Denae looking at her, already only in thin white long underwear. Leah still wore her heavy flannel shirt and lined cords.

"Already down to your thermals, or are those silk?"

"Silk, and it feels good."

Leah started unsnapping the shirt. She'd given things a lot of thought after Denae had left two Sundays back and thought that if she didn't chicken out, she might try sleeping nude like Denae. She'd probably chicken out, though, but then again, she was already stripping down to her long underwear while Denae put more wood on the fire.

"You look great like that in the firelight," Denae said. "Now we relax until the fire goes back to coals. Then I'll make up some sausage and cabbage."

"Seriously?"

"I thought you liked them," Denae said, looking slightly disheartened.

"I do, but we'll stink this place up with our farts," she said with a grin.

"Oh," Denae replied. "Well, we'll stink it up together then."

Leah surveyed the inside. Yeah, it was about twenty feet in diameter and at least that tall. It was painted in yellows and oranges of different figures and animals most of the way up until black soot started covering it the top several feet. There was that sheet suspended over on the right, so the slit trench must be behind that.

The flickering red glow of the fire gave the whitish rock a warm glow, and with the extra wood on the fire, it was getting quite cozy, but something was missing.

"Hey, where are the beds?"

Denae flashed a grin at her. "No bed, but there's plenty of blankets and quilts and pillows, so you can make your own bed wherever you like. I usually bed down about where we're sitting, so this will work. Sorry that I don't have any buffalo hides, but the tipi is stone and not animal skins, so we're not really authentic here."

Leah laughed. With all the different quilts and blankets piled up, it could be more like *The Princess and The Pea* than anything rustic. This would be nice.

They talked a good half-hour before Denae declared the fire ready for cooking, pulled out a cast-iron skillet, and placed it on the grill. She dumped bacon grease into the pan. Once it melted, she dumped cut-up sausage, onions, and cabbage from different containers into the skillet. Soon the smell was making Leah's mouth water, and not too much later, they were digging into the meal, served on paper plates.

Leah looked around the stone tipi again. This was just surreal, eating like this and washing everything down with wine in red Solo cups. If she wanted water, she dipped it out of a pail of melted snow.

Denae wiped out the skillet, added a little more grease, let that melt, wiped that out, and set the skillet on the stone floor. The paper towels were tossed in the fire, flaring up instantly. Paper plates went next.

Leah slid next to Denae by the fire, feeling the warmth on her face and through her thermals.

"I know this is rustic, but I didn't see a tv at your house?"

"We don't have electricity," Denae said.

"What? You have a phone."

"Different wires, or so I'm told."

"Okay…I guess that's right."

"We do have some electronics, but they're all battery-operated."

"But you have a full kitchen."

"Yeah, and it's all done by magic." Denae grinned impishly at her. "The stove and the fridge are tied into each other. Some sort of thermodynamics. The more you use the stove, the better the fridge works. It's a symbiotic relationship between the two, and done right, they feed each other as a closed system."

Leah nodded. This sounded more like physics than magic, and wasn't symbiotic something biological? "You're making my head hurt again."

↢ ↢ ⊙ ↣ ↣

Denae laughed as Leah threw herself on the mound of blankets. She was so glad Leah was here. Denae slid onto the blankets next to her and felt a presence pushing in. She tensed, thinking *no, no, no*. Leah looked at her as she sat up, but Denae held her hand up, closing her eyes.

Denae. It was Mom.

What? It came out as a whine, though she knew only her mom could hear it.

Can you come home? There was a pleading there. *With Leah.*

But why, she replied, trying to suppress the whine.

Her mother's driving me crazy. She's called here three times already, wanting to speak with her, demanding it.

But she knows we went to a 'rustic cabin' with no telephone or anything.

She listened to the news and weather on the television, and she's in a total panic. Denae felt the frustration in her mom's sending. *Can you get her back here so she can talk to her mom and calm her down?*

She's not going to like this, Denae said.

If I don't say she's at least coming, her mom and dad will be driving up here, and we don't want that. Hurry, and you can go back to the tipi after she talks to her mom.

Have two big mugs of hot cocoa ready.

I will. How long do you think it'll take?

Fifteen minutes, but if she calls again, tell her longer, Denae answered. *That should give us time to warm up before Leah needs to call her back.* She sent another sigh out. *Leah's going to be upset when I tell her, and I'm already pissed off.* She paused. *Bye.*

Love you, came the response, and her presence was gone.

Denae opened her eyes, looking into Leah's face inches from her own.

"What was that…why are you so mad?"

"Your mother," Denae yelled, and Leah jumped back. "She is driving my mom mad because she keeps calling and is totally panicked about you being in a rustic cabin. If we don't come back so she can hear your voice, she's going to try to drive out to the house, so we need to go home now so you can talk to her and calm her down."

Leah turned red in turn. "She's not panicked. She's using this to control me like she always does." She moved back to Denae and rapped her forefinger into Denae's sternum. "She always tries to do this, making up something so I have to go," her finger thumping into Denae's chest with a steady beat. "I am not going to let her do this again…not this time…not this time." Leah was dissolving into tears.

"I told Mom we'd be back at the house. We'll get there, you make your call, and then we'll come back here. You can stay here as long as you like, but we have to go home."

"Tell your mom we're staying," Leah said through her tears.

"I can't," Denae explained. "Mom can do that, but I can't, so get dressed up completely. It'll be colder, so let's get there and back before it gets late and the storm hits."

They dressed hurriedly, putting on layer after layer, then the snowsuits over it all, and finally the helmets. They went out and started the snowmobile, stuffing the cover and its strap deep into a saddlebag before heading out. It was already darker, clouds now covering the sky.

They rode quietly about a quarter of the way to the lake when Denae felt a shift in the air. Trees creaked, snow dropping heavily from their boughs. Then the snow began to fall in earnest, her visibility dropping to only a few feet distance.

The storm was early.

Chapter 11

Snow-Blind

"This isn't good," came into Denae's helmet from Leah.

"No, but we'll make it," Denae responded, though she slowed down to a crawl as the snow blocked her vision.

"What are you going to do? Go back?" There was fear in Leah's voice.

Denae took a breath as she thought. It was so easy to become lost in a blizzard. She could find home, but there was a forest between here and there. It would be easy to get herself home in a second. Getting Leah there was more difficult. She couldn't teleport her there with her…she could do maybe one hundred pounds, but not more, and Leah definitely weighed more than that. She could try teleporting Leah separately, but it was exhausting, and she wasn't very good with it. She wasn't sure how far off her mark she'd be, and a blizzard wasn't the place to practice that. But there were other ways.

"I'm going to find points on landmarks along the trail and aim for those. The trail doesn't wind that much, and once we get to the lake, I can shoot a straight line for the back door."

"Sounds easy." Leah seemed reassured by that, which made Denae breathe a little easier.

"It should be," Denae said, or she hoped. She already cast a seeking on her first point along the way and drove slowly, barely able to see anything at all. She swerved around trees that suddenly appeared, trying to remember every inch of the trail and failing, but her point acted as a beacon. As she got to that point, she cast out for the next and started heading for it, knowing they'd be close to the lake where she could reach out farther in a straight line. She was halfway to that second point when she swerved another looming tree. The snowmobile rose out of the snow and flipped.

She felt Leah slide off the back as she clung to the handlebars, trying somehow to control it even as she felt her body try to follow Leah's. The snowmobile came down, and Denae felt something in her leg snap, then the engine stopped as it landed in the snow. Lights popped in her eyes as the sharpness lanced through her shin.

No, no, no. Not now. No. She wailed against the pain. Then Leah was pulling her, leg freed from under the snowmobile as she screamed into the helmet. Leah lifted her upright while Denae came back from what she hoped was a momentary blackness. She fought for balance on her good foot. Leah tried to say something, but Denae heard nothing. They were unplugged from the communications jacks.

She pushed forward the couple of feet back to the snowmobile, tugging Leah along to keep her balance on one leg. Between them, they righted it and plugged back in as they got astraddle. Denae fumbled, mounting it, and floated herself to get back on.

"Are you okay," Leah said first thing.

"I think…I broke…my leg," Denae said, panting against the pain. "But okay…otherwise." She took a deep breath. "Fix…when we get home. You…okay?"

"Yeah," Leah responded. "Okay…how are you gonna drive?

"Doesn't matter," Denae said, feeling the throb and flashing sparks behind her eyes keep time with her heartbeat. "I'll do it. Let me get it started."

She could feel the starter turning through the seat, but the engine didn't start…didn't even try to catch. She stopped and tried again. she could feel it keep cranking, hear the slight static through the speakers, but it didn't start. Again and again she tried until the battery started going down.

"No, no, no," she cried, beating the panel with her fists.

"What are we going to do?" Denae could hear the fear in her voice.

"Give me a…minute…to think. I will…get you home."

"Okay," came the reply. "I'm getting cold."

"Me too." Yeah, me too, Denae thought. Even in the forest, they could feel the wind. It would be worse on the lake. A lot worse.

"Get off, but stay close," Denae said after a moment. "Once we…unplug, we won't…be able to talk. There's a strap in the saddlebag…with the cover. We need to tie it around us so we won't separate. Snowshoes are in the saddlebag on the other side. Put those snowshoes on, and…I'll guide your walking back."

"But you can't walk," she protested.

"Don't…have to." Denae paused. "Remember Daniel…I can do that myself. I just can't carry you very far, or I'll tire out." I could just send you home, Denae thought, if I'd bothered practicing that, but I could lose you because I was lazy. I will get you there.

"Oh," Leah said. "Ohhh." Good. She understood. "I'm no good with snowshoes."

"One foot in front of the other, just keep doing that."

"Okay."

"I'm going to unplug now. Get off and put the snowshoes on, and we'll go on."

Denae unplugged and floated herself slightly into the air as Leah got off and into the snowshoes. She fought against the breeze and snow to stay brushing against Leah. Just the gravity pulling on her leg made her want to scream again, but she worked to put it in the back of her mind.

Leah was as bad as she said with the snowshoes. She tripped over and over, but eventually they got to the last downhill to the lake. Denae floated ahead of her, tethered like some strange balloon. She was getting cold now, her teeth starting to chatter.

Denae stopped as Leah picked herself up after another spill and got her out of the snowshoes. She forced Leah to lie down, then lay on top of her a moment before raising up slightly, adding more energy into her levitation, and started pulling Leah through the snow. Once Denae hit the lake, it was a straight line to the house. She cast a seek to there, then headed that way.

She drew energy from the beetle locket so she wouldn't tire herself too much in the cold. Trying to focus on getting home and not on the screaming pain in her leg was sapping her faster. She was pretty sure it was bleeding but couldn't do anything about it. The wind hit them fully now that they were out of the trees, the cold pushing through their clothing and snowsuits. The gale pushed her sideways as she tried to stay as low as she could without shoving Leah's helmet into the snow. Only having that point at the far side of the lake kept her from losing her direction totally.

Around the middle of the lake, the energy in the locket ran out. Denae started using her own energy, feeding the spell, continuing to travel forward at a walking speed through the utterly cold darkness. Her visor was so caked with snow that there was nothing to see beyond the helmet. The blindness caused panic to rise that she tried to beat down along with the pain. Focus on the point and nothing else. Focus.

Across the lake, then a slope up. She buried Leah's helmet there, but the snow was soft, and they didn't tumble like they had a couple of other times. Uphill was harder, Denae thought, but not nearly as hard as it would be to pick Leah up and carry her. She remembered the way up being a clear shot but hoped there wasn't a tree she'd forgotten.

Her energy was flagging, but that didn't matter. She would hurt herself however much to get Leah to the house. If she couldn't draw from her energy, she'd draw from her body, like with the bear. The snow could take her, but not Leah.

They hit a snowbank, and she knew they were close to the back door. Denae pulled upward. These were the steps, and then they were on the back porch, and there was light. And a voice.

Denae, ten more feet, she heard in her head. It was Mom. She pulled forward through the snow, it caving on their legs as they drew level. It was suddenly different, no wind howling with the shutting of the door, more light, but she couldn't see anything through the ice-caked visor. *That's good, you can stop now,* and Denae dropped the spell, landing and rolling off Leah with a gasp. *Jerok, check Denae,* and her helmet came off. Warm air hit her face.

Her teeth were chattering, she realized, and she was shivering badly. She heard a grunted "Good" from Mom and then sobs and scrambling on her left.

A choked, chattering, "I'm sorry, I'm sorry," repeated from Leah. At the same time, her own right hand was exposed to the warm air, hot fingers probing her cold ones, Dad checking each of her fingertips.

"Stay still, girl," Mom said, "So I can check you out," and she felt warm breath on her neck with the continued litany of "I'm sorry" coming through chattering teeth. Denae started to reach out, but her dad grabbed her other arm, pulled off the gloves, and checked those fingers.

"If they have any frostbite at all," Mom said, "I will kill that woman."

Leah suddenly rolled away from Denae, saying, "Get. In. Line."

Denae started laughing, guffawing. She shouldn't, but she couldn't help it. Everything was ludicrous, but everything was fine now. Leah was safe. They were warm or going to be. Then Dad pulled at her boot. She screamed, and the world went black.

↢ ↢ ⊙ ↣ ↣

Denae sat on the couch in the living room with her foot up, feeling the warmth of the fire. Mom dabbed the ankle with bits of salve while Leah's voice started to rise from inside Dad's office. She'd drunk a healing draught, so the foot and leg bones knitted up, but there was still some swelling…soft tissue. Leah's voice was loud enough Denae could make out words now.

"Why did you have to do this?" A pause. "We were fine in the cabin. We wrecked the snowmobile because we couldn't see in the blizzard. Denae hurt her leg but still dragged me until we somehow found the house—we would've frozen to death if she hadn't found it—her parents checked our fingers and toes to make sure we didn't have frostbite."

Another pause.

"Yes, we are safe now, no thanks to you."

A longer pause.

"Really, Mom. I am not coming home right now…it's white-out conditions. Nobody should be anywhere out of their house…or cabin—you don't get it, do you? I'm not at your beck and call, not now and never again."

Denae and Mom exchanged looks.

"Mr. and Mrs. Dassow have told me I can stay here as long as I like, so I will…probably no school on Monday, so whenever school does reopen, I will get up and drive there, and if you're very lucky, I'll come home. Until then, do not call, do not disturb the Dassows in any way. Bye." The sound of the receiver hitting the phone rang.

"I don't remember telling you that you could stay as long as you liked." It was conversational, but Dad's voice carried.

"She doesn't know that," Leah said. "I'd get my things, but they're at the tipi."

"You are, of course, invited to stay as long as you like," he continued. "I like how you handled your mom."

"There will be hell to pay when I do get home, so understand that I'm not in a big hurry to get there. I just feel sorry for Dad because he's going to have to put up with her and can't get away because of the storm."

"As long as you like," Dad repeated.

After a moment of silence, Leah said, "If you'll excuse me, I need to see how Denae's leg is." Denae watched her stride out of the office toward her, face as red as her flannel shirt. A blanket trailed behind like a cape, looking strangely like one of those superheroes in Binesi's comic books.

Denae was down to her long underwear, the leg slit up to her knee and bloody.

"Oh, that's looking much better," Leah said, kneeling to look more closely at the ankle. "What is that stuff?"

"It's healing salve," Denae replied. "But the healing draught I drank while you were yelling at your mom is what mainly fixed it…after it was set, I assume." She grinned. "I don't remember a whole lot about all this after Dad tugged on my boot. Mom's using salve to take care of some of the little stuff that's not worth using another draught." Denae thought Leah would rant about her mom, but instead, her eyes got teary.

"I need some of that," she said quietly.

"What?" both Denae and Mom said.

"You know that day I could've died?" Leah's eyes flickered to Denae and back to Mom.

They nodded.

"My best friend was in the café waiting for me. She's had several surgeries and still needs more." Leah was tearing up. "They don't know if she'll ever really be able to bend her knee much or walk normally." Leah looked beseechingly at Mom. "Would that help anything this much later, after the surgeries, screws, and pins?"

"I don't know, but I'll ask Oma," Denae replied. Mom gave her a quiet-down look, but she continued. "I'll see if there's a way we could do it so she wouldn't ever know." Denae looked at Leah still kneeling there. "It can be some sort of spontaneous miracle, but she must never know, assuming it can even be done. Understand that this late, maybe nothing will help. Okay?"

Leah wiped her eyes and nodded.

Denae saw Dad come out of the office and lean on the door jamb. "You two can take the living room for the night if you want. With the excitement, I think I'm going to turn in early." He gave a look at Mom and walked around to the hallway to their suite, waving goodnight. Denae stared after him.

"I can bring some more cushions in," Mom was saying.

Denae looked at the living room, fire burning. It was tempting, but no. "I'd rather be in my room tonight," she said. "Leah can take the bed—I'll sleep on some blankets on the floor." Leah looked like she might object, so Denae said, "I'm used to sleeping on the ground," and grinned. "Trust me when I say I brought a lot more quilts and pillows to the tipi since I knew you were going to be there."

Mom started to get up.

"Mom, could I have a bottle of wine? We left ours in the tipi."

"Sit there, and I'll fix you a snack plate, too," she replied. "And then I'm going to bed."

As she left the room, Leah turned to Denae and whispered, "You are not sleeping on the floor even if it's a squeeze for us." She glanced at the kitchen. "Was she doing that telepathy thing with him? They were definitely giving each other looks."

"No, I'm pretty sure she didn't." Denae looked over to where each of them had been. "No, definitely not."

"How can you tell?"

"Magic leaves a residue. If fades quickly, but if I concentrate a little, I can see that residue, and there was nothing new."

"I'm deep in that rabbit hole, aren't I?"

"Oh yeah," Denae said, "and you still have only scratched the surface."

Mom walked back carrying a tray with a bottle and two wine glasses on it. There was also a platter of cheese and sausage and a tube of crackers. As she handed the tray to Leah, Denae also saw the jar of salve. "If Denae's leg or foot still hurts," she said to Leah, "dab a little more of the salve where it hurts the most."

Denae stood, and Mom reached and steadied her while Leah stood next to her. "How is it?"

"A little tender," as she rocked to the right and put more weight on it, "but it's good."

"You have a good night," Mom said. "I'm heading for bed."

"You have a wonderful night," Leah said, and Mom stopped and turned.

"Thank you," she said, "I plan to." With that, she headed down the hall.

Denae took the stairs one at a time, using her good leg to step up to the next step until she got to the top, then stepped out a bit, hearing Leah still behind her. She pulled the cord that opened the shutter for the overhead light-rock as she stepped into her bedroom.

Leah turned a slow circle after she entered before setting the tray on the desk.

"Shelves of skulls and books," Leah said, looking at Denae. "Jars with snakeskin sheddings and I'm not sure what else, a stretched snakeskin over there on a board, and what looks like various tools of your trade, though I haven't a clue how you'd use some of them. I shouldn't be surprised, but I wasn't expecting the skulls or the snakeskins. Is that a bobcat skin?"

"It is, and I've been collecting skulls since I was little. Mostly from dead animals, though that deer skull with the antlers over the door—"

She waited for Leah's look and nod before continuing. "That was my first deer. Well…Bin found it. He'd turned up his hearing, and we snuck up on it. I made a big rock and shot it at the buck and broke its neck." Denae beamed at Leah.

"A rock?"

"Yeah. I'm a good aim with a rock or a knife, though I was only twelve then. It probably was a lucky shot."

"So you skinned it and...."

"Justin showed Bin and me how to dress out the deer, and then he presented me with the skull a few weeks later. He'd asked if I wanted the whole head mounted, but I didn't want those glass eyeballs staring down at me, so I went for the skull."

"Right, because that's less spooky than a full deer head staring at you."

"Exactly."

She smiled as she watched Leah shake her head and continue her inspection. No posters here, and shutters on the windows instead of curtains. The walls were natural wood instead of paint-covered. Leah was looking down in the corner now.

"Beanbag chair? Really?"

"Is there something wrong with it?"

"No." Leah chuckled. "It's just...never mind, it is so you," and continued her scan.

Leah stepped over to her messy desk, then reached out to touch the large crystal sphere sitting in the corner, looking over at Denae.

"Vision?"

"Yeah," Denae replied.

"Seen anything since?"

"I haven't even tried."

Leah's brows furrowed. "Why not?"

"Too scary. The crash, the screams, the blood. I couldn't stop it. I'm afraid what else I might see."

Leah lifted her hand away and sat on Denae's oversized twin bed. "Is this a real feather bed, like in the John Denver song?"

Denae smiled because she knew that one. "Yes, but it's mine, not grandma's."

She stepped over and joined her when there was a knock on her door.

"Who is it?"

"Bin."

"Go away."

"Why are you back?"

"Long story."

"I have your belt."

Denae sighed. "Okay, bring it in, but make it quick."

Binesi stepped in, doing a quick scan around, spotting the tray, and held out Denae's snakeskin belt to her.

"On the peg over there."

Binesi hung the belt on the peg next to the head of Denae's bed, then turned, holding an empty wine glass in his left hand.

"I feel naked without those," Denae said, eyeing her belt with the knife and pouch.

"No," Bin replied. "You don't feel naked when you're naked…you'd rather be naked than wear clothes, so that feeling is something else."

"What are those, anyway?" Leah pointed at the belt.

"Massasauga snakeskin belt I made myself," Denae said. "The one on the board is for Bin if he ever decides he wants to make the belt."

"It's a type of rattlesnake," Binesi added. "She killed it, skinned it, tanned it, and made it into a belt. Same with the rabbit-skin pouch."

Denae nodded. "The knife is made by relatives in Germany. My dad gave me mine when I was ten. All of us have one."

"Denae wears that belt almost all the time, except when she's in town." He glanced at Denae, then continued. "In the summer, she'll be out in the woods, and that's all she'll be wearing. She's got salve, Off bug spray, snacks, a Bic lighter, and a few other things in there. With those, she can live out there for weeks if she wants."

"Oh?"

"Oh yeah. You'll have to be careful, or she'll have you out there that way too. Speaking of out there, I'd like to stay a little while." He gestured at the tray with his wine glass.

"Why?" Denae wanted to be alone with Leah. Another girls' night.

"Snowsuits, helmets, and some of your clothes lying by the door in a wet heap, along with a good-sized length of ratchet strap mixed in. There's an empty draught bottle drying by the sink and salve right here. I saw bloody rags in the trash, and from the looks of your long underwear, you had a compound fracture of probably both your tibia and fibula. Plus, you didn't bring up your belt…that must be a first." He gestured at them. "And just the fact that you two are here instead of at the tipi means there's a story."

"Let him stay for a few minutes," Leah said. "And you need to get that ankle raised while I put more salve on it. "

"Pour us all some wine then, bring the tray over, and find a place on the floor," Denae ordered. "Bed's taken."

He dragged Denae's beanbag chair over, then took care of the other things and sat.

"We'll tell you the story, but if the wine or food runs out before the story, you will fetch more."

Binesi nodded, and they started. Binesi mainly kept his eyes on Leah's face, Denae thought, his gaze only drifting down a couple of times. Maybe the talk helped.

As their story wound down, Denae stood up, trying her foot now that Leah had put more salve on it. It felt fine.

"Bin," Denae said. "Go do whatever you need to do in the lavatory, then go to your room and stay there. It's girls' night, and that includes the hallway and lavatory."

"And tomorrow?"

"This is Friday night," Denae explained. "Her school isn't until Monday at the earliest, so each night will be girls' night while she's here. Get used to it. Now out. I want to get Leah in a bubble bath. She deserves one, and so do I."

Bin nodded and was out.

"Bubble bath?"

"Oh yeah. We need to soak in hot water and get the last of the cold out of our bones."

"Won't it be cramped?"

"You haven't seen our tub yet."

Chapter 12

Home

"Why did you wash me?" Denae smiled at Leah's question. Leah lay beside her in bed and hadn't bothered putting on her sleep shirt.

"You were stressed by everything that had happened today. I wanted you to relax some. It took a bit, but you did. Besides, you washed me next, and that felt wonderful."

"Yeah, it did. You sure nobody's going to walk in?"

"Why would they?"

"I keep expecting your mom…or mine to open the door and yell at me to put something on."

"That's not happening. You're safe from your mom here." Denae started rubbing small circles on Leah's stomach.

"Now, what are you doing?" Denae felt her shift slightly but not move away.

"This is how you woke me up from my nightmare. It felt good, so I'm doing it to you."

Denae continued rubbing the circles, feeling Leah slowly relax and her breathing slow. This was nice, she thought, but Leah tensed and looked at her.

"You should probably stop that."

Denae stopped her hand. "Why?"

"It's feeling a little too good. If you keep rubbing me like that, I might not want you to stop."

Denae stared at her for a moment, then started rubbing circles again.

"I don't want to stop rubbing your belly."

↢ ↢ ⊙ ↣ ↣

Denae watched Leah stir and dropped her aura reading as Leah opened her eyes and smiled at her.

"Good morning."

Leah glanced at the shutters where the winds rattled the window. "Storm's still blowing?"

"Oh yeah. It's still bad out."

"This is so weird."

"The storm?"

"Everything. I woke up in the middle of the night and had to pee, so I just crawled over you…you were dead to the world, by the way…and went to the bathroom like I owned the place. Like Bin wouldn't walk out any time."

"He wouldn't unless you went downstairs."

"Downstairs?"

"Yeah. He puts a tripper on the staircase at night before he goes to bed. I didn't think he'd do it tonight, but he did."

"A tripper?"

"So he'll know if anyone goes up or down the stairs."

"And you went down the stairs?"

Denae nodded. "I got your bag and the food we took to your tipi."

"You went like this?" Alarm punctuated Leah's question.

"No, which is why I woke Bin. I went downstairs and put my snowsuit and helmet on, and he came down while I was doing that."

"He couldn't talk you out of doing this stupid thing?"

She laughed. "He didn't try…he knows better. He also knows that I could've been lying out in the snow naked if I was trying to escape my nightmare, so me going fully awake with a snowsuit on was a relief to him. He did wait until I got back. There's an area near the front steps that's swept fairly clear from the storm, and I came back there, then blipped back to just inside the front door."

"I thought you had problems inside buildings."

"If I can see in a window or am familiar with what's inside, like here or the warehouse, it's not a problem. Usually, it's simpler to just open the door, but with the storm, this was better."

"So, I've got all my clothes?"

"Yeah. We could be at the tipi instead of here if I wasn't so stupid and lazy." Denae didn't bother disguising her disgust with herself.

"Stupid and lazy?"

"Yep. I know how to teleport others, but I'm not very good at getting people where they're supposed to be. Last night, if I'd tried, I might've gotten you to the house or a quarter-mile away, but I wouldn't know which or where exactly. It's exhausting, too, so trying to find you afterward would've been a problem. So instead, I dragged you. I'm going to practice so I can get you where you're supposed to be. This won't happen again."

She watched Leah nod thoughtfully but stay quiet. "I didn't think I'd take anyone with me like that, so I quit practicing. That was so stupid. I could've lost you."

"You didn't, and I'm fine, and it wasn't your fault we left the tipi. This isn't so bad, though I did like the tipi. Now about last night after the bath. I'm not sure that was a good idea."

"I liked that. I thought you did, too."

"I…I shouldn't have…I shouldn't have kissed you."

"But it was nice. So was everything else."

"That was a lot more than just kissing."

"Yeah." Denae smiled at that, but Leah didn't return her smile.

"I like guys."

"And I think I like them, too, but I also like you."

Leah sighed, and Denae felt her smile falter.

"I like you too, but I may have liked you too much last night. I didn't mean all that to happen."

"I'm glad it did."

"I don't know. Last night it was great…you were great, but this morning…."

"You're scared."

"You're watching my aura again?"

"No. I stopped that when you woke up."

"You were watching me while I slept."

"Yeah." Denae smiled again. "It was nice…peaceful. You dreamed of something for a while, but it was good things. I wanted to be in that dream with you."

Leah shook her head. "You're doing it again, making me want to curl up with you and never leave. We should get up and fix breakfast."

"In a minute. What did I do wrong?" She wanted to look at Leah's aura again now, but that wouldn't be fair.

"That's just it. You didn't do anything wrong, except maybe kiss me back. It was my fault."

"Do you still like guys?"

"Well, yeah. Of course."

"Me, too, so this isn't about that. It's only about us."

"What do you mean?"

"Someday, you'll have a boyfriend, get married, and have kids. I won't stop that. Maybe I'll get a boyfriend someday, and that will happen to me too. It's not happening right now, but you have me, and I have you…if you want that." Denae rubbed her side a moment. "I thought about it while I watched you sleep, and I want this."

"I'm still trying to figure out what happened. If we do this like you want it, how do we keep it secret? You might not care, but my parents would freak out totally. So would everyone else around. It's not just us."

"I do care, and everyone thinks I'm too weird without adding this to it. We'll keep it private…just us…a secret. We can do that. It's pretty easy for me, anyway. Nobody pays that much attention to me."

"I don't know…it's all so crazy, and I know I started it. I'm going to have to think about all this."

Denae kissed her shoulder. "It's fine. It really is. Let's get dressed and fix breakfast."

↢↢⊙↣↣

The storm abated on Sunday morning, much to Leah's annoyance. There would be time to plow the streets, so school would be open. Denae wasn't happy either, but Leah was doubly annoyed because she'd have to go home and face her mother's wrath, and it wouldn't be pretty. She wanted to delay that as long as possible.

Leah wished she could stay here, and not only because of Denae. There was something different here than at home. They seemed to honestly like each other rather than simply tolerate one another. She knew they did some sort of magic here, but this was magic of some different type. She was more intrigued with this one…an even better rabbit hole than the one she initially fell down.

She was Denae's…lover…maybe…they'd fooled around a good bit, in any case. She wasn't sure it was right, but she'd agreed to keep it going in secret, and it was some kind of wonderful, as the song went, but it confused her.

She liked guys.

When she and Jessica were twelve, they'd kissed each other's breasts once on a dare and giggled for the next five minutes. She'd never desired to do that again with Jessica or any other woman. Why Denae? She was definitely touching Denae and being touched back.

Binesi talked intelligently to her, his eyes only occasionally drifting to her body, and when the conversation drifted to Olivia, he was obviously smitten with her. She remembered Olivia mainly from when she and Cheryl were still friends, and Olivia was little. From the little they'd talked at the arcade, she'd grown up a lot, and she danced where Jessica danced…had danced. She'd have to ask Jessica about Olivia the next time she was with her.

She was putting on her snow gear in the living room when she heard an engine start. That would be Binesi and Jerok starting up the snowblower. Jerok also had a small tractor with a plow but said it could be persnickety, and he wasn't sure if he could get it started. She knew they were doing this so she could drive to school, and the driveway was at least a quarter-mile to the road.

"You really don't have to clear the driveway just for me."

Riann smiled indulgently at her. "Bin and Denae will be skiing off tomorrow for their lessons, so they won't be here, and if Jerok can't get the driveway clear, he'll take you to school on the other snowmobile."

"He is a much better driver than I am," Denae responded brightly, patting her leg.

Leah laughed. "At least he won't have to drive by echolocation like you did."

She watched Denae head out the front door to go around as the snow had drifted against the back porch higher than the top of the doors.

"Give her at least 10 minutes before we go out," Riann said.

"Why?"

"You'll see," Riann replied mysteriously.

"Mrs. Dassow," Leah began. It was the first time the two of them had been alone, so she had to ask.

"Riann, please," Riann said.

"Riann," Leah corrected herself. "Thank you for having me. I feel more like family here than when I'm at home."

Riann lifted a finger, shushing her. "We do like you, and when you walked through that door," nodding toward the front, "in a way, you became family. Further, you are acting like family, even fixing supper last night, which was quite tasty." She smiled, looking Leah more directly in the eyes. "I'm glad you and Denae met. Denae is happier than I've ever seen her. That's even though she's having problems focusing on her studies, and I blame you entirely for both." Leah saw a slight smirk form. "She also suddenly seems to have matured in some way that I haven't figured out, and I'm sure you're also to blame for that."

"How are things going to be with your mother? Your Friday night phone call was quite impressive," Riann continued, a concerned look on her face.

Leah shrugged. "It's not going to be pretty. She'll be angry that the storm hit early, so I couldn't come home. That didn't go according to her plan. She'll be angry that I work at Fred's tomorrow night, so she can't berate me all evening, so she'll be angry at Dad for some real or imagined reason. He's been cooped up with her all weekend with her ranting, so I'm sure he'll be happy to get to work."

"What does he do?"

"He's an optometrist. Owns the business and has a second optometrist working for him, plus the staff. It does well, though he's doing things lately to make it worth less…at least on paper, in case he divorces Mom."

"That seems extreme."

"She gets the house. He keeps the business. Makes sense to me."

"I guess it does at that." Riann was nodding, but Leah wanted to change the subject.

"If I can ask, what's with Denae's hair and eyes? She's very sensitive about them."

"You mean the 'I want to cut it all off and go bald' type of sensitive," Riann asked, laughing.

"Something like that," Leah said, "I really like them, though when she looks at me, it can be unnerving sometimes."

Riann nodded.

"Jerok has a white streak in his hair, and Bin has a silver streak," Leah scanned Riann's hair though she knew she hadn't seen anything there.

Riann lifted a few strands of her hair. "None here…that comes from Jerok's side of the family. Denae got a whole lot more than a streak."

"But the color—"

"Is something she's been pissed about all of her life," Riann said. "The same with her eyes. That's why she wears those tinted glasses when she goes to town."

"Yeah, she told me."

"But like her brothers, those physical features mark a part of her ancestry."

"It's more than just physical," Leah asked. "Especially in her case."

Riann sighed, her shoulders sagging. "You are very astute, Leah." She stood up and looked down at Leah. "Jerok and I were very upset when we discovered that Denae told you about us."

"She only confirmed what I'd already figured out," Leah countered.

"Exactly," Riann said, "but now I'm glad she did. It made everything much easier in the long run."

"I don't understand," Leah said.

"What would you have done if Denae had clammed up like she was supposed to?" Riann crossed her arms in a defensive posture.

"I would've followed her, and you guys all over town trying to find out what really was going on," Leah said. "I'm nosy that way."

"We now think this is better, you simply knowing," Riann said, relaxing her pose slightly. "We trust you to not say anything about this to anyone."

"I won't," Leah promised. "Nobody would believe me anyway. I'm the science fiction-fantasy nerd, so they'd just think I was confusing my books with real life," she finished, grinning.

"What I mean," Riann continued, "is to keep our secret for the rest of your life, even if you and Denae are no longer friends."

Leah nodded. "I wouldn't say anything. I wanted to find out more, but that was for me, not anyone else. I'm good at keeping secrets. Besides, I don't want one of your family altering my memory."

"Denae told you that?"

"Yeah." Leah swallowed. "She said that it could mess with my other memories with all I know. If I think about it, you guys are more than a little scary."

Riann smiled. "We try not to be, but we will do what's needed to protect ourselves and, in turn, other practitioner families. We have to have your trust."

"I'll be quiet about this."

Riann nodded, seemingly satisfied.

Leah thought about this other new secret. She still had some misgivings about this, though she had given in to Denae…rather quickly, though Denae had started the kissing last night…and this morning.

"Zip up, and let's get out there. Denae should be about done with the top level," Riann said, pulling her hood over her head.

Perplexed, Leah zipped up and followed Riann out and around the house. Denae floated, moving slowly forward with a snow shovel, using it like a Caterpillar blade clearing the top level of the drift.

"She can do this through the light stuff fairly easily, but it looks like she's starting to get into the more packed stuff where it isn't worth it."

Leah watched in awe, seeing her float, knocking a thin layer of the snow off with the shovel. "She pulled me that way like a sled, all the way from where we crashed to here, with a broken leg, not being able to see, hitting branches and stuff all along the way."

"She would've killed herself to make sure you got back," Riann stated flatly.

"Literally?" Leah felt shaken by the calm way Riann had said that.

"Yes," Riann replied. "She has a strong sense of loyalty to people she likes."

Leah nodded slowly, realization sinking in as Denae turned and waved to them.

"Denae is not allowed at your house if your mom is there or anywhere with your mom," Riann ordered.

"I don't want them together either," Leah asked. "Mom made things rather…awkward," she finished lamely. "But there's something else, isn't there?"

"Yes," Riann said, "there is. If your mom says the wrong thing, and in my limited experience with her, she will…someone will get hurt. Denae will act before it occurs to her that the rest of the world doesn't have healing draughts and salves." Riann gave her a meaningful look. "Ready with the shovel? I think it's time for the muscles."

Chapter 13

Spark

"Mom tore all my posters off my bedroom walls and threw them away," Leah said over the noises and music and talking in the arcade. It'd been almost a week before Leah could get together with Denae for any time at all.

Leah continued. "She blamed me, of course, and Dad for not going and getting me."

Binesi walked over from a pinball machine, no doubt wanting in on the gossip, Olivia's hand in his. Leah caught Denae slipping her town glasses on and paused until Bin sat down and Olivia perched on his leg. She was brunette with brown eyes, small and slender, though still a couple of inches taller than Denae, a dancer's physique in miniature to Jessica. She wore a western-style snap-up red and white plaid shirt and lined jeans based on the flannel showing where they'd been cuffed up.

"So what was the aftermath?" Binesi asked. "The town's still standing…I was surprised at that." He gave a sly smile. "I told Olivia about your phone call."

"Really?" Leah said to Binesi, then looked at Olivia. "I'm sorry…he's an idiot."

"Sometimes," she agreed but smiled and ran her hand through his hair, right near his streak of silver. She also seemed interested in the talk, maybe because it was older girls dishing the dirt.

"Anyway," Leah started again, casting an annoyed look at Bin. "Mom tore the posters down, blamed me for not coming home in the storm, grounded me for a month, and said I'd be moving out as soon as school was out."

Denae goggled a bit but was thrilled, knowing where she could go.

Olivia broke the brief silence. "You don't look very grounded."

Leah looked up at Olivia. "Dad ungrounded me and told my mom that if anyone was moving out, it was her. He wasn't pleased with me because I told Mom what she could do to herself somewhere along the line."

Olivia gasped. "You used the 'F' word to your mom?"

Leah turned, leaning close to Olivia. "Yes, more than once." She raised a finger at her. "This is a private conversation, and I don't know you very well these days…only from when you were little. Bin likes you, and that's a point in your favor. However, if you breathe a word of this to anyone, especially your sister Cheryl, you will regret it. If Cheryl knows, she'll make sure I know she knows. Understood?"

Denae stood up, glasses off, and glared at Olivia. "Not a word," was all she said, but the way she said it unnerved Leah. Binesi also stiffened, raising his free hand, saying, "Olivia's good…she won't say anything, will you?"

Olivia turned on Binesi's leg like she was going to flee, then turned back and nodded. "I'll be as quiet as a grave," raising her hand as if taking an oath.

She looked about to leave but stayed. Leah wondered if Binesi had done something.

"Anyway, she's not moving out, though I don't know how much more my dad can take." She glanced briefly at Olivia and continued. "Those weekend marriage conferences aren't working because my mom won't change. I think my graduation will be the breaking point." She looked totally at Denae. "And I'm not allowed to see you."

"That's working as well as the grounding, I see," Denae said.

Leah waved that away. "Obviously, you can't come over," she continued, "I'm going to be visiting Jessica a lot."

"Oh," Olivia said, her voice suddenly sad. "How is she?"

Leah took a deep breath. "She had another surgery on Tuesday and was supposed to come home earlier today. She's getting a late release, so that hasn't happened yet, but as far as anyone is concerned, I will be over there a lot."

"That reminds me," Denae said, "you forgot your lip balm," handing her a small Carmex jar. "I tried some, and it works well."

Leah looked blankly at Denae until things clicked, and she hurriedly pocketed it. She tried to hide her happiness if this was what she thought it was. It could help Jessica.

Leah realized that Olivia had understood that something more than Carmex had passed across the table but hoped that she'd think it was drugs or something and that Bin could keep his mouth shut.

"Jessica always was nice to me and helped me at dance and elsewhere," Olivia said. "Even though Cheryl didn't like her. She didn't think Jessica was worth anything."

Leah turned to Olivia, anger rising. "Can you leave—"

"Olivia's not in Cheryl's good graces right now," Binesi said, putting a hand up. "She punched Cheryl in the face."

"I broke her nose," Olivia said proudly. "I punched her in the face and broke her nose. She bled all over the place and had to go to the emergency room to get her nose set and—"

"Has it taped in place," Leah finished. "I saw her at school, and the bruise went from cheek to cheek." Leah looked at Olivia, smiling. Maybe she was okay after all. "I've wanted to do that for years, but why did you do it?"

"She said she was going to tell Mom that Bin and I were doing…well…you know…the 'F' word." Color rose on her face. "We're not…we're not doing anything like that." That last was said directly to Denae. "I do need to go to the lavatory," and she ran off.

Binesi watched her go while Denae waited for her to go in. "I think that was awesome," he said, "Punching out her sister for saying something like that."

"And you're not?" Denae asked.

"She won't let me touch her much of anywhere for more than a few seconds," he said, slightly disappointed, "so definitely not, but I would've loved to have seen that punch…Olivia said she went down and didn't move for about 15 seconds." Binesi made a punching motion. "She cold-cocked her sister. She's grounded but snuck out because she was supposed to meet me here. I didn't think dance would build up the arms for a punch like that."

"We need to leave," Denae said to Leah. "I'll walk with you partway to Jessica's."

"Uh…sure," she said, looking at her watch. "She should be getting home around now."

"What about Olivia?" Binesi demanded. "I can't leave now. She risked a lot to come see me."

"You stay," Denae said. "Come back to the shop later." She looked up at that silver streak that glowed slightly in the black light. "Do you like her stroking your hair?"

"It gets annoying sometimes," he said, shrugging, "but she likes doing it, so I let her."

Leah said, "Say bye to Olivia for us, and tell her I love her right hook." Denae followed her out.

"Is that healing salve you gave me?"

Denae flashed a smile that thrilled Leah. "When I talked to Oma on Wednesday and told her what you wanted, she said it wouldn't hurt Jessica, and it might help, then told me all the reasons why this was a bad idea. When she was done, she transferred about a third of a dose of the salve into the Carmex jar, so it was still half empty. Oma said she didn't want to give any more out to mundanes than necessary. This should be enough to help Jessica's knee, but not too much."

"Thank her for me, please."

Denae nodded, looking serious. "She'll be doped up from the surgery, and it wasn't on her knee, was it?"

"Probably…and no, it wasn't."

"Good. Put it on either side of the kneecap and behind the joint, too, but do it when she's asleep and nobody's around. This has to be kept secret."

Leah nodded. This she could do. "I could kiss you. We could hide behind the warehouse fence for a few minutes."

"Another time, and we'll do it."

Leah almost stumbled as she looked at Denae. This wasn't like her, but then she'd wanted to leave the arcade and seemed very focused now. "Is something wrong?"

"I don't know, but something's strange…not quite right."

"Something with Olivia?" Let it be Olivia and not me, she thought.

"Maybe," Denae said. "I need to see her family."

"You want to meet them?"

"No," Denae said. "Just see them, preferably without their coats on."

"Hmmm…church."

"Church?"

"Yeah, they'll be there, and they should take off their coats once they're inside," Leah said, "but be careful because I'll be there…with my parents."

"I'll keep my hood up or something," Denae said.

↢ ↢ ⊙ ↣ ↣

Leah gave Denae directions and time, so Denae waved bye and headed that way to find a suitably hidden place near the church where she could arrive without anyone noticing. She studied the area around the church and wandered into the copse near the parking lot to find a spot suitable for her to show up. The branches above were dense enough, and there was no drifting snow. She peered out, barely able to see the church buildings through the trunks.

She aimed for the fenced-in area behind the shop, providing a safe place for her and Dad to arrive quickly if they wanted to. She should've come here with Leah, she thought belatedly. She could've done all this later, but Olivia had unnerved her, and she hadn't thought past that.

Olivia acted like she could tell that what was in the jar was something special, so Denae looked at her aura. Olivia had a spark of sorts. It was different but definitely a spark. That meant that she was a practitioner, and from how she looked over Denae, she knew Denae…and Binesi were, too. It looked like she could see auras. And there was more. Something small, nebulous, and greenish in the aura, near the spark, but not a part of it.

She had run her hand along Binesi's streak…always her middle finger exactly along where the streak grew on the scalp, not where the hairs ended up. How could she tell? This was all very strange.

She'd wondered if Binesi was doing anything, but everything looked normal for him. Or, as expected, with Olivia sitting on his knee. She wasn't affecting him unduly, but somehow, she seemed affected by it quite a bit. Enough that she had to leave for the lavatory.

Denae needed to know more about Olivia. Things were not adding up.

And Jessica. She hoped that Leah's comment about seeing Jessica a lot meant she'd be seeing Leah for some of that, but she wasn't sure. She knew she was selfish, and Jessica needed Leah, but she didn't like it. She should've come here with Leah for at least a few minutes. She'd been so preoccupied with Olivia that Leah's suggestion had barely registered until it was too late.

Denae went into the warehouse and found her mom in the break room. "Do you like rubbing Dad's white streak?" She thought she knew the answer, but she had to be sure.

"I like running my fingers through his hair, but you mean his streak specifically?"

"Yes, his streak."

"The streak's a little different texture, but no," she said, staring at her daughter. "Why are you—"

"I don't have a good answer for you yet," Denae said, "but something strange is going on." Denae paced the confines of the break room, then looked up. "Can you put my braids back in Saturday evening? And I need to wear my most feminine dress."

"What on earth?"

"I'm going to church," Denae said, smiling.

Chapter 14

Church

About fifteen minutes before the service was supposed to start, Denae got to the church, making a trail in the snow coming out of the grove of trees onto the parking lot between two cars. Inside, she was greeted by a couple of women who seemed pleased she was there visiting. They showed her where to get some coffee and donuts. One of the ladies introduced her to a man in formal robes who turned out to be a priest who everyone called Pastor Jonathan. He talked with her briefly before being interrupted by an older woman.

She'd just got a small Styrofoam cup of hot coffee when she heard her name whispered.

"What are you doing here?" It was Olivia, her eyes wide.

"I'd never been here and thought I'd come."

"Did Bin come?"

"No."

"Good. I don't want to punch Cheryl in church, and I'm already in enough trouble for leaving the house yesterday."

Denae managed to bite back a retort.

"We sit about two-thirds of the way up on the right side," she whispered. "Don't sit too close to there. I want to talk to you after service. Classroom C upstairs should be empty if I can get away from my family for a few minutes. Um…stay on the right side, though. Leah usually sits on the left." Then she was gone.

Denae added some cold water to the coffee, drank it down, and headed to where the sanctuary should be, being stopped a couple of times. She wore her town glasses, but people seemed friendly to her despite them and her hair color and braids. More people she didn't know welcomed her before pressing a bulletin into her hand.

She found a pew down the middle right along the center aisle. Organ music played something she vaguely recognized, but not from when.

She took off her coat and set it next to her, revealing her pink blouse and red skirt that some aunt had given her. The blouse clashed horribly with her hair, which was precisely what Denae wanted at the moment.

After a couple of minutes, she could hear vigorous whispering coming up the aisle behind her. Olivia and an older tall blonde girl came even with her, the older girl's nose taped with yellow and green showing slightly through the makeup she wore. Both were staring at her, though Olivia winked while Cheryl seemed angry. Their parents walked directly behind them, her dad sandy-haired, graying a bit on the sides with a slight belly, while her mom was heavy-set and blonde like Cheryl.

Denae looked all four of them over, seeing nothing she was expecting from any of the rest of the family. Only Olivia had the spark. Usually this ran in families…strange.

A minute later, Leah and her father walked by, Leah wide-eyed, shaking her head while her dad winced a bit upon seeing her but smiled and waved weakly. He started talking with Leah and saw a shrug. Where was her mom? Was she too upset to come, or maybe she did leave? Neither of the other two gave that latter appearance. If her mom wasn't here, Leah definitely wouldn't have looked like she did.

"Excuse me, young lady, but you are in my seat." The voice sounded ancient and a bit like Oma-ma's. An elderly woman in a pale blue dress, pearls, and matching hat stood in the aisle next to her, leaning on an ornate cane.

"Oh," Denae said and slid over, giving her plenty of room, pushing her coat further down. "I'm visiting."

"I paid for this entire pew, but these days I sit only here as most of my family has moved to the cities. Paid for the choir pews and the organ, too. I used to play the organ, but my fingers don't work well now, and I need the arm here," she patted it, "in order to get up and down." She smiled at Denae as she slowly sat.

"You do look familiar, but I'm not coming up with a name. I know you live north of town a little ways."

Denae shifted uncomfortably as a powdery scent wafted over her.

"I'm Agatha Christensen," she said, offering a clawed hand.

"I'm Denae Dassow," she replied, taking her hand and squeezing it lightly.

"Oh yes," she said. "One of Sofia's great-granddaughters, named after the unfortunate woman that Zeus misted on." She cackled lightly.

"Are you family?"

"Oh, dear no," Agatha replied. "But you could count me as a friend, as I do know your family. I bounced Hanna on my knee when she was little."

This lady bounced Oma on her knee?

"Jerok's daughter?"

Denae nodded.

"It's starting to come back," Agatha continued. "My memory, bit by bit."

Two children in ill-fitting white robes walked past and were now lighting candles up front.

"Oh, I always like to see the choir come in," Agatha said as robed people started filling an area near the organ.

Denae watched them come in and take their seats and spotted Leah's mom about the time she saw her. If looks could kill, Denae would be dead on the floor.

"Oh my," Agatha said. "What grievance does Anne have with you?" She lifted up her gnarled hand and waved at Leah's mom. The effect was dramatic. Leah's mom blanched and suddenly turned away to talk with the woman next to her.

"I'm friends with Leah, and she doesn't like it," Denae spat.

"Oh ho," Agatha said, a slight laugh in her ancient voice. "But then, Anne can be a real bitch when it suits her."

Denae glanced over and saw a smile on Agatha's face as Pastor Jonathan started welcoming the congregation, and the service started.

↢↢⊙↣↣

All the ritual of the service didn't surprise her, but the power did. It was palpable, and with a slow scan, she could see people who showed this power strongly. Not many, but some. Some others showed lesser amounts, but many showed little to nothing.

Denae pondered this.

Her family had their ceremonies because they had their own power and gathered together at special times to share and enhance that power. Here, though, they massed not because they had power but because the power was here, and they might gain it?

Strange.

Olivia had been stealing glances and smiling at her several times. Denae smiled back automatically, but whatever Olivia's power was, it wasn't this. That little thing swirled green and mottled, and Olivia had problems sitting still even when she wasn't looking at Denae.

"That Olivia has ants in her pants this morning," Agatha said as the organ and choir started some song, "and she seems to like you."

"She's my little brother's girlfriend," Denae said, letting the music start to wash over her, "and she's nice." She realized that Agatha had a steady glow of that power.

"How do you like the service so far?"

"It's impressive," Denae said sincerely.

"There is power in the blood," Agatha said serenely and turned her attention back to the music.

↢↢⊙↣↣

After the service, Denae assisted Agatha to the foyer. Agatha stopped to talk with some other elderly friends, so Denae ran upstairs to find classroom C and Olivia but found the classroom empty. There were posters with empty crosses and obvious religious writings, and a blackboard with writing from a class about people named Peter and Paul. But what caught her interest was a decorative sign above the other door to the classroom.

'Faith, Hope, and Love, But the Greatest of These is Love,' with '1 Corinthians 13' below. That was intriguing. Maybe she'd try to find this Corinthians book sometime.

"Ah, there you are," Olivia said, closing the door Denae had come through. "Nice saying, eh?"

"What did you want?"

"You were sitting in Agatha's seat," Olivia said, smiling.

"Yes, but I moved over," Denae said. "She's nice."

"Oh yeah," Olivia agreed, nodding, "She teaches Sunday school sometimes. She's very knowledgeable."

"She has power," Denae said, wondering what response she'd get.

Olivia's eyes widened some, and she nodded. "That's what I wanted to talk to you about."

Denae wanted to do the same, but not yet. She had her own questions she needed answered.

"Why did you run to the lavatory at the arcade?" Denae pulled off her town glasses, staring intently into Olivia's eyes.

Olivia covered her mouth with one hand while groping for a chair and sat down.

"How…what…," she stuttered through her hand, not breaking Denae's gaze. After a moment, she dropped her gaze to the floor. "I was…I needed to go pee," she said shrilly, her head drooping.

"Why did you see Bin yesterday," Denae continued.

"I wanted to see him," Olivia said to the ground.

"You were grounded," Denae reminded her.

"It didn't matter," she said. "I needed to see him. We'd planned to meet then."

"You needed to see Binesi," Denae said, sarcasm in her voice. "Or his hair."

Olivia looked up, fire in her eyes. "I like Bin. I really do like him."

"And his streak," Denae continued as though she hadn't heard her.

Olivia broke eye contact, dropping her head and looking at her toes.

"Is it addictive?" Denae asked this a little more gently.

Olivia nodded. "I don't know why," she replied. "Can Bin come over this afternoon? I can sneak him in." She looked up and gave Denae a coy look.

"You are not allowed to see Bin," Denae said coldly, "and he is not allowed to see you."

Olivia looked like she was about to pounce as Denae continued. "Not until we have all of this sorted out."

Olivia broke down completely, sobbing loudly, which was annoying. Denae still had questions.

She waited a moment, then, "Olivia, dry up."

"I'm…I'm…trying," came the response between sobs.

"Look at me," Denae ordered, swinging her braids to the front and letting them dangle in front of her.

Olivia looked up, face wet, eyes red and puffy, a bit of snot running down her upper lip.

"Grab my braids," Denae continued.

Olivia looked a little dazed but complied. Olivia stared straight for a moment, then her eyes widened as fear crossed her face. Denae saw the beginnings of a change in that mottled part of her aura, it writhing.

"No," Olivia yelled, dropping her braids like they were electrified.

"No," she said, knocking her chair over as she stood.

"No," and she turned, fleeing out the door they'd come through.

"So it's not just Binesi," Denae mused quietly. "Very strange."

The door behind her squeaked open, the one with the Corinthians saying above it. Leah walked in.

"That was dramatic," she said.

"Uh," Denae began, "Yeah." She didn't know she had an audience.

"I didn't hear much except for Olivia's last three words," Leah said, "What was that all about?"

"Can't tell you," Denae said.

"Can't or won't," Leah said evenly.

"I can't tell you enough to even make sense to me," Denae continued, "So I won't tell you." She shrugged apologetically.

"Fair enough," Leah considered. "But some time, though."

"Maybe," was all Denae could offer.

"This was about Bin?"

Denae glared at her. "A lot more than just Bin, I think, but drop it."

"Serious?"

Denae nodded, lips pursed tight. "For now."

"I…uh." Leah looked at the door. "I need to leave."

But instead of leaving, she moved forward and kissed Denae on her lips. Denae's lips relaxed as she returned the welcome kiss.

"We shouldn't be doing this in church," Leah said suddenly, breaking the kiss but not letting go.

"Why not?"

"It's a sin."

"How is it a sin? Nobody's getting hurt."

"I don't know," Leah replied, gave Denae another brief kiss, and then released. "I'm going over to Jessica's for the afternoon."

She turned to go.

"I need to meet her," Denae said, her tone flat.

Leah turned back around. "I'll ask, but don't expect anything. Any particular reason?"

Denae nodded. "Right now, I don't like her. She is some nebulous being who takes you away from me, and I hate her for it, and yeah, I can be selfish like that." She realized she was glaring at Leah and tried to soften her gaze. "If I meet and talk to her, have a face and voice and…person, maybe it won't be so bad."

"But you talked to your Oma about her," Leah said. "Even gave me that ointment, which helped…a lot."

"I want you to be happy, and she makes you happy," Denae said. "That doesn't mean it makes me happy." Denae felt her eyes smart, and a dawning understanding crossed Leah's face.

"It will happen," she said. "I will make sure it happens."

Chapter 15

The Braid

Denae was antsy, pacing along the sidewalk near the front of the high school. She was taking a risk but thought what she had in the paper bag would be worth it. She'd talked to a few adult family members about Olivia and Binesi. Each had a different theory, from 'Leave them alone, it's young love' to that she should be kidnapped and taken to be examined in a safe place. Denae was trying for a middle ground.

Binesi looked like he hadn't slept well. After some prodding, he resentfully confirmed that Olivia was in some of his dreams. He colored a bit. She thought she knew why but wouldn't embarrass him by verifying it. He had changed a lot in the last couple of years, mainly for the better. She didn't want to lose his trust.

She'd slept better, not going to the tipi at night nearly as often. Leah's trip out to her home had been good for that. They'd talked at the arcade. She was relieved that at least some of Leah's 'Jessica' time would be for her, but most of it wouldn't. It couldn't be helped, so Denae tried not to dwell on it and take what she could get. Leah said she'd gotten up to a 'Maybe' from Jessica, so things were progressing toward a meeting.

The bell rang, and kids started coming out. Denae was surprised at the number of kids now that she was up close instead of back in the trees when she was waiting for Leah.

Like the church, it seemed a little overwhelming. Also, all the different sizes. Denae hadn't considered all the changes that went on during those years. Still, almost everyone was taller than her.

A group of girls was going by when one of them stiffened and walked over to Denae, pulling down the hood of her blue parka. "Denae?"

"Yeah," Denae replied. It was Olivia.

"Why are you here? To apologize?"

Denae looked at her, perplexed. She had nothing to apologize for. Those were questions that had to be asked to help matters. "No, but I have another question or two and something I want you to do."

Olivia scowled but turned to the girls waiting on her. "Go ahead. I'll see you guys later," waving them on. "I'll be here a little while."

Denae took advantage of Olivia's distraction to scan her and the others. The heavy coats muffled everything, but the others showed nothing unusual, while something seemed different about Olivia's aura. Through the parka, she couldn't be sure.

"You handing out candy to children this afternoon," Olivia sneered. "What's in the bag?"

"It's a length of my hair," Denae replied. "I cut it yesterday evening and braided it together, so it's been disconnected from me for almost a day. Once you get alone this evening, hold it for a moment and see if it bothers you like it did yesterday, then put it back in the bag."

"Bother me?" Olivia said, her eyes blazing. "That's one way to put it. What are the odds of it…um…bothering me?"

Denae shrugged. "I don't think it will, but it could, so if you feel anything at all, put it back in the bag."

She snatched the bag from Denae, looked in, then rolled it up and put it in her coat pocket.

"You don't know, so you're using me as a guinea pig," she accused.

"You could do it right now," Denae said, "and get it over with."

Olivia looked at the students still trickling out. "No way," she said. "What if I don't want to let go?"

She gave her a sort of smile Denae had never seen before, then her face went back to normal. "We need to talk about other things, too, but not here. Sometime soon, though."

Denae was starting to doubt the wisdom of this idea now, but Olivia had turned away. "I'll check it out before I go to bed," she called back and waved goodbye.

A few flakes fell as Denae walked back to a small grove near the school. Once there, she moved to the trees behind Olivia's house, shifting slightly to get a good view of the door. She'd put a trace on the braid before she brought it to Olivia and was happy Olivia had brought it home.

She'd toyed with the idea of checking with her at night, but Binesi said her bedroom was upstairs. That could make planning awkward, having to float in the air to tap the window, and he wasn't sure which room was hers. Denae could determine that once Olivia got home, just following the trace, but she'd wait to see if that was even necessary. Olivia was in this too deep already. She needed to know as little as possible until her issue was solved.

Denae studied the house a good bit more before shifting back outside her own home as the snow started steadily coming down. She'd have to wait until morning to get a report back from Olivia, so this was as good as it was going to get.

↢ ↢ ⊙ ↣ ↣

Denae woke gasping. Her dream was weird and intense, shifting from Leah as Olivia intruded, time and again.

She lay there in the darkness, letting her breathing slow, confused by visions already dissipating. It was very different from the other dreams that woke her. Those could be disturbing, but they didn't leave her like this. She tossed the covers aside, stood up, and shifted back to her spot near Olivia's house, gasping as her bare legs hit the cold snow.

She really should think about clothes and a coat before she made these side trips. She peered, wondering about her late-night sanity standing naked in the snow, looking at an apparently dark, quiet house on an equally dark and quiet street. Well, let's get done with this madness and get to the tipi, she thought, and sought her braid, then began to rise out of the snow.

She floated into the air and out of the cover of the trees. No breeze to speak of, but the air and light snow were a frigid combination. Didn't matter, she thought. Soon enough, she'd be at the tipi, getting a fire back up from coals and sliding under thick covers. This was what was important now.

She floated up to Olivia's window, looking for any opening in the curtain that she could see through, even a little. If there was even a tiny nightlight in there, she could see just fine, but the curtains seemed fully closed against her and the outside cold.

There was something barely discernable there. It was more a feeling than anything else, or maybe she simply imagined it as an afterimage of her dream. Then something reached out, calling *Denae* in her mind. She gasped and jumped for the tipi.

She arrived, catching a face full of snow.

She gasped—backed up fast.

Things scratched, slashed into her back and legs.

Snow dumped down her body.

Forward, but something tripped her.

She fell, all concentration lost, and bounced from bough to snow-laden bough until she dropped into deep snow.

Her feet hung above her head, held there by a fir branch while her body screamed from a dozen scrapes and slashes.

She kicked free from the limb that held her legs up, totally disgusted with herself. She'd really screwed this up, teleporting into trees because she panicked, not thinking about being fifteen feet in the air. She dug herself out of the snow and saw the tipi next to her.

At least she'd only missed vertically.

She looked at herself as she limped to the flap, blood seeping down from lots of different cuts…so stupid. Her teeth were in full chatter by the time the fire caught from the mass of coals that glowed there. She came and started a fire from the embers every evening, so if she needed to go here in the middle of the night, she could just throw some wood on. It'd catch easily, plus it kept the whole tipi warmer.

She sat with a blanket held out to capture as much heat as she could as it slowly caught. Her body stung from all the lacerations. She'd even left without her belt, so she didn't have any salve or anything.

Stupid, stupid, stupid.

She was tired from the teleports and didn't want to pull from her amulet, so she had to rest before going home. That meant she might as well sleep here.

Once she was warm, she moved back to the flap and scrubbed herself with snow, drying off back by the fire with a dark towel so the bloodstains wouldn't show. She noticed the partial bottle of wine left behind from the aborted weekend here, opened it, and took a deep swallow.

She started dabbing the red wine on the gashes and cuts, taking an occasional swig as she went. She didn't know if she was doing anything more than dying her skin red, but she was beginning to feel better. Of course, it might've just been the wine.

If only she had a mirror…she probably looked like she'd warpainted her entire body. All that was missing was the braids. Leah liked her hair down more, so it would stay that way most of the time. She crawled under some blankets and closed her eyes, wishing that Leah was there, then glad she wasn't because of her stupidity with all of this.

↢↢⊙↣↣

Denae woke, stretched, and bit back a scream, stopping mid-stretch. She could feel partially healed gashes give way and didn't want to move, holding her breath against the pain. She had to move, stand, leave, meet Olivia and get her hair back. And go home and get dressed first, a small voice in the back of her head reminded her.

She slowly stretched each limb separately, biting her lip as she did. Rolling onto her hands and knees, she managed to get to her feet on the second try. Warmth ran down from a few opened cuts…she'd deal with them later. She had a feeling it was later than she thought and needed to move now.

She jumped outside the front porch, ignored the expected coldness from the snow that went partway up her calves, strode inside and up the stairs. Binesi's door opened, and he stepped out, eyes opening wide as he saw her.

"What happened to…you're bleeding," he stuttered.

"I don't have time right now," she said, turning into her room and pushing the door closed.

Binesi caught the door and followed her into her room. "Why are you painted up?" He waved a hand in front of his nose. "You smell like the bottom of a wine barrel."

Denae stayed quiet, throwing on clothes as fast as she could.

"You're not even going to clean those wounds first…not even some salve?"

She slammed her feet into tall boots, not bothering with socks, and strapped on her belt before grabbing her coat.

"You didn't even have your belt," he stated, staring at her.

"So I'm stupid," she said. "Stupid, stupid, so stupid." She was in his face by the time she was finished.

"Just tell me what happened?"

"This," she said, pointing to the slightly bleeding gash that ran from her forehead to her cheek, "was from panic teleporting to the tipi while hovering twenty feet in the air." She stomped her foot. "So stupid…I should've just broken my neck and saved everyone the bother."

"This involves Olivia, doesn't it?"

"Not everything involves your precious Olivia," she snapped, slamming her town glasses on, "but yes, this does. I don't understand it, but stay away from her." She waved a finger in Bin's face. "Do not go to the arcade…you probably shouldn't even go into town."

"Why not?" He pushed her hand away.

"I don't know, except she needs to be kept away from you right now," Denae stated. "Something is dangerous, to you, to her. Probably to me, too, now since I did something stupid. I need to fix that right now." She shifted away, leaving Binesi alone in her room.

↢ ↢ ⊙ ↣ ↣

She was back in the trees by Olivia's house. The coloring in the sky told her she'd panicked for nothing…she was early. She turned then, looking for her prints from the night before, but enough snow had fallen to erase any evidence that she'd been here, even in the protection of the trees.

Then she saw movement going away from the house. It looked like Olivia's blue parka…she'd left early? She shifted to the grove by the school, then pushed through the knee-high snow to the bench where she'd waited yesterday. She knew she had a couple of minutes before Olivia would show, so she grabbed inside her coat for the jar of healing salve and dabbed it on the gashes on her face.

She was dabbing her ear when Olivia came into view, kicking through the new snow. She crammed the jar into a pocket as Olivia stopped, obviously seeing Denae.

Olivia continued after a few seconds, stopping again when she got to Denae.

"What are you doing here," she demanded.

"I came to get my hair back," Denae said evenly.

"I forgot it," Olivia snapped.

"Where is it?"

"In my night stan—" Olivia said, suddenly dropping off and glaring at Denae.

This gave Denae a better look at her. Olivia looked like she hadn't slept.

"It affected you?"

"Oh yeah," Olivia said sarcastically. "It affected me."

"Did you get any sleep?"

Olivia let out a barking laugh that didn't sound like her and shook her head.

Denae stared at her, dumbfounded. How?

Then a glint came into Olivia's eyes, and she smiled. "Since you're here, I can do it at least once more." She pounced, knocking Denae into the deeper snow.

Olivia ripped off one of her mittens, trying to get under Denae's hood and toboggan to her hair. Denae grabbed her arms, rose in the air slightly, and flipped them over, Denae on top, knocking snow down and grinding it into Olivia's face.

Olivia coughed and sputtered as Denae got off, but there was a grin on her face. "You were outside my window last night," she said in that slightly different voice. She gave an ugly smile that Denae had never seen before.

"What is going on over there?" A figure tromped through the snow toward them. "You'd better not be fighting."

Olivia stood quickly, saying, "Did you have a fun trip" with a wide grin before turning. "Mrs. Offenheim, we weren't fighting," in an almost little-girl voice, "but she didn't like it when I said the 'F' word and was trying to wash my mouth out with snow."

"Olivia!" Mrs. Offenheim sounded affronted by that. "Then you got what you deserved. Now get inside."

She turned to Denae. "You don't look familiar."

"I'm," began Denae, thrown off by these changes. "I'm home-schooled."

Mrs. Offenheim wrinkled her nose like Denae had just said the 'F' word. "Well, you go home then…to your…school." Distaste rang on that last word.

Denae turned and started to trudge away through the snow when Olivia's voice rang out. "I'll see you tonight."

Not if I have anything to do with it, Denae thought sourly. Now how was she going to get her hair back?

She decided simply to walk to Olivia's house. Three jumps that close together, plus the quick flip, had her tired out some, and she could rest a while in the woods somewhere before going home. She could feel some stickiness inside her clothes. That flip with Olivia had gotten some things bleeding again. She hoped Binesi would still be there to help put on the healing salve…she didn't want her mom to see her like this. At least her face didn't hurt now. Minor, but something.

She passed Cheryl walking with a group of girls, but Cheryl was busy talking and didn't notice her. No cars were in the driveway, so the house should be empty.

Denae tried the back door. It was locked. Not a big deal. She could see through the window and moved to just inside the door, entering a mudroom with galoshes and raincoats hanging on hooks. She'd knocked off as much snow outside as she could, then again in the mudroom to not leave too many tracks, then closed the door into the rest of the house softly as she entered. She would've pulled her boots off, but she might leave bloody tracks if she did. If things went well, she wouldn't need to go out this way. Of course, if they didn't go well, that would probably still be true. She didn't think her boots would drip, so she lifted herself up a few inches before floating down the hallway.

There was no noise in the house aside from the ticking of a grandfather clock. She was up the stairway and found Olivia's bedroom after looking in a couple of rooms. Her trace was gone, but as Olivia had said, her braid was in the nightstand's top drawer, on top of the paper bag. It appeared intact, if a bit frayed.

She went to the curtains and parted them slightly. She wasn't sure she'd ever be outside that window again, but just in case. There was an orange nightlight glowing from one of the electrical sockets. Olivia would know…might even already know…that she was in her room. She might leave that part open as a trap for Denae should she come looking. She wasn't sure what that was last night and didn't really want to know.

She scanned the room, looking for anything magical.

Nothing.

Nothing to explain all of this.

Then she sat in her desk chair and rested, fighting the urge to doze. About ten minutes later, she heard a car crunch up into the driveway.

Time to leave.

↢↢⊙↣↣

She felt good enough to make it home, so she shifted there, noticing that her mom's car was gone, tracks in the new snow heading down the driveway. Dad was supposed to be doing stuff at Uncle Aldo's, so she should be in the clear.

She wasn't sure she wanted that. She had questions and needed answers. That last teleport tuckered her out again. Maybe she'd bled more than she thought, and no breakfast surely didn't help. Still, she'd rest a bit, hit herself with more salve, and be good.

She let herself in, trudged up the stairs, and went into her room. Binesi was sitting on her bed, obviously waiting for her. He was holding the crystal ball in both hands.

"I'd hoped that somehow I'd see you in this," he said, looking at the ball. "Nothing until you came up the stairs."

"Had your protection tripper thing going?" She took the ball from him and replaced it on its stand.

"Always, when you're blipping around," he said crossly. "So, are you going to tell me what's happening?" He stared at her intently.

She felt a tug on her back when she slipped off her coat and cried out as she started to pull her top off.

"Stop, stop, just stop," Binesi yelled, pulling her hands away from her shirt. "You are a bloody mess back there, so leave that alone, don't touch anything else…don't move until I get back."

She froze as he dashed out the door, then relaxed a bit as she heard the water for the tub turn on, and in another couple of minutes, he came back. She started to reach down to take off a boot.

"Stop," he said. "Do nothing. Bathroom."

Once there, he moved in front of her and started taking off the boot, looking intently at her face. It slid off, and he looked over her foot, seeing only tiny scratches.

"This one is going to be worse," she said.

She knew she had a pretty good gash that had split the webbing by her big toe. However, the boot slid off easily enough because it was a bit gooey in there…still kinda wet.

"Denae…really," he said with some disgust. "It would've taken so little to fix that before you left."

"I couldn't think which to fix," she said, shrugging. "It's good."

"It is not good," he cried. "This is not…and you said you did something even more stupid?"

Denae pulled the length of hair out of her pants pocket and held it out.

"Your hair…so what," he said, "and stand on this towel." Then his eyes widened. "You gave it to someone, and they used it to direct something back at you."

She nodded while he pulled the snow pants down. Her long underwear was spotted with specks and blotches. "Denae, the back is worse than the front. Who did you give the hair to?"

"Olivia," Denae replied.

He paused, blinking, then stood up, taking one of her arms. "Into the tub."

He balanced her as she swung her leg over, getting it high enough on the third try. "Seriously. You got this bleeding again by lifting your leg that high. I'll bet the inside of your snowsuit is a bloody mess." Disgust rang in his voice.

Denae knew he was still trying to figure out how his sweet Olivia could be doing anything wrong. She sat down in the tub, warm water soaking into her bottoms. "She or whatever's in her went after me last night, and it's because I gave her my stupid hair."

"She or what?" Binesi exploded.

"Whatever likes stroking your silver streak," she continued.

"I…don't—"

"Did you kiss before she started playing with your streak?"

"I usually wore my toboggan outside," Binesi answered, "and we kissed while I wore it, and…what are we even talking—"

"I'm talking about your streak," she said, sliding and wincing. "That streak you said you sometimes found annoying that she kept rubbing." She tried to stand, and he held her down, keeping her seated.

He looked furious and said, "Lie down…get your top soaked, too. That is actually something fairly new that she does."

She slid down, in part because the pressure of his hand hurt a bruised area. He splashed water on her front since the level wasn't high enough to cover her yet.

"Either her or whatever's in her. I'm betting on the thing." She spat as water splashed on her face. "It likes your streak…a lot, and not just yours. She touched my hair on Sunday and totally freaked."

"You keep saying that," he said. "What's in her, and how would you know?"

"I can see it in her aura if I focus on her. I did that while she was making love to your streak, and I saw something nebulous and small." She stopped to grab his hand, which was coming down at a bruised spot. "Dear brother, your sweetest has abilities."

He froze. "She's family?"

"She's someone's family, though the rest of her immediate family is totally mundane," Denae said. "It doesn't look like ours or any I've seen. That thing could've been twisting it even then, but I don't think so. Oh, and she can see auras. I'm pretty sure of that, so she knows at least something about us. Have you done any spells or anything around her?"

"No. She's mundane, so we don't do that, or at least I thought Olivia was mundane." He glared at her like she was stupid.

"She jumped me in front of the high school this morning, so I had to do a flip and dumped snow into her face to get her to stop. At that point, it wasn't her, but whatever's in her caused her to jump me." She looked at the pinkly tinted water in the tub.

He followed her gaze, cursed, and grabbed something off the counter. After giving it a twist, he held it out to her. "Drink!"

"I don't—"

"It's open," he yelled at her. "Drink it, or I will pour it down your throat."

She glared at him to remind him what would happen if he tried it but took the bottle, drank it, and felt everything close up and heal.

He pulled the plug. "Stand up," he ordered. "Arms up."

She stood so much more effortlessly than she could have even ten seconds before. Her body was really okay now. She raised her arms.

Bin roughly yanked her bloody silk underwear top off over her head, almost toppling her. He wadded it up and flung it in the tub by the drain, where the flowing water from the tap poured over it. It slid off more freely than if she'd still had open wounds, and with no pain, which she was thankful for, even if she'd just drunk a valuable draught.

He yanked her bottoms down holding them so she could step out, then grabbed the top and wrung both out under the tap before tossing them into the sink. Denae moved to step out but stopped at his look. He dropped the stopper back into the tub, gesturing for her to sit.

"What—"

"No." He pointed a finger at her. "You are my dearest and only sister, but if you step out of the tub, I will strangle you."

Like he could, she thought. I could be at the tipi in a second if I wanted. He couldn't stop me, and he knew it. She smiled slightly and sat.

"When we get more water in there, I will add some of Aunt Bertie's bubble bath. When it gets high enough," he said, his voice rising in both loudness and pitch, "we will have a sane conversation."

"Okay," Denae said. "Then, youngest and most favorite brother, will you please go to the kitchen and get me something to eat while we wait?" She smiled innocently. "I'm starving."

Binesi nodded, added bubble bath, and headed down the stairs.

↤ ↤ ⊙ ↣ ↣

Denae explained everything she knew to Bin at least three times before he started believing her. He was smitten, but if anyone had tried telling her similar things about Leah, she'd act the same so she could sympathize. Her talking about her dream seemed to help convince him, though he didn't say anything about his own dreams.

He agreed not to go to the arcade. Not much of a problem if Olivia wasn't there.

They decided that the shop and Fred's would probably be okay since Olivia had never been there with him. Still, he should be careful anywhere in town on the off chance she might be able to sense them somehow.

He left the bathroom to get to class at Aunt Issa's. He'd be late, but it was just him and Art in the class, and Art was way behind Bin anyway. Denae doubted that Aunt Issa would mind very much.

Denae needed help with this. This was out of her league. She simply didn't know what was going on. Something was inside Olivia, but Denae didn't know what it was or what it really could do. Her imagination ran wild with nasty speculations.

Maybe Oma would know, or Oma-ma. They lived together, so she could kill two birds with one trip. She'd start by telling them about Agatha before moving to Olivia and whatever was in her.

Chapter 16

Answers

"You look beat," Binesi said as Denae shut the front door. He looked her over, concern on his face. He still wasn't sure about this thing with Olivia, but Denae wouldn't have been doing all of this, getting herself hurt, if something wasn't going on.

"You could say that," she agreed. "I'm fine, but it's been a tiring and frustrating day."

"What did you find out?"

She pointed at the couch. "Bring food and drink over there, and I'll tell you."

He went to the kitchen and put hot water and tea bags into a couple of cups. He added chips, French onion dip, and the other requisite accessories onto a tray before returning to the couch.

"So…how was your day?" He grinned as she scowled while she fiddled with her teabag. Dad said that to Mom most days, and Bin knew it would annoy Denae.

"Frustrating," she said after swallowing a chip with onion dip. "I went to Oma's first like I told you I might." He nodded, scooping into the dip. "She was definitely concerned but didn't have any good ideas about what to do." She squeezed out her tea bag and poured in some honey and cream. "I think Oma-ma knows something more, but she didn't say anything."

"Probably wanted to talk with Oma about it," he suggested.

"Yeah," Denae said. "That makes sense. She recommended I go to Aunt Audrea, so I did."

"And," he said, making circular motions with his hand while she sipped her tea.

"She didn't seem to think there was much besides adolescent wish-fulfillment dreams." She grimaced. "Still, she seemed concerned that I think Olivia has something in her, though it may just be that I'm threatened by her somehow because she's dating my little brother." She took another sip.

"That's cold," Binesi said. "You've seemed okay with her."

"She was quite interested that Olivia has a spark." Denae shook her head. "She didn't say, but I think that's when Aunt Audrea thought I became jealous of her."

"Well." Binesi hesitated. "That's when Olivia went to the lavatory, and you became…well…concerned about her."

"I know," Denae said, putting her cup down. "Anyway, she sent me to Uncle Otto." She rolled her eyes. "Can you imagine me talking to him about all of this stuff?"

"I just wish this were Leah instead of Olivia." He put his hands up defensively as Denae glared at him. "I—I just mean that everyone is going to know about my girlfriend, and Uncle Otto will never let me forget any of this. That's all I meant."

"Do you think I like doing this, talking to the grown-ups about possible possession and such?" She made a face. "Plus, he was fairly useless with his suggestions. He had me cast a few spells into some wands he was making, but he did tell me to see Aunt Gaia."

"She's weird," he said. "In the clouds weird."

"I like her," Denae said dismissively.

"Of course, you would. She's your sort of weird."

"I should've gone there first."

Bin perked up, not shoving the handful of chips into his mouth that he'd just grabbed.

"First, she believed me in a way the others didn't quite seem to." She paused to sip more tea. He could see some tension leave her with her shoulders relaxing. "She was interested in her spark and the other thing and had me describe them in great detail. She seemed disappointed that I lacked the finer detail on her aura." She gave him an evil look. "Seemed to think I should peek in on the two of you while you were—"

"Were what," he shouted and stood up. He could feel himself turning red but lowered his volume. "Were what?"

"You know how she is, going all drifty and her mind a thousand miles away," she said, smiling. "She missed parts of what I said, except probably a few choice words, so calm down." She gestured for him to sit, which he did.

"I repeated to her why getting the two of you near each other was probably a bad idea. It took two or three times to keep her attention from wandering about Olivia's aura," Denae said as she sipped from her cup before putting it down. "She suddenly changed…focused…and told me to definitely keep you away from her, and to stay away from her myself."

Bin shrugged and sat back down. This didn't really answer anything. Still, Olivia had gotten a lot more friendly the last time he saw her.

If Denae was right and it wasn't her getting friendly, but that other thing, keeping away was probably the best. It seemed nuts, and he wanted to be with her, especially after that last time. It must've shown on his face as she continued.

"I know…I'd already figured out we should stay away, but Gaia was the first one I talked to who said anything like that. She said this was very unusual, and what she was thinking shouldn't be anywhere around here. She thought she was probably mistaken, but she would do some heavy digging in her library instead of tutoring me on the Unseelie Court tomorrow." She picked up her cup. "I've got no idea what that meant, but she seemed to seriously believe me."

He felt that sudden pressure and put his hand up.

I'm running late here at the shop, and Dad's got things in town this evening, so you and Denae are on your own for supper. Everything okay there?

Um…everything's fine, he thought back and mouthed 'Mom' to Denae. *We'll fend for ourselves fine.*

Finish up whatever studying you have to do. Love you, and the pressure was gone.

"Mom's running rather late, so we're supposed to handle supper ourselves," he relayed, "and get any studying done, not that you did any of that today."

"I didn't like talking about all of this, you know. I feel terrible about it for you and even more for Olivia."

He stared at Denae. That was the closest he thought he'd ever heard her come to an actual apology in years, and this one wasn't forced. He put his arms around her in a tight hug. "I know you're doing everything in your power to help Olivia, and I want you to know I love you for it." He pecked her on the forehead, slid back, and dipped into the dip with another potato chip.

Denae looked down. "There's a good chance that Olivia will become family shortly, and this isn't a good introduction." Binesi jerked slightly. He hadn't thought that far ahead. Sometime soon, his town girlfriend might be training with him.

"I was supposed to be at Aunt Gaia's today anyway, so I did spend some time on studies. I helped her with a couple of other things, then went to Great Uncle Mawk's to help him around the house." Denae paused. "He's getting up there but won't give up living alone." She shook her head. "We need to go help him out more."

"Easy for you," Binesi said. "You can just blip over there and say, 'Here I am.' It'd take me a half-hour to ski there.

"It's still tiring," she said.

"So you're blipping tired, is what you're saying." He grinned over his cup at her.

"Yeah, I am," she agreed, "and half the family now knows about this, and we have no better idea how to do this than we did before." She looked at the tray. "We can reload this, add some sausage and cheese and call it supper."

He nodded and followed her into the kitchen.

↢ ↢ ⊙ ↣ ↣

"Ow, Leah…that hurt," she said, opening her eyes, Olivia where Leah should be…had been. Binesi appeared behind Olivia, head up and eyes closed. Olivia smiled when she saw Denae looking aghast.

"No," Denae screamed, and suddenly she was alone, in her bed, no longer with Olivia, no longer with Binesi.

Lavatory. She had to get to the lavatory and wash up, get clean. She jumped out of bed, swung the door open, and stepped into the hallway.

Something hit her…hard. She went sprawling to the floor, someone landing heavily on her. He rolled, saying, "Don't look at me," and ran into the lavatory, slamming the door.

Denae curled up in a tight ball, then pushed herself sitting as she heard footsteps on the stairs, but still held a fetal position, feeling ashamed of her body. The lightstone above her was uncovered. Mom knelt next to her.

No, not now, her body screamed. Go away.

Mom knelt down and reached for her face. "Don't touch me," Denae growled.

Her mother jerked her hand back like Denae had bitten it. She looked toward the lavatory. "What…did…he…," she started, standing to go there.

"Leave him alone," Denae snarled.

Mom turned back, hands on hips. "Always defending your little brother?"

"We ran into each other in the hallway." Tears started flowing, and she sobbed.

Her mother kneeled down, not touching but leaning in so closely that Denae could feel her breath on her face. She just stayed quiet for a few moments before gently saying, "Your nose is bleeding."

Denae didn't say anything. Her sobs had lessened, but she didn't trust her voice. She thought it'd just been snot. It didn't matter anyway.

"We need to talk." Mom's hand brushed Denae's cheek, and she managed not to flinch. "When you dry up and clean up your nosebleed, come down to the kitchen."

Denae nodded. Mom reached out to stroke her hair, stopped, and stood instead, glancing at the light from under the lavatory door before heading back down the stairs.

A couple of minutes later, Denae stood facing the door in a bathrobe and finally heard movement from the lavatory. As he came out, towel around his waist, his eyes were down at the ground. She put out a hand, and he stopped and looked up, his eyes red and wet.

"We're going to the tipi, so get dressed."

"Why?" Disgust spewed in that word.

"I," she started, hesitating, "I'll explain downstairs. Mom will want to know, so I'll say it only once."

"She only wanted you," he said with a glare. "I'm not going—"

"Yes—you—are," she demanded. "You need to be down there."

"No." He raised up defiantly. "I'm—"

"It's your story much more than mine," Denae said rapidly. "You can tell your part better than me, and you need to."

He suddenly slumped, utterly defeated, then nodded. "Okay," and he shuffled to his room, the door shutting behind him.

↢ ↢ ⊙ ↣ ↣

"I wanted you dressed, but I didn't expect this much," Riann said as she grabbed a third teacup. They'd come down needing only to put the snowsuits on to be ready to ski to the tipi.

"She made me," Binesi said sulkily.

"We're going to the tipi when we're done with this," Denae explained.

Riann glanced at Binesi, who grimaced in agreement with a shrug. "Why?"

Denae took a deep breath. "Olivia, or whatever is in her," she hesitated as her mom's eyebrows went up, "came into our dreams tonight." She looked at Binesi, whose face had gone tight. "Jude says I somehow added some protection when I built my tipi, so I think we may be safe from that if we sleep there. At least I sleep better, without bad dreams, when I sleep there."

Riann looked from one to the other. "Okay, but you'd better start at the beginning."

Denae did, talking fast, trying to leave out anything that would hurt Binesi, letting some things slip by about Olivia. Her mom put up her hand. "Denae, you're bullshitting me."

"What," Denae stuttered, "I'm tell—"

"Denae," Riann said. "You never could lie your way out of a wet paper bag, so don't even try. Oma and Uncle Otto called, and I talked with Aunt Audrea, too."

She glared at her mother. Of course, they'd call her. She was stupid not to realize that. She glanced at Binesi, who looked like he was about to throw up, but he nodded. "Okay," she said after another moment's hesitation. "Back to the dream or vision or whatever it was."

Denae left little out of the dream, telling how they ran into each other in the hallway, and she then knew they were in the same nightmare.

"That explains why you were in the lavatory," Riann said, looking at Bin, who went even more crimson than he'd been at the end of Denae's telling.

"I'd had a similar dream last night," Denae continued, "though only with Olivia, but I woke up and went to the tipi and slept well the rest of the night."

"Denae," Binesi said gruffly.

"Okay," she said, glaring at Bin. "I took a side trip first. I went to look in Olivia's window to see how things were with my hair—"

"Your hair," Riann said, alarmed.

"Yeah, I was stupid," Denae said, "But let's not dwell on my stupidity, or we'll be here all night. I gave her a length of my hair, thinking it wouldn't affect her away from me, but I was wrong." Denae spat.

"Your hair," Riann repeated.

"To Olivia, my hair is all streak," she said, looking contemptuously at her mother.

"Well, of course," Riann mused. "It definitely is that. Your hair and eyes…you draw most directly from that primal ancestral line, your great-grandfather being the next closest I've seen, but still nowhere close."

"Oma-ma's husband?"

Riann nodded.

"He died around the same time you were conceived. Maybe the same night," she said. "This is for another time…go on with yours."

Denae continued, leaving little out, with Mom occasionally asking for clarification here and there. At the end, Riann said, "So you think that Olivia, or rather whatever is inside of her, wants to control Bin."

Denae nodded. "And me, because she knows I will stop her…it…if she doesn't control me, too."

"And the rest of us?" Riann waved about the house. "We are nothing?"

"I don't know." Denae shook her head. Her dad walked up the hallway in his bathrobe, and she froze.

He walked up behind her, kissed her hair, then did the same to Binesi. "Get out of here. Go to your tipi and get some sleep. You both have permission to be a couple of hours late to your studies in the morning, so get your suits on and go."

They did as he said and were soon skiing through the moonlit forest.

Crossing the lake, Binesi spoke. "When you close your eyes, what do you see?"

"I see the dream, waiting to suck me back in," she replied. "And you?"

"Same thing," he said. "You didn't tell Mom that."

"She knew," Denae replied. "She knew."

"Do you think this will work?"

"The tipi," she responded. "I think so, or at least for me, but I'm not completely sure about you."

"And if it doesn't work for me?"

"I'll keep you awake until she's done for the night."

"Okay," he said, silent until they got to the tipi.

"And if this doesn't work at all?" He peered through the open flap to the darkness inside.

"I'll teleport back to the house," she said.

"And leave me there?" He sounded a little panicked.

"And if I stayed here close to you," she said softly. She heard a sharp intake of air from Bin.

"That could be bad," he replied. "I wouldn't want you here."

Inside, Denae quickly got a fresh fire going. Lots of hot coals from her nightly trip here before bedtime.

"So, what do you see when you close your eyes now?"

"Nothing," Binesi said. "Only darkness."

"Yeah, same here," Denae said with a smile, stripping down. "Let's go to sleep. Get undressed and come over here," gesturing Bin to come to a spot where she lifted a blanket above loose earth.

"Earth bath?" He had a disgusted look on his face.

"Facedown works best," she said, nodding.

"Seriously. Now?"

"It's calming," she said. "You know that."

"This is stupid," he said but pulled off the rest of his clothes and lay face down in the dirt. "You're much more the earthy type than me, and this is chilly."

She wanted to move some earth on top of him but felt she was pushing her luck as it was. It helped him relax, but he didn't like it. "Turn your head to the side, and you're right. It doesn't do as much for you as for me, but it still helps."

She dropped on top of him, laying her hands over his, feet on his. This was getting harder now that he was so tall. He might end up as tall as Anton. She felt herself begin to relax, start to melt through him to the earth.

"How long do I have to lay here," broke the silence. Denae forced herself to answer.

"As long as you like, but even five or ten minutes should help," she said.

She wasn't sure how much time had passed, but she felt him move and slid off of him. He got up, and she waved a hand, the dirt dropping off him. He curled up into a different area of quilts and blankets.

"Better?" She knew it was better for her, and she was going for more.

"Some," he allowed. "Good night."

Denae wallowed into the earth and let herself drift. She'd wanted to show Leah the earth bath and would once they could get back out here. Here, she was safe. As Binesi would say, she was in her fortress of solitude. She'd worry about Olivia in the morning.

Chapter 17

Olivia

Denae finished her studies with Aunt Issa and teleported inside the warehouse fence to help Mom, and whoever else was there. Aunt Issa never asked anything but kept giving Denae sideways looks and asked her to help by casting a few spells on some things she was working on.

She and Bin both had slept relatively well the rest of the night, though waking with a jolt on occasion, anticipating something that wasn't there. But the dreams were dull, apparently not worth remembering upon wakening.

She helped at the shop with the packaging and readying for the next day's mail. Aunt Issa's rabbit-fur bags; Uncle Aldo's dried jerkies, pemmican, and fruits; Aunt Addie's bath products and other things that others in the family sold.

Mom acted as the broker for the family business. She'd already packed up the reserved items not shown in the regular mail-order catalog and only sold to a list of select families. They sold a lot less of those, but they were much more expensive. The specials and the mundane products made nearly equal total dollar sales.

They closed up and were almost home when the headlights landed on a figure in a blue parka struggling to walk in the snow up ahead. As Riann slowed the pickup, Denae said, "I think that's Olivia…looks like her coat."

Her mom nodded, her jaw tensing, then got out. Denae heard her say, "Olivia, you're almost frozen." After a pause, "Let me get you into the truck where it's warm."

Denae heard stuttering, "Thank you," as a response. It was Olivia, and she did look about frozen, teeth chattering. She slid haltingly into the center of the bench seat.

Denae looked at Olivia, who smiled back tentatively, shivering badly.

"Hi," she said through her chattering.

Denae's mom turned off the road down the long driveway.

"What are you doing out here?" Denae thought she knew the answer, but not precisely why.

"I wanted to see Bin…and you," she replied. "It has been a while."

There was nothing in her eyes or voice from the dreams or their last physical meeting. She seemed all Olivia.

"You could've called. We could've brought you over tomorrow on the way home."

She thought that wasn't likely, though we were bringing her home now, which wasn't a good idea either. Mom seemed to understand the risk, and Olivia really did look half-frozen.

"I should have dressed better," Olivia said, still shivering and chattering. "It was a longer walk than I thought, and…I think the clear skies…made it colder."

Mom stopped in front of the house as Denae agreed about the weather, then hopped out of the car, leading Olivia inside to the living room fireplace while Denae trailed behind. She wasn't sure what Mom's game was, pure compassion or something else. She seemed to understand, but Denae wasn't sure she fully grasped the seriousness of it.

Settling Olivia next to the fire, she turned to Denae. "Help Olivia out of her snowsuit so she can warm up faster while I grab some blankets." Denae caught her steely look. She definitely understood.

Denae helped Olivia out of her boots…she was shivering so severely she couldn't really grasp them. Denae unzipped the parka, revealing only a thin shirt. Olivia smiled, letting the parka fall while Denae hesitated, unsure. The smile wasn't Olivia anymore. The thing now shucked Olivia's snow pants and stood bare-legged in a short silk gown.

"Bin's in his room, but he's starting to come down. We will produce one who will rule over us." Olivia spoke in that not-quite-Olivia voice, then threw her snow pants into Denae's face.

Denae swept them away, and lights exploded as Olivia's fist smashed into her nose.

Denae fell…reached out…tagged Olivia's foot.

Olivia tumbled.

Mom jumped, wrapping Olivia with an outspread blanket.

"Help me hold her," Riann called out.

Denae pulled herself up, blood running off her chin.

She jumped on Olivia's ankles, trying to hold them still.

This seemed wrong.

She kicked her mother in the face and watched her topple away as she freed Olivia from the blanket.

Binesi started down the staircase, a smile blossoming while Olivia rose and waited for him at the base.

Denae stood, wondering at the blood smear on Olivia's beautiful leg. Binesi took a step back, undoing the belt on his pants. It will be a wondrous baby, she thought, one who will rule like in the old days.

Denae's legs gave way. Something had hit them hard behind the knees.

She fell, her head hitting the floor, lights exploding a second time.

Binesi's pants were loose now. He held them up so he wouldn't trip while going down the stairs.

Olivia stood waiting, arms outstretched.

Denae forced her hand out. She needed to stop Bin…keep it from happening…or did she?

It was confusing, but it was that thing, not Olivia, who was doing this.

She reached out.

He was farther than Denae liked for this, but she could do it—had to.

Bin looked at her, shock registering on his face. "No," he yelled, and he was gone.

Olivia screamed. It was primal, nothing girlish left in the shriek that echoed throughout the house.

It loped at Denae, ready to pounce, but suddenly stopped, shaking its head.

Denae focused, and Olivia froze on all fours, a snarling statue of marble.

Her head throbbed as she crabbed backward, one knee not working.

She'd drained herself of energy. Even her pendant was almost depleted.

Mom lay on the ground where she'd thrown herself against Denae, looking at Olivia, glistening white in the house's lights.

"Whut," Mom croaked, then groaned.

Denae stared, horror-struck. She'd broken her mother's jaw.

A probing reached out for her. She scooted farther from the statue.

"Mom," she cried, "it's not frozen."

What do we need to do?

Get it moved, Denae replied back. *Maybe Oma's.*

The door opened, and Dad stepped in, blinking in surprise.

"Dad," Denae shouted. "Out. Get away"

Instead, he moved forward toward her. The probing twitched away, and she gestured. A column of earth formed between him and the statue. His face widened in surprise, and he dashed back out the door.

Denae crabbed behind the column, dragging her bad leg.

I wasn't polite, Mom explained.

Get Uncle Otto. Have him bring Fred and Sarah if they're around, but not the others. None of the others. Fred was from his first marriage, Sarah, his wife. None of them were of Dassow blood.

Uncle Gunnar floated into her head.

No, Denae thought. *Nobody with a streak. You're a lot closer, and either it can't affect you or can't find you.*

Bin?

Is safe, Denae said with a sigh.

She felt the probing again.

I've got to get outside. It should be only me around whenever it's safe to bring Bin back. Okay, Mom?

No audience, she agreed. *I've got Uncle Otto, and he and Fred will be here in ten minutes. Sarah's at—*

That's enough for now. Dad and I need to get farther away.

I'll bring draughts out, her mom said.

She shifted, landing in a heap next to the pickup truck. This had to be far enough. She didn't have anything left.

↢↢⊙↣↣

Denae explained to her dad for the second time why it wasn't safe for him to enter his own house when Mom walked out, thrusting a small bottle into her hand. It was difficult to sound convincing when someone held a handkerchief to your bleeding nose.

Mom moved Dad's hand and the bloody cloth away. She rubbed her jaw, then reached down and yanked Denae's nose.

Denae screamed. Stars and sparks played through her vision, and the blood gushed out. She could barely see the smug look on her mom's face through the tears as Mom said, "Payback for breaking my jaw."

Denae lay there gasping a moment, fresh blood washing down her face. Her dad patted her on her good knee.

"She would've done that anyway. Much easier for it to heal if it's back in place." He moved, saying, "Speaking of which, let's straighten out that leg before you drink that." She gasped as he gently straightened it out, then broke the seal on the draught and brought it to her lips.

The nosebleed stopped, and the various pains faded quickly. She sat up, hearing the phone ring inside. Her mom went in, giving them a look to stay where they were.

"So Olivia and her thing came here," her dad began again after a minute, "and beat you and your mom up just so she could get knocked up by Bin?"

"She said they would produce one that would rule over us," Denae repeated, "as in days of old."

"I don't understand that at all," he said, his eyes narrowing. "How did Olivia damage both of you so badly?" He brought his hands together a bit. "She doesn't seem that strong."

Denae shook her head, glad it didn't hurt. "Dad, I broke Mom's jaw, and she hurt my knee." She pointed at herself. "That thing controlled me to attack Mom since she was stopping her. Mom body-blocked me to stop me from helping her…the pain helped me break free so I could entomb Bin before he could get to the bottom of the stairs to be with her."

"Be with her?" He raised an eyebrow.

"He was about to have sex with her, probably right there if it could control us," she said, eyeing him. "It's been priming both of them for that moment. A week or more, probably."

The front door creaked open. "That was Olivia's mother, wondering if we'd seen her." She sighed. "I told her that Bin isn't here, Olivia is not feeling well, so we put her to bed, and I'll call in the morning to make arrangements…this is a school night, after all." She squatted next to them by the pickup, a blanket around her shoulders.

Dad stood. "How are we going to handle this?"

"Olivia is a possessed statue," Mom continued, not moving. "We're taking her to Hanna's to try to get her…something." She shrugged. "And her mother wants to see her in the morning."

"We are supposed to get more snow before morning," Jerok said. "If there's enough, clearing the driveway could take a while. Tractor's cranky and all."

"Her mom's rather heavy-set," Denae said. "She might not want to walk up the drive if it's snowed in."

"Plus, Issa can always talk with her," Riann mused. "Issa's Dassow, so she can't help us free Olivia without the risk of it controlling her in some way. It controlled Bin and Denae tonight. And through their dreams last night, as you know."

"If this is going to take any length of time, using Issa might be best," Jerok said.

The sound of an engine came from down the driveway, headlights showing a moment later. Uncle Otto and Fred emerged from their pickup while Mom went to meet them.

Denae pulled her dad to the workshop while they loaded Olivia. "It's still searching for us, but I think it's hampered by Olivia being marble."

"That's disconcerting, the way it reaches out," Jerok agreed. "Distance definitely helps."

"We can go in now," Denae said. "Mom left with them, and there's a bit to clean up."

Denae dissipated the earth, which had collapsed minutes earlier from the column she'd called it in. Dad grabbed a cleaning wand and mopped up the blood with it while she went upstairs to wash up and change out of her bloody clothes. This was getting to be a daily event, and she wanted it to stop.

She soaked in the tub for at least half an hour, mulling over what had happened. She worried about Binesi but didn't have the energy to bring him back yet and didn't want to involve Dad. He'd probably want to be there, and she was pretty sure it'd be awkward enough with just her there. At least Dad didn't know the earth spells and couldn't bring Bin back up himself.

Once out of the tub and dressed, she made sure Dad was in another room before bringing Binesi back.

He looked around, saw Denae, and rolled into a ball. "What…where…"

"Pull your pants up, and I'll tell you," she said and threw a blanket over him.

He stuttered a few words, nothing comprehensible, then muttered, "Okay." He shifted under the blanket for a couple of minutes, and Denae wondered just how okay he was.

She sat with him and explained everything, including his coming down the stairs several times. He didn't even know Olivia was here. He didn't remember leaving his room or anything else about the last hour.

"And Olivia?"

"Should be at Oma's, with them working on something to free her from whatever that is."

"Can we go to the tipi? I don't think I could sleep here tonight. I'm not sure I can sleep at all, but I definitely won't be able to do that here."

"Yes," Denae said. "I think that's a good idea for both of us. I'll tell Dad."

↢ ↢ ⊙ ↣ ↣

Denae returned to the house in the morning to see if there was any news. She smelled the coffee, so she poured a cup, added sugar and cream, and went to the office to find her dad.

"I thought that'd be you." He came around the desk and gave her a long hug. "You look better this morning." He brushed some dirt out of her hair. "Earth bath?"

She nodded, realizing she hadn't even bothered to sweep herself clean. She set her cup on the desk and returned the hug with a tight one of her own, wondering why she suddenly needed to do this.

"Whoa," he said, returning the second embrace. "Everything okay at the tipi?"

"Yeah," she said. "Except, of course, Bin doesn't like the earth baths." she mimicked, releasing her grip on her dad. "Doesn't like putting his dick in the dirt."

"But you still made him," he said, chuckling.

"I'm still the big sister," she said, smiling up at her dad, "Even if he can lift me over his head now." Her smile dropped. "How's Olivia?"

"Not sure," he replied. "I've talked with your mom a couple of times. Everyone's gathered, but they're having problems getting that entity totally disassociated from her. They're loathe to bring Olivia back to flesh without removing it, whatever it is."

"Is Aunt Gaia there?"

"She's Dassow," her dad reminded her, "and you said nobody with a streak."

"But she probably has the best idea of how to do this," Denae said.

"I know," he replied. "I've tried calling, but it just rings."

"She unplugs her phone sometimes because she thinks it's being rude to her," Denae said, shaking her head. "And it just sitting there, quiet."

"Mom's tried, too," he continued, "but no response. The telepathic equivalent of 'Do Not Disturb.'"

"Arrgghh!" Denae grabbed her coffee and chugged, gasping a bit. "Still too hot, and that's probably my fault, too. Aunt Gaia, I mean."

At her dad's upraised eyebrow, she continued. "I told her all I knew about Olivia and that…that entity…is that what they called it?"

He nodded, and Denae continued before he could say anything.

"She was very interested in that…entity…and disappointed I couldn't give her more detail…I would've had to strip Olivia down completely to see her aura as clearly as she wanted, and well, I guess that's pretty well done. She was wearing only a silk top, plus the entity was in me. I remember it all, which Bin luckily doesn't…not even coming out of his room. They were going to create a baby that the entity would inhabit fully and become a ruler of some sort to rule over all of us…like in days of old? I'm not exactly sure who 'us' is or how long ago it means. Centuries, at least. That was all way too scary and too close to actually happening."

She winced.

"I can give her more detail now, but what I mean is…she said she was going to need to dig deep in her library to research this." Denae realized she was pacing in front of the desk. "That's what she's doing, and you know she's not coming up for air until she's done."

"She makes you seem reasonable about your studies at times," her dad said. "That's part of why she's my crazy sister, the youngest of my generation."

"She's what…twenty-six," Denae asked. "Only eight years older than me."

"And brilliant in her own way, though you're giving her a run for her money," he said. "At least you spend time outdoors. She'd be happy to stay in the family library and have people push food and drink under her door."

She took another draw on her coffee. "When I finish this, I'm going to see her," Denae said.

"If she's in deep dive with no patrons coming, she'll have the library locked up tight," Dad replied, sitting down. "You won't be able to get in."

"A few months ago, she left me out in the snow for a couple of hours while I was banging on anything that would make noise," Denae said. "I finally got her attention by banging on several second-story windows. After she let me in, she showed me how to unlock the security wards and said there was another way, but only you and her knew that."

"That there is," Jerok agreed. "If there's a reason, I'll teach you. There aren't very many who could even learn that method."

"I've already learned not to try to teleport inside the door," she said, flashing a quick grin. "If she doesn't answer, I'll let myself in with what she showed me. I am supposed to have class with her today anyway, so I should be there." She sipped at her coffee, then added. "Has Aunt Gaia ever had a boyfriend?"

"She's had a few but generally scares them off or discards them fairly quickly." He chuckled quietly. "If they're family, she out-competes them, and if they're mundanes, I think she weirds them out…maybe some of the family as well. Kinda like you."

"I've never even had a boyfriend," she protested. "How can you say that?"

'Your brothers are all scared of you," he said, smiling broadly now, "except Bin, maybe, but he'd drink milk out of a saucer if you asked him to."

Denae smiled, realizing there was some truth to that last part, but only Lucas had any reason to be scared of her, and he usually brought that on himself.

"Your male cousins are afraid to ask you out, scared of how you'd say no, or even more afraid you might say yes. Justin would still pee in his pants if you looked at him wrong."

"He would not," she shouted, and he laughed. "He's the only cousin who is my friend."

"That's good then," Jerok said, shaking his head. "I think Bin was ready to melt into the floor during that talk with Mom a couple of nights back."

"We were talking about him having dream sex with Olivia, and," her eyes opening wide, "her with me at the same time. How could that not be completely and totally embarrassing to either of us? It's not like either of us has done anything like that in real life. It was preparing him for last night and had been for at least a week. Why I was in there, I'm not sure, unless it was trying to bring me under its control. I suppose that was likely. It did it pretty easily."

"Yet you rarely broke stride discussing it with Mom," he said.

"After she called me out," Denae said back. "I was trying to be nice to Bin, trying to minimize his…," she groped for words. "His…actions, and mine, but I had to find out what was going on. I still don't know how or why, but the moment I had Olivia touch my hair, I knew that it was dangerous."

"And yet you gave her some of your hair?"

"I told you I was stupid with that. I like Olivia and couldn't put the two together well enough, even though I should've known. I'm sure I'll find something else stupid to do, but it won't be that."

Her dad laughed while she finished the last of her coffee, finally cool enough…barely… for her to swallow down. "I'm off," she said after putting the cup down on the desk, and with a brief vision of the front of the library, she stood there in the snow.

Chapter 18

Gaia's Deep Dive

Denae went through the obligatory politeness of knocking at the front door and pulling on the bell rope, knowing it would be fruitless. If she wasn't answering Mom's telepathic calls, Denae was sure she wouldn't even notice this.

The house was black granite, three feet thick on the ground floor, all made by some Dassow ancestor over a century ago…she wasn't sure which. It was supposed to be one of the oldest houses in the forest…her own house being another.

Denae looked at the granite, thinking of uncles Leonard and Mawk, who taught Denae and Lucas how to find, mold, and create the earth as they liked. Denae outstripped Lucas in the earth skills despite being three years younger. Lucas could stone and un-stone but never bothered with the entombing.

She took the first steps to ensure she was within the library's outer protective wards and said the word combination necessary to see the trip mechanism. She reached between the suddenly visible force lines of various colors, avoiding all of them except the peach-colored one, and touched it. This unlocked the inner wards, and Denae let herself in through the foyer.

She entered the living room and found the fireplace to be stone cold.

Aunt Gaia would be upstairs…hadn't even bothered keeping the downstairs warm. No lightstones showed here.

The only lights glowed from the staircase and the shuttered windows, but Denae could see quite well through the dimness. Dad's remarks about their similarities made her wonder if Gaia could see as well as she could in the dark.

Books were piled on the living room table, with bookcase after bookcase of the more requested books along the walls. Mom talked about the eighty-twenty rule in what they sold, and it seemed to apply here in the library for the books used for research, too.

Through the dining room, tabletop piled with books, and into the kitchen, Denae looked in the sink and counter. Dishes with cheese rinds, cut-off sausage ends, and a couple of empty boxes of Ritz crackers. No pots or pans.

Aunt Gaia was definitely doing a deep dive, not taking time to cook anything, not that she cooked a lot anyway. Of course, there were no visitors or library patrons if she'd unplugged the phone so they couldn't call and make appointments.

Denae turned to the lit staircase that led up to the library proper. She'd only been up there once, a couple of years ago, the first time she had been here for individual training. Aunt Gaia showed her around and spent over an hour describing the books, tomes, and other objects and what they were for. After that, she told Denae she was supposed to ask if she needed anything up here, and Aunt Gaia would bring it down.

There were three bedrooms upstairs and three more down, the house built for a slightly smaller family than her parents' house. However, the downstairs bathtub was larger and even more comfortable than at home. The upstairs bedrooms were full of bookcases and cabinets, no room for beds now, and only two bedrooms downstairs still functioned in that capacity.

The other was Gaia's workroom to work on her wands and such. She'd been trying to get the family to agree to give her the empty house next door…next door being a quarter-mile away…as her library annex, but with no luck so far.

Staring at the staircase, Denae steeled herself, unsure how Aunt Gaia would react to her entering her private domain uninvited. She stepped up and up, around the landing to the second floor. The main room was well-lit with lots of lightstones, the center table piled high with books. Denae turned to check another room when she heard scratching.

She stepped around the book-stacked desk and saw her aunt, left finger hovering above a line on a page of a bulky tome full of some sort of gothic script. She scribed with a fountain pen onto a ruled notepad with her right hand, apparently translating the script into English. She wore a gauzy gown of swirling reds and oranges that matched the two-tone colors of her hair. Denae started to speak but decided to wait until her aunt was finished rather than startle her. It was apparent she had no clue Denae was standing there.

After a minute, she quit writing and started to turn the page.

"Aunt Gaia," Denae began, and the change was remarkable.

Her aunt jumped, banging her knees on the table, gawking at Denae like she couldn't quite see her, then gasped, "Denae."

Another long breath.

"Oh, yes, you're here for class." She looked between books and her niece. "Oh, I've lost track of time."

Then she paused, looking at Denae suspiciously. "Didn't I…I mean…I thought I told you yesterday that class was canceled today."

"You're needed," Denae said, prompting further, "Now."

"But," she said, glancing more rapidly between that tome and Denae, "I can't come now." She waved a hand over the immense book. "That girl…that thing you told me about," she gasped. "I need to be here, to learn more, to know more…about it…about her."

"That's why you're needed," Denae said. "Olivia is at Oma's. They're having problems disassociating the entity from Olivia."

"Oh…things have escalated since yesterday…that was yesterday, wasn't it."

"Day before. That's why I wasn't here yesterday."

Aunt Gaia winced.

"Maybe I should've answered."

"Let's get you moving," Denae said.

"Not yet," her aunt said, looking through her notepad. It looked like she'd written at least forty pages, including some drawings, formulas, and such, stopping near the front. "What color of green was it?"

Denae wasn't good at describing colors. She knew the right line to get into the house was peach because Aunt Gaia said it was, and it did look peach-ish. She saw an illumination in the heavy tome with a green that was close in color, so she put her finger there. "Not shiny, but almost like that."

Her aunt closed her eyes slowly. "It could be worse, I suppose," she murmured, more to herself.

"So, what is it?"

"Too little time to teach you that," she replied, eyes still closed, breathing like trying to smell something very faint. "You don't know why it's here…or awake?"

"So Olivia can bear a child who will rule as in the days of old or something like that."

Gaia's eyes popped open wide.

"No," she said in increasing volume. "No, no, no, no, no!"

She started gathering papers and her notepad. She stood up, a head taller than Denae but just as thin, her gauzy clothing making it look like there was a breeze in the room. She stuffed wands into their individual spots in her roll-up bag, then pulled out a couple of others. She still uttered the occasional "No" and rolled up the bag, stuffing everything into an oversized handbag.

Then Denae followed her down to the foyer, following in her wake as her red and coppery locks seemed to float behind her. She was Dassow, but she didn't have a streak… the colors were a blended streak.

"You can't go inside," Denae said.

"Of course, I can't," Gaia agreed absent-mindedly, "but we have to free this poor girl."

She suddenly stopped at the stairs' bottom, Denae almost knocking her over. She was staring over her head.

"Did you hear me?" Denae asked louder. "You're Dassow, and you'll be the only Dassow descendent within a quarter-mile of Oma's right now. It goes after anyone with a streak. Olivia is marble right now, and that impedes its abilities some, but you can't get too near even with that. It almost got me and Dad before Mom had her moved to Oma's."

She looked owlishly at Denae. "You're right…I'll need something heavier."

Moving to the front door, she flipped off her gown and threw on a flannel shirt and thick sweater, pulling them from hooks on the wall. Her slippers flew halfway back to the living room as she kicked them off.

"How could it even be here? And that won't work," she suddenly said, pulling on corduroy pants, then snow pants. "It can't have freedom."

Again, she was speaking like Denae wasn't in the room.

"Denae," Gaia said so piercingly that Denae jumped. "There is a crock upstairs…room to the front right. Jade green, about two-foot-tall, with a wire clasp for the lid. It has several protections on it." Denae ran, taking the stairs two at a time. At the top, she brought her sight to bear and went quickly to the room.

So much magic, she thought, passing various objects on shelves. Protection, protection, protect...ah! She moved quickly, levitating the heavy crockery off the shelf and letting it settle into her arms before heading back down the stairs.

Her aunt was thoroughly bundled up by the time she got back, holding one of the wands in her hand, another now tucked behind her ear, the bag over a shoulder. She tucked the jade crock under her free arm, saying, "Make yourself at home…or whatever." Then she touched the wand to her head and was gone.

Denae went to the phone, plugged it back in, and called Dad to let him know Aunt Gaia was at Oma's. As tempted as she was to have full reign of the library and house, she needed to return to the tipi. Bin was surely awake by now, and she hoped he'd had the sense not to go anywhere. Maybe another time would let her explore here. Instead, she aimed for the spot just outside the tipi, ensuring she would be at ground level this time

.

Chapter 19

Burnt

"What's going on," Bin demanded as soon as she appeared. He was fully dressed, pacing outside the tipi, a set of skis and poles leaned against it. "Is she okay?"

"I don't know," she said. "I went and fetched Aunt Gaia. She wasn't answering Mom or anyone."

"You don't know anything?"

"They're having problems disassociating the thing…the entity…from Olivia," Denae said. "That's why I went to get Aunt Gaia. She wanded her way there but is staying outside to be safe if Olivia's not fully warded. She seems to know what it is."

"What is it?"

Denae shook her head. "I gave her a better description, and she freaked out…said it would take too long to explain, but it sounded like it shouldn't be from around here. You might as well go back inside."

"Me?" He glared at her. "What about you?"

"We," she amended, sighing, slumping. "I got no place to go. Why aren't you staying in there?"

"It's hard staying here." He pointed in the direction of Oma's house. "I want to be there, but I know I shouldn't. A part of me very much wants to be there to…." He let that trail off.

"A part of me wants you to do that," Denae said quietly. "That's why we need to be inside the tipi."

He glared at her. "And if I don't, you'll bury me or statue me or something like that, won't you." His voice was less accusing than stating facts.

Denae nodded.

"Then do it, so I don't even know anything until it's all over." He shook his head. "It's better than this."

"Get inside," Denae said firmly, undoing the flap. "You're stronger than this."

"I don't know. You'll do another earth bath, won't you?"

"It helps." She stared up at him, arms crossed. "Go in, get ready, and assume the position."

"That's in the wrong direction. I need to go to Olivia." He crossed his arms and stared steadily back at her.

"You won't help her going there," but suddenly, she wasn't so sure that was true. "She's still marble anyway."

"She's not," he said. "They just made her flesh. We have to stop them before they do the separation."

He was right. Olivia was flesh again. Maybe he was right on the second part. Something else had changed, too. They could separate them now…Bin couldn't get there in time, but she could get there and stop them but….

She screamed, fighting that urge to leave, willing herself to stay. It was Bin who needed to leave. To go far away.

He'd grabbed his skis but turned to look at her.

It stopped her.

She couldn't send Bin away. She screamed again and lifted him into the air. She could still do that.

"What," he shouted.

Denae fought for control and pointed at the tipi. "Get…in," she cried.

Binesi floated into the opening of the tipi but grasped at the entrance. He fought her levitate to stay out, but his hands slipped, grabbing the flap next.

She battled for her mind and forced more energy against her brother until the flap ripped. The torn remnants hung in his hands as he floated inside.

Denae staggered in and moved next to the fire.

"Everything…off…now…or…I…put…you…in…the…fire." He continued to stare at her. She squatted, shoving her hand into the flame, and gasped with the sudden pain.

"Denae," he screamed.

She stood and looked at her hand. It cried with pain but felt like it was separate from her. Not her pain…someone else's.

"Better," she gasped, watching it blister and her sleeve smolder.

"Put it in the snow," he said. "Let me down. I can help."

"Clothes off now, or I'll burn them off," she yelled. "That thing, that entity…it doesn't like pain." She grabbed a piece of wood from the fire with her burnt hand and pulled it out, holding the unburned end. Watching the flames jump, she stared at the bright red coals glow on the burning end. "My hand really hurts. I don't want to burn you. I don't want to hurt you, but I will do it. I will burn you as much as I have to so you won't or can't go to her."

Binesi struggled, floating, but wasn't undoing any clothes. His eyes flicked between Denae and the flaming stick, then over to the tipi opening and back.

He fought to enter her head, telling her to stop and drop the log. She squelched it. She was alert. He'd have to be a lot sneakier than that.

She blinked back tears as she pointed the flaming wood toward him.

Her leg twitched, trying to cramp, but she fought him away there, too.

She released the wood, launching it forward like she sent the rocks at rabbit heads.

It crashed into his face, his hands moving too late. He screamed as the coals hit, broke apart, scattered across his face, some dropping onto his shoulders and chest, burning holes into his snowsuit.

The rest of the log glanced away, landing in the bare soil where she did the earth baths. Her eyes tracked back to Bin, watching as his hair flamed up from the coals lodged in his scalp. It would heal if they lived long enough.

She released him. He fell, his face hitting bare dirt. Denae twitched a burnt finger. The log rose into the air again, floating, glowing end pointed down at him, ready to launch again. The flames began reigniting from the remaining coals.

Binesi writhed, wailing, a path of burnt skin and smoldering hair showing where blond hair had been seconds ago. Most of his silver streak was gone, too.

Denae tugged his boots off, snow pants following. She was undoing his belt buckle when he opened his eyes.

"Unzip your coat." Tears streamed down her face.

"Salve," he croaked, reaching out to her.

"No," she said. "We need the pain." She could hear his cries reverberate off the tipi walls but pulled his pants off, moving back for his long underpants as he fumbled with the zipper of his coat.

She helped him get the rest of his clothes off and face down in the dirt. More dirt moved over him, covering him from mid-shin to his wrists, only his head uncovered. Then she stripped down and settled back onto the soil. She felt him shudder as she relaxed. She wondered if his head hurt more than her hand.

"This works better," she said.

"I wasn't strong enough," he said, bitterness in his voice. "It hurts. It burns a lot."

Her tears fell on his face.

"I…I almost went to Oma's," Denae said, then she was sobbing again. "It was...so hard…and its hold…it…was greater…on you…. I could…see that when…you wouldn't…wouldn't…."

"Wouldn't go in?" He started to turn.

"No," she protested. "Stay."

He shifted back. "You screamed. Over and over."

"It kept it…away…long…enough for me…to get you…and me…in." She seemed to be getting more in control. "The fire…the fire, it did the rest." She took a deep breath. "It does burn. It hurts a lot."

"Why," he started. "Why could it reach us like that?"

"Desperate," she said, realizing as she said it. "Drew from Olivia to get us. Especially…." Denae swallowed. "Once she came back to flesh."

"Drew what," Bin said, his voice shaking.

He already knew the answer, but she said it anyway. "Her life essence."

"Is she?" He felt him swallow.

"I don't know," she said softly. "I don't know." She took a breath. "The fire. It broke the connection. She was alive then."

"Yeah, she was," he agreed.

"When we broke the connection, it couldn't call us, wouldn't draw on her," she said. "Maybe."

She felt his chest heave under the dirt between them, sobs coming strong. She shifted slightly, the char of his burnt hair strong in her nose as her hands sought his, the insides of her arches rubbing his calves. Tears ran down her face again.

After several minutes, his breathing eased. "Right now," he said, "a part of me hates you."

"Part of me hates me, too," she said. "It'll either go away, or I'll have to get used to it." She sighed. "I wish you hadn't ripped the flap…my butt is about frozen."

He brought his hands in, doing a pushup, rolling Denae away from the fire. Then he caught her leg, dragged her across him, and sat her roughly in front of the fire. He threw a blanket over her shoulders, breathed heavily, and got up, dirt falling from his body.

"What—"

"I'm fixing your flap," he said, picking up what he'd ripped away. "Maybe not. I did a number on this," he concluded, holding it up.

"It's okay," she said. "We'll fix it later."

Bin shuffled directly behind her, tossing some quilts down before half-falling, pulling more blankets over them. "Where's the salve?"

"Not yet," Denae said. "Not until we hear that they succeeded."

"If they remember to tell us," he mumbled.

"They will…eventually."

"And if they lost," he said quietly.

"Then it'd be best if you were dressed," Denae said.

"Where are you sending me?"

"Jude," she said. "That would be better than Lucas, I think."

"Why not Anton?"

"Wrong direction, plus he'd want to come home and do something stupidly brave. If you show up at Jude's apartment like this, he'll do what you tell him."

"What am I telling him?"

Good. He was starting to be intrigued.

"Drive south," she said. "Florida's nice this time of year."

"Florida," he said. "Seriously?"

"It's probably overkill," Denae admitted. "The entity may hunt you, or it may grab someone local…Uncle Leonard, Dad, Bradley, one of the others. I don't know."

"If it grabs someone local, you'll probably find out, but it seems fixated on you. This is Thursday, and if you have to run, be especially careful every four weeks from yesterday…probably change states or something before then." He looked puzzled, but Jude could explain it to him if needed.

She pointed off to the side. "Drag my bag over here."

Binesi winced but dragged it over, and Denae fished inside with her good hand, pulling a baggie out with money in it. "Here's two-hundred twenty-three dollars, plus some change, if you have to travel."

Bin pulled it over and peered in. "Hey, there's like four draughts in here," he said. "Why," and then his eyes widened.

"Yeah," she said. "I didn't know how badly I'd have to hurt you…or me."

"But you would've held me over that fire as long as it took, wouldn't you?" He said it softly, gently reaching over, pushing the blanket aside, and touching her shoulder. She didn't break eye contact but could feel her tears welling up.

"I'd still be alive, if barely, and you could bring me back…at least enough." He smiled slightly, wincing from the pain.

"I would've cut your balls off with my knife and thrown them in the fire to keep her…keep it…." She straightened up. "I'm so scared. I tried to send you to Jude outside, but she…it kept me from it. I could still levitate, so I did that instead and burned my hand until it let go completely." She looked at her hand, blistered and blackened in a few spots. "I thought it'd be worse."

"By then, I knew she wasn't free on the trail to get to us, so I simply burned you instead." She slumped.

"Instead of sending me to Jude or castrating me?" There was no sarcasm in his voice when he asked that.

"Preferably the first, but that was the second reason I wanted you naked."

"The draughts?" He looked at them thoughtfully.

"It'd heal the area, but it wouldn't regrow them," she said. "You'd need stronger magic for that. It doesn't regrow hair, either."

"Yeah, I've got some sort of reverse Mohawk going right now," he deadpanned, then looked a little green. "By stronger magic, you mean the people with Olivia right now."

Denae nodded.

"And if she controls them, it no longer matters." He slowly hung his head. "So then, you'd have to slit my throat."

Denae's eyes opened wide, and she shook her head.

"No. I'd cut off your balls. You'd be useless to her…it. Of course, it might retaliate by slitting both of our throats."

Then she felt a familiar pressure.

Denae raised her hand, letting her mother come through. *Are you two at the tipi?*

Maybe, Denae thought back.

Oh, Mom replied. *Of course. We were successful. It's contained in Gaia's crockery, and she's put extra wards on it. Pastor Jonathan and Agatha were instrumental in the final part…both say they met you recently,* a question riding on that thought. Denae realized she never thought it important to mention either of them to her.

Bin cannot come, she continued. *Right now, I don't think we could keep them from…consummating things…if they were together, or at least I'd rather not make the effort. I think the crisis is over, but Binesi does not need to be a father at sixteen, and that would probably happen. Tell him to stay at the tipi until I tell him to come home.*

You do need to come. Pastor Jonathan has come up with something to tell her family. She sighed. *For some reason, he wants you, Agatha, and Hanna there. Once you get dressed, come here, and how are you two, anyway?*

Nothing a couple of healing draughts won't cure, and we'll down those in a moment.

Do I want to know?

We'll tell you later, Denae sent, *but Bin will be sporting a buzz cut for a while.* She opened her eyes briefly and saw that he was slipping on his snow pants. She waved him to stop. *Anything else? I need to get dressed.*

No, she replied. *Love you both,* and she was gone.

"You're not going anywhere yet," Denae said.

Bin stopped, looking at her. "But everything's good, Olivia's okay, and all that?"

She nodded, watching his smile grow and wondering if he'd learned to mind-read recently. "And how many clothes do you want Olivia to be wearing when you see her?"

He hesitated.

"What do you still really want to do with her?"

"I…," he started, his smile faltering. "I see where you're going with this."

"She still wants the same thing," she said, "so you're not seeing each other until you can be civil. Otherwise, you'll be doing her on the pool table in the arcade."

"I'd at least take her outside, so it'd be private," he countered, the smile returning too brightly.

He handed her a draught and took one for himself. She one-handed hers and drank while holding her burnt hand high over the fire. The burns scabbed over, then started crumbling off into the fire as she flexed her hand.

"Denae," Bin shouted. "That stinks."

"You preferred *eau de* burnt hair," she said.

"At least I'd gotten kinda used to that. I'm staying, remember."

"And I'm probably sleeping here, so be careful what you do with your burnt hair," she said as he bent his head forward, brushing scabby dandruff and burnt hair into the ground where they'd lain.

"Maybe I'll hide out here for a month or two until my hair grows back. Besides, everything's good now, right? Bad thing gone and all that?"

"Let's see," Denae mused. "In the last twenty-four hours, Olivia told me she's going to bear your child, then broke my nose. I broke Mom's jaw, and Mom did something to my knee where I couldn't walk. I buried you, then turned Olivia into a statue that looked more like a snarling beast than a girl. I put up a mound of dirt in the house to block it from Dad, then shifted outside into the snow so it couldn't get me. I was controlled once, almost twice, held my hand in the fire on purpose until…," she breathed heavily, "and burned your face and head badly to break its control on you." She looked him full in the face as she pulled her long underwear top over her head.

Her shoulders slumped. "And those dreams…something else I'll never unremember."

Binesi just stood there quietly while she continued dressing. She stood after she pulled on her boots. He grabbed her around the waist from behind and gave her a bone-crushing hug.

"Thanks for saying all of that," he said. "I've been nothing more than a stud horse being prepared for when the mare was in heat." He started bawling, big wracking sobs.

Bin had released Denae slightly, and she forced herself around and slowly pushed him down until he was flat on the floor, pulling her head on his shoulder. There were places she needed to go, but not yet. She needed to wait here with him until he was good enough to be alone with himself.

Chapter 20

Apprenticeship

Denae stood on Oma's porch, watching the car with Olivia, Oma, and Agatha heading down the driveway. Pastor Jonathan had already left. Oma and Mom convinced them she'd be at the appointment in plenty of time.

Denae briefly relayed what happened at the tipi to Mom and the others, including Binesi's revelation about being little more than a stud horse. She assured them that he was perfectly happy now to stay in the tipi until the snow melted, if necessary.

Her mom took Denae's hand and looked it over, nodding. "It looks completely healed, but you've lost your tan there. I'm guessing that Bin's head is about the same."

Denae nodded.

"It could reach out that far?"

"You were about to separate it, and it knew you could even before you turned Olivia back to flesh. Bin had been fighting it before I got there. Then it tried to get me once Olivia was flesh. I could get there in time to stop you. I almost went. It's scary…scary…." The tears came, and her mom pulled her tight. "How close…how close I came to…to…going to it." The embrace tightened, and she felt herself being rocked as she sobbed.

Once she dried up, Denae asked about Gaia since she would've been a lot closer than either her or Binesi.

"I warded her in another room," Oma said, "so we could confer, but sent her back to the library before we brought Olivia back to flesh. We had no idea it could reach out that far."

"I'm pretty sure it was drawing directly on Olivia to do that," Denae said.

"It was, and we had to act more quickly than planned to excise it. Not pretty, but it did the trick. Pastor Jonathan and Agatha helped to contain it in Gaia's crockery. It's well sealed away now."

"And Olivia is okay? She seemed fine when I saw her."

"It hadn't drawn much," Oma-ma replied. "I was able to block that flow into the entity. Otherwise, we couldn't have separated them."

Denae nodded. She had wanted to use the broodmare analogy on Olivia, but she seemed so sweetly confused. She knew less about everything that went on than Denae thought. Olivia knew she'd been controlled, but some were dreamlike, and she couldn't account for the time for others.

Given the chance, Olivia would readily have sex with Binesi. Denae had asked her that in rather graphic detail and got a broad smile and a "Yes." The only good thing about it was that it did seem to be only with no sign of the entity showing. Still, she'd be just as pregnant if that happened today.

When she could get her thinking about other things than Binesi, she seemed herself. Considering Binesi's feelings, it probably wasn't surprising that this would be her reaction.

Thoughts popped in, causing her to wonder if Olivia was light enough to pick up and carry back to the tipi with a teleport. She might be petite enough, or maybe she could send Olivia there alone to be with Binesi. She hadn't practiced teleporting other people much yet but knew the front of the tipi very well. She could….

No, she couldn't. She hoped this residual urge would fade quickly.

She had misgivings about parts of the plan for the next few days. Olivia would spend Thursday night at home but stay at the tipi with Denae for the weekend. It had protections, and more scarily, they'd decided that since Olivia had some sort of spark, she should be Denae's apprentice.

Denae protested that she wasn't ready for an apprentice, but they all disagreed, saying she was being too modest. Her own modesty was her concern, scared that she'd wake up in her sanctuary with Olivia acting like in the dreams. She didn't voice them, couldn't find the words. Mom gave a concerned look while she sputtered about not being worthy of Olivia's apprenticeship.

Different family members continued to hang around Oma's, and they applauded her for astutely discovering this being living within Olivia and getting her to family so it could be taken care of.

A few took her aside, wanting more details about the entity and the reason for the final liaison. Denae used the broodmare/stud-horse analogy that Bin had come up with, saying only what they already knew about a ruler, like in old times. Aunt Gaia was the only one who understood much about that and had whatever the entity was safely stashed away at the library.

Oma-ma made a batch of sugar cookies for her and Bin, which she took back to the tipi, though with the instructions that he could go home, but not to town, if he liked.

Bin nodded, asking, "Where are you sleeping tonight?"

Denae shrugged. "Probably here. Dreams aren't going to be good, but they might be better here."

"Yeah," he said. "I want to be alone, but I'm not ready to go home, face Mom and Dad, hear their pity or pep talks. I cried like a baby." His eyes started tearing up. "That was so stupid, and I made you late."

"They couldn't do anything until I got there, so I couldn't be late." She gave her brother a sly smile. "Nobody complained, either."

Then she dropped her smile. "I have an apprentice."

"No," he said.

"Yes," she said. "Mom apparently didn't provide them with some of the nasty details about why this isn't a good idea."

"She's probably wanting you to be there to help keep her away from me until she's out of heat," he said, looking nervous. "How long is that, anyway?"

"Not something I've really had to worry about. Three or four days. You're the one who went through anatomy with those body spells."

"I was eleven. I didn't pay that much attention to that lunar cycle. It wasn't anything I thought I'd ever be involved in."

"You might want to brush up on it now. At least you know for Olivia that it's most likely every four weeks from last night."

She looked at his splotchy face and bare scalp and sighed. He'd tan again, and the hair would grow back. "I will have Olivia all weekend from Friday after school until late Sunday, so you need to clean up and vacate here by noon tomorrow."

He nodded.

"Why don't you spend the weekend with Art or Larry," she suggested. "Less temptation if you're farther away. Plus, she can't find you if she doesn't know where you are. She did think that screwing you on the arcade pool table was a good idea, so she's definitely not right in the head regarding you yet."

Bin swallowed hard. "Neither am I."

Chapter 21

At The Manse

She shifted to the stand of trees by the church, looking for the best way to step out while leaving the fewest fresh prints in the snow. She didn't know if it mattered, but she was trying to keep things mundane and unnoticed. The church was large, at least two stories, and made of red bricks. It had a pointed steeple with a cross on top and bells that rang on Sundays. The manse sat well behind the church, a house made from the same red bricks as the church.

They said Pastor Jonathan had an office in the front of the house, so she looked that way. Nobody seemed to be out, and Oma's car was there, so she knocked and, after a moment, was let into Pastor Jonathan's office.

Olivia's parents weren't there yet, so they talked amongst themselves. Olivia asked if she'd seen Bin, and when she said she had, Olivia's face brightened, and she started talking about him.

Olivia didn't want to get pregnant until she was married and out of college, but she would try to get that way if she saw him today. That made her sad because they couldn't see each other.

Denae asked her to change the subject, and she immediately asked about what she would be learning this weekend, suddenly sounding her usual sharp self. Denae stammered, not having thought about it yet, and went with the earth bath. She explained how it can help center their minds and relax, something everyone could use after the last few days.

Olivia went a little pink on the concept of taking her clothes off, then looked Denae up and down and whispered, "That's already happened, hasn't it? You've already seen me with my clothes off."

She seemed more surprised by the words coming out of her mouth than by the implications it might have.

"I was almost naked under a sheet when I woke up, and they said you turned me into stone to stop me from…from…." She looked confused and blushed.

"Yeah. Not naked, but what you were wearing was pretty sheer." Olivia seemed relieved, and Denae didn't want to say more, thinking the memory was best suppressed. She was pleased that she was saved from more answers by a knock on the door.

Olivia's parents came into the office, followed by Cheryl. The bruising had faded but spread farther and was still apparent through her makeup. Denae looked them over well before glancing back at Olivia, who looked amused.

"What do you see?"

'Later,' Denae mouthed as Pastor Jonathan began introductions while Cheryl and their parents gave Olivia hugs. After introductions, Cheryl glaring over their handshake, Pastor Jonathan started the discussion.

Denae noticed each of the three showed a couple of empathy-style magic spells affecting them. Most likely, the spells made them more agreeable to whatever was discussed here. Aunt Issa probably met them when they drove in, and it was probably a good idea under the circumstances. This would be shocking to Olivia and her mundane family.

With Olivia distracted, Denae looked her over, only half-listening to Pastor Jonathan's opening remarks to the family. A blackness showed near the center of her aura where the thing had been removed. Her spark was the same, so it wasn't the entity but something else. Maybe it was some other family trait, like the Dassow streak. She perked up when Pastor Jonathan started getting to the meat of the issue and paid more attention to the discussion.

"Olivia had some sort of an entity or spirit inside her which had to be removed," he said. That caused the expected uproar and questions, which he patiently answered, along with Oma and Agatha speaking up occasionally.

When pressed to explain, Pastor Jonathan said, "I would say that a demon was exorcised from Olivia. Hannah has told me that neither term is accurate. However, for purposes of this discussion, we can use those terms to save confusion."

"Who put it there?" Cheryl seemed ready with questions while their parents were still trying to form them.

"My dear," said Oma. "That is a significant part of why we are having this discussion. We don't know, except she has had it for many years, possibly since shortly after birth." She looked at each of them and said, "It is also virtually unheard of in the New World and very rare even in the Old World."

Olivia's mom seemed to be trying to form words while her dad was wiping his glasses to give him a moment to think. Cheryl, however, leaned forward, asking, "Who found it?"

"Denae did," Olivia said, startling everyone in her family. They all stared at her, glancing between Olivia and Denae in a way that Denae found dizzying. "She saw it while I was looking at her, or at least she seemed upset about something about me." She looked at Denae. "Am I right?"

Denae nodded. That wasn't quite what dismayed her, but she did notice it then.

"How?" Cheryl looked puzzled.

"Certain people can learn how to see auras," Denae said. "It's an emanation that everybody gives off, but only a few can be taught to see it."

"Who taught you?"

"Nobody, I don't think," Olivia responded quickly. "I've done this as far as I can remember."

"I was asking Denae," Cheryl said, annoyed, "but you do that, too? That explains a lot."

"Same for me," Denae answered. "As long as I can remember."

"You used to ask me about colors you saw when you were little. Was that it?"

"When I realized you couldn't see them, I quit asking," Olivia said. "I only asked Mom and Dad a few times before I realized I was the only one who could see them."

"And then," Oma continued, "there are those even fewer people who could do this innately from when they were very young." She gestured to the corner where Denae and Olivia sat. "There are the only two living people I know who can claim that honor, and they are both in this room."

Denae stared at Olivia, who seemed thrilled by the accolade.

"Living?" It came out of Denae's mouth without her meaning it.

Oma smiled a tight smile. "Your great-grandfather."

"What was disturbing about this…this thing in …her aura?" Olivia's dad brought the discussion back, slipping his glasses back in place.

"Not disturbing at that point, but…out of place," Denae said, looking at Olivia. "It's definitely gone now."

"We think it was very small, probably dormant. It probably wasn't readily visible until recently," Oma explained. "At the same time, it was most likely attached before she was three."

Olivia's mom and dad looked at each other while Cheryl asked, "What was the catalyst then?"

"Binesi's streak," Olivia said.

"Bin had a streak of silver hair that ran through his blond hair," Denae explained to the family's confused looks.

"Had?" Olivia suddenly paled.

"It'll grow back," Denae stated.

"My fault?"

"Entirely," Denae agreed.

Olivia went very quiet.

It wasn't really her fault, Denae thought, but this was easiest right now, and she did blame Olivia for having to hurt her brother like that.

"This explains some things," her dad said into the quiet. "She loves to watch people, especially at the swimming pool. When I was stationed in Germany, she would run in…well, people are more relaxed about nudity there…and just look at people, young and old. She liked the old people more…there was more to see."

"We adopted her during his third tour in Germany," her mom said, "though her birth certificate says she was born in Czechoslovakia."

"Could I get a copy of that birth certificate?" Oma asked. "It could be very informative."

"Certainly," her dad said. "I'll Xerox it at the office tomorrow."

The discussion continued. Olivia stayed quiet now, except to answer a few questions quietly and tell her sister she only vaguely remembered hitting her and was so sorry. She looked at the others and apologized for everything before lingering on Denae and bursting into tears. She didn't cover her face but just sat there stiffly, tears rolling down her face.

Her mom turned quickly to take a hand, pulling her into her bosom, Cheryl sliding into the space between her and Denae. Her dad looked slightly chagrined but stood behind his family, looking down on Olivia. He took a protective position with a hand on his wife and another on Cheryl.

Denae smiled at this. Cheryl seemed different from what Leah said about her or her impression of why Olivia broke her nose. How much was the entity affecting her even then?

Family.

She wished that Leah had more of this and wondered what had happened.

After a couple of minutes, Olivia had dried up. She kept casting furtive glances at Denae but looked away whenever Denae glanced back. Everyone regained their seats, and Pastor Jonathan resumed, detailing the significance of what had happened and what would be happening with Olivia.

Their heads jerked to stare at Denae when Oma told them Olivia would be apprenticing under Denae. Denae smiled instead of yelling what she thought of the idea. Olivia reached over and took her hand, beaming.

Her dad came next to Denae, squatting to get eye-to-eye, and took her other hand. "You seem to be the hero of this tale, spotting Olivia's issue and taking charge to find out what it was. Then you got the experts," he glanced at the others, "to excise or exorcise it or whatever was needed." He squeezed her hand firmly. "Would you come join us for supper tonight?"

Denae jumped.

After stuttering a moment, she found her words. "No," she said. "Tonight is the four of you…just the four of you. I would be intruding." She couldn't stop herself from continuing. "This whole weekend should be just family. I shouldn't be interfering, but…," she looked at Oma, who smiled sadly at her, tiredness showing in her eyes. "But the others feel it best to start Olivia tomorrow evening, so I will."

Denae fought back tears. Why was she tearing up now?

More words were said, then everybody started hugging each other. A warm, hearty hug from Olivia's dad, a soft one from her mom, and a weird one from Cheryl, tight, warm, but with a sudden release.

Then Olivia hugged her, whispering, "Keep Binesi far away. If I think I can find him, I might not be able to keep myself from going after him."

Denae stiffened. Olivia's hug lessened for a second, then regained its hold.

"If he were in town, you could find him," she whispered.

"Yes," she said. "Bin gave me this a few weeks ago."

Olivia reached into her parka pocket and pulled out a beaded necklace that Denae recognized. She'd made it for him a couple of years ago, and he usually wore it. She hadn't noticed it was missing with all that had happened.

Denae grimaced, trying to turn it into a smile as she thought back, moving her hands to Olivia's shoulders. According to Binesi, it'd only been a little over a week ago when Olivia had started on his streak, so it was from his heart instead of this other thing.

"Yes, you could," she replied.

Denae suddenly realized everyone was looking at them. She fought the urge to drop her hands, squeezed Olivia's shoulders instead, and said, "Broodmare," a little more loudly than she intended. Olivia gave her a confused look, and she felt eyes turn to her.

"Bin said that to that thing, this entity, you were nothing more than a broodmare to his stud horse." She shook Olivia slightly. "You were nothing more than a womb to bring forth a child for reasons known only to it, but probably not for anything that would do you, Binesi, or any of us any good."

Olivia's eyes widened as she thought about it.

Denae continued with, "So think about that if you have any urges to go out and find Bin to fuck him." Her voice had gotten even louder, and in the echoing silence, she heard Olivia's mother gasp.

Good.

She hugged Olivia tightly and formed a trace in her head. It showed on Olivia like it had the braid.

She whispered harshly, "If you leave your house tonight, I will find you. You won't want me to find you," then released her.

Olivia looked stunned but nodded and tucked the necklace back away.

Pastor Jonathan started herding everyone out, though Denae sat down again, feeling tears in her eyes. Not again, as she fought them back.

A moment later, she felt eyes on her and looked up, seeing Oma and Agatha smiling down at her, and stood up quickly.

"You ready to leave?" Oma shrugged on her coat.

"I guess," Denae agreed, "but I think I'll walk. I have some things to do in town."

Oma nodded and looked at Agatha, who took Denae's hands in her gloved ones, smiling at her. "You have such a wonderful way of getting to the point of the matter."

Denae felt the color rise to her cheeks.

"That last was for her mother," she said.

"Oh, it got through." Agatha laughed, her weariness showing through the laugh. "I wouldn't be surprised if Patricia hogties Olivia to her bed after that."

Oma chuckled at that. "Well, if you're walking, we'll be leaving. It's been exhausting, so I'll have an early supper and go to bed."

Agatha nodded in agreement, dropped Denae's hands, and leaned heavily on her cane. Oma assisted her out.

Denae slipped on her coat and followed them, Pastor Jonathan patting her on the shoulder, then closed the door behind them.

↢↢⊙↣↣

Denae rounded the corner of the church to find Cheryl standing there. Cheryl advanced, grabbing her and pinning her against the building.

"You'd better not hurt my little sister," she growled.

Denae stared into Cheryl's eyes and lifted her about three inches off the ground, then swung her around so she hit her back on the building. She gasped, dropping her hands from Denae, and looked around in fear.

"She is so torn up inside right now you wouldn't believe it," Denae shouted. "She has been through so much, she might've died."

Denae realized she'd raised her fist to rebreak Cheryl's nose and dropped it, lowering Cheryl back to the ground, and watched her tremble.

"You saved her?" Her voice shook.

"I don't know about that," Denae said, looking down. "I did keep her from being that broodmare." She raised her eyes to see Cheryl looking at her, puzzlement growing.

"How?"

Denae closed her eyes, the scene playing in her head. She felt slightly sick.

"No," she said.

"She's my sister," Cheryl pleaded. "I can't help if I don't know."

Denae considered momentarily, then opened her eyes, pointing her finger in Cheryl's face. "If you ever tell her that you know this…if she ever finds out, I will hurt you…hurt you bad."

Cheryl tried to take a step back but hit the wall. She nodded.

"I don't think she remembers any of this. I hope to this God," Deane said, slapping the brick wall, making her hand sting, "and any others that might be around that she never remembers."

She felt her stomach shift.

"She'd walked to the house because the entity made her. She was fertile, and it controlled her completely. It had Binesi compliant, ready to be controlled. Once inside, we discovered she only had that long silk undershirt under her snowsuit."

Denae shifted uncomfortably, unease stirring inside her.

"She was standing at the staircase, waiting on Bin to come down and fuck her."

She saw the horror growing on Cheryl's face.

Denae swallowed. "I was cheering them on. I don't know what I was saying, but I was happy. It controlled me, too."

"Mom body-blocked me, and the pain freed my mind." She wiped her eyes, feeling her stomach churn. "I stopped Bin, put him away where he couldn't…. He had been so close to…." She took a deep breath, trying to finish before the inevitable happened.

"She…it charged me on all fours like some beast. I turned her into marble, but it still tried to get me, make me undo it all. I had to get out of the house to get away."

Then she felt it coming, turned away from Cheryl, tripped, caught herself with her hands, spewed all over the snow-covered sidewalk, and then again. She gasped for breath, at least not feeling the sobs she feared would follow. As she caught her breath, she felt a hand on her back, rubbing up and down.

"Done?"

Denae nodded, a bit of puke dripping off her upper lip. Cheryl helped her sit and wiped her mouth with the end of her scarf.

Cheryl was wiping the splatter from the sleeves of Denae's coat when Denae said, "You're getting it dirty," trying to pull her sleeve away.

"It'll wash," Cheryl said, hanging on to the sleeve. "What happened to Bin…Binesi's hair?"

"No," Denae said. "I can't go there…not now."

Her hands began shaking at the memory, the screams.

"Fair enough," Cheryl agreed. "Some other time."

"I need something to cut his hair," Denae continued. "Something battery-operated…no electricity where he's at…buzz-cut."

Cheryl nodded.

Denae started to get up, but Cheryl put a hand on her shoulder.

"You okay to get up."

"I think so," Denae replied, and Cheryl pulled her up and steadied her.

As they walked, Cheryl said, "Try the dime store…maybe a beard trimmer would use batteries. Otherwise, use a razor and shaving cream and shave his head."

"I don't know," Denae mused. "I'd probably cut him. I've never used one."

"Not on your legs?" Cheryl stared at her. "Your pits?"

"No," she replied and explained. "I've never…well…felt the need."

"That's a little…weird," Cheryl said, looking away.

"I'm a little weird," Denae said, bringing a chuckle out of Cheryl, then continued before Cheryl could comment. "Speaking of weird people, could you be nicer to Leah?"

Cheryl stopped and looked at Denae. "I'm mean to her?"

"You and your friends do things to her. Call her names," Denae said, staring into her face.

"Yeah, yeah, yeah," Cheryl said, hitting her hand against her coat. She took a deep breath. "I haven't thought about it. I guess we've done it for so long, it's become a habit," she continued. "God, that sounds awful. I can't vouch for my friends, but I will try to stop. We used to be friends. She went her way, and I went mine. I don't dislike her…I don't know, but I'll try."

"Good," Denae said and started walking again, Cheryl easily keeping in step with her longer stride. They were quiet for a couple of minutes.

"Does Olivia find things very often?"

"Oh yeah," Cheryl answered. "Misplace something, and Olivia will find it for you."

"Really?"

"Last winter," Cheryl continued. "The neighbor's three-year-old boy was lost…fell through a crusty snowdrift and couldn't get out. Olivia went straight to him, under that snow, and pulled him out like she'd put him there. It seems like…can you do that?"

"Yes, but I had to be taught," Denae said. "I didn't have to be taught to levitate, though."

"Daniel's been right all these years," Cheryl said.

"Yes, but please don't tell him. That was my mistake when I was seven. I've never really lived it down. You're practically family now, so don't say anything about this to anyone."

"Family?" Cheryl sounded shocked.

"Olivia is my apprentice, apprenticed as a part of my rather extended family," Denae said, smiling. "You are her family. Ergo, you are now, in some ways, part of our family."

Cheryl thought about it for a moment. "That's a different way of thinking about things. What does this apprentice thing mean?"

"Usually, you apprentice to your parents, but that's impossible here. For reasons I don't understand, they decided that she should be apprenticed to me, and no, I don't know what I'll be doing this weekend since I just found out about it. In general, I'll assess Olivia and decide what she needs to learn, when, and in what order. She has some serious innate affinities and abilities. Until very recently, I was the only one I knew who could do auras innately. I don't know anyone who can seek and search innately, but then I'm the only one who can levitate innately, so go figure."

Cheryl looked like she was trying to form her next question.

"We have family members who teach different areas. Most of us specialize in only one or two areas. I started younger than most, so I have more abilities than cousins my age, but I'm sure I'll be handing Olivia off to some of my aunts and uncles to learn more. I'm just not sure of the details yet…and no, I don't know of any way you could learn any of this."

Cheryl gave her a sheepish grin. "I didn't think so, but I was going to ask anyway. Did you read my mind?"

"No," Denae said with a smile. "It was written all over your face."

Cheryl chuckled as they continued walking.

Denae pointed toward downtown. "I'm heading there," she said.

"And I need to give someone a hug," nodding her head to the left.

"Lots of hugs," Denae corrected.

"You betcha," Cheryl said and waved.

Denae waved back and walked on to town. She wondered what would've happened if they'd been able to train Olivia from when she was younger. She also wondered how Olivia had even come up for adoption. That entity had been put into her for a reason.

Denae doubted that her birth parents or whoever actually put the entity there would have wanted to give her up. Things came to mind, but they all ended up with Olivia becoming an orphan and somehow abandoned.

Denae shook her head and sighed as she got to the edge of downtown. She wondered how long it would take for Olivia to come to that same conclusion.

Chapter 22

At The Warehouse

Denae found a battery-operated beard trimmer she thought would work well enough, then went to Fred's for supper. She wasn't ready to face home yet, or even the tipi. She hoped Leah would be working and was pleased to see she was. Denae sat in her section, seeing Leah's face light up when she saw her there.

Leah took her order and plopped down after delivering it. "Are you okay?"

Denae told her briefly about the last 72 hours, covering mainly the final success and what this weekend would entail. It seemed like a quiet night at the diner, with nobody sitting nearby.

"That blows any chance of us getting together," Leah said, patting Denae's hand in sympathy.

Denae had no appetite, pushing her food around more than she ate it. She glanced at her right hand, pale compared to the tan of her left, and shook her head. The tan would return once it warmed up to where she wasn't wearing gloves outside.

Leah came back and looked at the plate. "I guess dessert is out of the question."

Denae nodded.

Leah left again, coming back a few minutes later.

"Give me the check, I guess," Denae said. "Just not that hungry."

Leah cleared the table and had her coat on when she returned. At Denae's questioning look, she said, "Your check is covered, and since it's a quiet night, I can take off the rest of the evening. The only question is where to go. You need to talk."

Denae's mind whirred, trying to get into gear. "The warehouse should be empty," she said, and Leah's face lit up.

↢↢⊙↣↣

Inside the fenced-in warehouse courtyard, they stood at the door. A light was on over the back door and others around the outside, but the inside was dark.

Leah asked, "Key?"

"Don't need one," Denae said, shifting inside the building by the door. She turned off the magical and mundane security before letting Leah in. Her mom was the only one who might come through that door, and even that was unlikely this late. And if she did...well...she probably wouldn't be too shocked, or at least Denae hoped she wouldn't. Leah might not realize it, but Denae didn't need to talk nearly as much as she wanted to be held.

Leah looked in awe at the shelves of bottles, jars, pelts, and pouches as they walked hand-in-hand to the break area. There were stacks of folded boxes of all sizes, bins of packing peanuts, rolls of brown wrapping paper, and bubble wrap. She'd seen the office in the front and passed the loading area at the back of the building.

They went past a thick steel door and into a kitchen area where a couple of bunks were folded against the wall. Denae unlatched and lowered the bunk down.

"We have these and some cots in case we get snowed in."

Leah nodded, then looked back into the warehouse area.

"That's a lot of stuff. I had no idea."

"This is the main family business, which means all the family."

"Everyone contributes items here?"

"Most everyone. My mom runs it, so she rarely makes anything, and Aunt Gaia runs the library, so she doesn't need to, but she does a few things anyway. Oma takes care of our injuries and ailments and makes many healing draughts and salves. Everyone has a job. I've worked here for years, as have all the bubs. I've even made a few salves that were sales-worthy. I haven't learned enough about the various draughts yet to begin making them, but someday I might. Other aunts and uncles will help, generally part-time, and many also teach. I guess I'll be earning money this weekend for teaching Olivia. I hadn't even thought about that. That means I should try to do a good job introducing her to all this. I want to, but I don't have a clue."

Denae slumped down to the bunk. Leah put an arm around her and pulled her close. "You've been doing it all your life and said you've taught some kids the basics. It shouldn't be that hard."

"I'm scared."

"Of teaching Olivia?"

"Of being alone with Olivia. It should be okay, but that entity controlled me. It…she was in my dreams. It was a totally different sort of nightmare."

"But you said that Olivia's okay now."

"She remembers very little, and that's a good thing. She's been hurt enough without knowing that. It's better that she's confused and concerned."

"So, it'll be okay?"

"Yeah. It's me…I'm not. I'm so scared it'll come."

"Like the bear?"

Denae stared at her.

"Your nightmares about the bear. It's chasing you. You didn't run from it when it was real. I think you're afraid of it coming back, and now you're afraid of the same thing with this green entity thing. Didn't you say your aunt had it all locked up and magically secured?"

"Yeah, she does."

"Then you're safe, and I'll keep you safe here."

↢↢⊙↣↣

Denae opened her eyes, wondering where she was. It took her a moment to focus, realizing it was Leah. She was at the shop.

A gentle caress across her shoulder blades. "Back with the living, I see," Leah said quietly.

"I slept," Denae croaked, her mouth dry.

"You drool," she said, amusement in her voice.

Denae lifted her head, cheek peeling away from Leah's chest. "How much time," she said, working her mouth to get spit in it.

"It doesn't matter," she said, stroking Denae's head. "That was amazing, by the way."

"What," Denae said. "Oh." She pushed up to look at her better. She was smiling.

"That's assuming you didn't injure yourself," Leah said.

Denae thought, flexed, and shifted a little. "No," she said. "I don't think so, but I may be sore tomorrow." She looked back down at Leah.

"That was seriously intense." She brought both hands up, caressing Denae's cheeks. "And the sobs, those came from deep inside you…deep. I think you fell asleep before you quit crying."

Denae nodded, then brought her hand slowly down Leah's stomach.

"Denae, please," she pleaded. "I need to go home, and if you do that, I'll never leave."

Denae slid her hand lower before stopping. "What time is it?"

"Almost ten," Leah replied.

"You're in trouble," Denae said. "My fault."

"It was worth it," Leah said. "Every minute of it…including the drool. I might get away with telling Mom it was a messy closing."

She chuckled as she sorted through the clothes on the ground, tossing her panties on the bed but ignoring them as she dressed and finally wadding them up in her coat pocket.

Denae lay on the bed, feeling the chill air in the shop but not bothering to get her clothes. As Leah finished dressing, Denae got up and kissed her, then stopped her at the door to kiss again hard and long. She resisted the urge to drag her back, securing the door once Leah went out, and waited until the gate latch clicked. Denae folded the bunk up before pulling on her coat. She put her boots on and threw her clothes over her arm, ensuring the trimmer was secure in her coat pocket.

She knew her destination was the tipi, but she had a couple of stops first. She shifted beside Fred's, moving to the corner to watch Leah walk past, listening to the crunching footsteps recede in the distance. She hoped this trimmer would cut a full head of hair on the one set of batteries and wouldn't break partway through.

She jumped again, near Leah's house, moving to a dark spot where she could see Leah come up to the house. Once she went in, yelling started from her mom and Leah.

Denae wanted to go in but knew nothing she could do would help. Leah would have to handle this on her own.

She double-checked the lump in her pocket and sighed. She'd never cut anyone's hair besides her own. That was only when she had wanted it all gone, and she'd botched that badly. She hoped the trimmers would work better than scissors, took a breath, and shifted.

↢↢⊙↣↣

Denae sat at home waiting for time to pass when she heard the phone ring in the office. Dad was probably a hundred miles away with Bin.

The trimmer had worked well. She couldn't do anything about the pale, newly healed skin on his face, but the blond stubble was practically invisible compared to where it was burned away.

Mom was off with Oma to pick up Olivia for the weekend. She and Olivia would be skiing to the tipi from Oma's. Mom wasn't ready to have Olivia back at the house after the last time. Denae had cleaned up the tipi and packed it with food and drink for the weekend. Everything was as ready as she could make it, she hoped, as she went into the office to answer the phone.

It was Leah. She rarely called, so her mom must not be home. "What did you do to Cheryl?"

"What do you mean?"

"One of her friends said something snide to me at lunch, and Cheryl told her off, then said she was sitting with me instead, so the other two went off in a huff," she said, amusement in her voice. "Did the same with her jock boyfriend, saying he was an asshole."

"Good."

"Good?" Leah laughed. "What body parts did you threaten to remove?"

"None," Denae said seriously. "I asked nicely. Really."

"If you say so," Leah said, not convinced. "We had an interesting talk, especially since she didn't know I knew about this weekend or the stuff about Olivia."

"You didn't tell her you knew?"

"I asked how Olivia was," she replied. "I was concerned…I like her, but of course, Cheryl didn't know that."

"Oh," Denae said. "So, how much does she know?"

"Enough," Leah said. "She knows that I know about you and your family. I didn't mean to, but I hope that's okay…since she already knows."

"Sure," Denae said, rolling her eyes. "Why not…." She let that thought drop away. "How much trouble are you in?"

"For last night?" There was a smile in her voice. "Not as much as she'd like. The messy closing worked, but she didn't like my attitude, so she grounded me for that." She laughed before continuing.

"When you told me of your weekend plans, I swapped with Renee, so I'm working both shifts on Saturday. I was working Sunday anyway, so I'm grounded, and I'll have to stay home the rest of the time and read or something. Some punishment, eh?"

Denae laughed. "Next weekend?"

How's this apprenticeship going to work?"

"There is that," Denae said slowly. "Not sure, but with Olivia in school during the week, it may interfere with any weekend plans."

"There is the shop now, isn't there…the warehouse, but a nice enough place." She paused. "Did you put the bed back?"

"Yeah," Denae replied. "Not sure I tidied up enough."

"You want your mom to know?"

"No," Denae answered, "but she'll figure it out in time if we keep going there."

"But until then," Leah said, "go make sure it's tidy."

"I will," Denae assured her. "When Mom sends for me, I can jump from there almost as easily as here."

"Good," she said. "I'm glad we went there last night. You needed it so badly."

"So did you," Denae countered.

"No, I didn't," Leah said, "but that doesn't mean I didn't want it." She paused. "I have to go. My mother just pulled up. Bye." Denae heard the smack of a kiss, then a click.

Denae hung up and gathered her snowsuit, skis, poles, and backpack when the phone rang again. Sighing, Denae piled everything back and answered the phone again.

"Denae?"

It was Cheryl.

"Yes," Denae replied.

"What's with you and Leah?"

"What do you mean?"

"How did you meet?"

"At Fred's and the arcade."

"And she knows about you."

"Yeah. I let some things slip, and she figured it out."

"Okay," Cheryl drawled out. "Olivia swears she and Bin haven't done anything much more than kiss."

"That's my understanding," Denae said, annoyed.

"How do you know for certain?"

"Why do you think she isn't?"

"I got up in the middle of the night last week and heard noises coming from her room," Cheryl began. "The things she was saying, how she was moving, and she said Bin's name over and over. It scared me. It sounded like he was in the room with her."

"It should have," Denae said. "That thing was in her dreams and Bin's as well. It was setting the stage for last Wednesday night."

"And you know this how?" Cheryl's voice had gone shrill.

"I was in a couple of them," Denae yelled, "and I'm more afraid of what I may wake up to in the middle of the night than you need to be of what I might do to your sister."

There was breathing on the other end for several seconds, then an "Oh." Then more breaths. "I'm sorry," she said. "I'm so scared for her."

"So am I," Denae said, still loud.

"Listen," Cheryl said, quieter but still agitated. "She's scared to death about this weekend."

"Then she's not alone," Denae said, but in a more normal voice.

"Your mom and Hanna just arrived," she announced. "I need to go see Olivia off. This is all so very weird." Then there was a click.

Denae hung up, sagging against the desk. She hoped this weekend would be relatively quiet and that Olivia would indeed be Olivia, whatever that meant. She'd only ever talked to her a few times at the arcade when Olivia was entirely herself, so she really didn't know Olivia at all. She gathered up her gear and landed in front of the shop door. It was locked, so she took the slight shift inside after knocking as much snow off her boots as possible.

She set the gear by the door, pulled off her boots, returned to the break area, and dropped the bunk down. She plopped down and pulled the sleeping bag over her. Leah's scent was still on it. She held it tightly for a while before folding everything up and latching it in place. She wondered if it mattered, if her mom already knew what was going on between them, and if they'd think of this place to meet to avoid Leah's mom. Mom couldn't mind-read like Bin or Aunt Issa, but she always seemed to understand what was happening, sometimes better than Denae did herself.

Denae debated about going early to Oma's and visiting with Oma-ma but decided on solitude instead. For the first time, she tried to formulate what she should be doing with Olivia this weekend…work on how to begin training Olivia rather than letting her fears run free as to what Olivia might do to her.

Chapter 23

History Lesson

Denae grabbed the gear and was at Oma's within a minute of her mom's contact, long before they pulled in. She had the skis and poles leaned against a shed wall, ready to head to the tipi. Maybe she'd build a kiosk for Oma a little down the trail once the snow melted.

As they exited the car, Oma told Olivia not to worry and that she would be in good hands.

Denae realized she'd never even been alone with Olivia except for those brief times she had interrogated her. Olivia looked worried but flashed a quick smile at Denae as she approached.

Mom dropped her smile when Olivia turned away, looking instead at Denae. Denae flashed a smile at Olivia she hoped didn't look like a grimace. Maybe not, she thought, since Olivia brightened afterward.

Oma watched them as they started putting on the skis. "Back here around three on Sunday," she said. "Your mom will take Olivia back home then."

Denae nodded. They'd been over all of this.

"Olivia's mom seems much more reasonable about the lack of communication over the weekend," Mom said. "Despite some probable snow this weekend, I doubt I'll need to contact you."

Denae nodded again.

"Still, I'm going to look into getting some of those walkie-talkie radio things so you can contact us if you need to."

"Mom," Denae said. "We'll be okay."

She saw Olivia's head bobbing in agreement.

"Not for this weekend, but for the future," she said.

"If you have to," Denae agreed. Now that her mom had this idea, she was sure it would happen. "Lots of batteries, then. We have problems keeping batteries for the boomboxes, and I'm sure those walkie-talkie radios use much smaller batteries."

"Denae," Oma said. "This is all very new to Olivia, so if things get too intense, bring her back here."

"I will," Denae said, and at the concern showing on Olivia's face, "I'll keep her safe."

She smiled at Olivia, who smiled back shyly. And who's going to keep me safe from her, Denae thought, flashes of the past week popping in her head uninvited. Almost two full days and nights with her…it should be okay, but what if it wasn't?

And why was Mom so quiet? She didn't give any coaching or anything, and that's not like her. She saw Mom glance nervously at Oma as they grabbed their poles, but Oma only smiled. Denae sighed and smiled faintly at Oma, who nodded. This was going to be one of those learning experiences for Mom, letting me go off alone with a girl who'd caused them a lot of pain and suffering…what…two days ago.

Then they said their goodbyes and were off down the snowy track. Denae had Olivia take the lead. There weren't many side paths until this merged with the trail to her tipi.

Olivia skied well and not so fast that Denae had problems. It didn't take long to make the half-mile to the merge, then left and a few hundred yards to the tipi. The light was fading when they got there, but Olivia gaped at it. "It's gotta be twenty feet tall," she said.

"More, but about that in diameter," Denae replied.

"You could live here. When they said we were staying in something you'd built out here, I wasn't expecting this." Olivia touched the side of the tipi. "What's it made out of?"

"Stone," Denae answered. "I used a white granite. I was trying to do it with limestone and marble but had problems with those."

"How…what?" She stared at Denae. "How would you even…I guess I'll be learning about that, huh?"

"In an abstract way to begin with, but possibly more hands-on, if you have a talent for it, and if not, then you'll be doing other things."

Olivia looked around.

"You and Binesi left here this morning." There was a longing in her voice as she looked down the trail toward home. "He's been up and down this a few times, and…you and Leah on a snowmobile?"

Denae nodded, feeling stunned. Closing her eyes, she sighed, trying to remember if anything had happened between her and Leah inside the tipi before Mom had called them in—nothing that came to mind…all that was later.

"You didn't stay long?" Olivia looked perplexed, but it was a reasonable question.

"Leah's mom is not reasonable," Denae groaned. "As Leah said, she can be a real controlling bitch, and that was no exception. The blizzard hit before we got home, and I had to use a good bit of magic to get us home alive."

Olivia opened her mouth in a silent 'Oh,' then started looking back along the way they had come.

Denae said, "You can follow our trail tomorrow since you do history." At her look, Denae continued, "I want to know what all you can already do, but for now, let's get inside and get comfortable."

This was something else new, Denae thought. I can view the past, but she sees history innately, like her aura and seeking. She will be good at the knowledges, or rather, she's already good at them. She needs to be taught the understanding of how she does these things.

"How far back can you see?"

"Days, even a few weeks, I guess," she replied. "I can go back a little more, but I have to concentrate, and it gets hard to see anything." She'd started looking around inside as she unzipped her parka.

"Can you turn it off?"

The irritation must've shown in her voice as Olivia looked at her with surprise.

"It's hard to keep it off," she said, apology in her voice. "It can be annoying at times, but once I've seen a person or a place, I can usually shut that off with no problem."

She reddened slightly. "Some people don't trust me because I've let slip things I shouldn't have known."

She looked at Denae.

"You have secrets here you don't want me to know?"

"Not really, but it is my place of solitude."

Denae stripped off to her silk longjohns, finding Olivia watching her constantly as she followed Denae's lead. "What?"

"This is your comfortable?"

"No, but it'll do for now." She smiled at Olivia's confusion. Keep it slow and easy, Denae thought. "Can you keep from looking around while you're here?" She was pretty sure of the answer as they each removed their socks.

Olivia shook her head.

"Leah and I had gotten comfortable, me more than her, so don't be embarrassed by any of that."

Olivia looked around, her eyes widening. "You're—"

"Comfortable," Denae finished with a laugh.

Olivia turned as she continued, "Am I supposed to get that…comfortable? I'm not…." She jumped back, a hand going to her mouth. "No," she wailed, then turned her head to the left. "Nooo!" The scream reverberated through the tipi as she dropped to her knees sobbing.

Denae dropped next to her, realizing what had triggered this. She'd been thinking about Leah coming in and forgot about the rest…blocked it from her mind. Stupid.

Amid the sobs now wracking her body, Denae heard occasional words. "Hand…burn…Bin…face…my…fault." Denae rubbed her arm and back, trying to give solace.

After a few minutes, the words had gone away, but pulsing sobs continued unabated. Denae gave up rubbing and grabbed Olivia by her ponytail.

"Get up," Denae shouted, pulling her to her feet but still bent over.

Doubled over would work, and Denae guided her to the opening and out. She pushed Olivia into a snowdrift and fell with her, driving her farther into the snow.

She began coughing, so Denae climbed out, grabbed Olivia by the waist, and yanked. Snow in the mouth, up the nose, or both, Denae wondered with grim satisfaction. Olivia wasn't at fault for what happened there, but this was some small measure of payback for having to push a burning log into Bin's face. After several attempts, she pulled Olivia out.

Olivia stood up and looked at Denae, snow-reddened face scratched, looking forlornly waif-like, stray hairs wet and stuck to her cheek. She turned to face the dark trail and started walking.

"Stop," Denae said, but Olivia continued down the trail.

Denae stepped up and grabbed Olivia's ponytail again. "I will put you in another snowdrift if you don't stop."

"Whatever," Olivia said slowly, but she stopped. "I'll just stay out here so you don't have to see me."

Denae yanked, pulling her backward into another drift, then straddled her.

"You will go back into the tipi," Denae said.

"Why," Olivia countered. "You hate me."

"If I hated you, you wouldn't be here."

"You should hate me," she said. "I…I…." She waved her arm in the general direction of the tipi. "I made you burn yourself, burn Bin, and God only knows what else."

"A lot of 'what else.'" Denae pulled snow over Olivia, dumping it onto her chest and pressing it in. "But it wasn't you. It was that thing in you."

Olivia's face screwed up again.

"If you start crying again, I'm going to knock this entire drift on top of you, pull you out by your ankles, and throw you back in over and over until I start to feel better." Denae stopped to catch her breath as Olivia fought a losing battle against the tears. Denae knocked an arm's worth of snow on Olivia.

"I don't hate you. I don't even dislike you." Denae shoved a handful of snow down inside Olivia's waistband. "I hate that thing that was in you," she continued. "I hate what it did to you."

Another handful of snow, this time up under the long undershirt. "I especially hate how it took over Bin." She pushed the shirt up again, sweeping an armful of snow onto Olivia's belly. "And me."

She kept sweeping snow down on Olivia, pushing more into her pants. "It's not your fault at all. I'm doing this to you because I can, and it's not making me feel any better."

The tears came in a rush.

Olivia pushed through the snow to sit up and held her while they both cried.

After a minute, Olivia said in a weak, shivery voice, "Can we go back inside? You'll have to answer to Binesi if you freeze off any important parts."

Denae pushed herself up and helped Olivia stand. She started laughing at her snow-stuffed pants despite her chattering teeth.

"Your plan worked if you wanted me to be as comfortable as you like," Olivia said, joining in. "I'm going to have to take these off before I go in."

"Well, at least something worked," Denae said, pushing her back toward the tipi. "You okay?"

Olivia shrugged. "You?"

"No," said Denae quietly, watching Olivia waddle back to the opening. "Not yet."

↢↢⊙↣↣

As Denae started dinner, Olivia idly pushed a stick in and out of the coals, a blanket over her shoulders. Denae reached over and pressed her hand on Olivia's belly.

Olivia jumped.

"Why'd you do that?"

"Checking your core temperature," Denae answered. "You're fine."

"Aren't there other places to check that?"

"Yeah, but I'll save the best one for Binesi." Denae flashed a wicked smile that caused Olivia to blush, and they fell silent for a few minutes.

"I…it caused Bin to dream of me? To dream of us…uh…doing it." She was still blushing but looked determined. "I remember dreams with him, but not going…that far."

"He does," Denae said, "so when the time comes, he may be more aware of things about you than you expect." She looked at the skillet and stirred. "His awareness may be wrong," she continued, "so if he does things you don't want to do, stop him."

"And I was…." She looked worried. "You, too?"

"Stop," Denae said. "I shouldn't have said that. You don't want that memory."

"But I…." Olivia stopped, Denae holding her hand up.

"I'll do anything that will help," Olivia continued.

"Tell that to Bin," Denae retorted. "But talk to Oma before then. We don't want you pregnant at fifteen."

"I'm sixteen," Olivia said, nostrils flaring. "My birthday was in December. I'm going to take my driver's license test next week."

"Which means..." Denae tossed Olivia's blanket back and pinched her nipple hard, "you'll still be sixteen when a baby's sucking on this, and Bin won't be seventeen yet, either."

Olivia glared at Denae while she grabbed her blanket and pulled it close. "I don't want that until I graduate college," Olivia replied. "Can we talk about something else?"

↢↢⊙↣↣

They did manage to talk about other things, in fits and starts, as Denae finished cooking supper. After they ate, Denae pulled the mat aside, uncovering the earth as Olivia watched with interest.

"Bin was lying on top of you there?" Olivia was trying to make it sound casual but didn't manage it. Binesi didn't know about Olivia's history ability, so he wouldn't expect her to be familiar with him naked, except maybe from those dreams.

"Yeah," Denae agreed. "His idea…he came up with it this morning, so we tried it. Me on the bottom, then a layer of earth, him on top so he doesn't get chilled." She gestured at the area.

"I generally lie in the earth…I can sleep there all night and feel good. Most everyone else is done after about fifteen minutes." She ran a hand rake through the area, though it was still pretty loose. "It seems to help them some, but not like me. The cool earth saps their body heat, especially this time of year. Not me, though. I draw warmth from it."

She shrugged as she set the rake aside.

"Bin wondered if I could transfer the centering to him if we switched places, with him on top, so we did. I thought he wanted to do this because I'd keep the cold away from him, but it did seem to work better."

"It looks weird."

"It felt weird," Denae agreed. "but I felt the earth centering begin to flow, and he did, too. We lay there at least an hour, and he felt much better when we left."

Olivia nodded. "Someone else has been here…longer back. Over a month ago," she said, focusing near her feet. "Hard to see…shorter but broader than Binesi, dark hair." She colored slightly at that.

"That's Jude," Denae said.

"Your older brother?"

"Yeah, next older than me."

Olivia pulled her blanket tighter and looked at the opening. "So, where is he?"

"U of W Milwaukee," Denae said, "doing something interdisciplinary studies combining anthropology, philosophy, and sociology to understand the different mythologies of the world, or that's the plan, which goes into graduate degrees, but he's only in his sophomore year."

"Oh." She blinked. "He could walk in here any time?"

"He's in Milwaukee," Denae responded, "so not likely."

"But it's possible?"

"And if so, he'll see your nice, pert breasts," Denae said, letting her blanket drop. "He'll see them sooner or later anyway."

"What!" Olivia pulled her blanket tighter.

"Lesson time," Denae said louder. "We have ceremonies, some periodic, others called when needed. At most of these, we go sky-clad, dressed in nothing but the stars and sky. Wards are set to keep the temps at least somewhat comfortable."

Olivia's hand went to her mouth.

"Everyone in our family is naked," Denae continued, ignoring Olivia's look, "from potty-trained toddlers to Oma-ma, with her boobs hanging past her navel. It's not a big deal…you'd be the weird one if you weren't naked."

Olivia didn't look convinced, so Denae continued. "My mom came from a different family, and they don't do sky-clad. She was freaked like you are, standing naked for the first time at Ceremony in front of her soon-to-be-husband's family. She did it and realized within a couple of minutes that nobody cared. After that, she was okay with it. When you drop your robe, nobody will notice."

"Bin won't notice?" Olivia looked a little disappointed.

"He'll notice but won't say anything to you until later. If he doesn't say you have the best breasts and butt, kick him in the balls."

Olivia giggled.

"So drop your blanket," Denae said. "Might as well practice."

"I…," she said, "I…."

"I helped you get out of your Frosty the Snowman costume," Denae said. "I was a lot more up-close and personal than I am now, and," she glanced over at the area of earth, "we're going to be much more than that in a few minutes, so get up without the blanket and stretch."

Olivia looked Denae in the eye and stood up, letting the blanket fall. She spread her arms out and slowly turned in place, making eye contact again near the end of the turn. She turned again faster using two steps, then quickly on her big toe several more times, regaining eye contact each time before stopping. She stopped, staring at Denae, who applauded.

"I forgot Bin said you were a dancer."

Olivia flushed, then said, "I…uh…need to pee. Do I need to go outside?"

"Behind the sheet back there." Denae saw Olivia brighten. "Don't get too excited. It's only a slit trench, it's chillier in there, and if you fart, I'll definitely hear it."

↢↢⊙↣↣

Denae was standing by the area of dirt when Olivia came back. "Grab your blanket and come on over," Denae said. As Olivia returned, Denae dropped and laid face-down, calling a thin layer of earth to move over her. "Lay down, your feet inside my arches, hands on my hands, and my head as your pillow." Olivia hesitated, then moved forward, dropping down above Denae, slowly easing herself down, placing her hands and feet as Denae had said.

Denae could hear her rapid breathing. After several seconds, she could feel Olivia's heart racing. "You okay?"

"I don't know," Olivia said. "I'm…scared." Denae could feel her entire body trembling.

"It's just me…nothing to get worried about," Denae coached. "Just take deep, slow breaths."

Her breaths weren't deep, and they weren't slow, but they did begin to slacken. Denae seemed able to relax more than she'd thought possible with Olivia so close. The earth helped, but she was in control, not Olivia. The tenseness seemed to leave, little by little. The trembling had stopped, and the breathing was slowing.

"Better?"

"A little," Olivia conceded. "I'm still working on my breathing."

"You can cover up with the blanket if you get chilly."

"Ummm…I think I'm okay right now."

Olivia's breathing continued to slow until Denae could match it and felt the earth rise into her. She heard a slight gasp by her ear, and Olivia melted into her as she drifted further.

↢ ↢ ⊙ ↣ ↣

Denae woke, noticing the glow of the coals had lessened a good bit. How long…how many hours, she wondered. She felt Olivia stir as she came fully awake. Much better, she thought. Hopefully….

Olivia pushed up, and Denae turned under her. "Feeling any better?"

"Oh," Olivia seemed disconcerted to see Denae's face inches from hers, "un…yeah. Yes, I do." She sat up and rubbed her stomach. "It doesn't hurt as much."

"Hurt as much?"

"Where they ripped that thing out," she said. "It hurts, but not as bad now. It's healing or something."

"Lay back."

Olivia did, and Denae waved the dirt off both of them, then leaned over and looked at her aura. There was some emptiness she could see better now than earlier. "Yeah, I see it."

"And," Olivia said after a breath.

"It's an opening, emptiness, something like that, and I think it's smaller than when we were at the manse, though I couldn't see it as well with your clothes on. I'll look at it again on Sunday and see if there are any changes. And ask Aunt Gaia about it during the week."

Denae looked up through the tipi's smoke hole. "It's still dark. I'll throw some wood on the fire and get it going, and then we'll roll up in some blankets and go back to sleep for a while."

"I…," Olivia began. "Okay, that sounds good."

Denae placed a few pieces of wood on the coals, watching them slowly catch, then moved over to the area piled up with blankets and quilts near where Olivia had covered up.

"I had horrible dreams the night before," Olivia said. "Cheryl slept with me most of the night. Will you sleep with me?"

Denae slid next to Olivia, pulling a blanket over herself and sliding an arm around Olivia, who took her hand and held it. After a moment, Olivia said, "Where am I?"

"Safe," Denae responded. "I have you, so you're safe." At least, Denae hoped that was the case.

Chapter 24

Blood

As Saturday morning progressed, Denae noted that Olivia seemed more comfortable and relaxed, even though she still wore nothing more than a blanket. They'd do another round with an earth bath later with Olivia on top. Binesi seemed to have gotten that one just about perfect, but there were other things she'd come up with for today. She was ready to face the bear, so to speak, plus some of the basics that Olivia should know about.

Denae told her some of the foundations of the magic she did, explaining the basis for what Olivia learned by instinct. She told Olivia about the many different areas of learning and how a personal affinity could affect your ability to work in those spheres of influence, like weather or fire. As she talked about health and healing, she brought out a small jar of salve.

"This is a salve of healing," Denae said. "I made several of these a few months ago as I got more comfortable with the area of alchemy, though I haven't progressed much past that yet." Olivia picked up the jar, looked at it with her sight, then opened it.

"You gave some of this to Leah in a Carmex jar."

"We all carry one to handle cuts, scrapes, and burns. There are other kinds of salves, but these are easy to make relative to most salves and draughts."

"How much will one fix?"

"A fair amount of cuts and scratches," Denae said, taking the jar. "Lean back on your hands a bit while I grab something."

As Olivia settled back and the blanket slipped off, Denae turned, grabbed her knife, and swung it in an upward arc. The blade slashed Olivia left-to-right across her ribcage and sternum into the lower part of her opposite breast. She then quickly set the knife back down behind her.

Olivia's eyes went wide as she followed the bloody trail of the knife, then to the blood flowing down to her stomach. She gave Denae a shocked look of betrayal as she pushed herself upright. "You…you…you…."

Denae saw her go pale and caught her, laying her down as she went limp before grabbing a towel to staunch the bleeding. "Well, that went well," she muttered to herself.

Olivia stirred a moment later. Denae continued mopping her face with a cool rag. "You…," Olivia started after her eyes fluttered open.

"I laid you open," Denae said.

Olivia pushed herself up, saw the bloody towel on her, lost the little color she'd regained, and dropped back down.

Denae slapped her cheek lightly. "Don't pass out again," she said. "If you can't stay awake, you can't heal yourself."

Olivia stared at Denae a little bit, eyes seeming to go out of focus before coming back. Understanding started to show in her eyes, along with a wariness.

Denae shifted around and pulled Olivia to a close sitting position, working on an idea that had just struck her. She grabbed her knife and put it into Olivia's unresisting hand, then brought it to her breast where it would match Olivia's cut breast. "Cut me here," she said. "About three inches or so will do."

Olivia stared at her, shaking her head.

"The knife's very sharp, so it won't hurt hardly at all," she lied, pressing it into Olivia's hand. Something about being cut with her Dassow-made blade hurt a lot more than a regular kitchen knife.

She gasped as she guided Olivia's hand, a searing pain erupting as it sliced in and downward on her breast toward her sternum. She took the knife back and set it down behind her as she felt warmth flow down her chest. She then patted Olivia's face again.

"Stay with me."

Olivia slowly nodded as Denae pulled them together so the blood would mingle.

"Repeat after me," Denae said. "I am the master. You are my apprentice."

"You are the master," Olivia repeated weakly. "I am your apprentice."

"You will follow where I lead," Denae continued, and Olivia repeated the line. "You will achieve mastery," and this was repeated.

"You are forever family," Denae continued, pausing for the repeats, "and as our blood comes together, we are forever sisters."

Olivia looked at her strangely but finished the last line. There was a jolt within them, briefly holding them together. Shocked, they looked at each other as they released, their bloodied skin reluctantly peeling away from one another.

"What was that?" Olivia looked shaken.

"I'm not sure." Denae felt the quaver in her voice. "This was supposed to be a little fun thing to say, but I'm pretty sure something more happened. I think we are now blood-sisters, and I'm not even sure exactly what that means." At Olivia's look, she continued. "I like the idea, and it should be a good thing, but I'm not sure about the details."

"That last part," Olivia said, her voice shaking. "That sounded Germanic. You said something similar to *Blutswiestarn,* which I think is blood-sisters. Cheryl is taking German and trying it out on me, but I don't think that's the type of German she's learning."

"I don't speak German," Denae said, looking but not seeing anything different with Olivia. "I don't remember speaking anything but English."

"What do we do?"

"We go back to your lessons," Denae said quickly, "which currently is using the salve to heal yourself before you bleed even more."

She handed the jar to Olivia.

"Take just small amounts," Denae began, "and simply put it up to the wound. It will almost hop off your finger to start its work. You don't have to rub it in for something like this. If it's internal, you do, but just go up the cut a bit at a time."

Olivia dabbed and worked up her ribcage, paling again as she could see a bit of the rib bone in a couple of spots. Her fingers followed up and across her damaged breast, watching it heal. She was very pale, and her body had broken into a cold sweat, but curiosity seemed to win over her tendency to faint. When she was done, she reached over and dabbed salve on Denae until her cut was healed.

"Will all your lessons be like this?"

"No," and Denae flashed a grin. "Some will be worse."

"Oh," Olivia replied quietly, "I see."

"That was a joke," Denae said, grabbing her hands. "Mostly a joke. This isn't easy stuff. Like in life, you're likely to get hurt now and again. Me slashing you like that was for you to know how to be hurt and care for yourself."

"I flunked that then," Olivia replied, dejected.

"No," Denae said, "you did not. You did about what I expected. You passed out, regained your senses, and healed yourself. Just ignore that middle stuff. You feel okay now?"

"I'm still a little light-headed, but I think so," she replied.

"I'll give you a minute or two, and then we'll scrub off in the snow. I need to get a fresh pot for water anyway."

She wiped her knife clean as Olivia said, "This is so not what I thought this weekend was going to be." Some color had returned to her face.

"I know," Denae said with a grin.

↢ ↢ ⊙ ↣ ↣

The rest of the day went well. Olivia seemed over the shock of being sliced open, though Denae noticed she kept an eye on where the knife was. They'd donned their snowsuits and went out for a while in the afternoon. It continued to snow, falling heavily with little wind, lighter and fluffier earlier than now. Denae had wanted to see if Olivia could see the bear, but it was too far in the past for her to see.

Denae felt a little smug in that Olivia would at least have to learn to see that far back if she could even learn the spell. Many people had problems understanding how to do something so close to their innate ability. Denae struggled with learning to fly rather than her innate levitate. Then, one day, something clicked, and she could swoop and soar rather than simply float and turn at a walking pace.

They donned skis and went down the trail following the snowmobile ride. Since Denae usually just teleported back and forth, she hadn't bothered looking before. Plus, she'd had other things on her mind when she came back and forth with Binesi to even think about it. She knew where they'd crashed from when she helped Dad dig it out but asked Olivia to take the lead.

Olivia seemed to ski the exact path Denae took like she was following them on their trip. Once they hit where the blizzard started, Denae was horrified to see how off the trail she went, surprised they'd made it as far as they did before she wrecked out. It could've been so much worse.

Olivia stopped where Denae knew she would and stared at Denae. "You're screaming," she whispered.

"I broke my leg, but Leah couldn't hear because of the helmets and the blizzard." She patted Olivia on the shoulder. "If she'd heard me screaming, she might've stopped, and we might've died," then Denae shook her head. "No. We wouldn't have died, but I would've had to do something riskier, and Leah might've died." Denae's voice trailed off. "No, not true. I would've made sure she'd make it somehow."

"You floated after that."

"Yeah. I couldn't walk."

"Can you do that to me?"

Denae raised her up several inches above the snow, swung her upside down, skis in the air, and lowered her head slowly toward the snow.

"No," Olivia yelled, laughing. As her parka hood entered the snow, Denae raised her up and brought her back down skis-first.

"Oh wow. Can you teach me to do that?"

"Probably not," Denae replied. "It's innate, so I don't think I could teach you." At Olivia's puzzlement, she continued, "Can you teach Bin how to look at auras or do your history?"

"I don't know," Olivia pondered. "I'm not sure how I do it."

"Exactly," Denae said. "I had to learn all the history stuff so I can teach that. I can maybe teach you how to look back years, even centuries, and I can teach you how to fly, but not levitate, or slow fly like Bin likes to call it."

She shrugged before continuing. "Those are different somehow, and flying was difficult for me to learn until I understood the concepts behind movement. Just because I could do it innately didn't mean I understood it, but it's all different and works differently. If I give it more energy, I can lift more, but I don't move faster with levitation. With actual flying, more energy makes me go faster, but I can't carry more."

Olivia looked impressed. Good. This was probably more what she was looking for, Denae thought. So let's go for some practical exercise on this.

"Okay, let's ski down to the lake. Just follow the trail."

Denae stopped them as they got to the edge a few minutes later.

"First, an experiment. Get out of your skis."

Olivia undid her ski bindings, leaning the skis against a tree trunk. Denae followed suit and led her to the edge of the snow-covered lake.

"You and Leah went over this. You were pulling her."

Denae nodded, then stepped behind Olivia and put her hands around Olivia's waist.

"What?"

"We're going to try teleporting to the far side of the lake. I don't know if you're light enough that I can carry you there.

"Um…okay."

Denae focused on the far bank, and they jumped, landing short by about thirty feet.

"That answers that," Denae said. "Now you're really going to be my guinea pig."

"What do you mean?"

"I'm going to teleport you back to by our skis…I hope."

"Um…."

"I know how to teleport other people…in theory, but I haven't practiced it like I should have. If I had, I could've gotten Leah to home no problem, but I'd been lazy with that."

Like she had with the crystal ball. She was still afraid of what she'd see the next time. Would she have seen Olivia and her entity?

"What happens if it doesn't work right?"

"Then I'll have to go find you if you go very far in the wrong direction." Denae pulled off a glove and reached into her pouch, pulling out a bloody piece of paper towel. "I have your blood, so I can locate you easily. You'll most likely end up somewhere between here and there, but just in case. I couldn't risk it in the blizzard. It's very tiring…again because I haven't practiced it much. You're lighter than Leah, so that will help keep me from being as tired. It won't be as tiring once I have it down well. I can see across the lake, so now I'm practicing."

Olivia looked dubious as Denae said a few words with a gesture and touched her, feeling the sudden energy loss. She saw Olivia not quite where she'd envisioned, but close…not close enough for the blizzard, but plenty good for the moment. She'd practiced a little with Binesi and would practice more now. There couldn't be another episode like with Leah.

Denae paused, catching her breath. Olivia wasn't that heavy…this shouldn't take much effort, but she simply didn't know it very well. Not like teleporting herself. She would've been face-down in the snow if she'd tried the tipi. She definitely needed to practice more…a lot more.

She shifted herself next to Olivia and, breathing heavily, pointed out where she had wanted her to go. Olivia shrugged at the twenty feet.

"Not good enough. Leah couldn't have found the back porch from there. I have to be exactly on. Where would you be if I'd tried to put you next to the tipi? That's a lot farther away. You might've been somewhere out in the woods."

Olivia nodded.

"That's the thing. Close isn't usually good enough with magic. It can get you in trouble, especially if you rely on being close to correct. I will practice this with you. I obviously haven't mastered this, and there are many areas I don't know at all, and you'll have to learn from others. Let's grab our skis and go a little while I catch my breath."

She led Olivia down a side trail about a hundred yards to her kiosk, which was half-buried in snow.

"We can rest here." Denae watched Olivia look it over and grinned. "I built this when I was fifteen, off the main trail so I could strip down and hang my clothes here so they'd stay dry while I hunted and ran the trails. That was before the bear or the tipi."

Once they'd rested a while, Denae asked, "You think you can stay on the path and find the tipi?" She knew the last part wouldn't be a problem for her.

"I don't think I could miss the tipi, even in a blizzard," Olivia said. "It's so tall."

"Good," Denae agreed. "Strap your skis and poles to my pack, and I'll let you fly back."

Olivia looked scared and thrilled by the idea. Denae touched Olivia, and she rose in the air slightly.

"Now go and see if you can beat me back."

Olivia pulled her scarf over her nose and took off down the path.

Denae smiled, watching her go, then realized she hadn't given her any warnings and sighed. Binesi had broken his arm when he did this the first time, and she'd gotten in trouble even though it was because Bin didn't listen to her. Hopefully, Olivia would be more cautious and not run into a tree or something.

Denae waited until Olivia was out of sight around a bend, then shifted in front of the tipi. She had the skis and poles secured and was out of her outerwear before Olivia swooped through the opening.

"I knew you were going to teleport back," she accused, laughing. "It's so Star Trekkie."

Denae was glad Leah had talked to her about Star Trek, so she got the reference.

"Yeah, but no whirring or flashing lights," she agreed. "A lot quieter." She gestured at the opening while pulling her sweater off. "Secure the flap, then get out of those things."

Olivia closed the flap, securing it in place, and stared at it for a few seconds before turning back and seeing Denae in her long underwear. "All the way?"

"Your choice." Denae shrugged. "After getting splattered with hot grease cooking the bacon this morning, I'm staying in these until after supper." She laughed. "I'll probably forget by morning and have to learn it all again."

They laughed as Olivia continued undressing, hesitated momentarily, shrugged, and skinned off her underwear.

"Feeling at home, are we?"

"Yes," Olivia. "Totally weird, but I feel safe, at least so long as you keep your knife in its sheath."

"I will hopefully never cut you again in my life," Denae said. "That should be a one-time thing."

"Good," Olivia said, pulling a blanket around her. "Why do you like being naked?"

"I feel free. Clothing binds, it itches, it constricts. There's nothing much better in the summer than swimming in the lake or running along a trail. Or sitting here talking with a friend any time of the year."

Denae stopped, then reached down, pulled off her top, and slid off her bottoms.

"What about splattering yourself cooking supper?"

"It stings for a few seconds." Denae shrugged. "This is better. Plus, it stains the silk. This silk is about the closest thing to naked. It doesn't itch or chafe as much as other clothing."

Olivia shook her head. "I guess, but I can't imagine myself running through the woods naked."

"You will frolic through the woods naked this summer," Denae said. "And swim in the lake."

"But what if Bin or someone else is—"

"You've forgotten the ceremonies," Denae said, some exasperation in her voice. "Bin will be there, as will the others. He will know what you look like…like that," Denae finished, waving her hand at Olivia. "And you'll know what he looks like, too."

Olivia reddened slightly but nodded.

"He'll probably swim with us and even frolic in the woods. If you two are frolicking together, I may not want to be there."

"I've seen him here," Olivia said slowly, "so I already kind of know what he looks like, I guess."

"Not nearly as good as the real thing," Denae said with an evil grin.

As Olivia reddened more, Denae dropped the smile and sighed. "I wish I had breasts like yours. I look like a twelve-year-old boy."

Olivia laughed but kindly. "Stand up," she said, and Denae did. "Turn around, slowly," and Denae did so.

When she'd done a complete turn, Olivia lifted Denae's hair onto the top of her head, sweeping it up a couple of times and catching the strays.

"Hold your hair up here." She stepped away, gesturing with a finger for Denae to turn around again.

Denae did that, feeling more self-conscious than she ever had naked. Olivia smiled again, sitting down on a pile of blankets. "No, you definitely don't look like a twelve-year-old boy."

She waved Denae to sit down, so Denae let her hair fall and sat near Olivia, but not too close.

"No," Olivia continued. "You have a dancer's trim figure and strong legs, even if you don't dance. If I had to call you anything, it'd be, I think, a pixie." She nodded. "Yes, I think that works."

"A pixie?" Denae was unsure if Olivia was making fun of her.

"Yes," she said, "at least from the drawings I've seen of them in the books." She grinned. "Now they are supposed to be like six inches tall or something like that, but if you cut your hair short, you could model as a pixie. You don't have wings, but you can fly," she ended with a giggle.

"I'm not sure how to take this," Denae said.

"What I'm saying," Olivia continued, "is that you are perfect like you are. You are so slender that bigger breasts or butt would look wrong on you. You'll find some guy that likes you just the way you are."

Denae put some wood on the fire. "I pity whoever is dumb enough to marry me…I'm not an easy person to be around."

"I don't know why you say that," Olivia started, smiling and holding her hand up. "In the last 24 hours, I've been dumped in snowbanks in my long underwear twice, and you stuffed them with snow the second time."

Two fingers were up. "You slashed me with a knife, then made me heal myself and scrub clean with snow naked afterward."

Two more fingers went up. "You sent me looking for a bear I couldn't find." Her thumb popped up.

"I slept naked on top of you and dirt for hours." The forefinger on her other hand waved vaguely at Denae. "And again with you the rest of the night," she continued with a second finger.

"Somehow, we're now blood sisters, and I don't know what that means, and neither do you." She laughed a little wide-eyed, holding a third finger out. "I flew back here from the lake and had to figure out how to steer on my own. I hit one of the pine boughs and got a face full of snow."

The pinkie jutted out. "And I'm sitting here naked, hungry for supper and whatever you'll throw at me afterward." The thumb came out, and she waved both hands in Denae's face.

"A weekend with you, and I won't know how to act around normal people."

"And your point," Denae drawled out, wondering where this was going.

"You're my master or mistress or something. You're my role model," Olivia yelled. "My fucking role model," and fell over laughing.

Denae leaned over and peered into Olivia's once-again tear-streaked face. "Are you saying I set the bar too high?"

↢ ↢ ⊙ ↣ ↣

The rest of the weekend went by more quietly. When they arrived back at Oma's, Oma-ma studied Denae and Olivia for several seconds before nodding and sighing after Denae told them they had maybe become blood-sisters.

"You definitely are," she said with a slow shake of her head. "Denae, you should've waited a few years before doing this."

"I didn't know I was doing this until it happened."

"She said the last in German or something like that," Olivia explained. "She says she doesn't know German, and I only know a few words, but…I…really had no problems repeating everything. None at all. Now that I think of it, even that part was weird."

"Then there was some sort of bond between you even before then, and I don't mean that entity. I don't know what it is, but maybe this will help with the apprenticeship. You will feel this strengthened bond in different ways. It will be quite palpable at times. It doesn't matter if you're inches apart, like now, or a continent away. You will have to discover the forms it takes in time, but it will always be there. You two must make the best of it because it's a lifetime vow."

Mom drove them back to Olivia's, and Olivia hugged Denae before going inside.

Once Denae returned, she said, "I need to talk to Binesi before they can see each other. Bin doesn't remember ever leaving his room, but I don't know what he does remember. She remembers very little of those last few days, which is very good for her."

"Oh, and she does history as well as auras," Denae continued, then explained how she saw the snowmobile trip with Leah and freaked out about Bin being burned, among other things. "She could see barely far enough back to make out Jude."

"Jude?"

"When he was home during Christmas break," Denae answered. "He stayed at the tipi a few days, investigating that whole native vision quest thing. Bin and I went out there with him for a little while, and he asked me if I had experienced anything like that. I haven't, or nothing like that, anyway."

"Ah…right."

"Oh, and because of her history thing," Denae said, "she's not coming into our house for a very long time. For her sake."

Her mom nodded but stayed silent, and after a minute, Denae started again. "I wasn't very nice to her some of the time."

"That's why you cut her?"

"More like laid her open," Denae said. "A jar of salve took care of it, but just barely."

"And you did this blood-sister thing while she was laid open?"

"Yeah, and I don't know why she let me. I didn't even think about it until she had come to, and I pulled her close. I was just making a silly fake master-apprentice pact, and then those final words came out of my mouth. She said they were some kind of German. I still don't know quite what I said, but she repeated them."

Riann gave her a sharp look before looking back down the road. "Definitely talk to Gaia about that tomorrow," she said. "This whole thing with Olivia is unsettling for me. At least she seemed happy when she got back. She put up a brave front, but she was scared to death to be with you."

"So was I," Denae replied. "I dumped her into snowdrifts twice after she freaked about me burning Bin and myself. I think I somehow killed and resurrected her in my mind on Saturday and maybe in hers. Things seemed different once we scrubbed off in the snow after the healing lesson."

"You were also blood-sisters then," she reminded Denae.

"Yeah," Denae responded. "There is that, whatever that is."

Mom gave a tight smile. That meant she had a decent idea of what it meant but wasn't going to say.

Chapter 25

Contained

Mom had dinner ready shortly after Bin and Dad arrived, and they ate, chatting about the men's weekend. Binesi seemed more subdued and kept glancing over at Denae. She wondered about a trip back to the tipi. If nothing else, it was apparent that both of them needed a parent-free discussion.

An hour later, they secured their skis and poles and got comfortable in the tipi. Binesi looked at Denae as she turned from the fire and sighed. She glanced back, thinking she might need to buzz his head again in a couple of days to even things out from the spots where the fire burned to the skin and the others where it didn't.

"It looks like your weekend wasn't as good as mine," she started.

"Lots of heavy conversations with Dad," Bin said, looking at the fire, "with him talking about family, responsibilities, feelings, protection, and other things. We did some other things, but that was the gist of it." He raised his head. "How is Olivia?"

"Better," Denae said, nodding. "A good bit better than Friday night."

"Good," he said, though he didn't look as happy as he sounded. "I didn't sleep well either night, so I wanted to come out here. I do sleep better here."

"And an earth bath," Denae added. "Your way. It worked for her, too."

At that, he did brighten. "So, it wasn't just me?"

"Nope," she said, smiling. "Your idea seems to work well. Now, back to you. What's up?"

"I don't know. Dreams. Strange dreams."

"Olivia?" He nodded.

"Not like those others," he said. "Almost the opposite," and he reddened. "This isn't easy for me, and I didn't tell Dad about them."

Denae slid over and hugged him. "Tell me if you want, and Olivia can see history, by the way, so she's seen the shadows of everything that's gone on here over the last couple of months. She has problems turning it off."

"So," he said, hesitating, "she saw what happened the last times I was here."

Denae nodded. "And Leah, and even as far back as Jude being here, though he seemed faint to her."

"That means—"

"That everything will even out on that next Ceremony if that's what you're worried about."

"No," he said. "She saw you burn me." He seemed shocked by that.

"And went totally hysterical. I dragged her out and buried her in a snowdrift until she calmed down."

"You did what," Bin shouted.

"I did a lot worse than that to her," Denae said, pulling her arms around him, "but she's fine, so let's get back to your dream."

"But—"

"Your dreams," Denae insisted, "about Olivia."

He slumped and took a deep breath. "With Olivia." He shook his head as if to scatter cobwebs. "We are getting friendly…friendlier than we ever were in person...I think." He glanced over at Denae, who squeezed him. "I'm suddenly naked and…and she is too, and I'm trying to…do it…but…I have nothing…nothing to do it with," he continued, a panicked look on his face. "It's…they're gone…nothing there at all."

Denae held back an urge to smile.

"I'm scared," he said. "I don't know what it means."

"Probably nothing," Denae said. "What did you do the last time you were with her?"

"We kissed—"

"How far did you go?" Denae gave him an exasperated look.

"More than kissing. I'm not sure how much. It might've been part of one of the dreams. I know I came out of the warehouse, and she was waiting for me…took me behind the arcade. We were inside each other's clothes. If that was real. She wanted—"

"She wasn't sure if that was a dream or real either."

"Studhorse," he spat out. "That's all I was to that thing."

"Yeah," Denae said, "except that the broodmare wasn't in heat yet, so it was preparing you so you'd be ready when the time came."

"Yeah," he grunted. "And now?"

"Are you fully functional down there?"

He blushed slightly. "Yeah. Any more personal questions?"

"It was your dream," she retorted. "With the last week, it's probably residuals from that thing controlling you, plus your own insecurities."

He snorted, and Denae swung around, straddling him. "You're barely sixteen, and I was still a mass of insecurities even before all this crap, so I know you are." She plucked at his long underwear. "Besides, you didn't take this off."

"Neither did you," he said, pulling at hers.

"Because you didn't," she said, looking him in the eye.

"When has that ever stopped you before," he said with a sneer.

"Never," she said, "but this is different. Everything seems different."

"Yeah," he said. "I've done things I wouldn't have. I've done things I don't remember."

"Be glad for that not remembering part," Denae said, letting go of his shirt. He looked at her with irritation.

"And I remember what I looked like when you unearthed me," he said, anger coming to his voice. "And you standing there like it was an everyday thing."

"No, it wasn't," she fired back. "I knew it'd be bad for you. That's why nobody else was around when I brought you back."

He glared at her momentarily, then slumped and nodded, continuing like that part of the conversation hadn't happened.

"And Dad talking to me like Olivia and I had already done it." He looked disgusted. "It was like I already knocked her up, telling me about the responsibilities of fatherhood and diseases and how everything down there is supposed to work."

↢↢⊙↣↣

It was several hours later when she woke and broke contact. Bin stirred and woke partially. She slid behind him on the blankets to protect him from his dreams…and her own. She wanted him to wrap his arms around her and protect her, but she was the big sister, and this was part of it.

Between the nights with him and Olivia, she wasn't sure how her dreams would be if she were alone. The tipi and bodily contact seemed to nullify any dreams they might have. Eventually, she'd need to go home and sleep alone in her bed, but she didn't relish the idea. She'd rather just live here, at least at night. They both had classes in the morning, but if he slept in, she'd stay with him until he woke and they got back home. He needed it.

↢↢⊙↣↣

"It's well contained in this," Aunt Gaia said, placing her hand on the green crockery with the wire lock. Denae looked more deeply and saw various protection spells that made a far more formidable seal than the actual crockery. Olivia watched as well, though with disgust on her face.

"That's what was in me?"

"It was," Gaia assured her. "You're safe from it now. I doubt it could find its way back into you on its own."

"So what is it?" Denae pulled on her hair. "Why does it like our streaks?"

"I don't have a good answer yet," Aunt Gaia said, sweeping her hands around the library. "Not even within the entire family library. I believe with a fair amount of certainty that it is something within the Alfar that was locked away. Based on Olivia's birthplace and origins, the information may be locked away somewhere behind the Iron Curtain, though much more ancient than that political construct."

She shifted on her stool as she looked at Olivia. "How and why you gained this, I am at a loss to explain. I think there is a great likelihood that your birth parents' demise may somehow be attributed to the entity. Either it was being implanted into you by them, or they were attempting to keep that from happening."

Gaia hopped off her stool and started pacing in front of the bookcases. She seemed much more focused than usual. "From what I've learned from the two of you and others, and what little I've found here…." She slapped a book that stuck out slightly, her two-tone orange hair sparkling in the lights. "It appears that you were simply to be a host for the entity, nothing more than storage for it until some planned event happened. Meeting Binesi was not that planned event. In fact, I'm pretty sure you were never supposed to leave Europe for America. Whoever initially had control of you lost that control at or around the time of your parents' deaths."

Olivia sat silently, seeming shocked by this revelation, so Denae spoke into the silence.

"And this means what? Especially now that we have it, safe in a jar."

"In the short term, we're safer, obviously," Aunt Gaia said. "For the long term, not so much. It is powerful, as I'm sure you know. It is testing the protective wards placed over the space confining it if you didn't see. You said it was to be Binesi's progeny to rule as in days of old. Once born, Bin may have been discarded as the entity joined with the baby. And there's the rub.

"I'm not sure what this whole "rule" thing means. Is it ancient or small enough within history that it's not making a blip on our modern historical radar? Or is it something more specific to the Alfar…the White Ones, or possibly the Black Ones, that we've lost the link here in the New World?"

Gaia reached over and ran Denae's hair through her fingers. "If it's the latter, that may be even scarier for you since you are close to that particular link in our ancestry. To borrow from a recent movie I saw, 'The Alfar is strong in you.'" She smiled at Denae's bewilderment while Olivia giggled. "You really need to get out more, Denae. Escapism is good for the soul."

"Anyway," she continued. "I've made some phone calls to distant families here and abroad to see if they know anything based on this. I've tried to be discreet and haven't said we have this thing in a jar, but we'll have to see what they can come up with. I believe we'll have to destroy it in the long run. A large amount of Essence of Fire will probably be necessary. This will probably need to be a Family Ceremony, though there are certain dangers to that as well. I'm not sure its current container would be strong enough to destroy the entity without it escaping. But again, I'm uncertain about what it would mean for it to be uncontained and hostless. That combination might be enough to kill it, or it might become ghostlike and wander around until it secures a suitable host. We'll meet to discuss this matter, probably several times, and Denae, you may join us if you wish."

Denae pondered it a moment. "No," she said finally. "You guys discuss it and let me know what the decision is. I don't think I'm ready for that yet."

Aunt Gaia switched over to talking about different esoterica. It seemed to cover in passing the White Ones and Dark Ones in a manner different from what Denae had heard before. Aunt Gaia said that the Alfar of mainland Germany and the Northlands and the equivalent fey or fairy or elf were pretty much all the same sorts of beings.

There were equivalents in Asia, Africa, and even the Americas. They seemed somewhat different but were still similar to even the nymphs, dryads, and pixies of various legends.

"Olivia said I looked like a pixie," Denae said, and Olivia nodded.

"Lucky guess or maybe some intuition," Gaia replied.

"What?"

"With the studies we've had, I thought you'd figured it out by now," Gaia said with a grin. "Where do you think the Dassow streak comes from? Our forefathers dallied with some of the Alfar or whatever you want to call them…not pixies, as they're more Cornish, way in the southwest of England, but yeah, some sort of fey…or sorts. Our family history gets way confusing back in the old country. Still, human and fey blood are mixed in our family.

"All of what we know is mixed with myth and legend, so it's hard to pull the truth out from the fiction…to understand what exactly is in our lineage. So much of our Old World history was lost to us when our forefathers came to America. That first ancestor here married a Ho-Chunk chief's daughter and traded for a lot of what's now our family lands.

"From what I can find, babies were brought into our family from outside. Our forefathers dallied with some North German nymph or pixie equivalents and brought the progeny home. If I read it right, it wasn't uncommon for practitioner men to do that and bring the babies to be raised as family. This was to increase the power of the family. Women may have done similar, but those are harder to discern with any certainty. Whatever the case, we seem to be good examples of those genes coming back in full fruition, you even more than me or Opa."

"Opa?" Denae remembered some talk about her taking after him.

"Your great-grandfather Dassow. He was full-streak like you, though silverish, and was about as likely as you to be off naked in the forest, even in his older age. He and Oma would even frolic naked with the animals out there, or so I heard, though I don't know if that was true. Probably, they were just enjoying each other's company in the woods, and the story grew with the telling."

"So my hair and eyes—"

"Are from some rogue gene that cropped up from days of yore to manifest in you. Either that or Opa's death coinciding with your conception is more than just talk…or both."

Gaia gave her such a grin that Denae wasn't sure how seriously she should take it and told her so.

"There's something to some part or parts of this. Exactly what has truth to it is the big question. And to ask another question, what is the earth bath you mentioned?"

"Denae lies down on the bare earth," Olivia explained, pantomiming the actions, though not lying down. "Then you lie down on top of her, and when she does her earth thing, you get all nice and relaxed and fall asleep and feel much more rested when she's done."

"How do you do this earth bath again? I've done something like that, but that's not at all how I've done it," she said, looking at Olivia.

"Bin suggested trying this back right after Olivia was freed from that thing," Denae said. "Before, I'd have whoever was with me lie in the earth, and I'd lie on top of them. It worked, but not as well as this way." She sighed.

"Bin could never last over 15 minutes before he got cold," she continued. "He said he didn't like his dick in the dirt." Olivia giggled. "I can lie there all night. I draw warmth from the earth. With me on the ground, they can sleep on me for hours, though they don't follow me."

"Follow you? How? Where are you going?"

"I'm going nowhere," Denae said, "yet everywhere. I can reach out, feel the life in the soil, in the tree roots, for at least a hundred yards around, maybe farther, I don't really know. If animals or people are roaming above the ground nearby, I can feel them, too, though I can feel them much farther out than when I was younger. I—"

Gaia was gaping at her, then closed her mouth and started scribbling on a notepad.

"You are a pixie," Olivia squealed, "or a nymph, dryad, or something like that. I knew it!" She started laughing until Denae started chuckling along. Denae looked back at her aunt, who repeatedly pointed at Olivia, her mouth open but not quite making words. After a moment, she found her speech.

"There…there is some truth to that," Gaia said. "Exactly how much truth has been a topic of discussion about you, Denae, since you were born, and me, too. With your puzzling hair and eye color, we knew you were special, but so much has been lost since we came to America." She took her two hands and placed them on Denae's cheeks. "I will be researching this—I definitely will be."

"While we're on this subject, there's something else I should show you," Denae said. "Let's go to the living room, where I have a good view outside." Everyone moved over to the living room, Denae grimacing in remembrance as she passed the stairway. "No, this won't do unless we rearrange the furniture so we can sit. I can do it standing up, but you two should be sitting. Let's go out to the porch. We can sit there."

They put on coats and boots and went out. Denae pulled three rough bentwood chairs side-by-side close to the porch railing and sat in the middle.

She had misgivings about this. Only two people knew about this besides her…she'd kept it secret, and so had they. It was strange that she could do this from a distance without any contact with the earth. She guessed it was something not earth-based, but if not, she didn't understand.

She gestured for the other two to sit in the other chairs and take her hand. Aunt Gaia looked owlish behind her glasses, staring unsure at Denae's proffered hand. Olivia looked excitedly and grasped Denae's hand eagerly.

Aunt Gaia's unsure taking of Denae's hand seemed like the better way. She at least seemed to have some slight idea of what would come. Olivia was going to have a shock. She opened herself up to the forest in front of her, and all that was out there.

Two flying squirrels mate in a tree hollow. Marten births to four kits. Gray fox bloodily rips open cottontail. Cougar snaps fawn's neck. Birds kill, eat insects by scores, hundreds, thousands—insects do same. Raccoons break eggs, eat the partially formed chicks. Other eggs hatch. This dance repeats many times.

She never knew how much time had gone by when she emerged, but it appeared to be about noon. As she broke contact, Gaia was gasping, slowly turning her head toward Denae, at a complete loss for words.

Like when Denae had sliced her, Olivia looked pale to the point of passing out, tears streaming down her face.

Denae freed her hand from her aunt, slapped Olivia's tight grip, and sighed. That was becoming a habit, but Olivia turned to her, mouthing, "What?"

When she turned back, her aunt was scribbling again in her notepad. Denae didn't want to know what she was writing. She pulled Olivia out of her chair and into the forest.

Olivia still looked stunned when Denae finally stopped and turned back to her. "What was…was all…that," Olivia stammered.

"Life," Denae said. "Raw, unadulterated life."

"How can you…," Olivia lost her words.

"I've always been able to do this, since before I can remember," she said. "Like you and your history sight, though I have it off almost all the time, like you need to learn. We simply don't see this, all the deaths around us, all the births, most of which are to feed others, with only a few reproducing later. Of the larger animals, sometimes we find their remains, occasionally find one in mid-meal. Sometimes we are the hunter, but rarely the hunted. We're almost immune to it."

Olivia nodded. "You don't know why you do that anymore than I know why I do my history sight."

Denae shook her head. "I've only shown this to two other people: Bin and my cousin Justin. I was seven, and Bin was five. I was out by our lake, staring into the forest, when he disturbed me, wanting to know what I saw, so I showed him. When I was done, he was bawling. He wanted to run but didn't know where to go. Once I calmed him down, we talked about it. I told him it was a secret I gave him, a scary one, but something he should think about. He told me never again, but a month later, he wanted to and has seen it plenty of times over the last decade."

She turned around, arms spread before she continued. "Justin was almost your age when I showed him. He freaked like you, but we did this a couple of other times, including last summer. He wanted to do it again to help him with his biology and other animal stuff in college. He still freaks but said it was worth it."

Denae looked into Olivia's eyes, who shivered at the contact. "You will see this again, so think about what you've seen and what it really means. This is part of everything…I can't explain, but I can feel it, just as you did. Do you understand?"

Olivia stared for a few seconds, then shook her head from side to side.

Denae laughed. "Good, because you'd have to explain it to me if you did. Aunt Gaia had some idea of what would happen but didn't understand it until now. Maybe she'll be able to explain it, but I doubt it. Let's get back to the library."

Gaia hadn't moved from the porch, continuing to scribble on her pad, eyes still wide.

Denae patted her aunt's shoulder, saying, "Let me know what all this means," and got a vague nod while she continued to write. Denae was pretty sure Aunt Gaia hadn't heard a word she'd said and shook her head as they went inside.

Chapter 26

The Burning

For Denae, the following weeks became a whirlwind, punctuated at times by dreams of bears or entity-possessed family members that drove her to the tipi. Sometimes, she woke gasping in the snow, not remembering moving there, without even her belt. This wasn't a nightly event but every third or fourth night, which drove Denae crazy. She never knew when…nothing specific seemed to trigger it.

Other parts of the whirlwind were the stolen moments with Leah, usually in the shop after-hours but never long enough to incite Leah's mom more than necessary. Olivia's apprenticeship on the weekends was another. Trying to teach her at this comparatively late age was painful.

Denae was no teacher, at least to Olivia, and couldn't slash her way through some of the basics. Things that should have been easy weren't, and they both became frustrated. One good part was that many of Olivia's aptitudes and interests lay entirely outside Denae's areas. That meant she could pass Olivia off to those more expert in those areas…and better teachers.

Denae could do this one Saturday evening and then shift outside Leah's house. Her parents were off to another of those useless marital counseling weekends, so Leah was alone. Denae let herself in the unlocked back door to the smells of supper cooking. Pork chops, sweet red cabbage, and potatoes au gratin were soon served, along with a couple of glasses of wine.

Before Denae knew it, they shared a somewhat cramped bubble bath and much more. Denae left an hour before Leah's parents were expected home, exhausted yet filled by the time together, much more than those quick trysts a couple of times a week at the warehouse.

Classes from various family members recently focused more on spirits and the Alfar or fey or White Ones and Black Ones. Denae already had learned some about them. Other of it seemed to be things she always knew but became confirmation. Some of it she pondered, not quite finding in reality what should be according to the lore.

As a throwback, strong with this Alfar stuff, she should be able to attract those she wanted for her purposes. Gaia said she used it to her advantage regularly. She supposed that could've been the case with Leah but hoped not.

She wondered about herself and Leah. She had little desire for any of her male cousins, no matter how distant, whether they sported a streak or not, and even less for her female cousins. She'd seen a few guys in town from time to time who did catch her attention, but they hadn't noticed she existed. None of the girls interested her either.

That wasn't entirely true. Leah's friend, Jessica, was interesting and infuriating. She and Leah had such an easy friendship, obviously built upon years and years.

The first time Denae had gone over there, she wanted to throttle Jessica. After they'd left, Leah asked what was wrong. Denae practically melted down in the street before getting to Leah's car. She was so jealous of their friendship and wanted Leah for herself. As they drove away, Leah explained that if Denae forced a choice between her and Jessica, she would choose Jessica, but she didn't want to have to choose.

She told Denae to grow up and realize that people have more than one friend. She wanted Denae to be friends with Jessica, or if that wasn't possible, at least not get in the way of Leah's friendship. She and Cheryl were talking again, and Denae was okay with that, so what was wrong with Jessica?

Denae cried herself to sleep that night, but if she had dreams, she didn't remember them. The following day, she could hear Leah's calm voice still telling her those things. Somewhere in her gut, she understood.

Denae would at least try to be Jessica's friend. Maybe she could have at least a little of that connection like Jessica and Leah had with one another. What she had with Leah was something extraordinary and different from that. She didn't want that with Jessica, but something could be there between them.

Cheryl was weird with her. Denae didn't know whether it was friendship or something else. Sometimes Cheryl was so friendly, almost sister-like, and other times…well. Some of that Denae had inflicted on herself, she supposed, from that first weekend with Olivia.

Cheryl had cut herself slicing meat in the kitchen, and Olivia had used a little salve to heal her. Later, she told her how Denae had slashed her open so Olivia could heal herself. When Denae next saw Cheryl at the arcade, Cheryl dragged her out back and yelled at her, threatening what would happen if Denae ever cut her sister again. When Cheryl was done, Denae's face was wet with spittle, but she forced herself not to react. It was similar when she found out that Denae had dragged Olivia out by her ponytail, tossed her naked into a snowdrift, and sat on her, caving more snow on top of her.

Apparently, Olivia embellished it a bit. Denae was sure she was still in her long underwear, or she wouldn't have been able to stuff them full of snow. She liked Cheryl most of the time, but when that overprotective side came out, Denae was worried she might have to hurt her to keep from getting hurt.

↢↢⊙↣↣

Denae came to the library for her next class on the esoterica Aunt Gaia seemed to thrive on. She smiled because her brothers would be home from college that evening for Spring Break. Spring had started, with the usual amount of slush and wetness, occasional snow, and the ice on the lake was thinning.

As she pulled off her boots and coat, her aunt waited for her at the dining table. Several books were piled up, ready for use, and an old ceremonial axe next to them, probably for some esoteric reason of Gaia's.

As Denae moved to the table, she felt…sensed something…something different. She felt a wrongness, but Gaia grasped her hand before she could react, and darkness slid into her.

The entity.

It beat at her defenses, knocking them back as Denae faltered, penning her in. She curled her psyche into a defensive ball as it overtook her body.

Denae could still see and feel, but it wasn't her laugh that came out of her mouth. Aunt Gaia blinked and gasped for breath as Denae's hands grabbed the axe and swung it at the bitch's face. It cut into her cheek, ripped through her nose, and rose again. Blood trailed the swing, though not as deep as she'd…it'd wanted, but it was enough. Denae felt herself smile.

Gaia staggered, her hands grasping at the table as she fell, items raining down around her. On the floor, she tried to crawl. Denae felt herself swing the axe again, centering on her lower back, splitting through the backbone above the pelvis. Gaia collapsed.

Good.

Denae saw herself release the axe and stuck upright as blood spread from the wound, soaking the clothing. "Barren bitch," came from her lips as she turned away, heading for the stairs to the library.

There were things to retrieve.

I've been waiting for this, Denae heard as she…they trod up the steps. *Your aunt was…unsuitable. No eggs, no babies. Nothing for me to inhabit.* Denae could feel it spread through her, forcing her to retreat further.

It didn't have all of her.

You, on the other hand, are suitable. And, soon. Three days or so. There came a chuckle. *Your Gaia was gracious,* and there was another chuckle.

Gracious enough to provide me with a list of suitable mates. Uncles and cousins nearby. Plenty of time. Those of your blood are…susceptible…to me. Then you will destroy them.

Denae felt the hate build up in it.

No!

Yes.

They were at the top of the stairs, surveying the room. *And my last vessel, too. Binesi will have his way with her and then will choke the life out of her while you watch. Then we will kill him. Maybe we'll pull that axe from your aunt's spine and split his skull.*

Another chuckle.

B*athe in his blood.*

Denae trembled, and it laughed. H*ide your memories and abilities, but those will be peeled back, layer by layer, until I own them all. Every death by your hand will peel one back. Every eye gouged out, every slash, every throat slit. You will see it all and be able to do nothing.*

Denae tried to lash out with her mind but was beaten back.

What's this? You bonded with her, my little Olivia?

It seemed genuinely puzzled.

How?

Why would you do this?

She could feel it following that thread but couldn't stop it.

You didn't mean to, but it happened?

It seemed troubled by this.

Denae grasped at it. *Does this bother you?*

She was looking for an opening, anything to use against it.

She was simply my vessel, so why should she interest you, let alone give you a desire to bond? It seemed to ponder the thought.

Maybe she will need to die sooner…soonest.

Why her as a vessel? Denae tried to focus…to distract it as they gathered a few books and instruments. *What was the purpose?*

Silly girl, it responded. *To store me safely, of course. Gaia knew but was unwilling to submit a child to it and ignorant of the necessary rituals. She thought herself equal to binding me in that jar, if even for a short time.*

It laughed.

It takes a human body to hold me, not some object. They usually transferred me at or before the girl's puberty for reasons that should now be obvious. For centuries, I've been held such to keep me away from those I could dominate until now.

Binesi's streak?

Any opening, anything, to try to break back into her body. Keep it talking, she thought.

Hah, it responded. *Yes, that woke me little by little, so I encouraged it.*

By making her aroused by him?

She was already that, though she didn't know what to do with it. I knew, so I encouraged it more. It laughed again. *The contact started giving me control of him as well, also for the better.*

You have a timetable?

Denae worked to focus while she listened and questioned. It seemed time was so limited. It seemed to be peeling back layers of herself as it used her body. Focus and strike. She tried to build that within her, but it was so hard to do, and it seemed to have collected most of what it wanted up here. Focus.

Yes. With the seed your brother would supply, I would be freed to rule again. With him under my control, I would set up a kingdom. She felt something like drool from it. *Then I touched your hair.*

You went crazy. She could feel that from him but needed to focus on herself.

It…she…let go of laughs that echoed in the room. *You were an unexpected find, almost perfect but unattainable.*

Denae looked around, tossing a couple more small items into the bag with a *just-in-case* floating by. *I was trapped in the vessel, with my only escape being through birthing into a suitable host, but I was touching a very suitable host. I needed to control you, and then you gave me your hair.*

And you sent me those dreams, she spat.

You didn't like them, it chuckled. *Your body did. It gave me some control, but then you disappeared. Then the boy did, too. What did you do?*

Wouldn't you like to know, Denae thought, the words dripping with sarcasm. This gave her some focus.

Oh, I will. I will. It will only take a little time…a stone tipi? We'll have to go there when we're finished here.

They'd reached the landing and turned, stepping out to go down the rest of the stairs. Denae took her focused energy and shoved out to that leg, that foot, grasping control to miss the step. It worked. She…it missed the tread and tumbled.

The bag dropped. Books and other things tumbled. She felt her arm give way as it stuck out to break the fall, snapping instead. It fled from the pain.

Denae seized that broken arm, relishing in the agony of the shattered bones. They slid headfirst to the bottom of the stairs as Denae fought to spread the pain. Gain more control.

Control slid away as her head hit the wooden floor. She blinked as it pushed against her, forcing her to retreat, taking back some of the power she'd gained so briefly.

Aunt Gaia lay near the base of the stairs, axe still in her back but looking out of her undamaged eye. One of Gaia's wands pointed directly at Denae. As Denae took in the blood streak on the floor behind where her aunt had pulled herself, Gaia said a word.

Everything went black.

↢↢⊙↣↣

Light came back but was different. Diffuse. Close in. She was lying face up. Her arm pulsed painfully, and an ankle throbbed, but she didn't feel squeezed—pushed out of the way. She had control, but it was still there, somehow.

She wiggled her fingers and toes, still in clothes and boots. She felt a great stiffness under the pain and understood. She'd been stone, a statue in a rather unglorified position. She reached out to the light with her pain-free arm and found she was boxed in. Wards held her with only a few inches of movement in any direction.

You're back, she heard in her head.

The entity.

And you're not.

Not yet, it said, sounding pained, *but I will be.*

Be quiet, she ordered and felt it retreat. Somehow, she was in control.

She seemed to be on rough stone and could see vague movement beyond the lights. Things flashed through her mind, and she felt a familiar pressing in. She opened her mind.

Denae came Mom's voice. *Are you okay?*

Better than I expected to wake to, if that's what you mean, Denae replied. *Am I on the altar?*

Hesitation.

Yes, Mom said. *We are gathered.*

A chill coursed down Denae. She was the reason for a Family Ceremony.

They cannot separate us. The entity spoke this time. *Not totally. They will have to release us. They can't maintain this forever, and you will be mine when it drops.*

Denae, Mom said. *We're working on separating you, but what worked on Olivia isn't working. We're going to try some other things.*

Mom, Denae said, trying to keep the panic out of her thoughts. *It claims you can't do it. I'm too good a host. It was implanted in Olivia as a vessel but moved into me of its own free will. It inhabits me rather than controls me.*

Let us try, came back the shaky reply. Others were on the connection. There seemed to be a collective gasp as Mom dropped off.

There was gleeful laughing coming from the area of her gut. She shifted her head slightly, looking down her body. The entity rose from around her navel through a small slit in the wards. It vaguely floated in a separate box, mostly but not completely separated.

They can try, it chortled. *Your family has lost the skills to make the simple transfer from vessel to vessel, so separating me from you will prove impossible. They will let us go.* For being mostly separated, it seemed too happy. *Your Gaia didn't even know how to banish me, which would protect your family, but we'll be free before their wards come crashing down of their own accord.*

Denae had never heard of such a ritual, though there was plenty she still didn't know. Still, that was something she thought she'd have at least heard in passing in some class or another. How could she fight this thing, make it leave? How could she cause herself so much pain that it would release her? That was the only thing she knew about it. Denae reached inside her to see where it connected. Was it only the navel?

No, she realized. That was a central point, but tendrils flowed throughout her body. It chuckled at her realization. *Not that easy, eh?*

Hours streamed by. Denae felt occasional tugs and magics flowing across her, but nothing loosened its hold. The only thing that loosened its hold was her bladder when she could no longer hold it. Given enough time, the bowels would be next, but it didn't matter. Discomfort, but it could be cleaned up if they released her. Maybe they would find something to separate her from the entity, but she wasn't hopeful.

The entity stayed away from her broken arm and the throbbing ankle. The pain would make it release her, but she couldn't devise a plan to cause enough pain throughout her body to make it totally release her without killing her.

The darkness above was lightening, so morning was coming, she thought.

Denae? It was Mom. Denae knew what she had to say.

Mother, this thing is evil, she started. *It would have me kill off the Dassow line like I did Aunt Gaia.* Denae took a deep breath, knowing what she was about to say. *It must be destroyed. You must do this. Whatever else, this must be done. It can't be released.*

There was silence. The connection was there, but all was quiet for over a minute. Denae could feel the others there, even though they were silent.

Then, *Denae?* Mom's voice was shaking. *I love you.*

I love you too, Mom, Denae replied calmly. They understood, she thought. It was the only way. The connection broke.

What was that? What did that mean?

It means you're dead, Denae spat.

The fires came.

Denae screamed.

Chapter 27

Gone

She was floating…weightless…no pain. She looked down at the magical haze where she could make out people moving about. She was sure that what little was left of her body was down inside there. The entity was gone…she was sure of that.

Looking farther away, Olivia was wrapped around Binesi, both sobbing uncontrollably. Leah stood behind them, supporting Bin where he sat on a log, tears flowing down her face. She looked up as though she could see Denae, knelt behind Binesi, rubbed his shoulders, and whispered something in his ear.

Suddenly, he stiffened, his crying slowing, and he stood, taking Olivia's hand as she stared at him. Leah took his other hand, and the trio walked back to become blurs under the haze. Denae drifted momentarily, then felt a pull tugging her back.

↢↢⊙↣↣

There were visions, people moving, talking, pain, and blackness. This repeated, the pain different each time. There were dreams…or maybe more visions. More pain. More blackness.

Denae awoke.

There were still wards, but different, not dense, not confining. She floated slightly above the rough stone of the altar. There was no pain. She could hear the murmur of the people around her. A hand took hers, and she looked that way, seeing Olivia smiling at her through a puffy, drawn face.

"Am I okay?"

Olivia's smile widened, and tears flowed down her face. Denae pushed off from the altar, tender feet hitting the squishy ground, her knees buckling under her. Olivia caught and held her as she stood. She felt weak but good.

She wrapped her arms around Olivia as Leah approached, looking slightly less exhausted. Olivia started sobbing, and Denae shook her gently. "I don't see any snowdrifts, but I will roll you in a mud puddle if you don't stop."

"I'm…I'm trying," Olivia sputtered, fighting to control herself. She released Olivia and hugged Leah in turn as others gathered around.

"I don't know what you did, but it saved my life," Denae whispered. Leah looked at her, confused.

"Your mom called, so I came," she said and shrugged.

Denae looked over to the log. "You with Bin and Olivia. You saw me…something, then rubbed Bin's shoulders and whispered something that made them quit crying and join back in," Denae continued in a low voice. "That made the difference."

"I didn't see anything, but I knew we were needed," she replied. "How—"

"That was me," Denae said. "You brought me back to my body." Denae squeezed her tightly and kissed her cheek.

As others reached, touched, and squeezed her shoulders, Denae heard Olivia say, "Cheryl?" She looked around and saw Olivia's sister walking up, naked as everyone else in the area, with Olivia running over and hugging her.

Denae glanced at Leah, who shrugged. "Didn't know she was here."

"What's going on here?" Cheryl's voice was loud, so Denae released her hug, took Leah's hand, and walked over. "You look awful," Cheryl continued to Olivia. "You need to come home. Great-aunt Agatha is dying."

"Agatha? Was she here?"

Leah and Olivia both nodded as someone wrapped their arms around Denae. Binesi put his cheek against hers.

Cheryl looked at Denae, and her eyes widened, "Denae?" she stammered. "Where's your hair?"

"Smooth as a baby's butt," Leah said, rubbing Denae's bald scalp.

"It's all my fault," Olivia wailed.

Denae pulled away from Binesi, stepped forward, grabbed Olivia by the hair, and yanked back hard, swinging her into Bin's arms.

"If you keep saying that, I will yank you bald." Olivia stared at her, frightened.

Cheryl stepped up but stopped when Denae put a hand on her chest.

"Wait," Denae told her.

"Bin," she said, waving a finger at both of them. "Tipi. Now," then looked at Leah. "You, too. Don't come back until tomorrow. Actually, don't come back. I will come and get you."

She turned to Cheryl. "Where's Agatha?"

Cheryl stared at Denae, then pushed Denae's hand off her chest. "The nursing home, I think."

Denae nodded, picturing it and where it was.

"You," she said, "You stay here, right by the altar, so I can find you when I get back."

Denae shifted to the front entrance of the nursing home. It was easy to locate Agatha. She followed the path through the front door and down a hallway to a room with a few gray-haired people standing around a bed. Agatha lay there, eyes closed.

Denae slid in by the bed and took Agatha's hand, hearing gasps from the others as she came in. Agatha's eyes fluttered open, and she smiled weakly. "You made it," she said. "I'm so happy."

"It's my fault," Denae said quietly as someone draped something across her shoulders.

"That I'm going on a journey?" Her voice sounded slightly stronger. "No, my dear, it is not." She moved her other hand over slowly and patted Denae's hand.

"It is simply my time. I'm old. I've lived a good life here. It's time to find out what's next." She smiled more broadly. "It is that time for you, too. Find out what is next in your life."

Agatha moved her eyes, looking around the room at the others. "Since you have brought me back to life this one more time, I should say my goodbyes," and she lifted her hand slightly off Denae's. Denae leaned over and kissed Agatha on her forehead.

"Olivia is with me," she said quietly. "And so is Cheryl." At Agatha's slightly raised eyebrows, she continued. "She found her own way in."

"Did she. Now that is interesting," and squeezed Denae's hand slightly. Denae squeezed back, then let go, slipping the sweater off her shoulders and realizing for the first time that she was naked in a room full of clothed people. She handed the sweater to one of them and strode out of the room, spotting a side exit. She could make out her dim reflection in the glass door, staring at her bald head. She stepped outside into the cold darkness, taking several steps through the icy wetness of the ground. She felt her face with one hand while the other slid past her belly. No eyebrows, lashes, or anywhere else, she thought, and people thought she looked weird before.

She sighed and was back, about ten feet away from Cheryl, who argued with Leah and Olivia. Binesi stood behind Olivia, hands on her shoulders. Cheryl stopped, seeing everyone's eyes shift to Denae, and turned around.

"I want my sister," she demanded.

"You will have her," Denae replied, "tomorrow, at Oma's. Right now, they need to go to the tipi and rest, and you and I need to go to the house and talk."

A robe was thrust between them. Denae looked past the robe, then flung herself into her mother's arms. "You understood," Denae said.

"I tried not to," she responded, "but yes, I understood," and gathered Denae deeper to herself, stroking her head.

Denae started sobbing, holding Mom for several minutes before she could get control of herself, remembering that Cheryl was still standing there.

"I don't know if you've met, but this is Olivia's sister, Cheryl."

"We've met," her mom said, her tired face stained with tears, "but never here. How did you find us?"

"I was getting frantic," Cheryl said. "I hadn't heard from Olivia in three days. Not since she called and said there had been a ceremony called and she'd be away a while longer. She freaked out at school Friday morning, went home sick without permission, and left a note saying she was going with you," pointing at Riann, "to find Denae."

"I drove around most of the afternoon and finally saw a path when it was almost dark that I must've passed a half-dozen times before. I found several other cars parked together, so I got out and followed a trail to an arbor with several sets of clothes hung under it. I went a little farther and saw a group of nude people, so I went back and took mine off so I would blend in better."

"Then I found this," she finished, waving her hands around. "Denae won't let me have my sister and is sending them off to this tipi so they can sleep together or something, or maybe Leah's chaperoning…I don't know." She put her hands on her head. "Denae doesn't have a hair on her body, and I don't know what's happening."

"Of course you don't," Riann said. "I still don't know how you even got here. You shouldn't have been able to, but that's neither here nor there. You're here, and that's a good thing." She stepped over and hugged her. "That's my youngest son, who just headed out with your sister and Leah. I don't understand this either, so we'll have to trust Denae."

She released Cheryl, who backed up a step. "Even this is weird. We're all nude, and we're acting like it's nothing and—"

"If you hang around here long," Denae said, "it will be nothing, or maybe better than nothing."

"It takes a little getting used to," Riann said. "It took me a few ceremonies after I married into the family to realize that nobody except me cared, so I quit caring and relaxed."

"Now, if we're done worrying about no clothes," Denae said, "where are your clothes?"

"Back that way." Cheryl pointed back in the direction she originally came from.

"Good." Denae took the robe from Cheryl. "Let's get your clothes and car and drive to the house. You can call your parents, tell them you've seen Olivia. Let them know she's okay, you're staying with me, and you'll both be home sometime tomorrow."

"Seriously," Cheryl said.

"Yeah," Denae replied. "You have questions, and it'll take a while, so this is easier."

"I guess," Cheryl agreed.

"Plus, I'm starving," Denae said. "I feel like I haven't eaten in forever, and there's food and drink at home." Denae started walking off, throwing the robe around her, not waiting for Cheryl to catch up.

↢ ↢ ⊙ ↣ ↣

Cheryl wasn't sure why she was walking into this large log house, but Denae was in a hurry. In through the front door and up a set of stairs. Denae shed the robe partway up the staircase.

They had reached the top of the stairs when a man came out of the lavatory drying his hair. He looked up and shouted, "Denae," threw down the towel, and picked her up bodily. "We thought you were a goner," he said, his voice choking. "Are you really completely okay?" He squeezed her tightly. "You seemed little more than a cinder at one point."

"I'm great," Denae replied.

He gave her another big squeeze before noticing Cheryl.

"Hi," he said, "I'm Lucas," extending his hand while holding Denae off the ground with the other arm.

"I'm Cheryl," she said, keeping her eyes firmly up at Lucas's tired-looking face. She tried to ignore that he had just gotten out of the shower. "Olivia's sister."

"Olivia," Lucas said but was interrupted by more feet running into the hallway. Cheryl looked that way, seeing two other men, all three brothers by the similar looks, one in long pants and a t-shirt, the other as nude as Lucas.

Lucas tossed Denae a good three feet to the first one, who hugged her tightly, kissing her cheeks and forehead. He, in turn, tossed her to the third—taller, broader, and seemingly oldest- who did the same. Cheryl seemed not even to be noticed until Lucas asked, "Guys, who's Olivia?"

The clothed one, who looked to be the youngest of the three, replied, "Isn't she the little one who seemed glued to Bin but wouldn't leave Denae and also hung with that pleasantly plump girl with the nice jugs," gesturing what he'd like to do with them.

Denae wiggled out of the big guy's arms, shouting, "Hey!"

Once on the ground, she pushed the other dressed one against the wall, waving a finger in his face. "First, that little one is Binesi's girlfriend, my apprentice, and Cheryl's sister, so be nice."

"Second," she continued, "that pleasantly plump girl with the nice jugs has a name, and it's Leah, and she's my friend." She backed a step away from her brother. "Third, if you guys are through with the lavatory, Cheryl and I are taking a long bubble bath. She is with me for the night, so my room is private until we come down for breakfast, and," Denae pointed at Cheryl, "this is Cheryl."

Cheryl tried to keep a straight face, watching what looked like a little naked girl tell grown men what's what. She noticed Lucas grinning at her. As she glanced over, he said, "She has never taken any shit off of us." At that, they both burst out laughing. "By the way, the one against the wall is Jude and the other guy in his birthday suit is Anton."

Cheryl went pink, her eyes briefly dropping, before returning to their grinning faces. Denae grabbed her arm and pulled her into a bedroom, shouting, "Unlike me, Cheryl's not used to this much macho idiocy."

She heard Lucas slap Jude's shoulder. "Pile those plates up." At that, Denae stuck her head back into the hallway.

"You getting food?" then continued. "Bring a piled plate to the lavatory, plus a bottle of wine and two glasses."

"Denae," Anton called. "You really are okay?"

"We can talk about that at breakfast and not before," Denae shouted back. "Goodnight."

↢↢⊙↣↣

Cheryl was still puzzling over how she was in a bubble bath with a completely hairless Denae. Denae started to try to explain things when her mom came in.

"You okay?" Riann asked her, and she nodded uncertainly. "Sorry about the boys," Riann continued. "They weren't expecting company, let alone any of the fairer variety."

Cheryl pinked. "Yeah, I noticed."

"They didn't seem to mind that she was here," Denae said.

"I have talked to them." Riann smiled sympathetically at her. "Now that they know there's company, they will be decently dressed when they leave their rooms."

"Thank you," she said. "I wasn't expecting anything like that, but then I could say that about this whole day. I still don't know why I'm soaking in this wonderful tub with Denae, why she doesn't have any hair, what they meant when they said Denae was a cinder, where Olivia is, why she's with Bin and Leah, or anything else."

"That," Denae said, jumping in, "is why you are soaking with me in this tub. I wanted to take a bubble bath, and you needed to talk. So you're soaking with me so we can talk about all that other stuff."

"I guess," she said. "I never made that phone call home."

"Mom," Denae said, "can you bring more food up and call her mom to let them know everything is good and Cheryl's staying the night, too."

"I can," Riann said, "and anything else?" She smiled. "I'm afraid we're out of sanity at the moment, so you'll just have to make do with what you have," and walked out of the lavatory.

"What are the sleeping arrangements?"

"You get the bed. I'll sleep on the floor," Denae replied, then smiled, "though I have it under good authority that your breasts make nice pillows."

"What," she sputtered. "Who…she wasn't supposed to tell anyone about that."

"Relax," Denae said. "I'm not telling anyone, and I don't really care. Olivia was feeling more unsettled and confused than you are. That was somewhere after I dumped her in a snowdrift and stuffed her long underwear with snow."

Denae laughed and continued with that story, telling her about the last couple of months and answering her questions. By the end, she better understood at least some of what happened.

She balked at Denae's description of watching Leah stir Binesi and Olivia to pull her back to her body. "I don't understand," she said.

"Neither do I," agreed Denae. "Leah shouldn't have been able to discern that, let alone bring those two from hysterics to functional in a few seconds, but she did. You shouldn't have been able to find us…we had protections up specifically to keep that from happening, yet you found us."

Deane waved a forkful of sausage in the air as she continued. "Lately, things are happening that don't make sense. Even with Leah's thing, I think I should've been too far gone to bring back. I simply don't understand. Mom said it took the family three days to put this Humpty Dumpty back together again. No matter how broken, I've never heard of it taking more than one."

"Which also explains your pale skin and the hair, or lack thereof," Cheryl said. "Will it grow back?"

"I hope so," Denae said. "I don't like my hair color, but I like bald even less. Plus, hair down there was the only thing that kept me from looking like I was ten years old."

"I will admit that's what it looked like when you were dressing down your brothers earlier," Cheryl said with a laugh.

"That's what you were laughing at."

"I was laughing at the fact they were taking it," she replied.

Tears began to roll down Denae's face.

Cheryl drained her glass and stood up. "Time to get out," she said, wrapping a towel around herself. She helped Denae step out of the tub and started drying her.

She heard someone coming up the stairs as they got to Denae's room, so stopped and waited until Lucas appeared around the corner. "Dude, can you take care of the lavatory for us? I need to get her to bed."

Lucas nodded and turned toward the lavatory while Cheryl led Denae into her room and shut the door, pushing her into the bed.

She slid beside her and sang softly as she stroked Denae's bare scalp gently.

Chapter 28

Breakfast

Denae woke, a light of early morning coming through the window. Cheryl lay on her back next to her, both covered by a sheet and quilt. Denae's bladder was aching, so she climbed over Cheryl.

Cheryl stirred and opened her eyes. "Where you going?"

"Pee," Denae replied as she padded into the hallway. She wanted to cry, too, but didn't. She realized as she woke up that she had lost the necklace Papa had made for her. It was gone in the fire, like her clothes, boots, belt, and knife. She spent more time in the lavatory composing herself than peeing but forced herself not to cry over it. She was alive and shouldn't be.

↢ ↢ ⊙ ↣ ↣

"She cooks, too," Lucas said as he stepped into the kitchen with his brothers. Cheryl and Denae had dressed and started cooking breakfast before anyone else was up.

"Pancakes from scratch," Cheryl said, smiling at them as they poured their coffees and sat at the table.

"And a cheesy egg scramble with bacon," Denae added. Jude got back up and brought syrup and butter to the table. Their mom and dad both came out a minute later and joined them.

As they all settled down to eat, Anton said, "It's breakfast time, Denae," giving her a pointed look.

"Not until we're done eating," Riann said, "and I can leave. There are parts of this that I don't want to relive."

"Then tell the part I don't know," Denae said. "What happened after Aunt Gaia turned me to stone?"

Riann winced and sighed. "Fine. That bloody mess," she said. "Jerok called me. He'd gotten a frantic call from Olivia that you were in trouble, and she needed to get to Gaia's. I picked her up from her house, and we drove there. Olivia was a total mess, blaming herself for everything, so I knew it had to do with that blasted entity thing."

"We got in and saw…the smear of blood across the floor, and both of you turned into granite." Riann shook her head. "I should've kept Olivia from going in. She passed out when she saw Gaia and gashed her head. I made calls. We got Gaia out of there, and Oma and others started working on her while we discussed you. Once Gaia was healed, she gave us a few options." Her hand holding her mug of coffee started shaking, and she set it down.

"Once we got you in place on the altar and secured that thing, we set up what we would do to remove it like we did with Olivia. As you know, that did not work…not completely. Gaia said it wouldn't, but we had to try. We also sent everyone with Dassow blood off to Wausau based on what it tried with you and Bin when we turned Olivia to flesh. As you know, Gaia was correct, and you immediately shot down all the other options. You…you told us what we needed to do but were afraid to. Eventually, we ran out of options. You burned."

She wiped tears from her eyes.

"Somehow, you survived, and we…we rebuilt you. Regrew your limbs from almost nothing, restored your skin, and made you new. There's not much left in the draughts anywhere within the family, which was the smaller part of bringing you back. We were doing shifts to keep energy pouring into you, funneling it through Hannah and Ebby, who could do that heavy healing. Ebby's a total wreck right now. Her self-confidence was nowhere as good as her abilities, and she was sure she would kill you somehow, even after you'd turned the corner. Hannah's probably got her sedated, and Issa's got Flynn and Sasha."

Jude reached over and rubbed Denae's bald pate. "New you, baby soft all over, and we're so glad you're here this morning." Agreement was murmured around the table, with Cheryl staring around.

"Fine," Denae said, her voice choked and feeling her face turn pink. "Let's finish eating."

Once breakfast was finished and her parents left the table, Denae began the story. She started by telling them about Olivia rubbing Binesi's streak and went from there. All the guys looked into the living room as she described that fight. "This is why Olivia is not allowed in this house until late summer. She remembers none of this but does history innately, at least a couple of months back, and we don't want her to see what happened. I've worked with her quite a bit to get her past that, before this last thing with me—"

Cheryl started laughing. As all eyes turned to her, she said, "Yeah, Denae worked with her and was really gentle about it. She dumped Olivia naked into a snowbank, caved it down, and sat on her. Later, Denae slashed her open with that knife she carries—carried across the ribs and halfway through her breast. Yeah, real gentle she is," she finished as the brothers' looked back at Denae, gaping a bit.

"Somehow," Lucas said, "that doesn't surprise me. Denae is as subtle as a sledgehammer most of the time."

"Okay," Denae shouted. "That jumps ahead a little, but…," and Denae explained about burning Binesi and herself and how Olivia saw that and freaked out, hence the snow dunk, and continued to the end. When she finished, Lucas let out a whistle.

"No wonder Mom and Dad didn't try to tell us about this over the phone." Her other two brothers nodded in agreement.

"And that whole blood-sister thing?" Cheryl looked at Denae.

"That was it in action Friday," Denae said. "And now she's stuck with me." Her hands shook as she sipped her coffee.

"Then she's in good hands," Cheryl said.

"Wait," Jude said. "A little while ago, you told us how she almost killed your sister, and now you're saying she's in good hands with Denae. That sounds crazy."

"I did kill Olivia," Denae responded. "In a figurative but rather bloody sense, I did kill her. Then I made her my blood-sister in a rather bloody literal sense."

"She said you spoke the last part in some German language," Cheryl added.

Denae nodded. "Part of my…of our," she corrected, gesturing around the table, "heritage that reared its head and took over during that sharing of blood. Any of you ever do anything like that?"

Everyone shook their heads.

"Don't do it unless you've thought it out a long time, like years." She drank the rest of her coffee. "It's been driving me crazy all night that I'm not with her while she's hurting and blaming herself. Leah and Binesi are what she needed, but I need to get there to make sure. She's suffering because of me, and I can't stand it."

As the others stared at her, she looked at Cheryl and said, "You can stay here—meet us at Oma's."

"Like hell," Cheryl roared back. "She's my sister, and I'm going."

Chapter 29

Direction

Several minutes later, they quietly hiked down a slight slope through a wide opening in the forest to a small lake. Cheryl's tennis shoes started getting wet inside from the squishy ground.

Denae wore a well-worn leather belt her father had cut down for her waist, with a leather pouch on one side and a new knife on the other. Cheryl and the rest of the family had watched quietly as Denae and her dad choked up at this exchange. He'd given her his knife.

"How far," Cheryl said.

"A half-mile," Denae replied, "once we get over the lake."

"Get over the lake?"

"Exactly," Denae said, and Cheryl shook her head.

↢ ↢ ⊙ ↣ ↣

Floating across the lake was beautiful, Cheryl thought. There were small ripples and slabs of ice floated like miniature icebergs. She was disappointed when her feet squished into the ground, fresh water creeping in as her weight returned.

Denae stopped and unlaced her boots. Cheryl thought she was adjusting her socks until she put her bare feet onto the wet ground and hung her boots around her neck by their shoelaces.

"What on earth are you doing?"

"I lost my callouses," Denae replied. "My feet are as baby-soft as the rest of me, so I'm going to try to walk the last half-mile barefoot to try to toughen them up a little. The ground's squishy, so it shouldn't be hard on my feet. Besides, these are my old boots, and they're not very comfortable."

"And I was going to complain about the cold water getting into my shoes," Cheryl laughed. "Never mind."

After walking longer, she asked, "How can you stand it? My feet are hurting already."

Denae shrugged. "After everything that's happened to me and that I've done to myself over the last few months, this is nothing, but yeah, they're aching some. But the earth soothes me some, so…." She gave another shrug.

“I don’t know if Olivia will be happy to see me,” Cheryl said.

Denae turned to her and pointed her finger under her nose. “No overreacting. Even if…if she and Bin are…busy when we walk in, you will act as if this is natural and a good thing. You will be supportive of her no matter what.”

“And if I’m not,” Cheryl responded loudly.

“You will disappear until she’s at Oma’s, and then I will come back for you,” Denae said with a certain finality. Cheryl stared at her defiantly before dropping her gaze and heading down the trail.

After another minute, she asked, “Do you think they will be….”

“No,” Denae said. “But there’s a good chance you will see something unusual, and I don’t want you to do your usual over-protective thing when that happens. Anyway,” she continued, “it’s not like I’ve been right that often these last few months, so she may be on top of him shouting ‘Yeehaw’ for all I know.”

“I did not need that image in my head,” she said. “I don’t want Bin to get her pregnant.”

“That’s not likely,” Denae said. “She’s past her fertile period and should be starting her period in a few days.”

Cheryl grimaced. “You can see all that with your sight thing?”

“Yeah,” Denae responded. “I can see more with mine than the spell would show. So can Olivia.”

↢ ↢ ⊙ ↣ ↣

Another minute and the tipi was in view, and then they were outside, Denae loosening the flap. Cheryl looked up at its height, almost glowing in the dappled sunlight while smoke drifted out.

Leah smiled brightly as they stepped into the darkness. Cheryl was surprised at the long embrace Leah gave Denae but looked over Leah while they did. Pleasantly plump was an apt description, she thought. An anti-Denae. Soft as opposed to Denae’s skinny hardness, ample compared to Denae’s minimal.

Olivia got up and ran the few steps over to Denae and hugged her tight, then let go, screaming, “Cheryl,” and hugged her even closer. Binesi walked over and hugged Denae.

Denae looked at Leah, who shook her head slightly. “They did at least hold hands.”

“Seriously,” Denae looked at her brother and got a sheepish look back. “I guess that’s something after what we all have been through.”

“She thinks he liked her better when she was controlled, which is bullshit, and he’s afraid he’ll upset her if he does try to do anything, which is also bullshit. Try telling either of them that,” Leah growled. “They won’t even talk to each other about it. I don’t know if they’re too embarrassed or afraid they’ll embarrass each other.”

Cheryl peeled Olivia off of her and kissed her on the forehead. "Look at Denae," she ordered. "Look really good and close. Do you see anything wrong with her?"

"Uh," Olivia said, confused, then looked at Denae for several seconds. "No, she looks good. Really good."

"Look at Bin," Cheryl ordered again. "Is he okay?"

She looked for a few seconds and reddened. "He's fine, too. Great even."

"Denae," Cheryl said. "Look at Olivia and Bin. See if there's anything wrong with either of them."

After several seconds, Denae said, "Except for being very stressed and tired, they both look fine but frustrated." Both of them went pink.

Denae kneeled in front of Olivia, lifting her long undershirt, and touched her belly. "That ripped place is almost completely gone. It's barely even there now. You're doing good."

As Olivia broke into a big smile, Cheryl grabbed her arm. "We need to go have a talk. You two get dressed for outside, and Bin, don't move a muscle." Then she pulled Olivia out through the flap.

After a moment, distant yells came muffled into the tipi, words not discernable. Then came a scream, obviously Olivia's. Bin started forward but stopped when Denae held a hand out and blocked him as she peered out and down the trail.

Olivia was face-down in a mud puddle they'd skirted. She struggled and gasped for breath while Cheryl held her down. Denae grinned and pushed Binesi back to where he had been before. Leah looked at her, but she shook her head and zipped up her coat, Leah following suit.

Cheryl walked back in with a satisfied look on her face. She pulled a wet, muddy, shivering Olivia through the opening and thrust her at Binesi, who caught her, then picked up a blanket and wrapped her in it.

"Clean her up, dry her off, and warm her up," Cheryl said, looking at Bin. "Then either kiss her or tell her why she doesn't deserve a kiss."

Looking over at Denae and Leah, she said, "Let's go."

They walked farther down the trail a bit before Cheryl said, "I can't believe I just did that, but she was naked with him when I got there last night."

"What was that all about?" Leah asked.

Cheryl laughed a dry laugh. "I think I got through to her that it was okay for her to be with him. The devil-entity thing has nothing to do with how she feels now. It doesn't affect how Bin feels now. If she doesn't want to be with him, that's fine, but if she does, she should show it, at least by more than holding his hand."

Denae asked, "Did you really get through?"

Cheryl smiled. "Your methods are a bit extreme but seem effective on her right now. I told her that we'd give them at least fifteen minutes."

Denae laughed, and they walked for several minutes before turning around.

"Surely, they've settled things one way or another by now," Cheryl declared. "My feet are like blocks of ice."

When they returned, Cheryl went to the opening and hollered, "You done?"

"You can come in now."

They were bundled together under a blanket when the other three came in, looking flushed and embarrassed.

"Better?" Cheryl smiled as she unzipped her jacket, and Denae saw them nod their assent.

↢ ↢ ⊙ ↣ ↣

Leah gently shook Denae awake about an hour later, Denae breaking contact as she opened her eyes.

"We do have places to be," Leah said.

Cheryl began to stir and opened her eyes.

"I fell asleep," she said slowly, words slurring slightly. "What time is it?"

"You've been there one hour," Leah answered. "How do you feel?"

"Like I melted," she said. "Like I was part of the entire world, or it was all a part of me." Her words became clearer, her eyes more awake. "I don't know."

She looked at Denae like she'd forgotten she was even there. "Oh my," she said as Denae turned her head a little farther to smile back at her.

Olivia, Leah, and Binesi all looked at Cheryl in surprise.

"What," Cheryl said to their stares. "You've all done this," she continued. "You've felt this."

She pushed up as Denae struggled to turn over, and the others shook their heads.

Denae said, "No, they haven't. They feel good and relaxed, and maybe some of what you just said. You felt what I feel, one with the earth. And the weird part is, you shouldn't be able to do that, or at least I don't think you should have. No one taught me this, so I don't know."

Denae looked at Olivia. "We should discuss this with Aunt Gaia when we see her tomorrow." Olivia hesitated, then nodded but looked apprehensive.

Cheryl stood up, staggering a bit. Denae stood and kissed her on the neck.

"Why…what did you do that for?"

"I was with you, directing you," Denae said. "I've never been able to do that with anyone else. It was awesome. I didn't want it to stop."

"Oh," she replied. "Uh...and what...I dunno." She looked around. "Why are we out?"

"We need to go," Leah said. "I need to get home, and you need to get Olivia home. Denae and Bin need to go home." Olivia clung tighter to Binesi, and he kissed her. "Denae, this would be easier if you knew how to drive."

"What," Denae said, confused. "Why?"

"My car is at your house," she stated. "Cheryl's car is at your house. Olivia can't go to your house. You could buzz in and drive one of the cars to your Oma's place. Be there before us."

"She could stay outside," Denae suggested.

"No," Leah said. "Your mom was adamant about her not being anywhere around the house for several months. She goes to Oma's, but we need to get the cars there."

Cheryl held out her keys. "Leah, go with Denae," she said. "I'll go to her grandmother's with these two, and you drive my car over. I'll drop you off at the end of the driveway and take Olivia home. We'll try to get our stories straight for our parents."

"That will work," Leah said, taking the keys. "I don't think I've got a good enough story for my parents. I told my parents I needed to be with Denae after school because she was sick. I'm not sure it's flying, though. I know my mom doesn't want it to." She sighed. "I'll find out soon enough."

"At least our parents know about Olivia's...abilities," Cheryl added, "and that she's supposed to be here at times, though not skipping school like she did." She smiled. "At least it's Spring Break now, so no school." She glanced over at Denae as they continued to dress. "Same for your brothers, so you have them all week."

Denae shrugged. "You up to dealing with your brothers for a week, Bin?"

"Can you turn one of them into a statue as a warning to not get too nosy? I don't want to answer too many questions right now. I could mess with their minds, but that's supposed to be *verboten*, so I shouldn't."

"I'm not going to do that, but we'll see if we can't head at least some of that off," she agreed.

Cheryl stared at Denae. "Would you really turn your brothers into statues?"

Denae shook Binesi's shoulder and smiled. "I haven't for several months now. He behaves himself better than he used to."

"I was the last one she turned to stone," Olivia said suddenly. "Because...because of that thing in me."

"Yes," Denae retorted. "And it's gone. The next time I turn you into stone, it'll be because you annoyed me. Right, Bin?"

"I'll," began Olivia. "I'll try not to annoy you."

"Don't try too hard," Binesi said, laughing. "You'll just annoy her anyway. You can't win."

Chapter 30

Plans, Interrupted

"You really need to learn to drive," Leah said as they walked the long driveway back to the house. "All your brothers do except Bin, it looks like from the number of cars here," she continued. "I'm sure he will be as soon as he can."

"You betcha," Bin replied.

"Yeah, probably," Denae conceded, "and I should, though it's a lot slower than teleporting."

"But you need to know where the spot is to go there," Leah countered.

"Not necessarily," Denae continued. "If I study a picture well enough, I might be able to go there."

"Yeah, you told me how successful that wasn't."

When they stopped by Leah's car, Leah hugged Binesi, kissed his cheek, and hugged Denae tightly.

Denae felt Leah's lips at her ear. "Can you make nine o'clock at the shop?"

"Yeah," she said with a smile.

"If I can't, I'll call," Leah said, squeezing her.

↢ ↢ ⊙ ↣ ↣

As Leah's car went out of sight, they heard the front door open and clapping and whistling. Denae and Binesi turned to see their brothers cheering.

Denae felt herself go pink but saw Bin turn red, too. She went up the steps quickly, pushing through her brothers when Anton picked her up.

"Not so fast, sis," he said. "We want to have a sibling reunion this evening."

At her look, he continued.

"At your tipi, all five of us, away from prying ears and eyes. I need to go back to work tomorrow, though the others are on Spring Break. Since more people seem to be using your tipi lately, we thought you might open it up for all of us."

Denae felt flustered. She wanted to be with her brothers. The tipi would work fine for them. She'd left a fire burning since she and maybe Binesi would end up there tonight, but she was supposed to meet Leah.

"I told Leah I'd help her with Jessica this evening," Denae said.

At their confused looks, Binesi said, "She was hurt badly in that truck wreck in town back at the start of the year.

"Wait...wait," Denae said. "We'll figure something out. I'll take you there, but leave at nine to help Leah, then I'll come back." She looked at her brothers. "Will that work?"

"You should be relaxing with what you've been through," Lucas said, "but I think we can work with that. Just don't be the entire night."

"I won't," she said, relieved, knowing Leah would have to go home anyway. A couple of hours would have to be enough. She'd take her alarm clock just in case.

"Okay, that's settled," Anton said. "Granmama and Papa are inside and want to see you."

↢↢⊙↣↣

Denae had just started snuggling in with Leah when three sharp raps echoed through the warehouse, followed by three more.

Leah looked at Denae, who shook her head. "Cover up. I'll see who it is." Who even knew they were there?

She ran the length of the warehouse and opened the door a crack. It was Jessica.

"I need to see Leah," she said, pushing the door open, then her eyes widened as she took in Denae's hairless head before scanning down the rest of her body. "I saw her come in, but not you."

"What?" Denae started. "How?"

Jessica limped in using her cane. "You have a phone in here?"

Leah came up wrapped in the sleeping bag.

"What are you doing here?" "How did you know I was here?"

"First," Jessica said, annoyed, "call your dad. I stalled him and told him you had an upset tummy and were in the lavatory. You might've told me I was your alibi for this."

"But—" Leah said.

"Second, you're coming to my house the rest of the night." She glanced back briefly at Denae, who'd shut the door. "My mom answered the phone. She thinks you're on your way, so you will be, or all this is blown. Your little soiree is blown for tonight, and what the hell happened to your hair?" She limped back to Denae and looked closely at her face. "All of it. No eyebrows or lashes. Nothing."

Denae said nothing but moved over to the desk with the phone and started dialing. Leah dragged the sleeping bag with her and took the receiver.

"Hi, Dad," she said after the second ring. "I'm feeling better now, but...well...it wasn't pretty." She paused a moment. "Sure, hang on," and waved Jessica over.

"Hi again," Jessica said. "Yes, it's Spring Break, so we'll probably sleep late, but she'll be home by noon." She nodded her head. "Okay, bye." She hung the phone up. "Whew!"

"Now get dressed and get moving," Jessica said. "My parents don't know I snuck out the back door to get you, so I'm going to sneak in and announce you a minute later." She turned to Denae. "Sorry for breaking this up, but it's probably good if her dad doesn't find out about the two of you with all the other crap he's dealing with. You might as well get dressed, too."

Denae shrugged as Leah gasped out, "How did you know?"

"I think I figured it out the third time you had Denae over," she said. "The way you looked at each other, touched each other. It was something more than just being friends." She looked around the warehouse. "And then I saw you come here one evening about three weeks ago. The lights were on, and they were rarely on that late. I've seen Denae and her mom and brother come here a lot, and I can put two and two together, even when it seems like that answer must be five."

She looked back at Denae. "I look out my bedroom window a lot since the accident, and I can see that gate from the window." There was a lonely sadness in her voice.

Leah dropped all pretense of modesty as she tossed the sleeping bag to Denae and headed for the break area. Once there, she started pulling clothes on. She stuffed her underclothes into her coat pocket as Jessica limped in, Denae behind her.

"We have a lot to talk about, don't we?"

"You could say that," Jessica said.

"We need to talk, too," Jessica continued, though to Denae, who had watched everything silently. "Leah can tell me where your hair went, but there are some other things we need to get straight. I'll get your number from Leah and call you about when we can get together. Leah should've told me about this, but we'll get it straightened out. So, get dressed already."

Leah put her coat on, looked at Jessica, then went to Denae, pulled her close, and kissed her. "Go see your brothers," she said. "That's where you were supposed to be tonight." Denae nodded.

Jessica hurried Leah out the door, and Denae sat on the bed, struggling not to cry. Leah was right, of course. They'd tried to steal some time together, and it didn't work out. She'd wanted to yell at Jessica to leave them alone, but she'd come to protect her friend and was doing the right thing for both of them. Still, it hurt, and now she was supposed to talk to Jessica about this. How?

She walked over to where her clothes were and looked at them. She was going to the tipi, so she could just carry them.

Denae groaned. Her plan was not to be there until much later, but that was shot, too. She really didn't want to talk about this or anything.

She folded the bed and rolled up the sleeping bag before gathering her clothes. After ensuring the door was locked and protection was up, Denae turned out the lights, shifted, and stood on the cold, damp ground in front of the tipi.

Chapter 31

Siblings

Binesi opened the flap as Denae reached for it. Her other brothers laughed at something but watched her enter by the glow of the fire.

"What's wrong," Binesi said quietly. "I wasn't expecting you for a good while."

"Jessica was sleeping, so I came back."

"Oh," he said, a question floating in the word.

"Bin," Lucas's voice rang out. "Where's that bottle, and Denae, get your tiny butt over here. This party's in your honor. Isn't it a bit cold for you to honor your 'no clothes in the woods' vow?"

She dropped her bundle of clothes on some blankets as Lucas got up and tossed her into a fireman's carry before plopping her down on the blanket where he'd been sitting. "Kept it warm for you," he said, grinning before taking a seat on the other side of Anton. "Thought you were busy with your hurt friend."

"She'd already taken her pain meds and was out, so there wasn't anything to do," Denae snapped.

Binesi gave her another look.

Lucas laughed again, "You're touchy tonight."

Denae closed her eyes, put Lucas up in the air just because she could, and heard him yell. She didn't want to talk about anything with her brothers. Binesi, maybe, but not the rest. The problem was that they knew how to push her buttons until everything spilled out, and they would do just that. There was an odor as she opened her eyes, and a drink was held in front of her. Lucas was coughing now, up near the smoke hole.

"Put Lucas down gently, Sis, and you get this," Anton said. "We don't need any broken bones interrupting things tonight."

She lowered Lucas, took the Solo cup, and sniffed. Some whiskey plus the Seven-Up Binesi had brought from outside, so she brought it to her lips and gulped it down.

"Whoa," Jude said, grabbing her arm as the last went down her throat. "Slow down there, Sis." She handed it back to Anton, who was manning the drinks.

"That bad, eh?" Lucas tried brushing his back and looked at his hand. "I've got soot on me."

"Yes...no," Denae said. "I don't know." She waved a hand, and the soot fell off of Lucas. "I can't unsee attacking Gaia." They'd get this out of her anyway, so it was better just to say it. "I cut through her face. I drove the axe into her back so she'd die slowly. It laughed inside me, making me laugh…laugh at her."

"You know she's alive," Jude said quietly. The other brothers looked at her. Bin took her hand and gave her a look, but she shook her head. He could soothe her mind…numb it, but she didn't want that.

"I know, and I'm glad," Denae agreed. "But now it means I'll have to face her some time. I don't think I can do that."

"You need to," Anton said. "You need to show her that you don't hate her."

"Why would I hate her?" Denae stared at him. "She should hate me."

Anton and Lucas looked at each other. "She went more than a little crazy after the fire started," Lucas said, swallowing hard. "She blamed herself for everything and tried to throw herself on you…on the fire. Anton and I could barely hold her. She's stronger than she looks. Issa finally sedated her, but Gaia fought that, too. She has to use the wands because she has so little energy, but she has lots of defenses to fight the spells. Kind of like you, I guess."

She felt Bin's hand squeeze hers, and tears glistened in his eyes. This was tough on everyone, she realized. It wasn't just her.

Denae relaxed slightly and held out her Solo cup. Anton took it, poured more whiskey and pop, and started talking again.

"She's in another of her deep dives now. Dad talked to her today, and she's determined to learn more about that entity and how to protect us from it should we run across one again. You should talk to her when you see her."

"And what has been going on this year?" Lucas looked at Denae. "Bin's got a girlfriend who, it turns out, is an untrained practitioner, and you made her your blood-sister?"

Denae nodded.

"Your friend Leah's mundane but knows all about us and was even at the ceremony with us? The same with Cheryl, Olivia's mundane sister, and Mom said she somehow broke through the wards at the end?"

Denae nodded again. Lucas was getting on a roll, it seemed.

"You have her phone number?" He flashed her a grin.

She gave him a wicked smile. "I have her number, but you have to get in line. Right, Jude," she said, swinging around to look at him.

He had the decency to go a little pink. "She wasn't supposed to tell you."

"She didn't," Denae responded. "Dad overheard you and told me. Why not tell me?"

"She didn't want to bother you with anything else right now. She said you were pretty upset last night. Cried in your sleep," Jude finished.

Anton looked from Denae to Jude and back. "So if she's going out with Jude, what was with you dragging her off for a bubble bath, then into your bed."

"I wanted a bubble bath. Cheryl needed to know what had been going on. I combined the two. That's it. Why would you think otherwise?"

"Denae, you're the weirdest person we know, and you're our sister. You even outweird Gaia, and she's had girlfriends and boyfriends, so if you and Cheryl were an item, it wouldn't be totally unexpected."

Binesi squeezed her hand again. She looked at him and could see it in his eyes. He knew about her and Leah.

He smiled and gave the briefest shake of his head. He wasn't going to say anything.

"So," Anton said.

Denae tensed, wondering what was next as she looked back his way.

He waved a new walkie-talkie radio around. "Mom talked to us on this tonight instead of her usual way—wanted to make sure they reached here. I think she bought out Radio Shack and has an order in for more. Every household will get at least two, and we're supposed to have them on standby whenever we're out and about. Dad calls it a boondoggle, but Mom's insistent. It was pretty weak in here....hard to hear. There's a higher spot this side of the lake, and I think it's blocking the signal." He shrugged, setting it down, then leaned over and rubbed her head. "Hey, peach fuzz." He pulled her to him as the others came over, each rubbing in turn.

"That felt so weird, guys."

Lucas laughed. "Yeah, it did."

Anton poured more for everyone.

"Hey, mine's half-full," Denae complained.

"So's Bin's," he said. "Bin's underage and both of you have things to do in the morning. This won't help you figure out who or what you are. On the other hand, we can lounge here until noon if we want. Well, they can. I'm leaving with you."

"Mom will be with you so that she won't be calling them," he said with a grin. "Don't want you two hungover for class in the morning. What would Olivia think?" He winked at Binesi.

"I wouldn't know since I'm going to be schooling with Granmama and Papa tomorrow since they're here," Bin complained. "Denae and Olivia are staying at Aunt Gaia's tomorrow night, so I won't see her for a while. I just hope they don't decide to take me back with them for a week or two."

"Must be love," Lucas said with a laugh.

Denae froze. Did Gaia know she would be over there tomorrow?

↢↢⊙↣↣

The rest of the night did go well enough, with discussions about college in Milwaukee and Madison. She knew she wasn't going to college and hadn't even considered it, but listening to her brothers, she felt the desire to be there.

Instead, she'd work with family and possibly other families to investigate magic's inner workings. Right now, that seemed less important than whatever she might learn in college. They told her it would be almost the same when she voiced that, but she'd get personalized instruction instead of sitting in a class with a hundred other students. No crowded campuses, and she'd probably get stuck in a dorm room with someone she didn't know.

She knew they knew her well enough that they didn't think she'd do well around the crowds, and they were right. She'd visited them enough over the last four years that she knew she was always happy to leave the city and see the forests again. She was too weird for college but was ready for something else.

Not just learning the esoterica of magic. She didn't know what, and she didn't know if it had to do with what they were calling the burning…her burning…but things had changed. She had changed.

Leah would be leaving, and Cheryl, too. Jessica was staying. Her brother might not make his senior year because of her accident and the medical bills. She still had physical therapy, but at least she was done with her surgeries. If Denae had known her earlier….

She lay there for a while, wondering if she'd blown any chance of friendship with Jessica. She hadn't seemed angry with her, just Leah, so maybe, assuming she and Leah didn't break up over her.

What went on over at Jessica's house this evening? Would Jessica keep it a secret? For Leah's sake? Would they stay friends?

She could feel that selfish part of her and what it wanted, but she wanted Jessica and Leah to stay friends, no matter what. Jessica seemed friendly enough to her, so maybe she could also have another friend.

And Binesi. She guessed he'd keep it secret, too. He'd had plenty of opportunities to blurt it out to the bubs and impress them with his knowledge. Instead, he almost clung to her hand. None of them seemed to care that she was sitting there naked. Of course, they'd all skinned off their clothes when they decided to sleep. She could see their lumps under blankets in the glow of the embers, Bin being only a hands-breadth away.

Binesi started moving and moaning, and she automatically moved closer to him, listening. Was it the start of a nightmare or something else? She turned her sight on, seeing panic rise, and slid against his back, gently rubbed his chest until he quieted. She thought about sliding away but stayed, hoping she'd fall asleep and have no bad dreams with him close.

↢ ↢ ⊙ ↣ ↣

Anton stirred them up, Denae feeling like her tongue was stuck to the roof of her mouth. Binesi seemed the same, while Anton laughed at them. "Cozy," he said as they sat up.

"He was starting a nightmare," she said.

"You've always done that." Anton grinned at her. "Or jumped into one of your big brother's beds if you'd had one, assuming we didn't hear you first."

"Yeah," she said with a yawn, looking up. She saw the light coming through the top of the tipi.

"You should be turning that over to Olivia these days." he continued, humor in his voice. "I mean, she is his girlfriend."

"If she were here, she would've had him," she agreed, "but she wasn't, and it looks like I get her tonight anyway. Aunt Gaia's only got two beds."

Binesi groaned, sat up, and shook his head.

Anton laughed. "Better you than Gaia. That little girl won't know what happened if Gaia got her claws into her."

"What do you mean?"

"Gaia has an apartment in town for her conquests there, and from what I understand, she rarely goes home alone when she's on the prowl. She'll keep them until she gets bored, then go for fresh meat. She always has someone on her hook, but I don't think she's ever had a serious relationship."

"She could be a threat to Olivia?" Denae voiced it, but Binesi was staring at Anton nervously.

"I doubt it seriously, but we all have this ability to a smaller extent. It's subtle, but it does work. Has Dad told you about that, Bin?"

"Yeah, but I haven't tried it. I'm not sure I even have it."

"You do, or will, if it hasn't shown up yet."

"Same with you, though you should have it spades, like Gaia. Attract all the guys to you."

Denae gave him a dirty look. She didn't want that.

He laughed. "Or girls, if you swing that way."

She shook her head. Aunt Gaia had said something about this, but she didn't want to know. Maybe that was how she'd gotten Leah, and she didn't want to think that it was anything but herself that Leah liked.

Anton laughed again. "Either way, you should go to that new arcade Bin told us about and try it out. Find yourself somebody."

"I'd rather it was just someone who liked me for me," Denae said, glowering at him.

"It can be, but this can speed up the process."

"And nobody tells me about this stuff why?"

"Dad didn't tell me until I'd turned eighteen, though I already had some inkling about it. I was sworn to secrecy until each of the others of you were old enough, but Bin already knows more powerful ways to get what he wants—"

"And he'll lose precious body parts if he does it that way."

Anton looked from her to Binesi.

"You have him well-trained, I see."

"I've been his guinea pig for a lot of those spells. I know what devastation he could wreak on the local female population if he wanted to."

Anton nodded. "And you're sure he hasn't done this with little Olivia?"

"I'm not going to check Olivia's history. I lived it, and I trust Bin that he has done it the right way."

"And what about little Olivia? From what I understand, she's loaded with innate powers. What if she—"

Denae jumped up and hit Anton well below the belt buckle as hard as she could. He managed to dodge enough, and he put his hand on her head as she swung again.

"Sorry, sorry. I didn't think."

"No, you didn't," Denae shot back. She realized that Bin was standing next to her. "That entity had her doing things that she luckily doesn't remember. Bin and I aren't so lucky. Mom, too, for that matter."

Anton put his hands up, taking another step back. "I said I'm sorry, and don't make me wet myself, Bin. I see that look in your eye, and I don't have a change of clothes here."

She saw Binesi relax slightly, and she did as well. She looked around and saw that Lucas and Jude were watching.

"She obviously likes you better than me, Anton," Lucas said. "I would've been a pile of broken bones by now. She would've bounced me all over this tipi before shoving me out the smoke hole and dropping me in the woods."

Denae turned and smiled. "I haven't broken any of your bones in years."

"Last night was almost an exception."

"That was just a reminder that I could, not that I would."

"I thought I was going out of the smoke hole last night."

"I hadn't even thought about that, but now I'll add that idea."

She smiled at Lucas as he lifted a few inches off the ground, still under his covers, then set him back down as she saw his eyes widen in alarm.

He looked at Anton, who was laughing. "Why can't I ever fight that off? Just once would be nice."

"She has you totally intimidated," Jude said. "That's why. You've been able to fight Dad off when he's done that. He worked with you to be able to throw that off. Is Denae really any stronger?"

"No, but she's sneakier. She slips it in before you know it's there."

Like Bin's doing to me, Denae thought. He slipped a bit of calm into me while I was lifting Lucas.

"That's really not necessary," she said.

"I wasn't sure."

It went away. There was a difference, but she was only teasing Lucas anyway. She turned and was halfway to where her clothes lay when cold water coursed down her body.

She gasped and turned back.

"That's payback for last night when I wasn't even sure why you were sending me to Oma's, and the towels are to your right."

She stared at him a moment before nodding and going for a towel. She thought she heard a collective release of breath from all her brothers.

"You do like playing with fire," Jude said.

Lucas snorted in response.

Denae didn't like Lucas getting the last shot, but he was right. She'd done that for no reason. She wasn't twelve anymore and could let this go.

Anton slapped Binesi stingingly hard on his bare back. "Get dressed. Mom will have breakfast ready for us. If these other two want to sleep, they'll have to fend for themselves, though Mom will do another sending on them in a little while. Dad has some things he wants them to help with, so she'll call for them before you guys leave for Gaia's."

"If she's doing that," Lucas said, "we might as well get dressed and go with you."

They dressed, and as Lucas stepped out of the tipi, Denae said, "I need to practice one of my spells," and touched him.

He disappeared as she slumped from fatigue, dropping her hands onto her knees.

As the others looked at her, she grinned at Binesi. "I wonder how close to the house I got him."

Chapter 32

At The Library

"Leah did what?"

"Yeah," Denae said, "and it dried them both up." She glanced at Olivia before continuing. "They went back to the circle and drew me back to my body."

Gaia shook her head. "I need to get her over here and examine her," she said.

Denae bit back a response as to just how well she'd examined Leah. Instead, she said, "And Olivia's sister Cheryl found us shortly after my feet touched the ground Saturday evening. She spent a few hours driving back and forth, narrowing things down until she saw the path to drive to the parking area, then found the trail, stripped down where she was supposed to, and came up to us. That shouldn't have been able to happen."

"They must've been dropping wards."

"Mom says no," Denae insisted, "and she handles that part."

"Then I need to examine her, too."

"Should we pin them on boards so you can look them over at your leisure," Denae said, and Olivia giggled, which got them both glares from Gaia.

"Get them together, unclothed, if possible," Gaia said. "Maybe make up some initiation ceremony since they're both technically friends of the family now. I can give them a good looking over during it."

"Trust me," Denae said. "I've had ample opportunity over the last couple of days to look them over up close." And personal, she added silently. "If there's anything I can't see, you need to teach me."

"I got to see them quite well myself," Olivia added. "They are about as mundane as they come."

"Discernment," Gaia said, somewhat dreamily. Denae knew her mind was now only half-aware of the conversation, already trying to work things out. "Being able to see within the norm for the unusual."

She turned around, and Denae rolled her eyes, causing Olivia to stifle a giggle.

Later, they were all up on the second floor, Gaia walking them through the library's organization and quizzing them on it. Denae supposed this was today's lesson since they'd spent most of the morning doing this.

Denae had been antsy since she'd gotten here, knowing what she needed to say but unsure how.

"Aunt Gaia," Denae said, suddenly feeling awkward. "I'm sorry for what I did to you. I couldn't stop it, I couldn't—"

"You did nothing wrong," Aunt Gaia snapped, her voice suddenly cold. "It had told me in loving terms how since I was barren and of no use to it, it would kill me, but make sure it was a slow death so I would suffer as I died. It wanted me to slowly die so I could think about my folly of trying to keep it captured. It was my own hubris. I saw it poking, trying to find an opening."

Her eyes glared at Denae. "I even showed you that. I was confident I had it trapped, stupidly so, it's now apparent. It's my fault you almost died."

Olivia opened her mouth, and Denae slapped her hand over it.

"Don't you even start," she said.

Olivia nodded, shutting her mouth, though tears showed in her eyes.

"I knew about the child storage in theory," Gaia continued, "but as it gloated to me, I was totally ignorant about how it would be done."

She put her hands on Olivia's shoulders. "I'm not sure I could've done it anyway. The idea is to swap it from toddler to toddler every decade so the things that happened wouldn't happen." She pulled Olivia to her. "The very idea is repugnant."

"But killing Denae is?" Olivia pushed away from Gaia. "That's what your plan was."

"After it was in me, talking to me," Gaia said, tears coming to her eyes, "I knew there was only one way to destroy it. I wanted it to be me, but I lured Denae here, and it gave me the slow death I deserved." She smiled, but it wasn't pleasant. "But it didn't own me completely. I'd planned and plotted."

Her eyes snapped over to Denae.

"When it attacked me—it, not you. It had me put that axe there so I would see it all the time until you arrived. When it attacked me with that axe, I pulled everything I could down from the table, hoping the right wands would come down, and one of them did. It was too smug."

It thought I was too weak, too helpless," she continued. "I stopped it and saved myself. Us, I guess, though as soon as I turned you to stone, I knew you would burn. I didn't want that, but I saw no other choice. To save the family, the beast must die, which meant you would too."

She wiped her eyes. "I gave them contingencies I knew wouldn't work, and they did too." She looked Denae in the eyes. "You did too, bless you, and told us what we had to do. Your mom held out for something…anything…until you said that. Then she gave in."

Gaia heaved a great sigh.

"We saw you as the one who would become the magically strongest in the family, stronger even than your great-grandfather, who you resemble in many ways. You proved yourself to be exactly that, but in ways we didn't expect. And you lived somehow, and the entity was vanquished. And these girls, Leah and Cheryl, do things they shouldn't be able to. All in conjunction with this. Old Agatha and Pastor Jonathan, too. I don't understand. That is why I need to examine them. And you're right—I will probably find nothing, yet even that is an answer."

She turned to Olivia. "And you, inadvertent blood-sister to Denae, your lives intertwined now in ways neither of you fathoms. When Denae burned, where were you?"

"I burned," Olivia said with a shiver. "It hurt so bad. Bin held me, I think. I tried to make it stop, at least in my head. Then it did stop, and Leah told us to go back to her, and we did. She came back."

She started bawling, and Denae pulled her tight against her.

"I shouldn't have done that," Denae said, tears running down her own cheeks. "I didn't realize."

"It's okay," Olivia said, fighting through her sobs. "I like that you and Cheryl are my sisters. Sisters in different ways, but sisters all the same." She hugged Denae tightly.

Gaia broke the silence after a minute, or it might have been several. "You will be master of more, Denae, though I prefer the term Mistress."

As Denae and Olivia looked at her, she continued. "You are to be Mistress of the Dassow family library," she declared. "You will move in at the end of May, if not sooner, and I will depart at Summer Solstice, again if not sooner."

"What?" Denae wondered if she had heard correctly. "Why?" She blinked at her aunt, not understanding.

"I need to travel," Gaia said. "I need to talk to others. Go to the Old World. I'll start in Germany and try to find any family still there."

She smiled at Denae's confusion.

"Yes, we still have family there, those who survived the purges over the century, the last being Hitler's since they wouldn't aid him in his occult works, or so I'm told. There…Lubeck…Hamburg, that whole area." She stroked Olivia's hair. "I need to travel to where you, dear child, were found and adopted…and beyond, I'm sure. I need to learn German quickly, though I think I arranged that last night."

"Why do you need to go?" Denae thought she knew the answer but needed to hear it out loud. She thought Olivia would need it spelled out, too.

"I need to find out how to stop that thing or another like it," Gaia declared. "I need to know exactly what it is and if more of them are stored in children or out and about. I need to find out when, where, and how it ruled and how it was captured."

"Olivia will be your apprentice here for the library as much as for her other learnings." Gaia stroked her cheek. "You brought us grief and trials not of your making. Denae was pushed to make a sister out of you, a blood-sister, for reasons we don't understand. You, who have a sister not of blood, now have both."

She turned back to Denae. "This is now your place, and you need to learn it as I have. As I can, I'll send more books or notes and whatever else I can to build us up in areas we now know we're dangerously weak in. If we'd had our ancestors' knowledge, we might've solved the problem before it started." She looked at both of them. "I don't know."

"Maybe we would've put that entity into Sasha for an additional time until we found a better solution. I don't like that, but with more knowledge, we'd have more options."

She placed her hands on Denae's shoulders. "It will be announced more formally at Ceremony, but you are now the Mistress of the Library, so get used to it."

↢ ↢ ⊙ ↣ ↣

THE END

Made in the USA
Columbia, SC
27 January 2024

3ce2e63c-6d42-44b9-91cb-1f58bcf408f1R01